enguin Books

After Purple

Wendy Perriam was born in 1940 in an air-raid shelter and educated at a strict Roman Catholic convent where God was Judge and Sex was Sin. She escaped to St Anne's College, Oxford, graduating in History Honours in 1961. She worked as a waitress, barmaid, artist's model and carnation de-budder before embarking on a successful career in advertising, which she combined with writing poetry and short stories.

Her first two novels, *Absinthe for Elevenses* (1980) and *Cuckoo* (1981) were acclaimed as a heady mixture of sex, humour and religion. She has just completed her fourth novel – her most ambitious yet – which explores variations on the themes of power and procreation, family and fame.

A selection of the reviews for *After Purple*:

'An unabashed sexual romp' – *Book Choice*

'Its purple hot-pot of sex and religion . . . is boiling over with too much energy and talent to ignore' – *Good Housekeeping*

'Pagan irreverence and earthiness' – *City Limits*

Wendy Perriam
After Purple

Penguin Books

Penguin Books Ltd, Harmondsworth, Middlesex, England
Penguin Books, 625 Madison Avenue, New York, New York 10022, U.S.A.
Penguin Books Australia Ltd, Ringwood, Victoria, Australia
Penguin Books Canada Ltd, 2801 John Street, Markham, Ontario, Canada L3R 1B4
Penguin Books (N.Z.) Ltd, 182–190 Wairau Road, Auckland 10, New Zealand

First published by Michael Joseph Ltd 1982
Published in Penguin Books 1983

Made and printed in Great Britain by Cox & Wyman Ltd, Reading
Set in Linotron Ehrhardt by
Rowland Phototypesetting Ltd, Bury St Edmunds, Suffolk

one

'A *what?*' said Leo.

The telephone didn't answer, or if it did, it made sure I couldn't hear. Leo had it cradled in his lap, the phone-lead coiled across his stomach like an umbilical cord, both hands fondling the receiver. His dressing-gown gaped open, so that if I shifted slightly, I could see the whole line of his naked body underneath it. I crossed my legs and rubbed myself against the chair. It had a rough cane seat which prickled.

'Oh, I see. No, that's no problem. Late K'ang Hsi, you say. What shape? Mmm … sounds interesting. Is it just one phoenix or a pair?'

I tried not to listen. It was a phoenix I had smashed last night. The shattered pieces of the Chinese pot were still scalding and accusing on the floor behind me. It had broken right across the wings.

The base of the phone had slipped a little further down towards his groin. Leo's two thin hands were cupped around the mouthpiece as if it were a breast. He was joined, entwined, in full congress with a telephone. I was the intruder. I traced a picture with my teaspoon in the little puddle of sugar which had spilt on the breakfast table. It was meant to be a tree, but it came out like a prick. Leo's prick. I swirled the outlines round a bit, so it turned into a Chinese vase. That was more appropriate. He'd been talking for twelve minutes now, and this was Reconciliation Hour.

'*Where* did you say you spotted it?' Leo stretched an arm along the table, towards my cereal bowl. I thought he was going to touch me, squeeze my hand perhaps, acknowledge I was there, but the arm was stern, impatient – fingers tapping sharply on the table.

'Pencil, please.'

I got up and dug out a clutch of biros from the empty chutney jar. The first two didn't write. I handed him the third and kissed the space between the lapels of his dressing-gown. He brushed my lips away like flies. He also refused the biro. He had found his fountain pen and was already scribbling me away with it, jotting down dates and shapes and details on the back of the current issue of the *Listener*, a deep frown gashed between his eyebrows.

'Bermondsey Market? What, the chap we see in the salerooms? But the market's only open on a Friday. Oh, I see – his *shop*. I don't quite trust him, actually. Do you?'

The telephone cooed and simpered back at him. I couldn't hear the voice, but I knew it must be Otto. Only Otto was indulged so long. Usually some fancy vase or jar or snuff bottle or other he'd tracked down in a junk shop or a market stall and wanted Leo to buy.

'It's cracked, I suppose. What, just along the foot-ring? Oh, that as well . . . pity. Even so, it doesn't sound impossible. Look, I'd better get round and see it. Is the guy there now?'

I heard a purr or two and then a click as Otto put the phone down. Leo still hung on. He had pressed the receiver against his bare chest now. This must be the afterplay.

'So you're going out?' I said.

He didn't answer. He was staring at the back cover of the *Listener* where his bold black pen had lunged over rows of neat advertisements for Polish Programme Assistants or Secretaries for Audience Research. I passed him his toast, his cup, and the jar of peanut butter. The sooner we had breakfast, the sooner we might get to bed. Leo made his own peanut butter in a sort of antique churn he'd found in an auction room. He bought nuts cheap, in bulk, from a bird-food supplier, and ground them in a small machine marked 'Flagstaff, Arizona'. He never let me do it. I didn't cook at all. We didn't have that sort of relationship. Leo dislikes the word relationship.

I glanced across at him. If other men sprawled at the table with bare feet and bare chest, scooping peanut butter out of the jar with the wrong end of a paper-knife, they might well have looked slovenly, or even plain ridiculous. Leo looked magnificent. He turned breakfast into some dark, solemn ritual. He was dark himself, like an oil painting that needed cleaning, an old master with a crust of smudgy varnish daubed across it. His eyes went on forever. It was frightening, really, how little I knew about him. Both his parents were dead – that he *had* admitted. His mother was half Russian and a café singer. His father, twenty odd years older, had been thoughtless enough to die when Leo was still unweaned. That we had in common – no fathers. I doubt if his had even been married to his mother. I'd tried to probe, but Leo rarely answered questions.

'More tea?' I asked. He had opened the *Listener* now and was continuing his article on Bertrand Russell, a Reassessment by a Transcendentalist. I was eating branflakes. Leo despises commercial breakfast cereals, but I need them for the roughage. Since my divorce, I've suffered with constipation. I tried to eat them quietly so that my crunching wouldn't disturb his Reassessment. I never read The *Listener*. The print is too small and all the articles have a brown, musty, scratchy taste like branflakes.

Behind me, on the floor, I could hear the phoenix struggling to arise. It wasn't just the value of the thing, it was Leo's youth I had smashed. He'd bought that vase when he was more or less a stripling, the first in his collection. I could never imagine Leo as a boy, with only one bright bird between his hands. I suspect that after the phoenix, life had let him down a little, so in breaking the vase I'd destroyed the best bit of his life.

The kitchen was so quiet now, so innocent, it seemed strange that only seven hours ago, it had been spinning in black, bellowing circles, as I screamed at Leo and tore at his face and eyes, the rain sheeting down outside, the radio turned up to hurting, and Karma's fierce, hacking barks cracking through the room like gunfire. Karma always sided with Leo. He was Leo's dog and hated any rival, so if I cried, he simply drowned me out by howling louder. He hadn't appeared at breakfast yet. Karma was a sulker. If we upset his evenings, he skulked in his basket the whole of the next morning and refused all overtures. Not that I'd made an overture, not yet.

I pushed back my chair. 'I didn't mean . . .'

Leo turned another page. 'No post-mortems. *Please.*' A crumb was trembling on his lip. It didn't fall, even when he spoke. If it was still there by the time I'd finished my branflakes, then I'd take it as a Sign that Leo loved me. I was always doing things like that. Little tests, silly games. Since he never told me, I had to find out other ways. We hadn't spoken since the phoenix. Just fought and wrestled and hurled abuse and books, then slammed our bedroom doors and sweated and sobbed through the wreckage of the night.

Well, *I* had. Leo may simply have gone to sleep. I couldn't check, because once our doors were shut, we never made any contact till the morning. There were rules even to the rows. Curfew until dawn. Then fumblings, rustlings, trips to the toilet, freezing bathroom, stifling kitchen, strong tea, stale toast, Bertrand Russell or Bernard

Levin, according to what day and periodical it was, and – finally – the reconciliation. Which meant sex in Leo's bed, very long, wild, violent, still silent, but cleansing. Only then would one or other of us pick up the pieces – literally, I mean.

Breakfast is always a bit of an ordeal – stumbling and yawning from nightmares and unconsciousness to Sugar Puffs and Mother's Pride, trying to pretend the world is white and wholesome and sugar-coated, when you've just been dipped in dark and death. I'd found it unsettling even when married to Adrian (and he *was* wholesome – good-natured and sturdy like that sort of bran-enriched cereal which comes with a free plastic toy and a list of added vitamins). With Leo, the tension was unbearable.

To start with, it was always dark. Leo lived in the basement of his two-floor share of a five-storey Victorian house. I had the ground floor. They were both his, but he had assigned us separate territories. The kitchen was in his area. I had my own gas-ring upstairs and an electric kettle and even a sort of grill-cum-waffle-maker, but we mostly ate together (never waffles), sitting at the long, pitted pine table which was piled high with back numbers of all Leo's periodicals, and faded piano music without its covers, and expensive prints waiting for their frames. The high, narrow windows looked as if they were sitting up and begging for light. They didn't get much. A mulberry tree hogged most of it. Leo had bought the house for the tree. Mulberry trees are rare in Notting Hill. (My mother called it Kensington when she talked about me to the few brave bridge partners she still honoured with her conversation. 'Living with friends near Kensington Palace' was how she put it. She didn't know London and she hadn't met Leo. If she had, she would have put it differently. *Very* differently.)

Even if the sun was pouring its heart out in the street upstairs, we still breakfasted in gloom. It suited Leo, really. He looked wrong in sunlight, sort of cracked and faded. I'd met him in the dark. He'd been sitting with Otto and Karma in a gloomy basement wine bar, listening to an Indian sitar. I'd lost my job and my handbag on the same day and was drinking some rather scratchy red wine I had no means of paying for. Karma bit my leg, which solved the problem, because with all the fuss of blood and tetanus injections the barman forgot about my bill, and even if he hadn't, Leo would have been more or less forced to pay it, in simple compensation. When I met him for the second time, it was daylight and he looked a lot older, but he'd had me, then, and after that, things like age didn't matter.

There was a small grey puddle left in the bottom of my bowl and one waterlogged sultana floating in it. The crumb was still trembling on Leo's lip. He loved me. I pushed my nightdress up above my navel. Leo likes navels. We often did it on the kitchen floor with a pile of spread-out *Listeners* underneath us. I was used to being screwed on Bertrand Russell or Alistair Cooke or Letters to the Editor. Sometimes he rammed my head against the skirting. He always hurt. That was one of the reasons I lived with him, the recklessness, the scarlet-edged excitement. With Adrian, it was all pale pink candlewick and vaginal deodorants and *tenderness*.

The crumb fell off his lip at the exact moment I swallowed the sultana. That worried me. He was brewing a second pot of tea. He should have grabbed hold of my wrists by now and pinioned me against the wall. He's very thin, the sort of build you'd call gangling if he were anyone else, but so strong he's cut out of sheet metal, with steel rods where ordinary men have bones.

His dressing-gown had fallen open again. (He never wore pyjamas.) His skin was smooth, almost polished, with a dull, sallow tinge to it, as if he'd been painted in a bad light on a foggy evening. He didn't have vulgar things like body hair. He was like one of those ancient, precious icons of Christ the Saviour, where fuzz would have been sacrilege.

I held out my hand to him. He left it stranded, pawing the air like a limp, foolish thing without an owner. Leo gave me headaches – the endless tension, the unpredictability. I pulled my nightie down again. He had picked up his cup and was walking towards the door. He wasn't angry, just preoccupied. Bertrand Russell made him nervous. I heard his footsteps fade and vanish up the stairs, followed by the higher, brighter footsteps of the piano, racing and tumbling down again.

The piano was the most expensive thing he owned. It was a Bechstein grand in inlaid ebony, and twice as old as he was. The removal men couldn't get it down the narrow curving stairs into the basement, so it stood in my territory. In fact, I didn't have much territory left. Once the piano was established, that room became his living-room (which he and Otto called a drawing-room and my mother would have called a disgrace, since no one bothered cleaning it). That encouraged him to use my bedroom, too – not for sleeping in, but for storing the largest and most gloomy of his canvases. I often went to sleep surrounded by ruined temples or anorexic nudes, tipped on their sides and glaring. I could hardly complain, when it was all his house to start with. Even with Adrian, I'd never got my half. Other wives have joint mortgages and shared bank accounts. Adrian thought more in terms of pocket money, or presents of huge boring (improving) books he wanted to read himself.

Leo was playing very loud and fiercely. He had plunged straight into the middle of a piece, a general sort of pandemonium where his hands keep crossing over on the keys and he hurls himself about a lot. He'd been practising it for at least two months. It sounded fine to me, but then I'm not musical. (Another thing between us.) I hated Leo's music and yet I worshipped it. I can't even type, let alone play an instrument. I've never had the knack of doing different things with each hand, except in bed. When Leo first showed me his musical scores, I was dumbfounded. A hundred pages of squiggles was a whole crashing symphony, or the sobbing tangle of an opera. A murder or a deathbed or Man's Highest Aspirations crammed into five straight lines and a clutch of crotchets. It was like God in a grain of sand or the Bible on a silicon chip, and gave me that same sinky, trembly feeling as when I watched television programmes on 'Man and The Cosmos' and realized we were just a small, second-rate planet spinning towards extinction.

I shut the kitchen door. The music was crashing and pounding through the house, booming down the stairs, churning up my breakfast. I felt extinguished by it, excluded. I had no idea who the composer was. I never dared ask Leo things like that, in case the piece was so ludicrously well-known that even an ignoramus would have known it. I *was* an ignoramus. My lack of musical knowledge so appalled me that I always kept it quiet, which saved me from contempt, but never taught me anything.

It had been much the same with Adrian. He wasn't musical, but he wrote textbooks on medieval history and I don't know history, either. At smart dinner parties I used to say that Adrian divorced me because I thought Stephen and Matilda were a folk group. Adrian didn't divorce me, anyway – *I* walked out on him – but even if he had, he would have done it on the grounds of just that sort of flip remark, not because of my ignorance. On the other hand, if you don't know anything (I mean *really* know, like Leo and Adrian know things, or Bertrand Russell, or the man at the auction rooms) you have to get by on flip remarks, or by regurgitating chewed-up bits of other people's conversations. I stole whole sentences and served them up, not as stale and tepid left-overs, but as my main Dish of the Day. Their owners never noticed, because I changed things round or tacked bits on from someone or somewhere else. My vocabulary was already quite impressive, but it couldn't compare with theirs. They had whole freezers and larders full of freshly brewed opinions and ideas, jumbo-sized tins and packets, while I had only a few rinds and husks pinched from their plates and secreted in a paper serviette, the sort of thing you'd tip into the dog's dish.

It amazed me, really, how ordinary people could remember things. Adrian talked about thirteenth-century battles as if he'd been standing there in person, handing the king his breast-plate or picking up the arrows. He probably knew what Matilda ate for breakfast. Leo could play whole piano sonatas off by heart, without the music. If he turned on Radio Three in the middle of a concert, he knew immediately the name and dates of the piece and the composer. I could listen to an hour of it and still not guess whether it was Mozart or *The Merry Widow*.

I opened the door a crack. The music punched me in the face again. It was pouring down the stairs like lava, coating and choking everything with noise and heat and fury. Leo had me trapped. I could only escape by bolting out of the back door in my nightdress. If I wanted my clothes, I'd have to walk right up the stairs past the source of the eruption, that black, smoking, evil-minded Bechstein.

I didn't want my clothes – I wanted Leo – so I braved the stairs and stood deafened at the door of the drawing-room, watching his body lurch and plunge along the keyboard. The room was shuddering with the impact, objects trembling on the table, walls and ceiling wincing. I was totally shut out. I think that's why I resented Leo's music – he gave it his full devotion and attention, when I could never win them for myself.

I waited a while until he'd reached that section where the piano draws its breath and quietens down a bit, then I walked towards him and stood behind his shoulder. The music was merciful now, forgiving – armies kneeling in the snow and laying down their swords, brother embracing brother. I wanted to slip in underneath the notes and have

Leo's slow, dark, bony hands stroke and gentle me the way they did the keys.

'Leo . . .'

'What?' He leant away from me to rumble down the lowest end of the piano. 'Well, *what?*'

'Oh . . . nothing.' It was pointless, really. He was squeezing such feeling out of those notes, such *anguish*, my own petty little needs could hardly raise a murmur.

He paused a moment, flexed his fingers, closed his eyes. 'I'm meeting Otto for breakfast,' he said. He made the name sound grand and showy like the climax of the piece.

'You've *had* breakfast.'

'Lunch, then.' He was already playing again, Otto's name now frilled and furbished with a flurry of arpeggios.

'You said we'd have lunch *together*.'

'We could have done. But you just turned breakfast into lunch.'

'I *didn't*.'

He answered with a mocking little trill in the left hand.

'Anyway, you told me Otto doesn't eat breakfast.'

'He doesn't eat at all.'

'So why are you having lunch with him?'

'I'm not, I'm having breakfast.'

'Oh, *Leo* . . .'

Both hands were jeering at me now, turning their backs on me, jabbing the notes with a slow, lazy scorn.

'When are you leaving?'

'Now.'

'But you're not dressed.'

'No.'

'So couldn't we . . . ?'

'*No.*'

The music had turned loud and fierce again. He should have stopped by now. I think he'd tacked a new bit on, simply to shout me down. The right hand was darting like a lizard over the keys, while the left one kept on repeating the same phrase, the same phrase, the same . . .

I suddenly wanted to chop it off – that hand – smash it into pulp. All the fury I had ever felt towards him, all the pain, resentment, pique, humiliation, was pouring into that left hand. On and on it went, the same dazzling, murderous phrase; spinning, sparkling, screwing the room tighter and tighter, while the right hand raced and tumbled over it. The piano was throbbing, the whole room roaring and trembling. Leo had his eyes closed. He was communing with the souls of dead composers, deafening and insulting me in a language I couldn't understand. I hadn't a clue what key he was in, I didn't even know which century. It was like Adrian again. All those confusing battles in the Hundred Years War; strings of kings with the same name but different numbers, Henrys and Edwards whom I always muddled up. Feudalism, scholasticism, internationalism – all those impossible words with '-ism' on the end of them. The only one I understood was sensualism. I wanted to lie down under the piano, on my back, and have Leo's thundering hands play the same phrase over and over and over me, pounding me, dazzling me, in any key he chose. Eroticism. Barbarism. Steel rods rammed against my breasts, sheet metal gouging out my stamens. And there he was, vertical, not horizontal, making love to that dead, smug, preening slob of a Bechstein, pouring out lies about tenderness and emotion, (*dolce* and *grazioso, con somma passione*), when he was a pig, a brute, a thug, a . . .

I didn't slam out, just slipped into my bedroom, lay down on the mattress (which my mother called a divan), closed my eyes and snuggled up against my father. I hadn't seen him since I was a tiny kid, but I still knew what he looked like. He was so tall, I only came up to his thighs and he could pick me up with just one hand and sling me over his shoulder. He bought me sweets on Saturday afternoons, and when he read *Red Riding Hood*, he made his voice all frightening for the wolf.

I didn't want to think of wolves, so I moved on to my second father who was actually a step-dad. His name was God and He lived in the convent boarding school where my mother sent me to give herself what she described as breathing space. You had to be a proper baptized Catholic to claim Him as your *real* father. The other three hundred blessed girls all were. They feasted on His flesh and blood and wore His naked body on a chain around their necks. I was the only step-child. The difference showed, of course. My mother got as irritable with God as she had done with my father, so she moved me to a godless college where I first discovered Life and Lib and cheese-and-hashish sandwiches and mortal men like Adrian.

Adrian told me God was an irrelevance and replaced Him with

Philosophy. On Saturday afternoons, he bought Spanish plonk and Durex Gossamer instead of jelly babies, and read me history books in place of fairy tales before we went to bed. There wasn't that much difference, so I married him. Actually, I didn't have much choice. God was still cold-shouldering me because I wasn't a cradle Catholic and my father had long ago pissed off and married someone else.

I shivered in my nightie. Leo and the Bechstein hadn't relented yet. I tried to picture him and God and Adrian and my father, and even Bertrand Russell and Bernard Levin, all fighting over their claims to me, all begging me to give them one more chance. It didn't really work. They were much more interested in demolishing each other's theories than they were in wooing me. Instead of their impassioned pleadings, all I could hear was Leo's jeering music shrilling and scoffing underneath the door. I longed for my father to wrap me in his great-coat and pretend I was Goldilocks sleeping off the porridge. Or God to sneak me into bed with Him and pull the blankets tight. Or even Leo to simply stop his playing and prove I still existed. There was only Adrian left. I was crazy to have left him. I only did it because we'd had a row and I wanted him to come panting after me and beg me not to go. Instead, he had gone grovelling round to Janet's and asked her to marry him. (I didn't even know he *had* a Janet.)

I booted her out of my bed and set up house with Adrian again. Things had been safer then, predictable. He always came home (and left it) at the same time, and made careful unobjectionable remarks in the right order. Simple things like breakfast cereals never became reasons for contempt. He'd shared a packet with me, most mornings, and even helped me enter the competitions on the back. (Complete the line: 'We eat Kellogg's Ricicles because . . .') He took the competitions very seriously, juggled words, jotted headings. We might have won a trip to the Bahamas. Adrian would have taken the cash in lieu of, and then gone somewhere grey and cultured and boring, like Ephesus or Athens, which had history and temples instead of golden sands. We always had five or six different cereals, so we lived in constant expectation of new cars, world cruises, day trips to Disneyland. Most of the packets were too tall for our poky little larder, so we stood them in a row on top of the refrigerator. It was an old fridge with an intermittent judder, and every time it juddered, one or two of the packets fell on their backs. We never moved them to a safer place, just picked them up again. They were like our children, I suppose, bright and sweet and shared and always falling over. I suppose that's why divorce hurts so much. Not the obvious things, the division of the property, the haggling in the courts, but the loss of a plastic Batman in the cornflakes packet, or the chance of a cabin cruiser with two coupons from Puffed Wheat.

I longed to grab it all again – the sugar on the Weetabix, the honey on the toast. Oh, I know I'd only ruin it – I always mess things up again as soon as I've put them straight. But just to escape the music, just to have a breakfast without the silences, the strain. Leo was playing slower now, but the notes were still cruel and spiky, cutting into me with their sharp, jagged edges, reminding me of disasters and divorce courts, of last rites and lost fathers. I had to get away. I never felt safe with Leo. There were too many gaps in his life I couldn't fill. He was like one of those intricate, five-thousand-piece jigsaw puzzles with the picture on its box missing, so that you had no idea what it was meant to look like if you ever succeeded in sorting out the bits. Adrian was simpler. He'd be at home alone now, on the last lap of his Christmas holidays. Term didn't start till the second week of January. He'd be deep in some book or other, wrapped in two sweaters to save on the heating costs, and with a bag of Creamline toffees hidden in his box-file so that Janet wouldn't find them. She wouldn't find me, either. She worked in the City, half-past eight till five.

I didn't wash, just pulled on a sweater and a pair of jeans, without any bra or pants. My jeans smelt sort of raunchy in the crotch. Leo liked that. He used to sleep with them sometimes, when I wasn't there. My mother had always nagged about clean underwear. It wasn't so much the hygiene as the fear of my being mopped up after a car crash and discovered in dirty pants or greyish vest. I was going by train, in any case. I've never learnt to drive.

I dragged on Leo's sheepskin, the second, shorter one, which was yellowish like he was. I was still shivering underneath it. I went downstairs and made a wide detour round the broken vase. I slammed the door on Leo's playing, which had swollen up again like a huge black shadow stalking after me. I could almost see the shrill, black squiggly notes crushed and writhing in the door like mangled flies. I left them there to die, whistling my own defiant tuneless tune.

two

It was cold and grey outside. The mulberry tree was pressing its bare arms against the bright, lighted window, to keep them warm. The sky looked stained and creased as if someone had picked it up cheap at a jumble sale and tacked it up skewwhiff. It was still early. People were hurrying to work with their stiff grey morning faces on. Nice to have a job. I'd had nine in twelve weeks, and blued them all.

The underground was crowded. I stood wedged among a party of German tourists whose coarse pink faces looked as if they'd been moulded out of *Leberwurst*. (That's not original. I pinched it from a girl at a dinner party who had just come back from Munich.) At Waterloo, the crowds thinned. The morning crush was over, but had left the station seedy and bad-tempered, pock-marked with dirty footprints and with little pustules of litter erupting all over it. A businessman with a briefcase and a bowler was queuing at the Baskin-Robbins icecream stand. I went and stood behind him.

'A marshmallow sundae, please,' he said. 'To take away.'

I was almost disappointed. I'd hoped he'd order a double-scoop strawberry cornet, and suck it all the way to the Bank.

'Same again,' I said. That's typical of me. No originality. I don't even *like* marshmallow. But the thought of all those thirty-one flavours was almost paralysing. I could stand for ever, agonizing, dithering, trying to weigh Orange Sherbet against Chocolate Chip. Decisions like that are more or less impossible. There are no absolutes. It's like trying to decide between the big-bang theory or the steady-state, or limbo or nirvana, or Marx or Mrs Thatcher. Left to myself, I wouldn't have bothered much with things like that. There are enough imponderables in deciding when to wash your jeans, without taking on the universe as well. But people around me were always fretting on a cosmic scale. At Adrian's school, we used to be invited for sherry and sandwiches, and some master or other would rabbit on about whether Sartre's Marxism contradicted his Existentialism (all those '-isms' again), and at Leo's gatherings, everyone agonized about Buddhism or Bio-Energetics or how Christianity could be compatible with capitalism. There were always so many arguments on all ten thousand sides. It astonished me how normal people could settle for one opinion or another. How could they be that *sure?* I tended to follow whoever I was with. If he was an ecologist, I threw away my aerosols and wore a badge saying 'Save the Condor'; if a vegetarian, I shovelled in the nut cutlets. That's the only reason people like me, I suspect. I give them instant backing and support. I could have made a fortune working for Rent-a-Fan.

The icecream lady dolloped sauce on my sundae and sprinkled it with nuts. Actually, I'd rather have had a cornet. I like the way they melt on your hand through the aperture in the bottom. (Aperture is one of Adrian's words.) I once masturbated on a beach for twenty-two minutes, with a giant-sized Mr Whippy cornet dripping down my thighs like a sort of egg-timer. 95p the Baskin-Robbins cost. I could have bought a *meal* for that. The tube fare had been bad enough, and the day return to Twickenham almost cleaned me out. I should have bought a single. 'I'm sorry, Adrian, but I'll have to stay the night. I couldn't afford the fare both ways.' I grinned to myself. Adrian would take it seriously. That was his life's work, really – Taking Things Seriously. He'd spread out those gloomy beige pamphlets from the Social Security office, and ask to see my cheque stubs, and start explaining all over again how I could claim something-or-other benefit if I filled in a form which was so long and complicated, it would have been easier to take a high-powered job than try and wrestle with it. You needed at least two A-levels to cope with forms like that. I didn't care, really. If I had cash, I spent it, and if I didn't, I went through somebody else's. I never knew whether Leo had money. He did buy Chinese pots, but they were often chipped, from low-grade dealers or even junky stalls. He also owned two floors of a house, but it was only on a lease, and his Bechstein had been left to him by a Russian relative. We never talked about money.

My train was in, already. I found an empty carriage and started on my sundae. Any icecream called Baskin-Robbins must taste better than one with a boring name like Walls or Lyons. Take my own name. I've always felt special being called Thea. I mean, it gives me an immediate advantage over the Susans and the Janes. It's much the same with Leo. Any Leo is bound to be fascinating, where a Ted is merely common and a John plain dull. If we'd been a conventional couple, people would have talked about 'Leo and Thea', and we'd have sounded daring and decadent like Colour Supplement People. Names earmark you immediately. Vic-and-Brendas run ballroom-dancing schools in Penge, and Oliver-and-Emilys make their own duvet covers and send their sons to Bedales.

The icecream lasted only as far as Vauxhall. I licked out the carton with my finger and threw it under the seat. Someone had scribbled 'R.B. for me' just above my head. I wondered who R.B. was. Robert Bruce, Roger Bacon – Adrian sort of people. I could see R.B. slumped on the carriage seat, a tall, bony man with black hair. I unzipped my jeans. My pubic hair is a sort of reddish-brown and very coarse like wire. Sometimes I use conditioner on it, the stuff they sell for scalp hair, but it doesn't make much difference.

I licked my finger, ran it down my stomach and left it sort of poised above the hair. Leo hates it if I masturbate. I think he believes woman's only source of pleasure can be Man, so touching myself is an insult to his sex. He holds my wrists if I ever try to do it, twists them right behind my back, and then carries on with his tongue where I left off. (That's what makes me do it in the first place.)

Though now, I suspect it was simply a defiance. I never dared oppose him openly, so all I could do was break his rules (or fill his silences). Anyway, it's the only skill I have. Other girls can type sixty words a minute. I can come ten times an hour. It frightens me, my own sexuality. That's not my word either, but Adrian always frowned if I said 'randy'. Those '-ity' words are rather like the '-isms'. They're so bursting with prickly vowels and consonants, you can't tell one from the other, so that spirituality and bestiality land up sounding more or less identical.

It's the same with masturbation – God and slut combined. You soar beyond your own confining body and hit the electric fence which runs round heaven. It's all shock and heat and sparks – an angel or a rocket-launch zooming out of space and time and boundaries, towards the blaze and roar of the eternal. But afterwards, you find you're only Lucifer, belly-flopping back to earth, sore and stained and sweaty, with your wings and halo torn. And that rocket's just the damp, spent debris of a firework fizzling in the rain.

I don't know really why I go on doing it, except every time I think it will be different. Right, I vow, this one will be the clincher. I'll bump into God and *stay* there, spinning forever like a Catherine-wheel nailed on His front door, and that singing, panting, pleading, final climax will turn slattern into Soul.

I wriggled on the seat a fraction so that my jeans weren't cutting into me, and braced my feet against the floor. (There was no one in the carriage.) I wetted my finger again and pushed it up, probing very slowly and solemnly at first, and closing my eyes, to cut out all distractions like graffiti or no-smoking signs or five-pound fines for spitting. All my godlike feelings come to a sort of point an inch or so inside me. I touched that sanctum now, feeling it burn and quiver through my fingers, turning me from flesh to sacred fire. It was my own private morning service – lauds, or matins, or Mass in the vernacular – some new-style sacrament in which God's hands were on my thighs and His holy water welling up between them. My toes were clawing the floor, my face screwing up in total concentration, my whole body pierced and swooning like St Sebastian's. I used two fingers now, and then a fist, ramming more roughly as we rattled into Clapham Junction. I could feel whole chalices shoved high up inside me, bishops' croziers splitting me in two. The entire Roman Catholic and Apostolic Church had left the Vatican and set up court in Thea Morton's cunt. Wandsworth, Putney, Barnes – each station was a sacred shrine, a whistle-stop pilgrimage, thundering through my legs and out again. R.B. had slipped down from the wall and was pressed against my belly, in Communion with me, making me thump and judder on the seat. He was dark and wild like Leo, but had turned from mortal man to red-cocked cardinal, roaring into tunnels, leaping off the rails. I was so in awe of him, I thought I'd never come, but suddenly everything fizzed and purred and gloated and I heard doors slamming and feet trampling and we drew away from North Sheen at the very moment the cardinal shot his bolt.

Slowly, unwillingly, I opened my eyes and wiped my fingers on the rough accusing velour of the seat. I'd come so hard, I'd scratched myself, and my breath had gone all gaspy like a goldfish. I should at least have felt sated or relieved or even quits with Leo, but all I felt was squalid and depressed. The slut had won once more, the angel fallen. All I'd done was delude myself (again) that frigging was the fastest route to God.

Stupid tears were pricking behind my eyelids, trying to shame me further. I was wet both ends and I didn't have a Kleenex. I wiped my crotch with my shirt-tail and my eyes on my sleeve and sat there, hating myself, for the remainder of the journey. It was raining when I arrived at Twickenham, a stinging, ill-tempered rain which was almost sleet. It seemed strange that I had lived there five whole years, worked in the travel agency, belonged to the public library, swum in the municipal baths, shopped at Tesco's. I was divorced from the town as well as from Adrian. The Decree applies to streets, shops, cinemas, not just to the man.

I walked down from the station through the dingy main street and turned off by the river. Adrian had kept the marital home, as the judge kept calling it. It was a damp, cramped semi, with a small garden overlooking a dye-works. I'd been a couple there – Adrian and Thea. (His name always came first, like Leo's would if we ever became a couple, which we won't.) I stood in front of the prim French Blue door. Janet and Adrian had repainted it. (Her name came first, now.) It's a strange sensation, knocking at your own front door. Janet had planted snowdrops by the dustbins.

Adrian came to the door with a pencil in his mouth. I knew his pencils – 4Bs – very soft. He sharpened them with an old scout knife and left little coils and whorls of pencil sharpenings on his desk. They were soft, too. You could have made a pillow of them. He looked thinner. Janet rationed him. All his meals were gaunt and insubstantial now, but disguised with fancy French names and what Janet called 'garnishes', which meant half a slice of gherkin or a sprig of water-cress.

'*Bonjour,*' I said. It was the only French I knew.

'Thea!' Adrian sort of shrank back into himself as if I were a traffic warden come to book his car. 'Look, I *told* you not to . . .'

'I know, but it's important. How's your cold?'

'Better, but . . .'

'Can I come in? It's freezing on the step.'

'Well, I suppose so, but you really . . .'

I had already stepped into the hall. The house smelt different now. When I'd lived there, I don't remember it smelling at all, but perhaps you're unaware of your own smell. Now it reeked of television commercials – Daz, Harpic, Clean-O-Pine – a self-righteous, Janet sort of odour.

Adrian was looking like a dog who had messed the carpet, guilty and abject both at once. He still had the door held open. 'Look, Thea, I don't want to be unfriendly, but . . .'

He paused. Even now, he hated to hurt me. I finished the sentence for him. 'Janet doesn't like it.'

'Well, of *course* she doesn't, Thea. I mean, it's only understandable. I tried to explain to you *last* time.'

I was halfway down the hall. A small Christmas tree was glowering at me from a table, one of those green deodorized plastic ones which can't make a mess or drop their needles. Adrian was still agonizing between me and the door. The draught was killing both of us. I kissed him on the neck.

'Janet needn't *know*,' I whispered.

'No, but . . .'

The Christmas cards had been pinned to a piece of tape and then strung across the walls in strictly graded rows, small ones at the top. They were mainly small. Mingy things with undernourished robins on them, or spindly stage coaches with Gothic script and glitter.

'Merry Christmas to Jan and Adrian.'

'Greetings to Adrian and Janet from . . .'

I turned my back. Adrian and Thea had scattered their cards over every available surface in the house and used them as a reason not to dust for the whole six weeks of Christmas. Leo and Thea didn't go in for cards. (Xmas was a four-letter word as far as Leo was concerned. We'd spent most of Christmas day in bed and then got up and opened a tin of Epicure smoked oysters. Leo claimed he'd never eaten fowl in his life and didn't intend to start.)

Adrian had finally shut the door. The cards were blowing in the draught and I suppose he was afraid he'd disarrange them. Janet probably had her graded penalties. Loss of a roast potato for messing up her cards; no meal at all for letting in an ex-wife. I walked straight into the back room, which Adrian was still using as his study. It looked much the same, only tidy. His papers had been sorted into neat piles, the books banished to a bookcase, and five black biros stood to attention in a green plastic desk-tidy which Janet had probably purchased in the same shop as the tree. Clamped to the wall was a large black pencil sharpener, the old-fashioned type with a handle. The scout knife had been confiscated.

'Coffee?' Adrian asked.

I nodded. It would be instant Sainsbury's with 10p off and a money-saving voucher to go towards your next purchase, in a cup with roses on to make it taste superior. I followed him into the kitchen which looked scrubbed and white like a morgue.

'Well, how *are* you, Thea?' He really meant, 'What do you want and when are you going to leave?', but Adrian has always been polite.

'So-so.'

You can live with someone five whole years and suddenly find great silences springing up like traps. He tapped his pencil against the coffee jar.

'Found a job yet?'

'Sort of.'

He was wearing old corduroys without a belt. I stared at the bit between the legs. There were no bumps or curves. He could have been castrated, for all I knew. I inched my hand along the table and dropped it on his lap.

'Thea! Stop that immediately.'

Teachers always treat you like a naughty child. If you live with them, they turn into headmaster and you into the Upper Second. I noticed, though, he didn't remove the hand. There was a slight twitching through the corduroy. Sex is like masturbation. It makes you sacred – at least for half an hour. It also unites you to another human being. I always feel less alone and frightened when a bit of a man is corkscrewed right inside me, as if we're Siamese twins cemented at the loins, instead of just halves of people pining on our own. Even the nuns had allowed that sex was more or less permissible, so long as it was the married sort and without any contraception. That's why I still lusted after Adrian. Only with him had screwing been safe and sinless and smiled-upon, as if we had a sort of British Standards Kite mark stamped on our cock and cunt by God Himself.

I moved my hand a little further down. 'How's your book?' I asked. That always worked. Once Adrian got going on the Causes of the Black Death or the Decline of Feudalism, I could have raped him and he wouldn't really have noticed. 'You told me on the phone you were having a bit of trouble with John of Gaunt.'

He looked grateful, like a horse reaching out for a sugar lump. He loved me to remember names. If I'd thrown in a date as well, I think he'd have put 'good work, A +' on my report.

'Oh, he's fine now. In fact, I've almost finished. I've had an advance from Longmans, actually. They sent me a contract on the strength of the first five chapters and the general plan. Apparently, they're quite impressed.'

'Congratulations.' It was easier without a belt. He still had the stomach, but my hand had slipped past it, across the rough, curly hair, and down.

'Look, Thea, I don't really think . . .'

'I'm doing an evening class in History,' I said. I wasn't, but I knew it was the sort of bait he'd jump for, especially with a capital H. Meanwhile, I eased his underpants aside. It was the only way I could get close to him. He and Janet had barred every other route. I had to aim directly, knock him off his guard, dismantle his defences. I yearned to believe we were bound and tied again, that Janet was back in Devon, Leo still sitting quietly in his wine bar.

'Good for you! What period are you studying?'

'Er . . . Tudors and Stuarts.' They were probably safest. Television was always wooing them, and even I knew the juicier bits of Henry VIII.

'You should have started earlier.' He sounded disappointed, almost disapproving. 'You can't pick up history like a magazine and turn to the spicy bits without any chronological introduction. It's actually more or less impossible to understand Tudor government unless you've been strongly grounded in the Middle Ages.' He was stiff now, but trying to disown everything below his head. 'In fact, there's a new book on the Tudors which traces some of their achievements back to the reforms of Edward I. That's always happening. When there's a flowering, we have to examine the rootstock.'

I nodded. I had his own root cupped between my hands and was rubbing it between them. I knew what would happen next. He'd deny it later, deodorize it with historical facts, gloss it over with Latin land charters or thirteenth-century parish rolls, but at least I'd have had him for half an hour, defied the barristers, negated the divorce.

We went upstairs. I'd have preferred the kitchen or under his study desk, but sex meant bed for Adrian. It wasn't pale pink candlewick, it was primrose frills. Janet must have changed it. Her photograph was standing on the dressing-table in a fake-wood frame. She had plump arms and short blond hair, badly permed. I turned her round. I derived a strange sort of pleasure from the fact that she had made the bed that morning, between Adrian's breakfast and rushing off to work, and he and I were messing it up again. He turned the sheet back very carefully, as if it made the crime less heinous. They were slimy yellow nylon sheets, the sort that don't need ironing, but tangle round your limbs and make you sweat. Adrian had stopped talking now and looked embarrassed and furtive as if he was about to be examined by a bum doctor. A man with an erection is always comic, somehow, especially standing up. (Well, Leo isn't, but Leo exists only to be the exception to every rule.) Adrian touched my left breast very politely, as if he had been introduced to it at a formal dinner party. We both had all our clothes off. Undressing is always the trickiest bit. His zip could have stuck, or Janet phoned to remind him to switch the tumble-drier off, or war been announced on the radio. I wanted it so much, I think I'd have gone straight on, even with bombs and poison gas. It worries me, my greed. I read somewhere that the average woman in her twenties has it twice a week. I wrote to Evelyn Home, once, and asked her what was wrong with me, but she never answered. Actually, I may only have wanted Adrian, and not the sex at all. I can never really tell where men stop and their pricks begin. All I know is that if you want devotion, you have to get undressed.

Adrian's thing is short, but very fat. It's diameter which matters more than length. He filled me up like one of those tampons they show you in advertisements which puff up when you drop them into water. He let me lie on top. I rocked backwards and forwards against him and tugged at the hair on his chest and bit his neck. I was screaming out some nonsense or other ('R.B. for me, R.B. for me!') and the whole force and rhythm of the Southern Region was rocketing through the room.

'Hush, darling,' he kept murmuring. 'Not so loud.' He always called me darling when we did it. Otherwise, he saved the term for Janet. You lose your darlings after a divorce, like your housekeeping allowance or your joint insurance.

I knew he was worried about the party wall. I tried to quieten down, but he was slamming against me from underneath and we sort of collided with each other, out of time, in a delicious and reverberating shock. Fifty shocks a minute, a hundred, two hundred – he was hotting up the pace. The bed was creaking now. He was split between terror and excitement. All his 'Hush's' kept turning into gasps. 'Quiet, darling. Not so loud . . . Aaaahhh . . .' He was coming now. I hadn't had enough, but I pretended to come with him, whipping him with my heels and screaming. There didn't seem to be a lot of sperm. Maybe he'd used it all up last night – shot it into Janet. I could feel her looking at us from a hundred little touches round the room – the frilled mats underneath her toiletries, the vapour rub and the vitamin B her side of the bed, her satin nightdress case with 'J' embroidered on it, the smell of mingled distaste and Devon Violets.

'Look, Thea, I think we ought . . . I mean, I don't really . . .'

The disownment now, the stuttering, the quick return to the Henrys and the Edwards. I climbed off his stomach and stood up. His thing was dripping and shrinking like an invalid. He was remaking the bed, before he had even dressed. I think he suspected Janet could see us from her office in the City fifteen miles away. He pulled the covers very tight and smooth, brushing off my pubic hairs and inspecting the sheets for stains. I refused to help. It was Janet who would climb in there tonight. Neither of us bathed. He dabbed at himself with a Kleenex and changed into clean grey trousers and another sweater, as if to prove he was a different, stricter person who didn't screw ex-wives.

That's all I was, an ex. We'd been joined for eleven minutes and then divorced again. I hadn't undone the past, hadn't pole-vaulted from his prick into his heart. The Siamese twins had been sliced apart in a law court and wouldn't fuse again. The sex thing hadn't worked. (It seldom does.) Sometimes I long to be a nun or a Vestal virgin or a prudish panda like Ling-Ling who doesn't even do it when you fly her mate all the way to Washington and bribe them with bamboo shoots. At least pandas have a keeper and a proper home.

We trailed downstairs to the kitchen. Janet had left cheese and Ryvita for him under a clean white tea towel, doled out two small slices and a mean-sized piece of Gouda. If I'd been her wife or sister, she'd have rationed me as well. I'm not exactly fat, only what my mother calls big-boned. I was sent to a child-minder once who always used to say, 'Eat your food up, love. You never know where your next meal's coming from.' I took that seriously. Every meal thereafter was a relief and deliverance, something which had saved me from starvation, but which well might be my last. I took to secreting food in handkerchiefs, sneaking things down sweaters, hoarding them for those rumbling years ahead. It was much the same with sex. I rarely refused a man, in case no one ever fancied me again.

Even now, I was gobbling Adrian's lunch. He had eked out the Ryvita with a bag of apples and a packet of bacon-flavour crisps. I suspect he bought the crisps himself, to supplement his diet. Janet wouldn't approve of Golden Wonder. He was droning on about a new interpretation of Magna Carta.

'Adrian, I want to talk to you.'

'We *are* talking, darling.'

That was a post-coital darling and probably a mistake. He flushed. Darlings slip out unawares after five solid years of them. He looked wary, haunted almost. He wanted to get rid of me. He didn't like the past, except in textbooks.

'Well?'

I leaned against the dresser and grabbed an apple from the bag. It was hard and very shiny, as if Janet had applied an aerosol polish to it. I was surprised, really, that she hadn't engraved a 'J' on all the fruit. Everything else seemed to be stamped with her.

'I want to come back to you, Adrian.' I didn't, not really, but I needed an excuse to stay there a little longer. It was too dark at Notting Hill. Nothing there was mine. It was Leo's house, his furniture, his friends, his meals, his music. We'd never be an us. Leo wouldn't compromise. I suppose it suited me, in some ways. I hadn't any home of my own, or friends, or even food, so I might as well use his. Anyway, I worshipped him. But not when he blockaded me with his Bechstein or made Bermondsey antique shops more important than my body. I was better off with Adrian, then.

'Thea, that's impossible . . .' Adrian's skin had gone white in patches, underneath the red. His eyes were trying to walk away from me, turn their backs on mine. 'I mean, there's Janet and . . .'

'Janet isn't right for you.'

There was a tiny silence. A Ryvita crumb dropped from his mouth on to the floor. He pounced on it, as if it were a used Durex. The floor was so clean, he could have written his textbook on it. I wondered if he missed me. Even with my sluttishness, my refusal to scrub floors or change sheets, all our rambling, well-mannered rows over God and money and history and my non-existent jobs, there'd still been a mutual ease and greed between us. We'd never bought Ryvita – just hacked great chunks off new white loaves and larded them with butter.

'Look here, Thea, I have no desire to hear your views on Janet.'

I was the Upper Second again. 'Put that stink-bomb *down*, Hargreaves. No, Hunter, the study of History does *not* include the making of paper darts . . .'

'Leo doesn't sleep with me,' I said, sort of carelessly. That was a lie, an outrageous scarlet screaming lie, but I was losing Adrian's attention. He'd be back to his book if I didn't stir him up.

It worked. He choked on his cheese, dropped a flurry of crisps, and looked agog and embarrassed at the same time. 'But you always said . . . I mean, I thought . . .'

'It's different now. Oh, Adrian . . .' I wanted his soft, flabby arms around me, his thick sandy hair falling in my eyes, his British Home Stores sweater chafing against my breasts. I still wore his ring, the nine-carat gold one he'd bought me in a sale. It made me less an alien. It shouted to the world that I was married, normal, dignified. That someone still desired me. I hated the thought of Janet taking over, barging into my house, my bed, my husband, gate-crashing our life. She even had a better ring than mine – eighteen carat at least, and twice the width. Adrian wore *her* ring now, smirking on his finger, padlocking his hands. I shut my eyes so I didn't have to look at it, leant against his shoulder, squeezed my arms round what should have been his waist. He tried to squirm away.

'Thea, look, there's something I ought to tell you.'

'What?' I took a large, noisy bite from my apple. His voice sounded tight and sort of solemn, as if he were about to lead the prayers in Assembly.

'It's about . . . Janet.' I felt scared, suddenly. I crammed in a chunk of cheese along with the apple. I felt I needed ballast.

'How are her parents?' I asked. I needed to distract him. Janet's father was a vicar, and with any luck, we could move away from Janet and on to the ecumenical movement or transubstantiation. But Adrian didn't even appear to have heard. He was fiddling with the cheese knife – tapping it, caressing it. He suddenly flung it on the table and turned around to face me. 'She's . . . we . . . er . . . I mean, we're . . . going to have a baby.'

I still had the apple cradled in my hands. It felt heavy, suddenly, as if I were clutching the whole spinning planet earth, struggling to hold it steady, while dark empty space plunged and roared around me.

'What did you say?' That was one of Leo's tricks, repeating the question. It gave you time and a sort of dignity.

'Janet's . . . pregnant.' The word sounded brutal, smug, uncaring.

I scraped my front teeth against the hard shiny skin of the apple, then yanked it away. I could see two neat little teeth marks breaking the skin. Pure cold white underneath. Apples don't bleed.

'Oh . . . nice,' I said.

He looked relieved. 'Yes, we're very pleased. Look, Thea darling . . .' (That darling was deliberate – a gift, an offering, a reparation for the baby.) 'It wouldn't work, you and me. We know that. We've tried it. You need a new start, a decent job. If you're happy in your work, other things seem far less important. Why don't you go to a proper employment agency? Get some help. Even do a course in something.'

'Yes,' I said. Janet used multi-coloured Kleenex. There were boxes of them everywhere, sheaves of tissues, yellow, lilac, pink. She'd probably have a pastel-coloured baby, zip him into lilac paper nappies, lay him on a primrose-crocheted doily. Her breast milk would come out pink and scented. Her baby would shit flowers.

'You mustn't let yourself *go*, Thea. You're attractive.' (I'm not.) 'There's no need to wear Leo's old clothes. Buy yourself some new ones.'

If Adrian had been the type to hate anyone, he'd have hated Leo, but he didn't believe in strong irrational feelings. He had visited me in Notting Hill and been suitably appalled.

'You ought to stand up to Leo, not let him take you over. It's as much your place as his.' (It isn't.) 'Clean it up. Take a pride in it. Assert your rights.'

'Yes,' I said again. It was the easiest word I could think of. Janet had installed a waste-disposal unit where I had had an overflowing bucket. You can see pictures in a bucket – landscapes of tea-leaves, still lives of lemon peel and tins.

'How many months?' I asked, as casually as if I were merely inquiring how long it was till Easter. I tossed a piece of cheese rind into the waste-disposal unit and listened to it spit and grind.

'What, darling?' Adrian was cutting up his apple into eight neat segments. He never cut apples when he lived with me. That's what teeth are for.

'Janet. How far gone is she?'

He handed me a piece of apple, as if I were a toddler or a chimpanzee. I knew he wanted to make it up to me, give me treats, distract me. I was already awash in darlings.

'Look, Thea darling, let's not go into it. I just wanted you to know, that's all. But I don't really like discussing Janet with you. It only upsets you.' (It doesn't.) 'Janet's all right. She's got a job. She knows where she's going. Frankly, Thea, you don't. You need to sort yourself out. Start again.'

'You mean leave Leo?' I shut my eyes and saw Leo lean and naked in his double bed. He had long, thin feet like that picture of Christ on the Cross in the Scottish National Gallery.

'Not necessarily. But don't let him rule you like he does. Establish some rights in the place. Tidy it, redecorate, cook proper meals, stick to a timetable.'

For five ruled and dotted years, I'd watched Adrian plotting out his own school timetables: first period – Hanoverians with the Lower Fifth; second period – Norman Invasion with the first formers. Janet probably had her own ante-natal timetable: first month – cells divide; second month – baby's limbs begin to form. I flung my half-eaten apple in the sink.

Adrian took my hand. He looked angry and anxious and tender all at once. I stared at his clean grey trousers. I could see his thing rearing up, tearing into Janet, leaving babies behind. Messy, almost careless. I wanted to hack the baby out of her, rip it out through her rose-scented frilly little cunt, the way it had got in.

'I'd better go,' I said.

Adrian's relief was almost comic. He hymned and scooped me to the door, pressed a bank-note into my hand, picked up the bag of apples and pushed it after me. Now I had my pocket-money, my tuck-box for the train. When I turned the corner, Adrian was still standing grey against his French Blue door. His and Janet's door.

I spread out the bank-note in the train and stared at it. It was a whole ten pounds. I wondered what it was for. Hush money, guilt money? Janet had Adrian and his (our) house and blond hair and a baby. And I had a ten-pound note. I stuffed it into the pocket of my jeans. I took out the apples and laid them in a line on the seat. (It was another empty carriage. Twickenham is much divorced.) There were five French Golden Delicious, all exactly the same size and perfectly rounded. Adrian and I had always eaten English apples, rough, blotchy ones in odd shapes and colours.

I picked one up and sniffed it, but it didn't smell. Janet deodorized everything, even apples. I pushed down the window of the carriage. The cold air rushed in and slapped me in the face. The train was juddering past rows of trim little semis, their neat back gardens running down almost to the edge of the railway track. Bare, cold, empty gardens, with only sooty privet or shivering brussels sprouts. The only colour was the washing, drooping on the lines. It was all Janet's washing – interlock vests and nylon overalls, everything non-iron and easy-care and pastel-coloured. Except the nappies. Rows and rows of nappies. Janet's baby's nappies. All smug, white, flapping, mocking . . .

I cupped an apple in my hands and aimed it at the nappies. Missed. It didn't even make the hedge. I flung another. Missed again. We had already left the nappies far behind. But there'd be more. There'd always be nappies. Other people's nappies. Other people's babies. I threw the last three apples so violently, they broke and squashed against the rails. I crumpled up the bag, kicked it under the seat and closed my eyes. Someone would wake me when we arrived at Waterloo.

three

I was almost back at Leo's, when I suddenly turned round again and trudged back to Notting Hill. There were half a dozen employment agencies just a minute from the tube. I stopped in front of the first one and stared at all the little white job-cards snowing up the window. They were tacked against a sheet of gold foil with coloured cut-out holly sprays prickling between them, and a reindeer or two nosing around the best ones. I suppose it was their way of jollifying slavery. Ruled and timetabled slavery is probably safer, anyway, than great lumps and voids of freedom. Adrian is often right. He'll never set the world alight, but he's the sort of man who keeps it ticking over.

'*Sous Chef*,' I read. 'For large West End Hotel. C. & G. training essential.'

'Maintenance Electrician. Must have own tools. Free meals and overalls.'

I had neither tools nor training. In fact, when it comes to jobs, I don't have much at all; no glowing references, nor strings of letters after my name, no father in High Places. Everybody wanted secretaries, or machine operators. Machines break down as soon as I go near them.

'Retail Clerk, Ledger Clerk, B.H. Clerk, Credit Control Clerk . . .' Between the rows and rows of clerks, I could see my own face gazing back at me. It didn't look good job material. My hair was tousled and un-brushed. The collar of my shirt (Leo's) was grubby underneath the shapeless sweater and the yellowing sheepskin. I knew already how the interviewers would look – long scarlet talons and eyes trailing three-tier lashes, trained to spot the ladder in your stocking or the hole in your story.

Lower down the window, a fully employed Santa Claus was emptying a pile of job-cards almost on to the pavement. 'Receptionist,' I squinted. 'Required for smart Mayfair firm.'

That was Janet's job. Only read City for Mayfair. Janet worked in a tall glass cage near Moorgate, with thick pile carpet even in the lifts. She was Indispensable. The partners and directors popped in and out, of course, but it was Janet at her twenty-foot reception desk who kept the whole firm going. Well, that was *her* story. Frankly, I suspect anyone can be a receptionist. You're just a smile strung between a blow-wave and a clean white collar. I'd work on myself tomorrow, and by Monday, I'd make that job in Mayfair. Just a matter of a change of style. Throwing out one face and clamping on another. You could be Maggie Thatcher and Madame Curie combined and still be shown the door, if you marched into the bureau in the wrong identikit. Thatcher would never have become Prime Minister at all if she'd worn a sheepskin or let her perm grow out.

I hailed a taxi. The driver looked at me suspiciously, but I pulled out Adrian's ten-pound note and waved it at him like a boarding pass. Taxis expect you to dress for them – like jobs. They stop in droves if you're wearing Persian lamb. It cost me £3.80 to the City. I almost enjoyed squandering Adrian's money on a visit to his wife. Janet could have bought three dozen nappy-liners with it, or a year's supply of foot deodorant. I knew I had to see her – well, not her exactly, but the baby. I suppose I hoped it would all turn out to be a gigantic hoax, some phantom pregnancy I could puncture with a pin. I over-tipped the driver who said, 'Good thing the snow's held off', which I suppose was a sort of apology for having looked suspicious in the first place. He set me down in London Wall. The buildings were so high, I felt dwarfed and dizzy. The whole area had a bleak, castrated look, as if the bulldozers had been in and smashed up anything that was cosy or homely or merely man-sized. Trees, clouds, colours, had all been confiscated. Even the sky looked like a slab of pre-stressed concrete. Huge cranes peered between the tower blocks, like spies, checking up that everyone was working. This was labour-land. They hadn't spent twenty million pounds on twenty-storey buildings just to let people live in them, or laugh in them, or play or fuck, or simply lark around. Those rows and rows of prison offices were all identical, with the same grey files, grey phones, steel desks, steel manacles. If there was a mural or a window-box, it was only part of the production drive, to cheer the workers and make them slave still harder.

Janet's block was so new and shining, it looked as if it had just been scaled and polished by a dentist. As I walked towards it, it grew taller and taller until the top half was bent back against the sky. There was a half-demolished building opposite, which was reflected and distorted in its glass, so that I felt as if I were walking straight into a pile of rubble. The automatic doors slid open, gobbled me up, and spat me out into the foyer. It had mock-marble pillars and a mock-stone fountain with plastic plants grouped round it. The pictures were mocking squares of colour, chosen to match the mock-leather chairs and the mock-silk wall hangings. There was real water splashing in the fountain and a real doorman with a real frown. I dodged him by nipping round the corner, up the stairs. Janet's firm was eleven floors up and I stopped at every floor and stared down at the City, until I gradually felt less like a human and more like a crane. At the eleventh storey, I paused for breath, then walked down the corridor and concealed myself behind the double-glass doors which said 'Mercantile Development and Investment Limited. Reception and Inquiries'.

I could see Janet clearly through the glass. Her desk looked rather like a coffin, in highly polished wood with lots of brass handles, and awash in flowers. There was nothing fake about the flowers. I could have fed myself for a fortnight on the price of just one bloom. They were re-arranged each morning by a girl in a magenta jumpsuit and a matching mini-van whose primary purpose in life was to set Janet off. It wasn't difficult. Janet had one of those television commercial complexions which never need to use the lotions they're advertising. She'd grown up in the country with extra milk and ballet lessons and badges from the Girl Guides for Stitchery and Housecraft. You could tell that her father was a vicar just by looking at her face which was all manna and ambrosia. Leo's father was probably a witch-doctor or ambassador to Satan. That's why he's dark and lean and sallow and has Armageddon in his eyes. Janet's eyes are the sort of blue you read about in Mills and Boon. She was simpering into one of the four cream telephones. Everything was cream – her blouse, her teeth, the thick pile rug, the hessian-covered walls. I could see her sitting in the country as a child, with pink ribbons on her plaits and a blonde buxom mother pouring double Devon cream on her all-milk porridge. She was made of double cream. It spilled down her cleavage to her soft, swelling breasts, which had always been large, but were now gallon-sized. (My own breasts are smallish and unspectacular. I haven't even got a proper cleavage, unless I fake one with what Adrian used to call an armoured bra.)

A man marched through the double doors and almost knocked me over. He was cream as well. Top-of-the-milk shirt, an exactly matching tie and a suit which looked as if it were pretending it was summertime in Acapulco. He and Janet exchanged double-cream smiles. Janet scribbled something on a pad, pushed back her orange. Dralon chair and stood up. And then I saw it. The baby. Janet's baby. Adrian and Janet's baby.

It was huge, monstrous, pushing out her stomach like some malignant growth, blocking all the space between her and Acapulco. I was prepared for one month (cells divide), two or three months even (baby's limbs begin to form), but not this vast, completed hulk, jutting out like a gargoyle, almost overbalancing her. It wasn't just a clutch of cells, but a living, breathing, kicking, finished creature which might drop out any moment and claim its name, its rights, its milk. It might even demand its father – *my* father, my husband, my Adrian.

Janet was still standing up. She no longer stood upright, as she had in all those years of Girl Guide Posture Badges and deportment lessons, but tipped back against the weight. She was totally transformed; not just her shape, her stance, her breasts, her breathing, but something else more subtle, more sublime. She had Entered The Kingdom, and been transfigured, glorified. Those preening hothouse flowers were nothing to do with Mercantile Investment. They were an offering to her alone – to fertility, to motherhood. Adrian had swelled inside her and sanctified her. She was growing round him like ivy round a tree, bursting into flower. I realized now I would never get him back.

Janet had sat down again and the baby vanished from my view. Only her flower face was left, and those lumbering milk churns weighing down the desk. The man from Acapulco was walking back towards me, whistling through the double doors. I darted after him into the lift and tried to stand close, so that some of Janet's glory would rub off on my own unhallowed, concave form. He had been in the Presence and was beatified. When we reached street level he shot away, and all I picked up was the tailwind from his expensive camel coat.

I turned left out of the building, across the road into Moor Street and along to Chiswell Street. The streets looked grey and empty, as if somebody had dumped all children, pets and people underground, and then tipped concrete over them. Not that I really cared about my surroundings – I was far too busy working out Janet's dates. That baby must have been in there before I'd even got the Decree Nisi. I'd thought I'd left Adrian, but really he'd already left me. He'd allowed me to play the role of deserter and destroyer, while he hung on to the house and his good name and the judge's sympathies, and Janet swelled and burgeoned on the sidelines. At least Leo had the decency to admit he was a swine, whereas Adrian confused you with ten-pound notes and darlingses and read the *Guardian* and *New Society*, and joined in all the agonizings about Northern Ireland and the slaughter of the seal, so that you *thought* he had a conscience. Yet all the time, he must have been sleeping with Janet and me in shifts. I saw it now. Janet had had the lunch and evening slots, while I got nights and breakfast. And while Adrian and I simply thrashed around like animals, he and Janet had been engaged in a sacred act. Easy for me to dismiss Janet's prowess between the sheets, imagining her wasting half her stint on douching, or refusing to remove her vest. In blazing fact, she and Adrian had been creating life – begetting, engendering, propagating – all those glorious, gloating, biblical words which kept the earth spinning and the grass thrusting and piled man on man on man.

I crossed the road and turned into Bunhill Row. I knew where I was going – St Joseph's church, a place of sanctuary when your stomach is a bombsite and your head a half-demolished building. It's one of the poorest Catholic churches in the whole of London. It isn't even consecrated, but God still lives there (when He's not at the Vatican or Lourdes or Knock or Compostela). I collect Roman Catholic churches like other people collect coins or stamps or Chinese restaurants. The only reason I know my way around, is because London for me is the bits between churches. St Joseph's is so hidden away and hard to find, that even a lot of priests have never heard of it. You can walk past it in the street and still be asking, 'Where's the church?' It's built in a basement, underneath a school which has now closed down, and all you can see is a door and a flight of dark stone steps with wild cats peeing on them. Most of the time, it's empty.

I slunk down the steps and into the church, which smells of chalk and ink and punishment and unwashed hands, like an old school hall in Dickens. There's nothing sublime about it – no towering nave, or shimmering mosaics, no Gothic tracery, or whispering arches. I didn't feel like splendour. I wanted a Cinderella church in a dark cellar, where I could hide away and be solitary and idle, after all the glass, the toil, the tower blocks. I was trying hard not to think of Janet.

I walked up to the altar and knelt down in the very front pew. I don't believe in humility. It only makes dominant people worse, and God, if

He exists, is bound to be a Leo. I say 'if He exists', but that's only in deference to Adrian who is what he calls an eclectic agnostic, which means he spent five years studying God in relation to anthropology, psychology, sociology, economics and historical geography, and still couldn't say for certain whether He was there or not. I knew He was, of course, because of my convent school. Step-fathers make quite an impression on you, especially when they're all you've got. Not that I talk about it much. People always assume that God and sex are incompatible, so that if you screw around, you can't grab God as well. That's rubbish.

Mind you, religion has always been a problem. My father was vaguely C. of E. and missing. My mother was an atheist with a private line to God. She railed at Him without believing in Him, and grudgingly accepted convent education as a sort of insurance policy against the bad vibes and worse morals of a world He hadn't created. That was the only concession she made to Him – entrusting me to the nuns – and I suspect it was more to improve my accent and my manners than to polish up my soul, or perhaps to put two hundred miles between us. She hadn't even allowed me to be baptized, although my father had booked the vicar and bought a silver christening mug (which disappeared when he did). The nuns at my school saw me as something between a leper and a freak. When they weren't struggling to fill the gaps in my religious ignorance, they were praying for my salvation. I feared damnation like other girls fear rape. Only Catholics were indisputably saved. I longed to be a Catholic, not only to avoid the horrors of hellfire, but also to be the blood-child of a close and legal Father.

Janet wasn't Catholic, but she had Adrian and her pregnancy instead, and parents who still celebrated their wedding anniversaries and sent each other cards with satin hearts and flowers on.

She kept squeezing her great swelling belly into the church, even though I'd tried to shut her out. The Blessed Virgin could have been her double – the same vanilla-blancmange complexion and social-worker expression in her eyes. And holding a baby, of course – *Janet's* baby – blond, blue-eyed and goody-goody, with her crinkly permed hair and stubby fingers. The church was full of hideous painted statues, all holding Janet's baby in their arms. One podgy infant was gurgling against St Anthony and another almost sitting on St Joseph's lily. It was a relief to turn to St Bernadette, who was holding nothing except a candle and who wasn't even looking at the Virgin, but staring up at the window as if she hoped she might escape. It's rare to find a statue of St Bernadette – that's why I liked this church. She's one of my favourite saints, in fact; a shabby, homely person, who was illiterate for years and never learned to spell. Saints make good substitutes for friends. They never let you down, or answer back, or pinch your boyfriends or your clothes. I always avoid the intellectual ones like St Thomas Aquinas, or the prigs like St Thérèse of Lisieux or the rigid toe-the-liners like St Ignatius.

St Janet was less easy to avoid. I could see her huge, misshapen stomach everywhere. In the swell of the tabernacle, the curve of the windows. The two fat pillars in front of the altar were nine months gone like she was. The halos of the saints were her white moon breasts. I wondered if it would be a son. Adrian and I had had a son, once. He's in a jar now, sterilized and labelled, a four-month foetus they saved for the students. It was a big teaching hospital and they asked me if I minded. How could I mind with a ward-round almost swamping me and the remnants of my baby still bleeding into the bed? We'd planned to call him Lucian. It meant light (I think). Adrian chose the name.

There was no light in the church, only a grey, musty film over everything as if chalk had been mixed with rust. The pews were scratched and grimy, and the kneelers looked as if some rodent had been nibbling them. It didn't really matter. It's like sex with a man who's got holes in his socks – it doesn't affect your orgasm. I could feel prayer oozing out of me – my soul lying back and opening, moistening to God's touch. I was almost scared to pray. I knew the prayer would be a savage one. But the words were forming in my mouth, squeezing through my lips, whispering through the church.

'Let Janet's baby die,' they murmured. Very simple, very unambiguous. I knew God heard, because at that very moment, all the lights went on and the church burst suddenly into life. The orange wall behind the altar glowed a deep sunset colour and the figures in the stained-glass windows fled into their backgrounds to escape the glare. Even the shabby wooden floor gleamed and shone a little. I turned round. A priest in a skimpy cassock was standing by the light switch. I think he was trying to flush me out, like you might shine a torch on a rodent to blind and startle it.

'Good afternoon,' I said, and added 'Father' to placate him.

'You shouldn't be here,' he griped. 'The church is locked. I've trouble enough with vandals, as it is . . .'

'It wasn't locked,' I said. 'And I'm not a vandal.' I threw in another 'Father' for good luck. I like to call them that. Fathers are rare enough, for heaven's sake.

He mumbled something about 'can't go away for two seconds without intruders', so I got up from my knees. Priests are often a stumbling block to prayer. They're more materially minded than most of the laity – always on about sex, or vandals, or the state of the church roof, or their own poverty. I made a giant-sized sign of the cross to mollify him and walked down towards the door. He was poking about by the rack of religious pamphlets, probably making sure I hadn't nicked one. I had, in fact, noticed one on Motherhood which I could have pinched for Janet. I knew what it would say – every new baby is a soul for God, and it's God who puts it there. I only wished He had, instead of Adrian.

The priest was walking up towards the altar. I strode after him, scrabbling in my pocket. There was still five pounds sixty left from Adrian's money, and twelve pence of my own. I poured it into his hands. 'Say a Mass for me, Father,' I implored. 'Special intention, something very urgent.' He seemed to hesitate. Could you still buy Masses, or was that only in the Middle Ages? Adrian would know, but I could hardly inquire of Adrian when it was his and Janet's baby I was bribing God to kill. Fortunately, a coin dropped on the floor. The priest bent down to pick it up (they never scorn small change), and while he was grovelling on the floor, I nipped through the door and out.

He'd have to say the Mass, now I'd paid cash in advance. After all, I'd offered all I had for it. I hadn't even left myself the tube fare. I buttoned up my sheepskin, stuck my hands in my empty pockets, and began the long trek back.

four

I was so chilled, blistered, and exhausted when I finally limped into Notting Hill, that I made straight for Leo's vodka, which he keeps hidden in his bureau. There was only a centimetre left, so I topped it up with Lucozade, then added the dregs from a dry martini bottle. It tasted strange, but comforting. I sat in the kitchen with my feet on a chair and tried to think of nothing. Leo wasn't back yet. The breakfast dishes were sticky on the table, the broken vase still weeping on the floor. I picked it up, tenderly, as if it were part of Leo. There were four main pieces and a little spray of chips. I fitted them together on the table, but the cracks still showed and shivered and there were tiny gaps and crannies in the phoenix. I had disfigured Leo, smashed his youth, clipped his wings. The vase was a sort of proof of his existence. That's why people have children, I suppose, to prove they were once alive (Leo hasn't any).

On the way back, I'd nipped into a bookshop and filched a book called *Mending and Restoring China*, in reparation to him. I opened it at the step-by-step instructions, spread a copy of the *Listener* on the table, and fetched glue, sandpaper, and a few of Leo's tools. There was a picture of the author on the back cover – E. H. Leatherstone Esquire – a finicky old fellow with a white moustache, which looked as if it had been daubed and stiffened with his own flour-paste. Mr Leatherstone suggested making a rest-bed for the broken object. I liked the word rest-bed. It had overtones of healing, care, compassion. I wished I could lie on one myself and have all my shattered pieces stuck together. The mending wasn't easy, even with the diagrams. The smallest chips fell off, and the glue squeezed out too quickly, and the phoenix seemed to have lost a lot of plumage. If I held it firmly in my hands against the table, it turned into a bird again and seemed even to be arising from the ashes, but as soon as I let go of it, it broke apart and moulted, and I was left with just a pile of random feathers.

The trouble with me is I haven't any staying power. As soon as I start something, I want to give it up. I really wanted Leo. I abandoned the vase and walked along to his bedroom which is the darkest room in the house. He always keeps his curtains closed and has lots of dark purple hangings and gloomy pictures of uninhabitable landscapes. I took off all my clothes and crawled into his bed which is high and covered with a tattered Persian rug with black and scarlet dragons woven into the border. It's so heavy, it's like another man on top of you. Sometimes, I lay beneath the two of them (Leo and the rug) and felt I was being crushed into a sort of dark, dragon-haunted past, which I dimly remember from some other, nobler, long-ago existence when I was perhaps a male and probably a Persian.

A blob of glue had dried hard on my finger. I opened my legs and touched the glue against myself. A man once told me I was over-sexed. That worried me. Men are never over-sexed – only virile. Adrian hinted it was simply boredom and said that once I found a satisfying job, I'd get sex into perspective (which I suppose means doing it once a week, at night, with a shower before and after and all the lights turned out). I haven't got a sister, or even a close girlfriend, so I've no idea how much normal people think about it. All I know is that when we do it, Leo likes me more. If he ever said, 'I love you', it would undoubtedly be in bed.

I was lying there, imagining him saying it, and trying out different approaches with the glue, when Leo came in. Or rather Karma did, with Leo on the end of him. Karma is a cross between a mastiff and an Afghan hound, which is more or less impossible. He had lost all the shaggy, silky, swanky Afghan bits, and retained the square solid shoulders and the black mastiff muzzle. He had the faults of both breeds – being aggressive, neurotic, temperamental and difficult to train. He was also a loner, a fighter, ruggedly independent and rare – all of which Leo is himself. If he weren't Leo's dog, he would have looked grotesque. As it was, he looked majestic – dark, large, lowering and explosive.

He came right up to the bed and sniffed me between the legs, which is one of the reasons I don't like him. He always knows what I've been up to, and then reports to Leo. If I lie in his bed, Leo usually comes and fucks me, anyway. It's our sign language. Proud men like him can't demean themselves by asking. My legs were already opening wider and my nipples sitting up and begging. Leo has that effect on me. Even if I see him in a supermarket, I start to moisten among the cornflakes and the Fairy Snow. That's why sex is so dangerous, I suppose. I'd worship Jack the Ripper or Idi Amin if either of them fucked like Leo does.

He hadn't even looked at me. He was standing with his long brown back towards me, dragging off his sweater. The hair grows very low on the nape of his neck and then stops abruptly, as that slope of pale, singing flesh plunges down, down, towards his buttocks. I lay very still and tried to think of Belsen and Cambodia and the sinking of the Titanic, anything to turn me off. Leo pulled another sweater on, a thinner one, and then a grey cashmere polo over that. And finally his sheepskin.

'I'm taking Karma for a walk,' he said.

Karma barked when he heard his name. I could almost see him gloating. He had plumed up his tail (which he probably shouldn't have had, being half a mastiff) and was pawing the ground with his great eager feet.

'But it's almost dark,' I objected. I dug the glue in hard, to try and hurt myself.

'So?'

'Can I come too?' See how I grovel? I should have shrugged and lain there, read a book, filed my nails. Instead, I was already pulling on my clothes, panting after Karma, zipping up my jeans, wailing, '*Wait*, Leo,' like a five-year-old. He always walked faster than I could. I had to half run to keep up with him, which is very uncomfortable, not to say undignified (which I suspect is why he does it). He strode, and I trotted, down the hill, round the corner, across three streets and into the entrance to Holland Park. It was twilight and they were almost locking up. Grass and sky were both grey, trees only shapes and shadows. It was raining again, the sort of thin, hopeless drizzle which somehow makes you wetter than an out-and-out downpour. I hadn't had time to grab my coat. I was wearing only a shirt and a sweater, and I could feel the cold sneaking its hands inside them, turning my breasts goose-pimply and clammy.

I prayed for Leo to speak. I had no idea what he was thinking, whether his breakfast (lunch) with Otto had gone well, and if he'd bought the vase. Sometimes, he was silent only because he was thinking, or working on a problem like the relationship of relativity to nirvana. He'd been reading a book on modern physics in relation to Taoism. It caused him a lot of anguish which I couldn't share. I dared not even raise the subject since the time I'd pronounced Tao wrongly. One mispronunciation could ruin a whole day.

Leo walked, too fast, down towards the Holland Walk entrance where dogs are allowed off the lead. Karma wasn't on one, anyway. He was swooping in proud, swaggering circles, like a race horse. He was so large, he made the grass throb. After every eight or ten circuits, he bounded back to Leo, rammed his huge black head in his master's hands, and then crashed away again. He seemed to be flaunting his own simple joy in rain and speed and motion. If I ever return to earth in some reincarnation, I hope I return as Karma. Only then could I be best beloved of Leo and yet spared his anger.

I didn't even know if he *was* angry. But the silence made me so tense, I filled the spaces with what I *imagined* was his fury, and then built it up, up, until I was almost choking in it. I was always doing that. Then, when I was all but dead with terror, he'd lean across and kiss me, or pick up a pebble in the shape of a heart and smuggle it into my palm, or ask me what I thought of Olive Schreiner.

It was like falling up a step you didn't know was there. I'd realize, then, the fury had all been mine, something I'd cultivated in my head like a patch of dark, spongy fungus. Often, I made him angry simply by assuming that he *was*. Even now, I could hear myself trying out phrases in my head, stupid, dangerous things guaranteed to wound him. I wanted to grovel, humble myself, lie at his feet and lick them, but all the loving, healing phrases had rotted away like summer leaves and there was only the thick black mulch we were squelching underfoot.

The sky was turning darker and darker. The clouds were like chunks of rough grey pumice stone, chafing and scouring the trees. I kept glancing at my watch and playing little games with it. If Leo didn't speak within one more minute, then I would stop in my tracks and scream. The minute passed. Two more minutes. If he hadn't broken the silence by another two, I would kneel in the mud and beg him to kick me, trample me, anything to prove I still existed. Three minutes, four. It was almost closing time. Any moment now, they would switch on the floodlights in the Belvedere Gardens, lock all the other gates, turn us out. The park was almost empty, anyway. Only the odd drenched dog with its owner, birds muttering their bedtime stories, a tramp growing on a bench like mould.

Only Karma was alive, pounding and streaking past us, throwing up the grass, barking to the sky. I had never seen such exultation in a dog, rolling on his back, shaking the water from his coat, pouncing on sticks, terrorizing trees. I knew he was mocking me, my misery, my silence, the strange, stupid fears I was piling in my head. I longed to race and flaunt like him, to bark, romp, flurry, chase my tail. All I had to do was break the tension, fling my arms round Leo's neck and yell out wild, singing, leaping, glorious things; tell him I loved him, loved the park, the rain, the sky, the earth, the cold. But somehow, the words wouldn't form themselves. They were broken, soggy, unravelling. Another minute passed. Leo's feet made blurred, sludgy noises on the path. The rain was drammering through the trees, shining and streaming on the holly leaves. Karma rocketed past, spattering me with mud. I tried again. It should have been so easy. The park was full of things I could pick up and present to him – the greys, the greens, the shadows, peacock feathers, skeleton leaves. Or if I could just say something *ordinary* – 'Was he tired, would it rain tomorrow, weren't the puddles deep?' I edged a little closer, cleared my throat.

'I went to Twickenham today,' I said. My voice had suddenly come louder, as if someone had switched an amplifier on. Leo hadn't answered. He was striding ahead, lashing into the branches with a stick.

'And Adrian screwed me on the kitchen floor.'

Leo stopped. I realized now, he hadn't been cross before, at all. He'd simply been meditating, or digesting his lunch with Otto, or watching the changing colours in the sky. Karma stopped, too. Even the rain seemed to let up for a moment – one brief, shocked, paralysing moment while Leo caught his breath. I could see the bare trees fidgeting and whispering behind him. He grabbed my wrist and twisted it behind me. Karma dropped his tail. He could pick up anger like a seismograph.

'You're a whore, Thea, a dirty little whore.'

His hand had made red marks across my wrist. I shook it free. 'I can hardly be a whore when Adrian's my husband.'

'He's *not* your husband. Not any more.'

That hurt. Marriage to Adrian was like saving with the Abbey National. It had made me feel cosy and protected, sensible, conventional, joined to all the other savers in the land. Now I was a debtor, a drop-out, who didn't have a number any more, or a little blue book which told me who I was and how much that was worth.

'It's your fault, anyway. If you'd screwed me first, I wouldn't have needed Adrian.'

He had pinioned me against a tree. Both my hands were trapped behind my back. He does that when we fuck. I love it then. He rams in and out of me while I lie disabled from the waist up, kicking and flailing with my feet and yelling. Sometimes he muzzles me, as well, so I can't even scream, only bite his hands. He loves me powerless.

I was powerless now. His face was very close to mine. I could see the tiny points of dark stubble pricking against the sky, the fine black hairs protruding from his nose, his full, brownish lips.

'If you ever sleep with Adrian again . . .' he said. I could almost see the stubble growing, hear his whole body breathing, digesting, excreting, beating, 'I'll *kill* you.' His voice was so soft, it was like a tiny beechnut dropping in a dense wood. I heard a twig snap underneath his shoe. 'I'll break you into pieces. Do you understand me, Thea?'

I nodded. I almost worshipped him because he could say things like that and mean them. Adrian would never threaten me, not in a thousand years, not even if I committed some atrocity. Leo let me go. It was raining faster now, almost in relief. We had left the formal centre of the park and were striding towards the woodlands. There were rustlings and cracklings in the undergrowth, sudden swoops of wings, the cackle of a rook, and, over everything, the hoarse, bad-tempered rumble of the rain. I loped along behind him, my shoes squelching in the mud, jeans clinging sodden to my knees. I felt horror mixed with pride. Leo had made me powerful like a woman in a Greek myth, dark, dangerous, monumental, driving men to murder. With Adrian, I was only the Upper Second, some scatty and exasperating urchin whose ear you tweaked or sweets you confiscated.

Leo turned into the avenue of chestnut trees, dark trunks lined up like guards, branches reaching out to trap us. It was so hushed, so gloomy, even Karma seemed subdued. He was padding along close to Leo now, both of them large, black, unpredictable. I suddenly realized we belonged, all three of us. We were all dangerous, all majestic, all from the same dark myth. I wanted to shout with triumph, hurl myself upon them and claim my kinship with them. I fell against Leo's back and smelt wet leaves, wet sheepskin.

'Leo,' I cried. 'Leo.'

He stopped and turned around. He was kissing me so roughly, my whole mouth had turned to pain. I could feel his hands moving further down. We were pressed against the fence which lined the wild, tangled enclosure beyond the trees. Half the fence was broken. Leo trampled it down and forced a passage through. I followed. I wanted him so wildly, I was already pulling off my sweater, fighting with my shirt. Leo pushed me down. The ground was soggy underneath my back, a briar scratched against my breasts, and I could feel cold, clammy leaves sticking to my shoulders. Leo was tearing off my jeans. The cold was so sharp it hurt. As soon as I was naked, it swooped in and stuck its fingers in all my secret places. Leo had entered me, too fast. Everything was pain, the tall trees rushing past me, the steel rain stinging in my eyes. I was shivering with cold and shock and sheer simple shouting ecstasy, like Karma's. Leo had only half his clothes off. His body burned against mine, yet was cold round all the edges, as the rain lashed in between us and tried to force us apart.

He was hammering against me, as I slid and slithered in the black sludge underneath. It was a wild, surrendering feeling. I was a leaf, a twig, a straw, crushed by his body, joined to all the earth. I could smell bright rain and bruised leaves and the strange oily tang of Leo's hair as it brushed against my eyes. A bird swooped past, an insect ran across my hand. I opened my eyes and saw the sky sweeping down towards us, clouds wrapping round our bodies like a duvet, stars and moon blanked out to keep us private. The bell was clanging for closing time. They were shutting all the gates, turning people out. They couldn't turn us out – they would never find us. The rain was muffling all our cries. It was joining in with us, slamming down on me in time with Leo, forcing its way inside me like another lover. The whole world was inside me, sky and earth, clouds, great trunks of trees.

Suddenly, the lights went on, further down the park. Leo stopped, sat up. I could have wept for those few lost moments before he entered me again. I was nothing on my own. But joined to Leo, I was a king, a priest, a god. My body only worked when it was under him, over him, sharing the same wild purple rhythm, the same crashing heartbeat.

He rolled me on my belly and licked the mud off my shoulders. His tongue was rough and humble at the same time. He was like a dog, a great, dark, dangerous animal mounting me from behind. His own dog was blundering through the undergrowth, but he hardly heard it. He had pressed my face against the earth. I could feel the sting and prickle of holly leaves, the nudge of a tree root underneath my breasts. My hair had fallen over my head so that I lay in a tent of drenched, soggy strands. The gardens were floodlit now, the park shut, but here everything was dark and open. We were in our own private park, which had no lights, no gates, no rules. Leo had twisted his body at an angle to my own. I was burning hot inside, freezing outside. My hands and feet were numb. Cold was darting through me like a snake. I hardly cared. Cold and rain were all part of it, part of us. I couldn't tell where Leo ended and I began, where the numbness at the edges melted into the scorching, spinning feeling, further in.

Leo refused to let me move. He knew exactly how to trap me, muzzle me with his body, until I was wild with having to be still. Any man can let you thrust. I worshipped Leo because he didn't let me, and yet he made my stillness more fierce, more frenzied, than any amount of movement. I could hear myself shouting out above the rain. I could also hear Karma howling for his master. His howls drove me on. I came three times just thinking of him jealous and outraged. We had snuffed him out, so that he was only a broken shadow at our heels. Leo was *my* master now.

He was coming. I clung on. Leo has great seething, swelling, violent, anguished comes which swallow up me and him and everything around us. It was starting now. I dug my fingers into the earth to get a grip. He likes me to squeeze and squeeze and yell out words and almost fight with him. I shut my eyes and saw a shadowy group of swarthy park-keepers creeping up on us, bending down to watch, the gold braid of their uniforms scratching rough against my back. Their flashlights were blinding me, the hot breath of their tracker dogs panting through my breasts. I was moving now. We were all moving, all coming. Shouting, pounding, bucking, hurting, coming. Karma was coming and the keepers coming and the whole world and sky and earth and world and Leo Leo Leo Leo Leo . . .

five

We slept together that night – I mean *really* slept, in the same bed, in the same bedroom, with all twenty dragons crouching and rejoicing over us. In the morning, Leo left for work like a normal man, and I sat down with a piece of paper, Adrian-fashion, and tried to make a plan. Normally, I hardly listen when Adrian rattles on about getting jobs and settling down. But things were different since the baby. I knew I'd really lost him now. He wasn't just a couple, but a family. There'd be other kids (all Daddy's boys); bright, shining, cheerful, jolly Christmases; parent-teacher meetings; football workouts in the park; bruised shins, broken legs. I sat and thought about the broken legs. I hoped there'd be a lot of them, fractured skulls as well, deformities.

Somehow, I had always thought of Adrian as being in the background of my life, like a sort of supplement, or back-stop, a universal comforter. Janet hadn't counted. Even with all those 'J's' on everything, I felt I could always peel them off. They were only transfers, not tattoos. But now, she and Adrian were indissolubly united. The baby had pooled their genes, tied them together with its umbilical cord, imprinting their new, combined formula for ever and ever down the generations. I shivered. I had only Leo, now. I would have to change him, mould him, batter against him until he let me in. Adrian was right. I couldn't drift and doze for ever, letting Leo keep me, own me, trample me, treat me like his second, smaller dog.

I stared at Adrian's wedding ring, mocking on my finger. I was married to Leo now. He'd never buy me a nine-carat noose from a high-street jeweller's. He'd never buy me a ring at all – full-stop. All the same, I liked it when people looked at us and assumed we were married because we both had the right bit of booty on our wedding fingers. Leo's ring was a heavy antique gold one he'd bought from a market stall. It was no more connected with me or marriage or mating than Adrian's ring united me to Leo, but people didn't *know* that.

I twisted the band round and round and round. I felt a racking spasm of energy like a labour pain. I wanted to scour out my life like a saucepan, sweep through all the mess and complications with a rough, scratchy broom. If pregnant women get the urge to purge and clean, then I was the one who was pregnant.

I swept my hand across the table and stemmed the tide of magazines and papers; stuffed them in a cupboard, weighted them down with the peanut-butter jars, the dictionaries, the playing cards, all the things which Leo had dug out weeks ago, or years ago, and never put away. I banished the bread and tea and branflakes to the larder. It was crammed with fancy, foreign delicacies – guavas and black-eyed beans, bird's nest soup and lumpfish roe – exotica he'd bought in Soho delicatessens and forgotten to enjoy. I threw out every tin and jar and packet which looked strange or stale or rusty, or was priced in old pence. I cleared the dishes, cleaned the sink. I didn't dust or polish. The kitchen was so gloomy, you couldn't see the dust, so there was no point in going to extremes.

I started on myself, instead. I washed my hair in Fairy Liquid, dried it with a drier, and secured it with a brown velvet ribbon, with long streamers hanging down the back. I got out all the pots and bottles and lotions my mother had been giving me (in mingled hope and reproach) for the last ten Christmases and spread a selection of them on my face. There was no mirror in my room upstairs and the bathroom one was always cracked and steamy, so I sat at Leo's dressing-table and stared at my reflection. My hair is my best feature. It's very thick and straight and reaches almost to my waist. It's the sort of middle brown which was described as dark when I was married to (sandy) Adrian, but looks almost mousy when I'm standing next to Leo. It's the same with my eyes. They started off a good, strong, uncompromising brown, but once I lived with Leo, they paled and faded as if someone had left them out in the sun for too long. My skin is sallow like Leo's, though not as smooth, but I have better teeth than him. I rarely bother with my looks. This time, though, I messed about with scents and salves and varnishes, until I felt very frail and precious and new-born, like something which had climbed out of an egg and still had damp feathers and shaky legs. I pulled on a dress sprigged in dark purple flowers, with a tiny collar and a row of fiddly buttons down the front. I looked modest and demure. I pinked in my lips and gave myself high Slavonic cheekbones out of a bottle. I stared at the woman in the mirror. It wasn't me. It wasn't even a Mayfair receptionist, more like the owner of a Bond Street picture gallery. I shivered. I know nothing about art. I'm the sort of person who muddles up Vorticism with

Expressionism and hasn't a clue what either of them mean. (There are probably more '-isms' in art than in any other field, except sex.) But I wasn't going to think about sex – not today. This was reform day, new-start day, get-a-job day, cook-a-meal day. I took off the dress and put on a suit in fine grey tweed which my mother had bought me in an attempt to wean me off my dungarees. I coiled my hair on top, removed the ribbon, and changed my lips from 'Dusky Pink' to 'New Dawn'. Now I was a receptionist, perhaps not quite Mayfair, but getting closer all the time. I didn't have a coat and it was January outside. Well, I'd simply have to freeze. Leo's sheepskin would only turn me into someone else.

I stood for a full ten minutes outside the employment agency before daring to go in. When I did, everything was mustard-coloured vinyl, including the plants. There were only two interviewers, but they appeared to be handling the entire London job market between them. Phones were screaming, temps jostling for their pay cheques and every available mustard-vinyl chair was in use. A Girl Friday who looked as if she'd just made it into double figures was trying to keep control. 'Temp or perm?' she asked me.

I paused. I would have loved to have said 'permanent', but it's not a word I have much faith in.

'Oh, temporary, I think.'

She handed me a form so long and detailed, I almost walked straight out again. There's never enough of me to spread on forms. I've only got one Christian name to start with, and that a mere four-letter one. They'd left so much space for your educational record, I doubt if Einstein could have filled it. I invented a few O-levels to make it look less bare. There were whole long lists of skills you were asked to tick or cross. Some of them I'd never even heard of. I thought of ticking every third one, just to show I was keen, but in the end, I ticked the four most likely. I'd like to have compiled my own list. There'd be ticks for praying, then, and for fellatio and making fudge, and being the only girl in London who'd eaten every one of Baskin-Robbins thirty-one flavours in the same week. (That was last July and cost me as much as half a pair of new jeans.)

I'd just put a zero in the box which said 'Number and Ages of Children' when the girl came back. I took my half-completed form and followed her over to a metal desk which had a notice on it saying,

'No time-sheet, no pay'. Behind it was a woman made of stainless steel with a smile on top. The smile was so insistent, it must have been cut right through her, like letters in a stick of rock.

'*Do* sit down.' The smile bent in the middle, but still stayed put.

I sat. The soggy vinyl chair was still warm from the last applicant. The interviewer scanned my form, still smiling. I wondered if she practised the smile at night, or switched it off the minute she got home, and started kicking cats or roughing up old ladies. So much charm seemed suspect. Every time the phone rang, she said, '*Do* excuse me, *please*', as if she'd peed on the carpet, and when a girl butted in to demand her pay cheque, she threw me so many extra little smilelets, I almost picked them up and started a smile collection. I found myself simpering back. I felt like a schoolgirl sucking up to the head prefect or the history mistress. Any minute now, I'd be offering to carry her books. She so inspired me, I concocted delightful and exciting little lies for her. We were going over my employment record now, and I told her tales of jobs I'd manned for gruelling and devoted years (most of them I pinched from Janet), and how I'd only left to nurse my (long-dead) grandmother. She must have been impressed, because she phoned the Mayfair job I wanted there and then, and even persuaded them to take me on without an interview. (It was Friday afternoon and they were desperate.)

I was to start on Monday, which gave me the whole weekend to get myself in order. It all seemed neat and businesslike, like one of Adrian's timetables. My boss had an OBE and a double-barrelled name, which I felt was even better than the luncheon vouchers.

Once I was accepted, the smile switched abruptly off, like a sort of 'file closed' sign, and I could feel the interviewer trying to edge me to the door.

'I'll have to take up your references on Monday, but I'm sure there'll be no problems.' She was already smiling over my shoulders at the next one in the queue.

'No,' I assured her. I'd given her the names of two ex-lovers, both of whom owed me favours.

I swept through the door, looking pityingly at the other applicants still grovelling for employment. I was now a fully-fledged receptionist, with my own time-sheet and introduction card, shoring up the economy, contributing to society – a success, a salary-earner, a slave.

When I got back, the receptionist and I sat down to a proper lunch.

It would be fatal to change my character too soon. I could ruin everything by flinging off my suit and munching a Mars bar, or scraping out last night's saucepans in my nightie. I made myself a dainty little *omelette aux fines herbes* (dried-up parsley I found in one of Leo's jars) and ate it with a chicory salad and a piece of Camembert. It all felt very Mayfair. I laid the table properly and used one of Leo's hand-painted Chinese plates which had a peony on it. As the omelette went down, the petals grew bigger and bigger, until there was no egg and all flower.

I was sipping my second cup of coffee (Melitta filter) when Leo rang. He said all sorts of luscious, creamy things until I felt I'd consumed a very rich, succulent pudding or been crammed with liqueur chocolates. Leo's like that. He can scream abuse at me one minute, and then pick every flower in paradise the next, and lay them at my feet.

'I'm bringing back some friends,' he added, almost as an after-thought.

I panicked. Leo's friends terrify me. They're all artistic and unpre-dictable and do things like shiatsu or batik or Reichian psychology or water-divining.

'How long are they going to stay?' I asked. I pushed my plate away. The peony was wilting.

'No idea.'

'I mean, will they want a meal?'

'Course. That's what they're coming for.'

'I'll cook it, then.'

'Don't be silly, Thea. You know you never cook.'

'I do. I used to. I'd *like* to cook this time.'

'Just make sure you're in, that's all.'

'I'm *always* in. Leo, listen . . .'

'And looking good.'

'Leo . . .'

'What?'

'I've got a job.'

'Congratulations. Where?'

I was starting to tell him about the employment agency when the pips went for the second time. He was phoning from a public call-box at a picture dealer's. I waited for the phone to ring again. I felt sure he'd call me back, but nothing happened.

My coffee had gone cold with a sort of scum on top, but I made myself sit down and finish it. Mayfair receptionists don't panic because a few odd friends decide to drop in for dinner. Leo always coped, in any case. He'd come in early and concoct complicated things, like bouillabaisse or dolmades, flinging in brandy and garlic, and using all sorts of exotic seasonings like dillweed and juniper berries. Or he'd storm the local delicatessens and return piled high with pitta bread and taramasalata, goat's cheese and salami, smoked eel and stuffed olives. I just hovered in the background, emptying waste-buckets and washing up the debris.

Not this time. This was cook-a-meal day. I'd already planned it, and if I had to cook for a crowd instead of two, well, all the better. It was more of a challenge, a more dramatic start to my new-year timetable. I wouldn't go too far. I wouldn't do a Janet on them and serve *Noisettes d'Agneau à la Française*, with lighted candles and the butter cut in little whorls. It would be aubergines in some form or other. There is something noble and classless about an aubergine. Somehow, you can't be criticized, even if they turn out wrong. And, most important, Leo likes them. If I wore my purple dress, I'd even match them. I could make the whole meal purple. Leo loves *themes* for things. He was always having Greek dinners (retsina and stifado) or Spanish ones (sangria and paella) or sixteenth-century feasts with mead and boars' heads. I'd have a *purple* theme. We'd have bortsch to start with, which would suit Leo's (probably) Russian mother, and something damsony to finish with. I'd spied bottled damsons in the larder, dark, swollen ones, bobbing about in brandy. Even though they were old, I hadn't thrown them out, because they'd somehow reminded me of baby Lucian, pickled in his jar.

An enormous purple strength was flowing through me like a blood transfusion. I felt almost equal to Leo, as tall as him, as strong as him, with metal in my bones. I took the largest basket and went out shopping to all his favourite shops and bought aubergines and olives and minced lamb and onions and fat hot beetroots and double cream and five different cheeses and black grapes. Money was a problem. In one of the Pakistani shops I got credit, and another accepted a cheque. (It would take them at least until Tuesday to realize it was only a boastful scrawl on a piece of paper.) I paid for the rest with two ten-pound notes I'd taken from Leo's bureau. It wasn't actually stealing. They were his friends I was feeding, after all, and I could always pay it back with my first week's wages.

When I returned, I removed my suit so as not to spoil it, but I kept the hair and the cheekbones. I had no desire to sink back into that over-sexed slut again, who couldn't cook and wouldn't work and let people walk all over her.

I overdid it, I suppose. I made so much food, there was hardly a dish or pan I hadn't used. I didn't even know how many friends were coming. It could be two or three, or nearer twenty. You never knew with Leo. I even tidied everything. I went through the entire two floors, scooping up clutter and confusion from every surface. Most of it was Leo's. Even in my part of the house, his possessions had gate-crashed and intruded. It was a strange sensation, stuffing Leo into cupboards, flinging him in waste-bins, shutting him in drawers. I draped a large purple shawl over the kitchen table and found some purple ostrich feathers which I arranged in a dark blue vase. It looked sensational. The food wasn't perfect. I'd never made bortsch before and it came out rusty rather than purple, and had little oily globules floating on the top. I hid them with some parsley I had left over from my omelette. The damsons curdled the cream. I'd whipped them together to make a sort of mousse which was a definite disaster, especially as I'd forgotten to remove the stones. But it would be dark by the time we reached the dessert, so people might not notice. The aubergines were better. I had stuffed them with the lamb and rice and onions, and they looked dark and smug and swelling.

By six o'clock, I was exhausted. I lay in the bath (Leo's – my part doesn't have a bathroom) and sipped the rough red wine I'd bought to moisten the aubergines. I'd only used a cupful and it seemed a shame to waste it. I was getting frightened now. My cheekbones had run into sweat, and my hair was falling down. Once I was naked, it was much more difficult to keep up the Mayfair receptionist façade. For one thing, I'm too fat. People who win are always slim (like Gandhi and greyhounds and Disraeli). For another, I was dreading seeing Leo. All very well standing up to him when I was safe in Adrian's semi. But supposing he came in angry or exhausted, or had splurged all his money on his own choice of food and was furious when he saw I'd done the same. Or had decided on a cold buffet instead of a hot sit-down meal. Or needed the twenty pounds to buy more wine. (Mine was only a trickle now.)

I stepped out of the bath and stared into the cracked and steamy mirror. I could see already that my face was slipping. The craven, shabby, jobless whore was sneaking back again. My double-barrelled boss would know immediately I wasn't a receptionist. I'd be sitting there, at my six-foot rosewood desk, between my Moyses Stevens orchids and the switchboard I knew I couldn't operate, and my past would show through like a tumour on an X-ray. No good pretending to be a Janet. Janets don't need to daub make-up on their souls, or draw themselves new contours. I might get by, first thing in the morning, but by 5 p.m., I'd have cracked and melted. All those creamy hessian customers would know I'd screwed a fifteen-year-old waiter, after only two small brandies, and had stolen a floral duvet-cover from Swan & Edgar's. (No one caught me. The waiter took six and a quarter minutes and I left the duvet cover on the counter of the next big store I came to. I didn't even *own* a duvet. But it was still a crime.)

I wrapped myself in Leo's rough black towel and rubbed myself almost raw with it. The flesh needed punishing. I must drub it down, deodorize it, force it into another mould. I dragged on a pantie-girdle which was far too tight and left red weals across my bottom. I heaved up the straps of a wired and armoured bra. Already, it was hard to breathe. I put on the purple dress with the fastidious little buttons. My fingers were trembling as I tried to fasten them.

'Liar!' they muttered. 'We know you're not demure. They'll find you out.'

I didn't listen. I picked up my lipstick and drew a cupid's bow. I made my eyes larger and more innocent. I painted health and wholesomeness on my cheeks. I pared down my face into more aristocratic lines. It was all a colossal lie. I was a sallow, base-born slut who had once masturbated with a Mars bar. I ought to ring them straight away and tell them I couldn't take the job. It wasn't fair to them, misleading them, lying in the interview, cheating on the forms. I trailed over to the phone. I could hear the bortsch spitting and glugging on the gas. I couldn't even cook.

There were two rings, two clicks and then an Ansafone. 'The Burton Bureau is now closed. Please phone at nine o'clock on Monday for the best jobs in London. The Burton Bureau is now closed . . . now closed, now closed, now closed . . .'

Nine o'clock on Monday, I was expected in almost-Mayfair. Mr Double-Barrel OBE would be peering at me through the flowers.

He'd have made me out a timetable, by then. First month, cells divide; second month, baby's limbs begin to . . . Adrian. I had to ring Adrian. He'd know what to do. He could tell Mr Mayfair I wasn't well again. I dialled his number.

'Oh, hallo, is that . . .'

'Sister, thank God! How *is* she?'

'Wh . . . what did you . . . ?'

'That's Sister Maddox, isn't it?'

'Who?'

'Oh, I'm *sorry*, I thought it was the hospital.'

He didn't even know me. Adrian thought his own wife was Sister Maddox. Anyway, what was he doing talking to a hospital, when *I* was the one who was ill? In all our married years, I'd never allowed Adrian to be poorly. That was my privilege.

'Adrian, it's me, Thea.'

'Oh, my God. Look, Thea, not now, I can't . . . It's . . .'

I could feel panic boiling up like bortsch. Adrian never said 'not now'. He was always there, like the English Channel, or the Houses of Parliament, or Harrods.

'I've got a job, Adrian, like you said. I've done *everything* you said, but it isn't working. The job's impossible. I can't stand it there. I'm working for a man called Moyses Stevens and he's . . .'

'Thea, listen, the baby's dead.'

'What baby?'

'*Our* baby. Janet's baby. It's dead, Thea. It was born dead.'

'Oh,' I said. 'Really?' I sat down on the floor. My legs had suddenly gone soft, useless, unformed like a foetus. Adrian was making whimpering and spluttering noises like the aubergines when I first put them in a hot oven. They sounded wrong on him. He never cried, or felt any strong emotion.

'It was a boy,' he stuttered. 'Perfect. Hair, toes, fingernails, everything. But dead.'

I tried to feel sorry for him, but all I could hear was the way he said 'our baby', meaning Janet's. If he hadn't put it there, sliding and runting on those yellow nylon sheets, I might have comforted him, put an arm round his shoulders down the phone. As it was, I just rang off. The room was very still, very silent. Even in the middle of London, with all the traffic screaming, you can still hear death.

£5.72 – that's what it cost to kill a baby – the sum I'd given to the priest to say his Mass; less, far less, than the bill for this evening's dinner. I shivered. God had got it wrong. I hadn't really meant kill. Just negate, erase, undo – something vague like that.

'I didn't mean . . .' I stammered.

There was no one there. Take responsibility for your own actions, Leo always said. Which meant I was a murderer. My body started shaking. I sat and stared at it. How could you take responsibility, when your own body was always sliding away from you, slipping out of your control, like a slimy nylon sheet. I didn't choose to shake. I didn't want to cry. It would only ruin my make-up. It was the same with sex. Somebody else made me wet between the legs, hard around the nipples. It was nothing to do with me.

'Stop,' I mumbled. My feet juddered on the floor, my hands drew zig-zags in the air. Perhaps it wasn't me. Maybe the earth had slipped its axis and was wobbling off course. I was crying myself away, melting into the carpet. When the phone rang again, I could hardly pick it up. I wanted to comfort Adrian, but I didn't know how. He had always comforted *me*.

'Adrian, I . . .'

'What the hell do you mean – Adrian? It's *Leo*.'

'Oh, I see, I . . .'

'Change of plan. We're going to eat at Otto's place. Can you get here, Thea?'

'I've killed Janet's baby.'

'Bring some wine, will you? You'll find two bottles of Beaune in the cupboard in my room.'

'I paid the priest to kill it. It was a boy. They called it Lucian.'

'I can't talk, Thea. I can't even hear. It's far too noisy. There's twenty of us here. Look, get over as quickly as you can. We're all waiting dinner for you. I tried to ring before.'

'Dinner's *ready*, Leo.' I was shouting now. 'I spent all day cooking it.'

'What are you talking about? You know you never cook.'

'First I killed the baby, then I cooked dinner. All the guests have arrived. We'll start without you, shall we?'

'Thea, for God's sake, be sensible. I've told you, everybody's *here*. It's only you we're waiting for. Libby's cooked a massive piece of beef – enough to feed an army. Just lock up and come straight over. Take a taxi, if you like. There's some money in my bureau drawer.'

'There isn't.' Voice petering out now, whispering.

'It's in the blue envelope underneath the blotter. I'll expect you in ten minutes. Right?'

I didn't answer. At least I wasn't shaking any more. I stared at my left thumb. It was purple from the beetroots. (I'm left-handed, which Adrian says makes for learning difficulties but Leo claims is a sign of genius, but only because he's left-handed, too.) I'd grated my thumb along with all the beetroot ends, and it was sore and feverish. If I was crying now, it was only for my thumb. The whole world's grief was throbbing in that thumb. I stuck it in my mouth and tried to comfort it. It looked fat and wet and helpless. Janet's baby was born with both its thumbs.

Slowly, I got up. It was dinner-time and everyone was waiting. My eyes were red and swollen, but if I turned the lights a little lower, they probably wouldn't notice. I was still well-dressed, well-corseted. My hair hadn't slipped its noose.

'Coming,' I called. 'Please *do* sit down.' I tried to copy the Burton Bureau lady. I walked into the kitchen, tipped the soup into a cracked Spode tureen and carried it to the table. It looked magnificent, blushing against the pale white china, a faint steam curling from its nostrils.

'Dinner is served,' I announced, and sat down in my usual place at the purple-skirted table.

six

I dipped the tarnished silver ladle into the soup tureen. 'Bortsch?' I said to the man beside me. He was a photographer with dark glasses and a denim suit. He didn't answer, so I ladled soup into his bowl.

'Start with the *ladies*,' hissed Leo in my ear.

I wasn't even flustered. I smiled at the out-of-work actress with no breasts, who faced me across the table. 'It's home-made,' I told her. 'I put almost thirty beetroots in.'

I filled her bowl. Strange how silent everybody was. I suppose they were concentrating on the bortsch. I sipped mine. It tasted thick and hot and sweetish, like blood. Janet's baby's blood. The telephone kept ringing, a brash, discourteous sound. I didn't answer. I knew I couldn't comfort Adrian, and anyway, they needed me to serve.

'More?' I inquired of the man with the velvet jacket and the goatee. He didn't seem to hear. He was probably meditating. All Leo's friends had a hotline to the East.

I had finished my own helping and felt ready for a second. I leaned across and swapped my plate for the borzoi breeder's, sitting opposite. I began to feel a little better as I sipped his untouched soup – warm and comforted and glowing. I could taste the mace I'd added and the juniper berries. It was an old Russian recipe which Leo always used.

'Aren't you going to try it?' I asked the photographer. He didn't answer, so I edged into his seat. His soup went down in seconds.

'Not hungry?' I said to the philatelist. It annoyed me, really, the way they wouldn't eat, when I'd taken so much trouble with the beetroots. I knew I shouldn't waste it. The mace itself had cost a bomb. I moved around the table, slipping into every seat in turn, finishing each plateful. I stopped bothering with a spoon, just tipped up the bowls and drained them. At the seventh bowl, I paused. The bortsch was cooling now, and a sort of heavy sediment falling to the bottom in little lumps and clots. It was difficult to swallow. Shreds of beetroot skin and onion were sticking their fingers down my throat. I swilled my mouth with water, then took a swig of wine. I had fetched the Beaune from Leo's cupboard, as he'd asked. It looked rich and blowsy, blazing in their glasses. It almost matched the bortsch.

'Try some wine,' I urged. 'To help it down.' Nobody even murmured. I think they were distracted by the phone. It kept ringing louder and louder, like an obstreperous and drunken guest. Adrian was getting frantic, I suppose, but there was nothing I could do for him, not when I was hostess.

There were only two bowls left. I tipped them into each other and forced the clammy liquid down my throat. A full, fat, bulging, burning feeling was surging through my limbs. I felt more important now, more substantial. I was weighted down, running over.

'Right,' I said. 'Now for the aubergines.'

I carried them in, in triumph. They looked dramatic, almost evil, with their rich purple gravy spitting and frothing in the baking tin. I smiled around the table. It felt good to be the hostess, for a change. I was coping single-handed. Leo himself couldn't have done better. I served the aubergines, gave everybody two, finished each plate with a slice of lemon and a parsley sprig. (Janet wasn't the only one who could manage garnishes.)

'*Bon appetit!*' I said.

I jabbed my knife through the fat black belly of my aubergine. Caesarean section. The placenta gushed out. I tried to staunch the wound with salt and mustard, but it was bleeding freely. I stuffed a forkful in my mouth and swallowed Janet's baby.

'I've got a job,' I said to the philatelist. 'A new one. Personal assistant to an OBE in Mayfair.'

It made me angry, the way he didn't answer. I fixed my total concentration on my plate. I wanted to shut out everything but the sensations in my mouth – the flabby little mushroom stalks which tasted like the fingers of suede gloves; the shingly grains of undercooked rice which gritted and scuffed against my throat; the smooth, oily skins of the aubergines with their fleshy velvet undersides, which stroked across my tongue; the fiery explosion as I crunched on a peppercorn.

I had cleared my own plate now and started on the philatelist's. Slowly, I bit into his huge misshapen aubergine. I could feel the stuffing oozing out of it, squashing against the back part of my throat. I crammed the rest of it whole into my mouth, pressing my hands against my stomach. I wanted to feel every morsel swelling up, slipping down. I was only a belly now, a mouth. Food was pumping round my body instead of blood. I felt warm, almost radiant. Little drops of perspiration were trickling down my body, underneath my clothes. The veins in my hands had swollen and were standing out, fat and mauve, like worms.

I moved round one more place. Now I didn't care if they were silent. My chewing had become a sort of conversation, a steady soothing rhythm of its own, which blocked out everything. I leaned across and speared the lemon slice from the untouched plate beside me. I needed it to counteract the grease. The aubergines were cooling now, little white flakes of fat clinging to their rumps, like dandruff, the stuffing congealing into a soggy mass. I'd mixed the rice with mushrooms which had turned it a dirty greyish colour, as if I'd been cooking with ink-stained hands. I sniffed my fingers. They smelt fatty, rancid, rank. The smell had got right inside them, pushed its way underneath my dress, settled on my hair and skin like sweat. The whole room stank of grease and spice and onions. All the subtle Leo-ish smells of precious books and musty manuscripts had been drowned in gravy, avalanched in rice. The entire house was a great black empty hole which someone was stuffing with heavy, soggy mince, packing it in, pressing it down, until there was no more room for even a mushroom stalk. I could feel my belly swelling up, up, up, in a sort of instant pregnancy. First month, cells divide; second month, morning sickness, often trouble-some. I had evening sickness. I lurched into the borzoi breeder's seat. He, too, had left his food.

'What's wrong?' I asked. 'They're not as good as Leo's, I admit. But I used his recipe.'

No answer. No one spoke at all, except the telephone. I began to count its howls while I went on eating. It helped me overcome my nausea. My ninth aubergine coincided with its twelfth bad-mannered scream. I pushed the plate away. Sickness in pregnancy can be very undermining – a bloated, distended feeling, loss of appetite, a retching sensation in the throat. I paused a moment, took a sip of wine.

'I believe you're interested in modern physics,' I belched to the literary agent. It seemed only fair to take an interest in her, now that I'd nabbed her food. Unfortunately, I'd got it wrong. It was the photo-grapher who had studied Heisenberg.

'More salt?' I stuttered. Safer, really, to stick to my hostess role. 'No, don't get up. I'll get it.' I smiled across at the actress. I think we could have hit it off, us both being out of work. She'd have called it 'resting', though, and I had never felt less rested. All the aubergines I'd swallowed were squatting in my belly like fat black babies, kicking me in the ribs, taking me over, sharing my lungs, my heartbeat. Multiple pregnancy. A clutch of smooth, rounded little foetuses, spawning in my stomach, squeezing against all my vital organs. I longed to lie down, excuse myself, creep away to my divan. But we were only halfway through the meal. There was still the salad, the dessert. I couldn't just surrender in the middle of a dinner party.

I dragged the salad into the centre of the table. I'd piled it into a huge china bowl, the sort the Victorians used for washing themselves, with a matching flower-sprigged ewer. The ewer held the vinaigrette. I slopped the dressing on to the lettuce leaves. My hands were very unsteady. Pregnancy unsettles all the nerves. The leaves turned wet and slimy, cucumber slices floated, waterlogged, tomatoes gaped and drowned. I felt too ill to pass it round. I used my hands as salad-servers, plunging them into the bowl up to the wrists and coating them with oil. It felt as if I were trying to grab a slippery, new-born baby. I crammed a fistful of lettuce in my mouth and forced it down.

'No, please don't talk,' I said to the philatelist. 'I don't feel well.'

I knew I had to finish it. Salad is very expensive, out of season. It was too much effort to chew, so I just shoved in bits and pieces whole and swallowed them, choked on cucumbers, squashed my lips against tomato seeds. Salad oil was dribbling down my chin, trickling into the spaces between my buttons. I fumbled my hands up beneath my dress and unhooked my bra. My breasts almost whimpered with relief. I held them a moment, felt them warm, full, and throbbing through my hands. They were almost as large as Janet's now, ready to suckle, bursting not with milk, but with vinaigrette. My whole body was swelling and distended. I had almost reached full term.

There was still a puddle of dressing in the bottom of the bowl. I could see the china flowers shining through it, as I tipped it up and emptied it down my throat. You always swallow oil before a baby. My mother had told me that. It acts as a lubricant, a laxative, eases the foetus out into a slippery world. I closed my eyes. The purple shawl was banging against my eyelids, the purple feathers swaying in my brain.

'Be quiet,' I begged. No one had said a word. My whole body was crammed and stuffed with food. I could feel it rising up to my neck, passing all the little notches like water in a measuring jug, slopping over through the waste-pipe of my lips. I went on chewing tiny morsels of bread. There were still little gaps and crannies to be filled, pin-holes in my wrists, chinks between my toes, small, forgotten spaces which would hold a quarter of a mouthful. Food was so muddled up with nausea, I could hardly tell them apart now. I pushed back my chair. We hadn't had the damsons yet, but Leo always liked a pause between the courses.

'Excuse me a moment,' I murmured, as I struggled to my feet, lurched outside to the bathroom and voided everything I could. I dragged off the pantie-girdle and kicked it in a corner, rolled down my stockings, took off my pants. Pregnant women should never wear things tight. I still looked reasonable. The purple dress had soaked up all the oil stains, so that they hardly showed. My face was flushed, but that could have been the make-up. All my little buttons were still demurely fastened. I hadn't disgraced myself. I was dry between the legs.

I returned to the dinner table.

'Dessert?' I asked. I could see my face distorted in the window and the dish of damsons wavering and shaking in the glass. The bowl was so heavy, I wanted to lie down with it on Mr Leatherstone's rest-bed and have him swaddle and support me.

'It's damson mousse,' I told them. I'd sprinkled nuts on top, so they couldn't see it was curdled. The damsons came from Otto's mother's garden. Leo doesn't have a garden or a mother any longer. Both his parents and Janet's baby (and what was left of Lucian) must be somewhere in the same shadowy place.

I spooned the damson mixture into eight sundae dishes and lined them up in front of me. I wasn't well enough to go moving round the table any more. I started with the actress's. She was the only one whose name I even knew. The mousse tasted very cold and clean. It had been chilling in the fridge all afternoon. Almost a relief to feel it melt and shiver down my throat, flushing out the aubergines, cutting down the grease.

The second one was harder. There was simply no more room. The mousse was lying just on top of my throat, waiting to spring out at me. Slowly, I stood up and shook myself, like Karma. Some of the mousse subsided. I picked up my spoon and started on the third. I wished they'd make conversation. Distract me from the obscene and vulgar things happening in my gut. Leo often played the piano after dinner. We hadn't finished yet, but I felt we needed music all the same. I unlocked the cupboard where I'd bunged the radio and tuned in to Radio Three. Like a miracle, they were playing one of Leo's pieces, very fast and pouncy with lots of swirls and flurries. It didn't help the damsons. I would have preferred something slow and merciful and soothing. But at least I felt a little safer with Leo there beside me, pounding and swaying on the keys.

I made a start on damsons number four. The sharp, tangy flavour of the fruit had somehow disappeared. All I could taste was onions now, and cream. Little piles of damson stones were beginning to hem me in.

'Tinker, tailor, soldier . . .' I began. It was impossible. Too many stones. I could see them piling up and up beside me, until I was buried in them, toppled by them. Damson stones reaching as high as the mulberry tree outside.

'Rich man, poor man . . .'

I fixed my gaze on the middle point in the wall between the windows. One of Leo's oils was hanging there, and the exact mid-spot coincided with the right buttock of a blue male nude. I kept my eye on this and my ear on the prancing line of the piano. That way, I retained some vestige of control. Damsons number six slipped slowly, slowly down. The odd piece of damson skin had eluded the mixer and tangled with my tongue.

'Beggarman, thief.'

The nude male buttock was swinging gently up and down, up and . . . I paused for a moment to allow the kitchen to stop spinning, then took another spoonful. The mixture was warmer now and heavier. I held a stone like a boulder in my mouth, then slowly spat it out, along with a slimy shred of skin. I stirred the mixture round and round the dish. That way I lost some up the sides.

'It was a marvellous year for fruit,' I murmured. 'Otto's mother bottles them herself.'

I belched again. The piano drowned it tactfully, by starting on a crescendo.

'Doesn't he play *beautifully?*' I remarked to the photographer. Mousse number eight had finally disappeared. I staggered out with the tray of empty dishes, the pile of ragged stones. It was difficult to walk. I wondered who was feeding Adrian. Janet wouldn't have had time to leave him his Ryvita. Perhaps he was sitting by her bed, nibbling on her grapes. Grapes! I hadn't even washed them. They were still oozing in their paper bag, fat and black, with a dusty purple bloom across them. I broke off a cluster and crammed them in my mouth. The pips crunched against my tongue like tiny half-formed bones. Leo was struggling with a phrase on the piano, tearing it to pieces, turning it inside out.

I felt the whole second movement churning and heaving in my stomach, notes squashing against my gut, like grapes. 'I'm sorry,' I spluttered. 'You'll have to excuse me. Leo will look after you.'

I dashed towards the bathroom, both hands cupped across my mouth. I slammed the door, and my whole fancy, curdled, purple dinner frothed and cascaded into the toilet bowl.

seven

I was still lying on the cold white bathroom floor when Leo returned. I'd no idea what time it was. It was still purple outside the windows, purple in my stomach. One cheek felt cold against the tiles, the other burned and flushed. I could see Leo's soft suede boots inching across the floor towards my nose. They stopped. If I'd put out my tongue, I could have touched them with it, but I felt too tired.

Leo scooped me off the tiles. I lay in his arms like a pile of dirty dishes. It was strange to feel him gentle. He laid me in his bed, underneath the dragons, and undid all my little buttons. He untied my hair and combed it with his fingers, washed my face with a sponge. I thought he wanted sex, and tried to move myself against him, but my body wasn't there. Only a gigantic throbbing head and a gaping hole somewhere lower down.

He undressed me like a baby. I felt terribly ashamed. My body smelt of sweat and salad oil, and there was vomit on my dress. I wished he'd rage and shout. At least I'd feel secure, then.

'I was sick,' I said. 'I'm sorry.' It was still difficult to speak. All the words were sticky with damson mousse. Leo held the sponge against my lips. I couldn't bear his kindness. I didn't know how to deal with it, what to say, how to move my limbs. I was like a virgin, unable to respond. I think I feared it would unravel him, lose him all his power.

'Look,' I said. 'There's no need to . . .'

'Hush,' he murmured, and laid his cool, sallow hands against my head. It was so beautiful, I could feel tears pricking against my eyelids. I wanted to break his hands off and keep them there, so that if he had to go away again, at least I would have part of him.

'Who was at your dinner?' I asked. I knew I had to talk to him, be worthy of him, stop him disappearing.

'Libby, Sian, Rowena . . .'

'Otto?'

'Yes, of course Otto.'

'Why "of course"?' It hurt to keep on talking. My body wanted simply to drift away.

'It was at his house, I told you.'

'Why didn't you *say* Otto, then?' The tension made me irritable, the tenderness. I wasn't used to tenderness.

'Oh, Thea, don't go *on* . . . Look, I shouldn't have left you. But I phoned at least a dozen times and when you didn't answer, I presumed you must have gone out. I'd have come straight back if I'd realized you were ill.'

'I'm *not* ill.' I had slumped back down again. The whole of my body between my headache and my feet was water-logged and churning. Leo hated illness. He was never ill himself. If I didn't sit up and talk to him, he might run back to Otto's. Libby, Sian, Rowena were always radiant.

'Leo . . .'

'What?'

'Do you *like* Otto? I mean really like him?'

'Yes.' There was a tiny pause, as if he were waiting for a star to pass, a tree to fall.

'I don't,' I said.

'I know you don't.'

'Does *he* know?'

'Yes.'

'Does he mind?'

'Yes.'

'Do *you* mind?'

'Yes, I do, Thea.'

I jabbed my foot against the coverlet. Four yes's in a row. Sometimes I didn't get a yes in seven days. But these were Otto's yes's. I wanted yes's for myself, strings of them, *years* of them. I always had to share him. Otto was like Karma, fawning on Leo, beloved of him, closer to him than I was.

'Thea . . .' He was stroking my hair again. It felt miraculous and terrifying. 'I wish you'd *try* and like him.'

'Why should I?' It came out curt, though I didn't mean it to.

'Because it's . . . important to me.'

I hated that word 'important', a hard, bony word when I was only a limp, crumpled sick-bag. I shut my eyes and tried to picture Otto – pale, flabby hands, fringe of soft hair falling in his wounded-mackerel eyes. All I could see was a white fish on a grey beach, gills gasping in and out, pale eyes staring, and a brown sea creeping up, up, up, on it.

'I don't like his eyes,' I said.

The brown sea was swirling through my stomach, the grey fish flapping in my throat. I could feel the waves rolling over and over the bedspread.

Leo had a strand of my hair pressed against his lips. My whole scalp was singing with it. 'D'you know what he said tonight?'

'Who?'

'Otto.'

Christ! Would we never be rid of Otto? Must he always be there between us, with those eyes?

'No,' I said. I didn't want to know. I wanted Leo wholly to myself, coffined in the bedspread of my hair, saying only yes yes yes.

'He told me he thought he was suffering for the persecution of the Huguenots. He's convinced that he was Louis de Gonzague in another life.'

'Who's Louis de Gonzague?' I asked. This was worse than Adrian. I wasn't well enough for history lessons. I was just an empty carton, kicked into a corner, leaking at both ends.

'Oh, a French nobleman who slaughtered thousands of the Protestants. His henchmen hacked them into pieces and flung the bodies in the Seine. He died in 1595, but Otto thinks he was Louis in a previous reincarnation.'

'I see,' I said. I felt like saying 'fuck'. Only Otto would claim power on such a scale. Other people fretted about being insects in another life, or cats, or rats, or cockroaches. Only pale, scaly Otto spent his pasts as noblemen, masterminding massacres.

'I don't think I *want* another life,' I said. Not if it was a life like this one, with divorce courts, and foetuses in bottles, and vomiting in bathrooms, and bodies in the Seine and only halves of people. An after-life was safer, a Roman Catholic one, where the soul was purged and the body purified, and one soared up, up, to where everything was free and white and shining, and God was legally and infinitely Father.

'You may not have much choice.' Leo had stopped stroking. He still had my hair twisted through his hands, but he wasn't concentrating. I could tell he was still haunted by the Huguenots. He and Otto had shut me out again, name-dropping in sixteenth-century France, believing in things I could neither prove nor leave alone. They'd been friends for years, long before I'd known them. Otto may have shared *all* his previous existences with Leo. Even as Louis de

Gonzague, he'd probably sat with him over a pile of hacked and steaming corpses, arguing about the authority of the Bible versus the Pope.

'Why don't you come to bed?' I asked. It made me uneasy the way he sat there, fully dressed. I didn't feel like sex at all, but I wanted him to want me. I had never lain naked in his bed before without being straddled and deflowered. Usually, we never talked for long, before he rolled me over and rammed into me. But now it was the early hours and he was still just sitting there, holding my hand as if he were a nurse. The room was full of other people, other things – all the friends and fears and fancies he had churning in his head. I wanted to split it open and tip them out, until his head was clear and clean and empty, and I could burst inside it and reign there all alone.

'It's late,' I whispered. 'Come to bed.'

He didn't answer. I felt tiny fingers of terror probe along my spine. He even had his boots on. It was as if it was all over and we had signed the divorce papers, divided the property, zipped up our jeans. Leo didn't desire me. I bored him, disgusted him. He could probably smell the vomit in my hair.

'I'm sorry,' I said, struggling out of bed. 'I'll go and have a bath.'

'Hush, Thea, go to sleep.'

That was almost proof he didn't want me. As soon as I was sleeping, he'd creep away again, return to his dinner party, clean Gonzague's sword. I was sitting up now, my breasts only inches from his face, yet he hadn't even glanced at them.

'I'm not tired,' I insisted. I took his hand and laid it on my chest, almost forced it there.

'No, Thea, it's late. Too late. I want to go to sleep.'

Even Adrian didn't say 'too late', or pull his hand away like that, or keep his boots on. I'd almost forgotten Adrian. I dragged the covers right up to my neck and lay back on the pillows.

'I had some people round tonight,' I said.

Leo only grunted.

'For dinner.' I could see the aubergines curdled with the damsons. I never wanted to think of food again. If I came back in another life, I would return as something which didn't have a stomach – a cloud, a stone, a flower.

'I invited Adrian.'

No answer. Only the sound of Karma's heavy breathing. He was

68

curled in a corner like a nerveless cat, paws across his nose, snuffling in his sleep.

'He said he couldn't manage it at first, but he turned up later, when everyone else had gone.'

Silence.

'You didn't know that, did you, Leo?'

'Go to sleep.'

At least I had made him nervous. He was flicking the fringe of the bed-cover through his fingers, one foot jab-jabbing the floor.

'His text book's been accepted. They gave him an advance just on the first five chapters. They're terribly impressed.'

'Look here, Thea, it's over with you and Adrian.' He was pacing up and down now. 'Why can't you accept that? It's finished, dead. Why d'you have to go on resurrecting things, creeping in underneath them and trying to prise them open when they're all nailed up and rotting?'

I shifted the pillows a little, so that they were soft against my head. 'He stayed for simply *hours*, Leo. Once he was here, I couldn't get him out.'

'I don't believe you. Adrian wouldn't come here.'

'Oh yes, he would. He did. He often does, in fact. He comes up when you're out.'

'You're lying, Thea.' The back of his neck looked very thin and spiky, as if I could cut my fingers on it. 'Adrian doesn't want you. He's married to Janet now. Perhaps you'd forgotten that.'

'Maybe he is,' I shouted. 'Maybe he is! But he doesn't fuck her any more. He can't. She's pregnant. Huge. Monstrous. He can't even get *near* her. She squashes him in bed.'

'Stop that!'

'That's why he came up here. He was *dying* for it. He'd hardly got in the door, when he . . .'

'Stop it, I said.' He was slumped against the desk now, elbows grovelling on the blotter, hands across his ears. 'I don't want to hear. I don't even want you *in* here.'

'I did say "no" at first, but he went on and on insisting. Then he undid my dress. I tried to stop him, Leo, but . . .'

'Get out!' Fists clenched now, grinding them against the wood, nails digging into palms, head down. At least it was safer than the tenderness.

'Actually, I didn't *want* to stop him. Not by then. We both had all our clothes off and . . .'

'Get *out*, I said.' Leo had picked up an old Victorian paperweight made of heavy glass, one that Otto had given him a hundred years ago, with tiny scarlet peonies painted on it in dainty little clusters. He was rocking it backwards and forwards against the desk. The noise went through my head. Karma had woken now and slunk over to his feet.

'He kept whispering things, dirty things. He even brought *you* into it. He kept asking about – you know – what we did in bed and everything. He made me show him all your things. I knew you wouldn't mind. He used your razor and your toothbrush. He even wore your dressing-gown. He seemed to want to sort of take you over. We did it in your bed. He forced me to. I was lying just like this and . . .'

'Get *out* of that bed, get out of it, get out of it . . .'

'It's all right, Leo, there's no need to be angry – I cleaned it up afterwards. It was quite a mess. Adrian thrashes around a lot and . . .'

Leo had jumped to his feet and was striding towards me. I could see his shadow stalking him along the wall.

'Then we did it standing up,' I whispered. There was no more need to shout. Leo's shadow was almost breathing on me. It had lunged across my feet and was creeping up towards my breasts. The paperweight was still between its hands. 'Adrian's very good at that. He . . .'

Karma was snapping and lurching at Leo's heels. His growl was like a low, crooning lullaby.

'He came three times,' I murmured. 'He would have come again, but . . .'

I could see the paperweight plunging towards my face. I even had time to notice Leo's yellow fingers gleaming through the glass. I opened my lips to tell him that I loved him, I desired him, and took the full force of twenty scarlet peonies in my mouth.

There was a sharp, sick, cracking sound, which must have come from outside in the street. It was nothing to do with me. Red petals were falling on the bed, like bright, crushed, mangled peonies. The pain was so bright, the room was heaving with it. A dog was howling somewhere, howling. Somebody else was crying. A dry, jagged, horrifying sound. It must be Leo crying, crying for my mouth. I hadn't got a mouth. Only a smashed, pulped, purple flower. I groped out of bed and stumbled to the mirror, stared at the person in it, almost laughed. She had a dumb black hole where her two front teeth should have been. The others streamed with blood. Her fat stupid lips were split apart and swollen, purple around the edges, her nose was so wide, she must have had Negro blood.

Somebody else had once sat in that mirror – an elegant receptionist with cheekbones, an ambitious Mayfair girl with white well-mannered teeth, an Abbey National saver with her own eight-digit number and her little savings book. Leo had destroyed them, bashed them all to pieces, refused to let them share his room. And now he was standing powerless, almost paralysed, shoulders shaking like a ninny. Terrible things were happening to my face, swelling, scorching things, which only he could stop. But he had turned his back, shut his eyes. I needed mending, restoring, staking like a broken flower, and there he was, broken down himself. The room was tipping sideways, sliding on its back. Leo could have righted it with just one finger, but his hands were clinging on to each other for their own support. He was drowning, floundering, snivelling like a baby, cowering close to Karma, impotent, unmanned.

I lurched across the tipping floor to Karma and kicked him, first in the flank, and then again, across his dumb, gloating muzzle. Dark paws reared towards my face and I heard the growl trapped and rumbling in his throat. Leo had come between us. I hit out at Leo, punched him, kicked him, tore at him. It hurt my mouth so badly, I was almost sick again, but I wouldn't have him cry, couldn't bear him weak.

He was warding off my blows, trying not to hurt me. I hit out harder. Red petals were still streaming on the carpet. Karma was there behind me, double-barred steel jaw protecting his master. Leo hacked him off. There was a tangled mass of arms, paws, petals, fur. I dodged away. As I fell, I saw the jagged teeth of Leo's cruel brass fender leaping for my forehead.

eight

When I came to, I was lying on a sort of high white table with a red stain on the pillow, and a white nun was standing over me, sponging the ruins of my face. I didn't have a body any more, only a deep purple pain somewhere where I should have had a mouth, and a huge throbbing lump on what had once been my forehead. I tried to feel my teeth. Most of the bottom ones were there. My tongue was thick and lumpy and seemed to be sticking to itself. I tried to pull it free.

'Leo . . .' I stuttered. It was difficult to speak. There was cotton wool stuffed above my gumline and something pulling on my lower lip. The nun smiled. Her own teeth were false, very white and thick like the stuff toilet-bowls are made of. I wondered if Mr Leatherstone could help me. I shut my eyes and tried to see his step-by-step instructions for repairing faces. All I could see was damsons. Something told me I'd been sick again.

I wondered where I was. It was difficult to see beyond the nun. She was bending over me, blotting out the view. She smelt of holiness and Dettol. She was so white, she hurt. I tried to turn away from her, to rest my eyes, but everywhere was white. White sheet, white screen, white ceiling. I picked up my own hand. White, pure white. White sick-bowl beside me on the white metal cabinet, white bandages, white walls. I closed my eyes. Purple now. White cream curdling purple damsons. I didn't want to remember. Some terrible, unbelievable thing had happened. I was a headline now, a statistic, a disaster movie. Leo was a brute, a batterer, a . . . No. It was nothing to do with Leo. Things like that only happen to violent, low-grade people you read about in newspapers, and then stuff into a waste-bin or abandon on a train. I must have got it wrong. I didn't really want to think about it. It hurt too much. I wanted just to crumple myself up into a ball and throw myself away. If I shut my eyes for long enough perhaps I'd disappear. There was a deep black well behind my eyelids. Easy to drop into it, and sink down, down, down . . .

Why did they keep dragging me out again, poking me with sticks, flinging me down rope-ladders and fire escapes? I didn't *want* to escape. It was too noisy and dazzling up there in the light. There were two nuns now and somebody else beside them. A man, I think, but still in that shining, blinding white. They were all peering down my well, and the nun with the teeth kept tapping my face and saying, 'Mrs Morton, Mrs Morton', over and over.

I shook my head. That was Adrian's name. It had never sounded right joined on to Thea. 'No,' I said. 'Dead.'

The nun smiled. She looked so friendly, I tried to smile back, but it wasn't possible. Whatever I'd used to smile before had now been confiscated. The man was rougher. He didn't smile at all, just mauled my mouth about and said, 'This won't hurt.' He was right, in a way. There was so much pain, it had all become just a shape, a colour, something vague and muzzy happening to a part of me which wasn't there. The nun kept passing him things, cruel, sharp-clawed instruments which only existed to inflict maximum damage on mouths. I wanted to forget my mouth, pretend I'd never had one, but there they were, turning it into the centre of the world. Soon, there wouldn't be anything left outside it. The whole universe would shrink to one huge black hole, with them all teetering on the edge of it and peering in. I couldn't even close it. They had propped it open, so that anyone could enter. Rude, clumsy people were clambering over my tongue, climbing up my teeth, knocking them with hammers, tugging at them with ropes. I tried to spit everybody out. I wanted to go to sleep. I'd no idea what time it was, but it felt achingly late, as if the night had gone on for about a hundred years, and was getting stained and crumpled round the edges. I could see a chink of tired black sky above the screen. There might never be a morning.

'Leave me alone,' I said. The words came out like one of those cramped and strangled noises spastics make. All the same, I think they must have heard me, because when I woke up again, there was no one there. Even the night had got fed up and crawled away.

I looked around. They had moved me somewhere different. I was lying in the centre of a small white room, very simple, like a cell; just a bed, a chair and a locker, a crucifix above my head and a picture of the Sacred Heart on the wall beyond. A nun came in and drew the curtains and everything turned whiter. There was a white square yard of sky behind the window, with white clouds lurching by, and the last white sliver of a faded moon. I could see a tree, just the top part, chopped off by the window frame, with one brave brown leaf left on it.

'Good morning,' said the nun. 'And how are we feeling?'

I wasn't sure. The rest of my body was slowly sneaking back. I could feel my legs now, very quiet and heavy, making two white curves in the coverlet, and my hair damp and sticky on my shoulders. I lifted up my hands and stared at them. They looked much the same as normal which surprised me. Everything was hushed, except the pain in my mouth which screamed.

'OK, I think,' I said. I didn't really have a voice, just bloody cotton wool. My head was throbbing underneath the lump. I think it was all the questions seething in it. What was I doing here? Why the nuns? How many teeth had I lost? I tried to break a question off and study it, but all the answers seemed dangerous and sharp-edged. They all led back to Leo and spinning, heaving, lurching things I didn't want to think of. Safer, really, not to think at all. I was just a head on a pillow, two hands on a coverlet.

The nun helped me out of bed. It felt odd standing up. My legs weren't really awake yet, and my head kept tipping upside down. She made me wash and pee and change my nightie and other boring things, which all hurt just because my mouth hurt. The pain was so fierce, it made the rest of my body feel grey and wet and soggy, like school cabbage. I was glad, really, to flop back into bed. The nun had re-made it and it was all crisp and white and snowy and smelt of dead Popes. She had brought tea and gruel on a tray. Eating seemed more or less impossible, like trying to squeeze a sack of set cement between stiff iron railings. My mouth was all puffed up, and one or two of my teeth were sharp and jagged round the edges and kept cutting into my lip.

'I'm not hungry,' I said. I never wanted to eat again, not after the aubergines.

The nun only smiled. She sat on my bed and eased a tiny plastic teaspoon between the corners of my lips. The gruel was warm and sloppy and tasted of blood. I forced down half a mouthful.

'Well done!' she said. The tea was in an infant's feeding-cup with a long plastic spout, like a straw. The nun was so gentle with it, I managed to swallow quite a lot. She kept mopping up my face and saying 'good girl', which made me feel very small and special, like a baby. Then she gave me medicine, which must have been a painkiller, because the pain started to whimper rather than shout, and soon everything blurred and fuzzed again.

Another nun took my tray and did something to the curtains. There must have been *flocks* of nuns. They all looked the same but different, like sheep, or angels. This latest one was small and frail and withered, like a skeleton leaf.

'Mr Rzevski will be phoning you at twelve,' she said. I frowned. I wasn't sure who Mr Rzevski was. The only name I could remember was Mr Leatherstone's and I knew *he* wouldn't phone.

Whenever twelve was, it took a long time coming. There were long, droning noises from vacuum cleaners, and short, jangling ones from metal bowls banging against taps, and people kept looming up and dwindling away, as if I were looking through binoculars.

I had just dozed off, when they wheeled in the telephone. Leo had somehow crawled inside it and been made smaller and more compressed.

'Thea, are you . . . all right?' His voice sounded strange and ragged, as if it had been caught on barbed wire and ripped.

'Yes,' I said. I almost added 'thanks'.

'Look, I'm terribly . . . I mean, I know I . . . Hell, Thea, I didn't . . .'

He had never stuttered before. I longed to help him, calm him, finish the phrases for him, but my own voice was equally disabled. It came out at an angle, as if it were squeezing past a series of impediments.

'I'm all right,' I repeated. I stared at the lone brown leaf. It took courage to cling on like that, when all your fellows were a brown sludge on the path.

'I wondered . . . I mean, if there's anything you want, anything I can . . .'

'No,' I lisped. 'Nothing.' There wasn't room for anything. The pain took up all the space.

There was a pause. I knew I should have filled it, but I felt too tired. Leo kept trying to say things. I wished he'd go away. I didn't really want him to exist.

'Are you alone?' he whispered, suddenly.

I looked around. It was difficult to tell. The white nuns and the white curtains round the bed were sometimes indistinguishable.

'Yes,' I murmured. 'I think so.' The Sacred Heart was gazing at me with blue, troubled eyes.

'Listen, darling,' Leo said. 'You fell down the cellar steps. On to stone. Do you understand?'

'No,' I said. He never called me 'darling'. It sounded dangerous.

'After dinner. You ate too much. Someone left the cellar door open and you didn't see. You fell all the way down and landed on your face. You remember now, don't you?'

'Wh . . . when did it happen?' I asked. I felt confused. I couldn't even remember whether we had a cellar, and if we did, whether the floor was stone.

'Last night,' he prompted. 'You weren't well. You were upset over Janet's baby and you missed your footing and fell.'

Janet's baby. I could taste the gruel again, bloody, slimy, sour. I saw Janet falling, falling, down the cellar stairs, landing on her womb. 'Yes,' I said slowly, 'I understand. She fell downstairs.'

'On to stone,' he urged.

'On to stone,' I repeated. I tried to picture the house at Twickenham. Did it have a cellar? It wasn't easy to picture anything. The pain-killers were fraying all the edges of my mind.

'They won't let me see you until tomorrow,' he said. He sounded relieved, reprieved.

I shut my eyes. I was so tired, I couldn't even hold the receiver. It dropped on to the bed and I heard the wreck of Leo's voice whispering to the blankets.

'Yes, I understand,' I murmured. The Sacred Heart had gone to sleep as well. 'I do understand. She fell.'

I think I dozed through lunch, but I had scrambled egg for supper and pink blancmange. It took me an hour and a half to coax a quarter of it down. Strange I had once liked eating. It seemed such hard labour now.

I felt better, all the same. The fog in my head had cleared, and all the nuns were very quiet and peaceful, and I'd somehow learnt to cut myself off at the neck and live in the bottom bit. It was not only less painful, it also stopped all the fears and horrors which were seething in my mind. Like whether Leo loved me and how many teeth I'd save. Girls in their twenties don't look good in dentures. The doctor had popped in just two hours ago, and droned on about loose teeth and lacerated gums and how I'd have to see the hospital dentist first thing in the morning. I hate dentists, so I didn't listen after that; just crawled out of my head and took refuge lower down. I decided to live in my legs, or my neck, or my stomach – anywhere where it was still safe and quiet and whole.

Sister Ursula came in after supper, with a form. 'Could you manage to fill this in for us?'

I nodded, I liked Sister Ursula. She was the big, bony one with the toilet-bowl teeth and the soft muslin voice which didn't match the rest of her. I glanced at the form. It didn't look as frightening as the Burton Bureau one. It was mainly boring things like place and date of birth and marital status. I didn't write 'divorced'. I hate the word. Where it said 'Occupation', I put receptionist. They also asked for your religion. Adrian always puts a dash. He said it looked pretentious to write 'agnostic', and I couldn't spell it, anyway. Leo never filled in forms and I doubt if his many-branched brand of religion would have fitted into the two-inch space they provided. I longed to write Roman Catholic, but I was scared they'd find me out. Leo said you could tell a person's class and religion by the merest glance at their teeth, their bookshelf and their medicine chest. I was fairly safe in those respects. I had no possessions with me, and my teeth were out of bounds.

'Catholic,' I wrote firmly in the space.

'So you're one of us,' smiled Sister Ursula when she took the form and checked it.

One of us – a beautiful and healing phrase. I gazed triumphantly at Sister Ursula's billowing white veil, the small gold ring on her engagement finger. One of them – white-robed, rustling, gentle-fingered, betrothed to Christ Himself.

'Still practising?' she asked.

I nodded. Not many other non-Catholics knew every Catholic church from Walton-on-Thames to Welwyn Garden City.

'Would you like to take Holy Communion in the morning?'

I shut my eyes. She was going too fast. I hadn't even been baptized. But if I didn't say yes, she'd assume I was in mortal sin. I shuddered. I remembered all those phrases from my schooldays – mortal sin, Holy Souls in Purgatory, flames of hell.

'You could have a talk with our chaplain, first,' she suggested. 'Father Laurence Sullivan. He's very nice.' Her head-dress was awry and a strand of grey wispy hair straggled through a gap in it. It made her look still holier.

'Yes,' I mumbled. 'Please.'

When she'd gone, I lay and trembled. A priest, a real Catholic chaplain, all to myself, a private audience. I'd never lost my respect for priests. I might mock at their intolerance or stinginess, in deference to Adrian, or make witty remarks about Papism when Leo's friends were listening, but secretly, I all but worshipped them. At my convent school the priest had been like a pop-star – mobbed and famed and dazzling, with his own private fan-club. I never got as close to him as his other three hundred fans – I was the leper, remember – but I prayed for cure and conversion as fervently as my classmates prayed for ponies or pierced ears or Rolling Stones records. My mother was the stumbling block. Catholic to her spelt Irish, traitor, slut. She'd only sent me there for the gloss and cachet all convent girls acquire, and because the fees were lower than at other private schools and the brochure mentioned 'discipline' eleven separate times and the place itself was miles away and difficult to visit. (The further away I was from her the better, since I reminded her of my father which was crime enough itself.)

She was highly disconcerted when I fell in love with the Faith. I could hardly fail to do so when the nuns put a Sunday shine on all the dreary weekdays and gave Life a capital L and loss a small one. Catholicism was all the swoony, soul-enchanting things life had lacked till then – the blaze of candles and the choke of incense in a hushed and shimmering chapel, the body of Christ exploding in a stomach or slithering down a throat, guardian angels following you around like faithful dogs, folding their wings around you when you went to sleep, priests in fancy dress dishing out God from gold and silver cups. Leo's music was in the Catholic church, his violence and his tenderness, and Adrian's history and all those early kings and queens. Joining that church meant receiving all the sacraments – birth and death and life and marriage duly sanctified. Water on your head and chrism on your brow, Christ's ring around your finger and His head against your breast, grace swirling through your soul like milk and honey. Being a Catholic meant going to confession – for me the most feared and envied thing of all. The prickle of terror as I knelt lonely and longing in the pew and heard the other girls' faint, scared voices whispering from the private palisade of the confessional box. Dredging up their sins. Fingers trespassing through knicker elastic, fumblings and touchings in the bath, magnifying mirrors shoved between their thighs to see if they looked the same as their best friend.

The thrill and horror of telling a *man* such things, a man in a black frock, who had nothing between his legs except the godhead. I spent my whole three years squeezing out the secrets of the confessional from all my friends. I swapped sweets and comic books for sins. I practised my own confession a thousand times over. 'Bless me, Father, for I have sinned . . .'

It made me sin much more, of course. Every time my hand went down, I imagined telling Father Murphy – his pursed, disapproving lips, the three small warts underneath his eye. I filled in all the details, almost drew him diagrams. He was the only man we had. There were no male teachers and boyfriends were taboo. Most of our sex-life was swept into the chapel. You could get an orgasm just by staring at the Blessed Sacrament. One of the girls even tried it with a candle, one of those long, fat white ones you were meant to light in front of the statue of the Immaculate Conception and which had been blessed by the Pope himself. She felt it was so holy, it would cancel out the sin. I only hope it did, because she never dared confess it. Father Murphy was very narrow-minded. Most of the time, the girls just whispered generalities: 'Father, I've had impure thoughts.' 'Father, I've committed sinful acts with myself.' I was committing more of those acts than anyone, yet I was the only one barred access to confession. I saw it as a violent deprivation. The more I gasped for the church, the more I felt excluded from it. God was deaf to my pleadings for conversion. Instead of finding a Father and joining His home and family, I returned to my mother's house and joined nothing more than a gang of blue-jeaned layabouts at the local (co-ed) College of Further Education. My mother told me she'd quarrelled with Reverend Mother over what she called religious propaganda, but I suspect it was rather the fees she quarrelled with. They went up as her maintenance went down. (My father's money was pouring into Another Woman, so I found out later.)

Anyway, that was the end of throbbing candles and bleeding hearts, of secret gropings with the butts of crucifixes, or rosaries trailing cold across my naked breasts. Now it was straight (short) sex in the backs of clapped-out Fords, or heavy necking under railway bridges. But I never lost my craving for confession. Often, I would enter a church and make straight for the confessional box. I never dared go in, just knelt in the pew beside it, feeling again that scorching mix of terror, lust and longing. Whenever I had it off with any man, half of the pleasure was confessing it afterwards to some imaginary priest. I never spared the details – which way up, how many times, had we used contraception?

And now, here was a real, substantial, unimagined priest, tapping at my door, shaking my hand, drawing up a chair. A priest in a stern black suit and a stiff white collar, actually leaning over me in bed. He was much better looking than Father Murphy, tall and thin and spiky, with hair the colour of a London pigeon.

Suddenly, I shut my eyes, turned away. I couldn't bear him to see me smashed and battered and hideous. I wanted to draw the sheet up right above my head, as if I were already dead. This was the first man I'd seen since I'd been here (bar the doctor), and the very first priest I'd had entirely to myself, and there I was, with a gap in my teeth, a hole in my face, a fright, a failure, a laughing-stock. The curtains were drawn close around the bed. We were in our own private confessional box. There was only a thin white nightie between my naked body and this living, breathing Father. And what a nightie. A hospital-issue one, which prickled my throat and imprisoned my ankles. He'd feel nothing for me, nothing. He'd laugh, puke, turn away.

He was already bending over me. I didn't know how he could bear to be so close. 'It's Thea, isn't it? That's a very beautiful name. It means "Divine", you know. You must have a very special relationship with our Blessed Lord.'

I could feel myself blushing. Was he being sarcastic? Had he guessed already I wasn't a member of his flock? It hurt to blush. My face was flushed and swollen enough, already. I hadn't dared to look at it. I'd shunned all mirrors, tried to forget I had a face at all. The nuns kept saying looks were of no importance, and I'd done my best to believe them. But this was a *man*. My body was on fire for him, sweat seeping between my breasts, trickling down my thighs. I had to see myself, check that I was still a woman. I'd been shocked enough when I looked in Leo's mirror, but his mirror often lied, and in any case, I might look better now. The nuns had spent a whole day and a night mopping me up and ministering to my mouth.

'I want a mirror,' I suddenly blurted out.

You don't ask priests for mirrors. That's a nurse's job, a menial's. It also smacks of vanity. You can beg a priest for Holy Communion, or a plenary indulgence, but not the tools and trappings of the sin of pride. Father Sullivan was looking round the room, but there was no mirror on the wall, not even above the wash-basin. Eventually, he rang for one, and Sister Anselm brought it. He wouldn't let me hold it but trapped it wrong side up against the counterpane. 'Now listen, my dear,' he said. His fingers were almost greyish against the stiff papal white of the bed-linen. I noticed they were trembling. 'You don't look too pretty at the moment, but they can do wonderful things these days. I know there's a lot of swelling, but you often get that round the face. It goes down very quickly. In a day or two, you'll hardly even . . .'

I wasn't listening. I had slipped the mirror from underneath his fingers and was staring at the strange, mottled, misshapen thing reflected in it. It wasn't a face. Its nose and lips were so swollen, they had merged into each other, its eyes were almost closed and ringed with deep purple bruising, its mouth was a car-crash.

I dropped the mirror back on to the bed.

Father Sullivan was trying to stuff comfort in his voice, like baubles in a Christmas stocking. 'Look, my child, it's really not as bad as it appears. A lot of that swelling is simply superficial bruising. It's a shame about your two front teeth, but the dental surgeon here is quite remarkable. He's a Catholic, of course – a knight of St Gregory, actually. He really does take trouble. Sister's spoken to him already, on the telephone, and he's coming to see you first thing in the morning. He'll make you look like new. Dentures today are so well made, you can hardly tell the difference.'

I touched my mouth, very gently, as if it was a foetus in a jar, some half-formed, wailing thing which still needed its mother. I wondered if you could kiss with dentures. I glanced across at Father Sullivan. He had perfect teeth himself.

'Try and remember, Thea, how Our Blessed Lord suffered. They crucified Him, pierced His side. We must strive to bear our sufferings as He did. In patience and resignation. Offer them up for the sins of the world.'

I must have sinned a lot – that was obvious, with a face like mine. It wasn't a dentist I needed, but a priest. I *had* a priest and all I was doing was wasting my time on mirrors.

'Father,' I whispered. My voice was a little black insect, crawling on the floor.

'Yes, my child?'

I paused. I could feel the earth turning slowly, very slowly, on its axis. 'I wondered if . . . I mean, would it be OK . . . ? Hell! Look, will you hear my confession?'

I think I expected a flash of lightning to strike me blind, a disembodied hand to write 'Not a Catholic' on the trembling wall. But Father Sullivan only nodded, then fumbled in his black vinyl hold-all and brought out a prayer book and a purple stole. My heart was beating so hard, it must have set up earth tremors twenty miles away.

This was my First Confession. The girls at school had spent months preparing for it. I had been banned from all those secret sessions, private instruction with the priest, blushing and whispering through the grille. Now I was a child again, face perfect, teeth untouched, no longer banned, alien, isolated, but one of the three hundred sanctified. Father Sullivan had called me child himself. I could see my short blue gym-dress, the ridged pattern on my bare pink knees where I had knelt too long, the warm virgin itch in my interlock knickers.

'Bless me Father, for I have sinned,' I whispered. I was sitting up in bed, head bowed, hands joined. There wasn't a grille, but there was a real, God-blazoned priest, and we were closer even than in the confessional box.

Father Sullivan was praying aloud, hands on his two black knees. The girls never saw the priest at school – well, not his lower parts – only an ear and a profile through the grille. I had all of him.

'May the Lord Jesus who learnt to obey through suffering, strengthen you, so that you may humbly confess your sins.'

I could feel myself going wet between the legs, my nipples swelling and stiffening. I remembered the fingers in the crotch, the crucifixes and the candle ends, the mutual masturbation with my twelve-year-old best friend.

Father Sullivan's voice was soft, like blue school knickers. 'The apostle Paul once said, "I am content with my weakness, for it is when I am weak, that I am strong."' He paused. He was waiting for me to speak, to tell my sins.

He tried to prompt me. 'How long is it since your last confession, Thea?'

I remembered now, you were meant to tell them that. The girls at school always said a week (or a fortnight, in the school holidays, when Reverend Mother wasn't there to chivvy them). I mumbled something indecipherable – twenty years, a century, half a dozen lifetimes. He must have thought I said ten days. He nodded, bowed his head. He was waiting for my *mea culpa*.

The pause was so long, I could feel a whole new continent forming in it, forests flowering, oceans drying up.

'And how have you offended Our Blessed Lord since then?'

I thought of the under-age waiter, the buggery under the railway bridge, the girl at work I'd paid to let me watch her. I shut my eyes. My hands were clasped so tightly, I could feel the knuckles crushing. I could see the keeper in the recreation ground, the fat pink knees of my best friend's little brother. My palms were clammy with sweat, my thighs sticking together underneath the sheet. I cleared my throat. 'I murdered Janet's baby,' I whispered.

There was a tiny pin-drop silence.

'You committed *murder*?' he said.

I nodded. I felt awesomely important. My schoolmates' first confessions had all been trivial stuff – talking in the dormitory, stealing chocolate bars. I was something different, someone outrageous and distinguished, a sinner he'd remember.

'I slept with a waiter,' I continued. 'At the Café Royal. Well, we didn't do it there. That's where he was working. He was only twelve and a half.' (The priest wouldn't know if I knocked a couple of years off. I had to make him listen, had to keep him there). I opened my eyes, saw a little drop of saliva bubbling at the corner of his mouth.

'Just a minute, Thea. I believe you said *murder* . . .'

'Yes,' I repeated. 'Murder.'

I liked the word. It had smooth, rounded syllables which slipped out softly like blancmange and didn't hurt my mouth.

'Murder is a very serious sin, my child. And a public crime. Does anyone *know* you killed this baby?'

He was frightened. I could hear it in his voice. He was worried about the police and public prosecutions, and getting mixed up with something he couldn't handle. He'd had thirty years of nuns' confessions: 'Father, I dropped my rosary in chapel.' 'Father, I ate meat on Friday.' He'd never met a crime before. His purple stole was clanging against my eyes. I shut them again. I'd had enough of purple.

'I'd like you to tell me exactly what happened, Thea. How old was the baby? Where was its mother?'

'I stole a duvet cover,' I stuttered. 'From Swan and Edgar. I trained Leo's dog to lick me when we made love.' I started to laugh. Karma

83

would never lick me. He hated the smell. He only sniffed and retreated. If it hadn't been for Karma, Leo might have loved me, might never even have hit me. No, he hadn't hit me. I only fell downstairs.

'I fell downstairs,' I shouted. 'On to stone.' I was crying. I didn't want to cry. It hurt my face. I wanted Leo. Leo's arms around me, Leo picking me up from the cellar steps, Leo's dog licking me between the legs.

Father Sullivan had sprung up from the chair. His face was sickly pale. His eyes had disappeared into two little slits, the frown lines above them cutting deep like cart-tracks. I hoped he'd put his arms around me. I wanted him to change me from a little black insect to a born-and-bred Catholic who'd been baptized with water and the Holy Ghost, and had swallowed God in a white Communion dress with roses in her hair. I longed to sob in his arms, collapse on his breast like John.

'I've committed the sin of vanity,' I whispered. 'Taken too much interest in my personal appearance. Asked for a mirror. Worried about my looks. Wanted people to touch me.'

The priest had slumped down in the chair again. He looked like a grounded puppet with its strings snapped. He opened his mouth and shut it, tried to mumble something, choked on a word and spat it out. I clung on to his arm. I could feel my nails sinking into his flesh through the thin black cloth of his suit. If he wouldn't hold me, I would hurt him, murder him. I could still see his perfect teeth.

'I've murdered a priest!' I shouted.

He sprang away from me, dashed to the door and opened it. 'Sister!' he called. His voice had gone high like a woman's. He *was* a woman. There was nothing there between his two black legs.

Sister came in seconds. She must have been waiting just outside. They spied on us like that, at school. Hovered outside dormitories, peeked through keyholes, caught our private lives in butterfly nets and then stuck pins through them.

He held me down while she jabbed the needle in my arm. The room smelt of sin and surgical spirit.

I struggled to sit up. 'I haven't had absolution,' I gasped. I craved his hands on my head, the whispered words of pardon, the 'go in peace'. None of the girls at school had ever been refused forgiveness. Three hundred girls multiplied by fifty-two. Week after week after week of absolutions. Sins wiped out, knickers washed clean.

'Father,' I whimpered. 'You haven't said the prayers.'

Something was happening to my voice. Black soot was muffling it, soft black snow falling on my limbs. I tried to shake it off, but my hands had turned to tissue paper.

'Father,' I mouthed. 'The absolution. *Please*.'

As I went under, I saw his thin black back dwindling towards the door.

nine

'Oranges and Lemons,'
Say the bells of St Clement's . . .

It was my fourth birthday and I was sitting on my father's knee, wearing a hideous dress in pink organdie. Well, it looks hideous in the photograph. I remember loving it. It had starched, frilly knickers underneath which scratched and rustled when I moved.

'I owe you five farthings,'
Say the bells of St Martin's . . .

My father's name was Martin. He was around for just four years. In fact, the last time I remember him was at that birthday party. He turned me upside down and swung me round and round, and my head started spinning and then the room and the whole world, and I knew he was God, then.

'When will you pay me?'
Say the bells of Old Bailey.
'When I grow rich . . .'

He must have been rich, because he bought me a rocking-horse with flaming nostrils and a real hair tail, and a red balloon you could sit on, and a dog on a string. At tea, he lit the candles on my cake and said 'damn' when he burnt his fingers. Then he cut the cake into fat little wedges and gave me the fattest bit with the 'T' on.

'T for Thea,' he said and kissed me. He had a kiss which prickled, like the knickers. He'd chosen my name himself. My mother wanted to call me Patricia Jane.

After tea, I climbed back on his knee and asked him to swing me round again. My mother said, 'No, Martin, not after all that cake.' But he did. The world span even faster then, and I kept saying, 'Again, again, again, again, again . . .'

When I was five, I didn't have a party and he wasn't there. My mother knitted me a cardigan the colour of manure. I asked her where he was and she said, 'Ask Josie Rutherford', but I didn't know anyone called that.

> Here comes a candle to light you to bed,
> Here comes a chopper to chop off your head.
> Chop, chop, chop, chop, chop . . .

I yanked my head off the block, fought my way through the trap of strangling arms. The candles had all burnt down and were melting the icing on the cake. Balloons were popping everywhere.

'Stop,' I shouted. 'Stop!'

I tried to sit up, but gravity had turned into gelatine. A face was swinging over mine. At first, I thought it was my father. I could see dark hair and feel the prickle of a chin, but the smell was different. My father smelt of birthday cake and Capstan Navy Cut. This was Leo's smell. Leo still brought with him the faintest odour of the Russian steppes, bare scrub and young horse.

'Hallo,' I said, when he'd stopped swinging.

'Thea,' he whispered. His voice was almost snivelling. He couldn't bear to look at me. His eyes had already left the room. 'How *are* you?'

'I'm fine,' I said. I was. I even knew it was Monday. I'd been to the dental room first thing Monday morning. The dentist had hot fat fingers which tasted of oil of cloves. He'd had to remove a root and a nerve or two, and put stitches in a gum, and file off two more teeth which were jagged round the edges. He gave me injections, so it didn't hurt at all. Sister Anselm stood beside me and squeezed my hand and passed him probes and forceps. And they both kept saying, 'Brave girl!', which was crap, really, because the injections made me feel as if I were floating above my own mouth on a fat pink cloud, and even if they'd attacked me with a pick-axe, I'd probably just have smiled. The treatment lasted about a hundred years, but I knew it was still Monday, because Sister Anselm had told me so when she tucked me back in bed and said, 'Now you rest there till lunchtime, dear, and I'll go and say three Hail Marys for you in the Chapel.'

Leo was trying to pick up the fragments of his voice. 'Thea, I don't know how to . . .'

'It's Monday,' I said. I had to say something. I couldn't talk about the weather. There isn't any weather in a hospital.

'Yes, I know.'

He'd brought me grapes. He dropped the bag at the foot of the bed, as if he couldn't bear to come too near me. I hoped they weren't the same ones I'd bought with his money for the dinner party. He edged a little closer. 'How are you, Thea?'

'I told you, fine.' I wished he wouldn't keep asking. My mouth was mostly numb. The lump on my head still throbbed, but I'd decided to pretend I was just a clock and that was the bit which ticked. I didn't inquire how *he* was. He looked too ill for that.

'How's Karma?' I asked, instead.

'OK.' He was scrabbling in a plastic carrier, bringing out books, biscuits, toothpaste, talcum – all the wrong things. I couldn't eat biscuits, I never use talc, and it was impossible to clean my teeth. I could have wept for him. He loathed shopping. It hurt his pride dawdling round Boots and Fine Fare with unwieldy wire baskets, trying to make contact with giggly shop assistants who had one CSE in General Studies. Yet he'd done it just for me. Filled a whole trolley with paperbacks I'd never read, sweets and grapes and Lucozade when I didn't have a mouth. He seemed embarrassed by them all. Boots and Fine Fare didn't suit him. The packets were too bright, too vulgar. The tin of talcum fell off the bed and clattered to the floor. He left it there. He kept staring round the room, shuffling his feet, clearing his throat as if he had something stuck in it. The backs of his eyes looked yellow. He hated hospitals. I knew we must both get out.

'Will you take me home?' I asked. My teeth were better now. I couldn't even feel them.

He seemed to have mislaid his voice again. He was always nervous when I called it 'home'. He had picked up the grapes and was pulling them off in little wounded clusters. 'They . . . er . . . won't let you go yet, Thea. They think you ought to see . . . well . . . a psychiatrist.'

'I won't,' I said. Leo had always told me psychiatrists were shit. He offered me a grape. I shook my head.

'They're shit,' I muttered. 'Not the grapes, psychiatrists.' I'd learnt to repeat the things he said. Usually I did it with more subtlety, changing his words around, so he wouldn't notice.

So they'd been ganging up on me. The Sisters intercepting him before he'd even seen me. I knew I must keep him away from them. They were weakening him, unravelling him. The smell of the hospital was seeping into him like acid and eroding him. He couldn't even sit down. His sallow hands kept clenching and unclenching. He didn't know where to put himself or what to do with his eyes. Every time they met my face, they retched and crept away. I couldn't bear them to have to cower like that, sneaking further and further back into their sockets, cringing under the lids. His eyes had always blazed before, not squirmed and grovelled.

'Why don't you draw the curtains?' I suggested.

'But it's still light.'

'Never mind. It makes it cosier.'

He walked over to the window and pulled them to, shutting out the cold white afternoon, as if it were a busy-body nun.

'Now pull the curtains round my bed.'

'But won't they think it's . . . ?'

'Who cares?'

He did it almost gratefully, as if he were glad of anything to do to fill the silence, offer restitution. It was darker now. My broken face could be dismissed as just a shadow, a shifting trick of the light. I turned it half away from him, pulled down my nightie, leant back against the pillows. I knew we must get out of there, return to his house, to peanut-butter sandwiches and arguments and normal conversations.

'Did you buy the vase?' I asked.

'Which vase?'

'The one in the Bermondsey shop. The phoenix one.'

He frowned. 'No.'

'Why not?'

He shrugged. 'Too expensive.'

'Was it a proper phoenix?'

'How do you mean, proper?'

'Well, like the other one.'

'Yes.'

'Rising from the ashes?'

'No.'

'I thought they all did that.'

'No, not the Chinese ones.'

'Why not?'

'It's a different bird.'

'How d'you mean, different?'

'Well, it's not a phoenix at all, not really. We only call it a phoenix because we haven't got another word. It's a sort of mistranslation. Look, Thea, Sister Anselm said . . .'

'What *should* you call it?'

'Call what?'

'The thing which isn't a phoenix?'

'Oh, Thea, let's not . . .'

'I want to know.'

'The Chinese word is *feng huang*.'

'Feng what?'

'*Huang.*'

'Oh.'

'There's no exact equivalent in English. I suppose we might have called it roc, or albatross, or . . .'

'The one you had *looked* like a phoenix. I mean there were flamy things around it.'

'No, they were only feathers.'

'Very fancy feathers.'

'Yes.'

'You even *called* it a phoenix.'

'Well – yes – one does.'

I leant across and took his hand. He had settled down at last, but had moved the chair as far away from me as possible, and was sitting opposite my feet. His fingers felt so cold, they could have been made of marble.

'Leo . . .'

'What?'

'You're *freezing*.'

'Yes.'

It was stifling in the room, windows shut, heating full on. Three yes's he'd given me, on top of all the shopping. He kept trying to make amends, offer me drinks, grapes – pick up things I'd dropped. It didn't suit him, really. The silences kept threatening us again. I knew I had to distract him, keep him talking. If the silence went too deep, it would lead us back to frightening hurling objects, dangerous things.

'Did they *ever* put the other sort of phoenix on their vases? The ones that rise from ashes?'

'No, they didn't even know about them. They're an Egyptian thing. The *feng huang* is a completely separate myth.'

I mistrusted myths – they're always so remote and complicated. 'You mean it's not a real bird at all?'

'No. It's like the dragon or the unicorn. A sort of symbol, I suppose.

It only appeared in a Golden Age. It was meant to be a sign that the gods were pleased with what was happening here on earth.'

'And *were* they pleased?'

'Not often, I suspect. Golden Ages have never been too common, except in retrospect. Though occasionally the bird appeared, even in a bad age. Apparently, it could be tempted down by music. It was a very musical creature, so if you played the flute, or sat with your friends in the garden, singing songs, it was meant to flutter down and join in.'

I closed my eyes. I could see Leo playing his piano by the open window, surrounded by Thea, Sian, Rowena, and above us all, the Golden-Age *feng huang*, pouring out its gold and scarlet song.

'What did it look like?' I asked. 'I mean, apart from on the vase.'

'Oh, beautiful, exotic.'

'Like a peacock?'

'Sort of. It was coloured like the rainbow.'

'Yes?' So long as he went on talking, we were safe, trapped inside the curtains in our own white bird-cage. Leo, too, seemed grateful for the bird. Its wings were sheltering us from sharp-edged, naked things. Without it, we had nothing to discuss but loss and shock and blame.

'It was the Emperor of all the birds, so the Chinese gave it the best attributes of all their creatures – you know, the throat of a swallow, the breast of a swan, the stripes of a dragon, the tail of a fish . . .'

I kept my eyes tight shut. Its beauty almost hurt them. '*Yours* didn't look like that,' I murmured.

'No.'

'I suppose they couldn't show it on a vase.'

'No.'

'Tell me some more,' I said. I was frightened by the no's. I wanted him there forever, sitting by my side, weaving me bright, exotic fables which matched the quivering colours in my head.

'It was a very good-natured bird,' he said. One long hand had edged towards me now, crawling up the counterpane towards my own. 'It never harmed a living thing. It wouldn't even peck at a grub or tread on a blade of grass. And in wartime, it simply disappeared.'

I smiled. The bird was so gentle, I could trust it near my mouth. I could almost see it hovering over us, as if Leo had brought it with him in his carrier bag, and then released it like a dove. I was still on my fat pink cloud. This was how the world should be – kind and bright and peaceable. I wanted to stop it there, freeze it forever like a picture in a story book, so no wars would start, nor mouths split, nor birds or vases ever smash again. The *feng huang* had already healed us. Leo had clutched my fingers now, and the pain in my mouth was hardly fluttering.

'Did it have a mate?' I asked.

'I shouldn't think it needed one. It was sort of male and female both at once. In fact, the Chinese poets used it as a kind of metaphor for the perfect union of man and woman.'

I picked up his words and held them in my hands like flowers. The perfect union. Joined, fused, indivisible. One pair of wings shutting out the world. No rows, then, no divorces, no separate beds, no sex. Or maybe endless sex, uninterrupted.

'So it couldn't lay eggs?' I said. 'I mean, there wouldn't be any young?' Even that could be a blessing. Man and woman and children all in one. No need to grow up, or apart or away, or become a disappointment, or an orphan . . .

Leo was pulling at a hang-nail on his thumb. 'I suppose it wouldn't *need* eggs if it was immortal. Though, actually, I did read somewhere it was connected with procreation.'

Procreation. That was a biblical word, a Janet word. I could see the *feng huang* carrying Lucian, very gently, in its beak. We needed it – for peace, for harmony, for offspring that were part of us and didn't abort, or die, or simply never happen.

'How?' I asked. 'I mean, why procreation?'

Leo tugged at the hang-nail with his teeth. 'No idea. There are so many different legends, I get confused. They say it's a creature which sprang from the sun, so I suppose it's connected with warmth and growth and harvest – things like that. I saw one on a tapestry once, gazing on a ball of fire, sort of pecking at the flames.'

'*Flames?*' I said, excited. 'So it *is* like the other phoenix.'

'Well, no, the fire wasn't really . . .' His thumb was bleeding now, and he had trapped it under the fingers of his other hand. Another silence. He tried to shovel words into it, like Polyfilla.

'Sometimes I think the Chinese made it a symbol of anything they fancied – fertility, the Emperor, peace, long life, married bliss – ideals of all the things that don't work out in grim reality. Perhaps that's what myths are for – to deal with what you can't explain or control or contrive or . . .'

'Leo . . .' I murmured. I didn't want to return to grim reality. I joined our two hands again.

'What?'

'Do you think it could be mended?'

'What d'you mean?' He was still a little irritable. It was as if his gentle, careful side had rusted up, and every time he tried to exercise it, it creaked and grated.

'The vase. The one I . . .' I didn't dare say 'smashed'. The word felt menacing. I knew I was responsible. I had brought war to the land, banished the *feng huang*. I could feel cold, sharp tears pricking against my eyelids.

'Oh, Thea, *don't* . . .'

He inched towards me very carefully, as if I were made of glass and even his footsteps might shatter me in pieces. I stretched out my arms to him, laid my face against his soft cashmere sweater, making a little nest for it in the hollow of his shoulder. I was safe again. Nothing had happened between us. It was so dark now, you couldn't see my mouth. The shadow on the wall had merged us into one. I didn't need a mate, because I was part of him, man and woman and child with him, immortal, feathered, joined.

'May I come in?' The voice was like a gunshot scaring away a bird.

'No!' I almost shouted. The door was opening. It was Sister Robert, furtive as a poacher, gun in her hand, torn and bleeding feathers at her feet.

Leo leapt up. He looked very dark and old against the nun. Someone seemed to have mangled him in their hands. He no longer stood as proud as I remembered him.

Sister Robert smiled. 'Dr Davies would like to see you both. He's waiting just outside.'

'I've . . . er . . . got to go,' said Leo. He was snatching up the carrier, shaking out his coat.

Sister Robert took his arm and steered him towards the window. 'It'll only take a moment, Mr Rzevski. Dr Davies is our hospital psychiatrist. He's very understanding.'

'Shit,' I murmured. 'They're shit.'

She'd ruined everything, lobbed a bullet through our perfect union, brought war and pain again.

'You see, it's really up to Dr Davies how long Thea stays with us. We've seen the X-rays and she's going to need a little operation on her mouth. But we can't do it yet. Not until all that swelling's settled down. She doesn't have to stay here. The immediate dental work can be done in the surgery, or as an out-patient. On the other hand, we think she needs a rest. She's very overwrought. Dr Parkes suggested . . .'

She was talking about me as if I were just a squiggle on the lino. Leo wasn't listening – backing away, shoulders hunched and steely, hand on the doorknob.

'Leo, *wait* . . .' His face was barred and shuttered, his eyes so dark, you could have lost your way in them. He had almost gone. He hadn't kissed me, hadn't said goodbye. The vase was broken again, the *feng huang* torn and writhing on the ground.

'Leo, I . . .'

Gone. He hadn't even left his smell. All I could smell was Sister Robert now – chloroform and death. The pain in my mouth came rushing in again, the lump on my head booming and pounding like a grandfather clock. The bed was littered with baubles – biscuits, bathsalts, cheap romances. There was nothing of Leo left.

Dr Davies must have passed him in the corridor. He knocked and entered before I could even say, 'Get out!' He was violating Leo's sanctuary, heaving back the curtains round the bed, unveiling the windows. The light strode in and raped us.

'Sitting in the dark, when the sun's trying to shine! It's a lovely afternoon.' His voice went through my head.

'It isn't now,' I said.

He wore a white nylon shirt which glared, and a shiny navy suit with tiny shiny lines across it, and horrid shiny shoes with shiny toecaps, and oily hair slicked down with Brilliantine. His skin was greasy and he had blackheads round his nose and glittery metal glasses. Even his voice was shiny.

'Well, young lady, how are you?'

'I'm not young.'

'An *old* lady, are you?'

'I don't want to see you.'

'But I want to see *you*.'

Silence.

'I understand you've spoken to Father Sullivan.'

So the priest had betrayed me, had he? All that crap about the Inviolate Secrets of the Confessional, and he'd already branded me as a public criminal. It would be on my case notes, next. Diagnosis: murderer.

'*So?*' I said. I wasn't going to be polite, not likely. Psychiatrists were shit.

He had plonked himself down beside me, without even asking. He was desecrating Leo's chair. There should have been a *row* of chairs – one for traitor priests, one for lovers who brought bright birds to your shrine, one for shitty shrinks.

'What happened to your mouth?' he asked. He was side-stepping the murder. It was probably a trap.

'I fell downstairs.'

'No, young lady, you did not.'

'On to stone,' I added.

'On to stone?'

I knew that ruse – repeating me. That was Leo's trick. And mine. 'I'd rather talk to Father Sullivan about it.'

'It was Father Sullivan who asked me if I'd see you. I'm a Catholic, too, you know.'

That was a trap as well. Psychiatrists were never Catholics. Adrian said it got in the way of Freud. He was merely hoping I'd confess more crimes, that's all.

'It's difficult sometimes, isn't it?' He cleared his throat as if he had religion stuck inside it. He was trying to suck up to me, suggesting we had common problems – spiritual crises, religious doubts. I had nothing in common with any psychiatrist. He had little black hairs on the backs of his thumbs and a dreadful mottled tie. Leo chose his friends on things like ties.

'I don't like your tie,' I said.

He laughed. 'You don't like *me* much, do you?'

'No,' I said. 'I don't.'

He faded the laugh into a smile, a sickly spaniel one which said, 'I'll still wag my tail, even if you kick me.' It made me mad. I tried to look haughty and unmoved. 'Anyway,' I added, 'I prefer to talk to priests.' I hoped it sounded grand, as if I had my own private confessor, or the Bishop came round to dinner every second Friday, like Sonia Jackson in the Upper Fourth.

'Psychiatrists *are* priests, Thea – in a sense. Priests for the mind.'

'Balls!'

He didn't even growl. Psychiatrists spend years and years learning never to react. It bores me, actually. What's the point of kicking spaniels, if they won't even show their teeth?

'Aren't you going to tell me how you're feeling?' He was fawning on me. If he *had* been a dog, I think I'd have had him skinned and made into a rug and then walked over him.

'You don't mind talking to the Sisters, so I understand.' He was sniffing at my skirts again. 'Sister Ursula tells me you're quite a little chatterbox.'

I didn't answer. Words like chatterbox make my stomach heave. I wiped my lips. A sort of yellowish scum was forming round the stitches. The pain had come roaring back now. He must have brought it with him.

He didn't like the silence, I could tell. He kept trying to plug it with feeble little openings, offering me a paw, or picking up his rubber bone and laying it at my feet.

'We're not too happy, are we, Thea?'

'Aren't we?'

'Perhaps you'd prefer to see Father Sullivan again?'

Silence.

'I *could* arrange it, Thea.'

I gave the most grudging nod I could. 'OK.' At least Father Sullivan didn't have black hairs on his thumbs, and he might even change his mind about the absolution. In fact, I think they *have* to give it to you. I remember hearing something like that at school.

'Good girl!' The spaniel had turned into a psychiatrist again and was nodding and smiling as if I had entrusted him with the entire story of my toilet training, with the odd Oedipus complex thrown in as well. 'Father may still be in the chapel. I'll go down there straight away and see if I can catch him.'

I didn't say 'thanks'. Why should I? He was trying to make a cosy little exit. He wanted handshakes from me, gratitude, goodbyes. I stared down at the floor.

'Take care, Thea. God bless.'

I shuddered. He made God sound like some nauseous Jewish uncle. On the way out, he helped himself to one of Leo's grapes. I chucked the whole bunch into the waste-bin. They were contaminated now.

When he'd gone, I closed my eyes. I wanted to make it dark and quiet again, to tempt the phoenix back.

'Immortal,' I whispered. 'Procreation.'

The words were like an ointment. I lay so still, I could feel peace falling on the land like rain, and the bright, good-natured bird hovering closer, closer, down towards my bed.

I looked beyond it, to where the wings of God enfolded the whole dazzling, spinning universe. I tried to make Him hear.

'Mend the vase,' I prayed.

ten

Two days later, I woke with my hand between my legs. I hadn't dared masturbate before, not with Father Sullivan on the premises. I was furious with the priest. He hadn't come to see me. All those parables about lost sheep and prodigal sons, and he was scared of the first real sinner he'd probably ever encountered in his life. Nor had Leo come again. I suppose he was frightened of meeting Dr Davies. (Not that *he* came, either.) Don't think I was lonely. There was a timetable as strict as Adrian's. I had more X-rays and more maulings about by a sort of sub-Pakistani dental surgeon. Sister Ursula took me to the hospital chapel and said a Hail Mary with me. (There were white chrysanthemums on the altar and a plaque which said '*Salus Infirmorum*'.) I had double blancmange for lunch and an enema for tea and a bath in a bathroom with yellow coal-tar soap. They gave me phoenix-coloured pills which must have blotted out a lot of things, because I felt smug and drifty and sometimes almost cheerful.

In the afternoon, a fat nun with a fair moustache arrived with a trolleyful of books and said hallo, she was the hospital librarian. The books were mostly lives of saints with brown musty covers and pressed rose petals fluttering from the pages. I chose St Cuthbert and St Philip Neri, then I grabbed a woman saint, in case she thought I was obsessed with men. Nobody mentioned men. It was like my convent school again – quiet and calm and orderly, but short on thrills. Even my food was censored. Toast and chops and apples remained strictly on the Index. I could only manage slops, and everything I drank, I sipped through straws.

I wondered who was paying for all those straws. I knew private hospitals were cripplingly expensive. And why a private hospital at all? Why a Catholic one? I should have questioned Leo, I suppose, but Leo didn't come, and even if he had done, I still wouldn't have asked him. Safer just to cut out that slice of my life between the aubergines and waking up with nuns – chuck it in the waste-disposal unit, like a piece of mouldy apple.

It was dark outside, as if the morning was suffering from a hangover and still struggling to get up. I removed the hand from between my legs. I had no idea how long it had been there and what it had been up to. Better, really, to start again from the beginning. Sister Ursula had left my morning tea and departed to the chapel for the Angelus, so I was safe for at least ten minutes. I dipped my finger in the cup and wetted it. I normally use spit, but I didn't fancy bloody spit. At least the tea was warm. My labia are rather long and droopy. Leo had clipped my dangly earrings on them once, one on each side, and then gone down on me with the earrings jiggling and swinging against his nose. I tried to think of Leo and the earrings, but I was really doing it with Father Sullivan. He was sitting in the confessional, fumbling with the zip, while I lurched sort of upside down on the prie-dieu, with my toes hooked through the grille. I don't know really why I bother with the acrobatics. I'm never simple in my fantasizing. I suppose I like it to be difficult or painful. That's what was wrong with Adrian. It was always such a cop-out – all the CSE positions rather than the A-levels. (Leo screwed me on a camel, once.)

'Bless me, Father,' I whispered. 'For I am about to sin.' I was so wet now, I didn't need the tea. Father Sullivan had his purple stole flung across his thing, and its fringed ends were sending amazing ticklish sensations down the insides of my thighs. Hospitals beds aren't built for masturbation. I tried to stop it creaking.

'Harder, Father,' I whispered as he tore me inside out. The grille was a gaping hole now, where he had thrust his thing right through it. 'Harder, harder, harder . . .'

The whole confessional box was shaking and groaning. He had wrenched down the partition and laid his bare anointed hands across my bum. I was panting and slavering like Karma. I had reached that hair-trigger moment when you *have* to come. Even if the Pope walked in, or someone shouted 'Fire!' and the entire Metropolitan Fire Brigade rushed clanking and slooshing up the stairs, I knew I'd still come before I packed my valuables or thought about escape. Why I like coming is that it's the only moment in your life when you're really committed to something. There are no ifs and buts, or analyses of terms, or parentheses, or maybes. Come is written over everything and goes through layers and layers and layers of it, like letters in a stick of rock. (I've done it with a stick of rock – in Blackpool.)

I came. And so did Sister Ursula. She was *running*. Nuns never run.

Even if a dozen fires had broken out, she'd still only *glide* from the inferno.

'What's the matter, Thea? What's *wrong*? I could hear you half a mile away.'

I tried to turn my gasp into a groan.

'I don't feel well,' I said. I didn't. There was a roaring in my ears, and the throbbing in my thighs had set my mouth alight.

'You're feverish!'

I placed my hands innocently on the outside of the counterpane, and tried to inch my nightie down with my feet.

She popped a thermometer underneath my tongue and took my pulse. It was roaring. Neither of us spoke. I was gagged and she was counting. She scribbled something on my chart. Her brow was all puckered up, as if someone was trying to make a pleated curtain out of it.

'I think I'd better get the doctor to take a look at you.'

'I don't want a doctor,' I peeved. 'I want a priest. Father Sullivan *promised*. Well, he didn't, but Dr Davies did. He said he'd send him two whole days ago.'

'I expect he's busy, dear. You mustn't let it upset you. It's affecting your temperature.'

'Well, it *does* upset me. Priests shouldn't break their promises.'

The puckering pulled tighter. A spiritual crisis *and* a rise in temperature. She pushed up her sleeves and hovered. 'Try and rest, Thea, dear, and I'll see what I can do. I know Father Sullivan's *around*, but . . .'

Of course I didn't rest. Coming once only makes me randier. As soon as she shut the door, I started off again. Father Sullivan was more or less insatiable. After fifteen minutes of the straight stuff, I decided to hurt him. He'd abandoned me, hadn't he, turned me over to a psychiatrist, refused to give me absolution? Right, he'd suffer for it. First, I bit his balls, then I changed the rhythm when he wasn't expecting it. I made him almost come and then lost contact. He was a gibbering idiot by the time I'd finished with him.

'Satisfied?' I said.

He slunk out of the door with his balls bleeding and his cassock torn, and someone else sneaked in. He looked like one of Adrian's part-time students at the Local F.E. College – youngish, shabbyish, and Leftish. He had raggedy red hair left free to do its own thing, and

National Health glasses perched on a pale, tense, shining sort of face which looked as if it were about to announce Universal Revolution to the world. He was wearing glum brown cords with shiny patches where they had lost their pile, and a green home-knit sweater balding at the elbows.

'Hi!' he said. 'D'you mind if I sit down?'

I wondered if he was the occupational therapist, except he didn't come complete with feltcraft kits or wicker baskets. He couldn't be a dietician or a radiographer – his nails weren't clean enough. He was possibly a friend of Leo from his earlier, less successful days, come to bring me a message or explanation. (I didn't fall on stone, I bumped into a brick wall.)

'How are you feeling?' he asked.

I wiped my wet and slimy fingers on the sheet.

'Shagged out,' I said. I knew with this one I didn't have to be too careful with my words. It was almost a relief. The strain of talking politely for four whole days was beginning to tell on me. Sister Francis had frowned when I'd let out just a 'damn'.

'Are they treating you OK?'

'Fine,' I said. I tried to see his eyes behind the glasses. They were a sort of muddyish-brown, like the stuff you find at the bottom of ponds. 'Except I think they regard me as a sort of nutcase.'

'Same here,' he said, cocking one leg over the other and balancing it at an angle on his lap. They were skinny legs, underneath the corduroy. His wrists were thin as well.

'You're Thea, aren't you? I'm Ray. That's a formal introduction.' He grinned, showing strong, sturdy teeth (though perhaps they only seemed that way, compared to the ruin of my own mouth. I peered at people's teeth now with a sort of fierce, fascinated envy, whereas before I'd hardly noticed them).

'I hear you've had a bit of a rough-up?'

I ignored the question. He spoke standard English, but with a faint undertone of northern dance-halls and a slight broadening of the vowels which Leo would have shuddered at. Leo never knew people called Ray, in any case. All his acquaintances had foreign names like Jochen or fancy ones like Jasper, and spoke either breathy Sloane Street or Middle European ponderous.

'So you're not a friend of Leo's?'

'No, I'm afraid I'm not. Were you expecting one?'

'Well, not *exactly*.' I'd learned from experience never to expect Leo or his friends.

'So who's this famous Leo?'

'My lover,' I said, sort of nonchalantly. I liked the word lover. It made me feel doomed and romantic, like Mary Queen of Scots or Judy Garland. I'd told Sister Francis that Leo was my uncle, but there was no point in lying to Ray. He was the sort of man you could say 'fuck' in front of, and he wouldn't turn a hair.

'The one who hit you?' he asked.

'No,' I said, too quickly. 'I bumped into a brick wall.'

Ray had taken off his glasses and was polishing them with a fag-end of the sheet. His face looked soft and vulnerable without them, like a clam without its shell.

'I think he hit you, Thea, didn't he?'

'*No.*'

'Didn't he?' The eyes were very gentle. You could have snuggled up inside them and gone to sleep.

I paused. 'Yes,' I whispered.

He took my hand. Both our hands were hot and sticky like slabs of toffee that had stuck together and melted in a sweet-shop window. I felt a tremendous lightness saying 'yes', as if granite had turned into candyfloss. I could feel tears sliding down my cheeks – somebody else's tears, distant and cleansing and permissible.

'It was my fault,' I explained, through sniffs.

He nodded. 'Bit of both, I expect. Always is.'

I stared at him. He had made my mouth acceptable, given us absolution. Leo was no longer a brute, a batterer. Nor had I driven him to violence by being a cruel and lying bitch. We weren't rough and dangerous delinquents any more, just two normal people who bashed each other up a bit. I suddenly felt starving. I didn't want slops for breakfast, but a roasted ox.

'I'm *famished*,' I said.

'So'm I. Shall we ring for breakfast?'

I laughed. He'd turned the hospital into a four-star hotel with room service. I hadn't believed I could ever laugh again. 'Ask for sausages,' I said. 'Pork ones. Fat ones. Not those mingy chipolatas.'

'Sausages,' he repeated to the nun. 'Big ones, please, with lots of fried bread. Oh – and some good strong English mustard.'

I thought she'd kick him out. It wasn't a doss-house for shabbysweatered drop-outs to give their orders in. But she brought the breakfast on a silver tray with matching silver covers over the food. It was usually melamine and lukewarm. There were three tiny little cereal packets, the one-portion size from Variety Pack. They reminded me of Adrian. (Though, actually, we'd never bought that size when we were married. They were too uneconomical and didn't come with competitions or free Bugs Bunnies.)

Ray ate my slops himself. They had brought me watery porridge, swamped with still more liquid until it looked like a greyish puddle in a builder's yard. Then he mashed my sausages into a sort of soggy paste with mustard, and fed me with the mustard spoon, which was small enough to slip between my stitches. The pain nagged away like a spiteful third person sitting down to breakfast with us.

'Sore?' he asked.

I nodded. Ray wasn't one for words, and those he chose were mainly monosyllables. It made me feel protected. He wouldn't try and outsmart me or give me history lessons.

'What *is* this place?' I asked him. I hadn't dared ask anyone else before. I was terrified the answer might lead back to paperweights. But with Ray I felt protected. 'I'm not even sure where I *am*, you see.' I knew he'd understand how strange (and yet safe) it felt to be living in a limbo where no one could flush out or find you on a map. 'I wasn't really with it when they brought me here.'

'You're in Surrey, Thea – the Walton and Weybridge bit – but nearer Weybridge. The hospital's called St Maur's.'

'St *who?*'

'Maur.'

'Never heard of her.'

'It's a *him.*'

'Oh,' I said. I liked the thought of a male saint called St More. It's one of my favourite words. 'Who was he?'

'A friend of St Benedict's. I think he's vaguely connected with invalids. I seem to remember a special St Maur's Blessing of the Sick which Benedictines use.'

'Nice,' I murmured. 'All the same, I can't really think why Leo brought me here. He's not a Benedictine.'

'He's a Catholic, though, I suppose?'

'Oh, no. His religion's sort of patchwork. A bit of this and a bit of that. You know, Buddhism and Beethoven and Bertrand Russell all cobbled up together.'

Ray looked a little nervous. I think he was frightened I was going to embark on Music or Philosophy or Eastern Mysticism like Leo does with me.

'Is he coming to see you today?' he asked. The 'coming' sounded oddly northern, as if Manchester had slipped down into Surrey.

'Maybe,' I hedged.

'It's a long way for him, I suppose?'

'Yes.'

'Does he drive?'

'No.' Leo rarely did things other men did. He'd never owned a car or played golf or taken out insurance policies. I felt I ought to excuse him. 'He's . . . er . . . very busy,' I explained.

'What's his job, Thea? What sort of work does he do?'

'Oh . . . things.' I hardly knew myself. There were the translations and the picture dealers, the buying and selling of manuscripts, the absences with Otto. I wished I hadn't thought of Otto. The breakfast tasted tainted now. I pushed the spoon away. 'Have you ever heard of Louis de Gonzague?'

'*Who?*'

'Louis de Gonzague.' I'd probably got the pronunciation wrong.

'No. Yes – wait a minute – isn't he the chap who scripted the James Bond films?'

'No,' I said. 'He died in 1595.'

'Oh, sorry. One of those early French kings, then?'

'No,' I said again. Adrian would have put him in the Remedial class. 'He's a sort of murderer. Leo's got a friend who thinks he's him.'

'Who, Leo?'

'No, Louis . . .'

There was a sort of prickly silence. Ray was holding my cup for me while I took slow and painful sips from it. His own tea was over-stewed and cooling.

'What are you reading?' he asked. I don't think he could cope with reincarnation. He nodded towards the pile of Leo paperbacks and saintly hardbacks jumbled on my locker.

I blushed. '*Life of St Bernadette*,' I mumbled. I'd picked her for my female saint from the hospital librarian. The only other ones I could have chosen were St Teresa of Avila who had A-levels in everything including ecstasy, and St Barbara who was martyred. Bernadette had asthma and a sense of humour and a shocking academic record. She didn't even know what the Blessed Trinity was and she hadn't learnt to write until she was fourteen and a half. I warmed to her for that. We even looked alike – the same dark eyes and long brown hair, the same heavy, undistinguished faces. I'd seen her photograph. She was small of course, but so was I, at fourteen. I only shot up after I'd left the convent.

'I've always rather fancied her,' I explained. 'We had lots of books about her at my school. Though this is a better one. Less sickly.'

Ray picked up the book and stared at the frontispiece, a picture of Bernadette, as Sister Marie-Bernard, in her black and white nun's habit. He frowned. 'I sometimes think she shouldn't have been a nun. I suppose they don't know what to do with people once they've seen the Blessed Virgin, so the simplest thing is to shove 'em in a convent. She was wasted, really.'

'Well she's not a nun *yet*,' I said. 'I've only reached page sixty-three.'

'Has she had the apparitions?'

'Yes,' I answered. 'Four.' I'd read them over and over again. The beautiful white lady appearing to her in the Grotto in a rush of wind. Dressed in a white robe with roses on her feet, bathed in light and holding a golden rosary. Invisible to everybody else, but entrusting heavenly messages to a shivering wreck of a kid who was out gathering sticks and bones to raise a sou or two for her starving family. A family who shared a converted prison cell with overflowing lavatories and lice.

'Do you realize, Ray,' I told him, 'they were so poor that her little brother was discovered in the church eating *candle* wax to try and fill his stomach. I tried it once myself, and it was so foul, I had to spit it out.'

Ray nodded. He seemed better informed on saints than murderers. 'One theory puts the whole thing down to hunger. Apparently, if you eat too little over a long period of time, you start to see visions merely as a result of semi-starvation. And there's another book which suggested Bernadette was suffering from ergotic poisoning. Ergot's a sort of fungus which contaminates the bread and causes hallucinations.'

I was thunderstruck. 'But it was a *miracle*,' I said. The girls at school had been to Lourdes every year. It was part of the convent calendar, like Reverend Mother's Feast Day, or the ice-cold baths and all-day fast on Ash Wednesday. They had stood on the very spot where St Bernadette had knelt, kissed the rock where Our Lady's feet had rested. I had never gone myself. My mother pronounced the name 'Lourdes' with the sort of shudder other people reserve for words like 'scab' or 'flasher'. While my classmates recited the rosary on the channel ferry or knelt in all-night vigils before the shrine, I would be dragged for quiet weekends to Harrogate or Eastbourne, to ease my mother's asthma. We came back with vapour rubs and woollen gloves and headaches. They returned with miracles – Tizer bottles full of holy water, magic mints made of Our Lady's toenails, Ave Maria inscribed on the head of a pin, musical boxes which played the Lourdes hymn and were strung with fairy lights, miniature television sets which flashed colour pictures of the apparitions to a tiny Bernadette trapped deep inside.

They pitied me, of course. They prayed for me. They even sent me cards. I had seen so many postcards of the place, I felt I almost knew it. One girl told me she'd counted the Virgin Marys in all the shops and had reached a thousand thousand before she'd given up – shelves and shelves of Blessed Virgins made in plastic, plaster, glass, wood, even mother-of-pearl. Puny Virgins shivering in little glass-ball snow-storms, plump Virgins basking in beribboned chocolate boxes, gigantic Virgins which cost you extra baggage on the plane. A thousand thousand Virgins couldn't be attributed to contaminated bread.

'But what about the *cures*?' I objected. 'There've been *thousands* of them. Eating fungus wouldn't make blind people see or cripples leap off their stretchers. One of my friends at school even *saw* a miracle.'

'I doubt it,' muttered Ray. He had hardly touched his sausages. 'There've been only sixty-four real, hard-and-fast, official accredited miracles in the whole history of Lourdes. Cures are different. There might always be another explanation for them – something like wishful thinking or mass hysteria or even a sort of self-hypnosis. I mean, in the nineteenth century, most illnesses were seen as strictly physical. Now, we're more aware of the psychological element. The mind has enormous power, you know.'

He was sounding more like Adrian, every moment. I turned away. I didn't want the wings pulled off those miracles, my classmates' wonders reduced to self-hypnosis. You can destroy anything if you have enough books and words and theories. Just talking about something can change its shape and meaning, and records and statistics take it by the throat and squeeze all the magic out of it. When Jesus said, 'Take up thy bed and walk', I bet a load of cavilling statisticians didn't pour in and start measuring up the mattress and pulling out the stuffing.

I think Ray sensed my irritation. 'Mind you,' he said, 'I don't deny there's been some pretty amazing events in Lourdes. I mean, I'm not opposed to miracles, as such. Some of them even happen sort of naturally.'

'Come off it,' I said. 'They wouldn't *be* miracles if they happened naturally.'

'I'm not so sure. I read in the *Sunday Times* only a month or two ago about a man who had been blind since birth. He was struck by lightning in a perfectly ordinary thunderstorm and regained his sight there and then.'

'Perhaps it *wasn't* lightning,' I objected. 'But a sort of flash from God. You know, like St Paul.'

'Perhaps.'

'You don't sound very convinced.'

'No. Anyway, does it really matter?'

I stared at him. Of *course* it mattered. Flashes of lightning and flashes from God were totally and fiercely different. One meant blind chance, the other meant a caring, healing Father.

Ray screwed the top back on the mustard jar. 'St Bernadette herself wasn't too happy about the miracles.'

'Oh?'

'She wasn't even cured herself, remember. She died in racking pain. With sores all over her body and raging TB.'

'You seem to know a hell of a lot about it. Have you read all the books?'

'Well, not really *read*. To tell the truth, I hardly ever read a book right through. I find it more or less impossible. I'm a skipper and a skimmer. Sometimes I read every other page, other times I just dip in here and there. It always seems to work. I mean, I've never lost a plot yet, or muddled up the characters.'

Adrian would have *killed* him. Skipping books was an Insult to the Author, a Danger to the Dissemination of True Fact and a lot of other Frightening Things. Adrian read not only the whole text, twice through, word for word, including all the commas and the semicolons, but also devoured indexes, appendices, bibliographies, tables of contents, acknowledgements, translators' notes, epilogues and footnotes to footnotes. I was liking Ray better all the time. Unfortunately, he seemed to have reached his own epilogue. He was pulling on his anorak, brushing down his knees. 'I'm sorry, Thea, but I'm afraid I've got to go.'

I grabbed his arm. 'No,' I said. I didn't know who he was or why on earth he'd come to see me, but I knew he mustn't go. He was a sort of minor miracle himself – a book skimmer who muddled up French kings and fancied Bernadette and didn't mind me swearing. And something of a saint. He'd tamed and softened all his breakfast and offered it to me, torn out the softest pieces from the inside of his toast and slid them gently between my lips. He'd even held my hand. Both hands.

'Stay,' I pleaded.

'I'm afraid I'm needed elsewhere.' He was probably going to fetch his wicker baskets, or take a class in potato-printing. 'But I'll come again – if you want me to, that is.'

'Of *course* I want you to.'

'OK then.'

'Promise?'

'Promise. How about tomorrow lunch?' It sounded like a date or an assignment. I remembered the waiter at the Café Royal. But it wasn't like that with Ray. He didn't turn me on at all. He was one of the plainest men I'd ever met. Red hair is fine in Titians or on Irish setters, but disastrous on men. It was something else I liked about him, something hidden. He was like a plain, serviceable coat with a plush fur lining.

'Make sure it's not blancmange,' he called. He was already halfway through the door. 'I *loathe* it.'

'It's *always* blancmange,' I shouted.

When he'd gone, I nicked the baby cereal packets and hid them in my locker. Perhaps Adrian would have brought them if we'd ever had a family. Children like things small. I sat and thought about my marriage. Mondays we had Sugar Puffs and Adrian took Assembly. Tuesdays, it was Ricicles and Dinner Duty. Wednesdays he put hot milk on the Weetabix to warm him up for soccer practice. Thursdays . . .

Adrian felt very far away. I picked up the spoon and dribbled an R in marmalade on the last abandoned piece of toast. I couldn't eat it, but I felt it kept Ray there a little longer. I needed someone. I was feeling rather lonely. I had a nasty feeling Leo wouldn't appear, and there was still no sign of Father Sullivan.

Sister Ursula glided in without him. She doled out my penicillin and my tranquillizers, and removed the breakfast debris from the bed.

'Well,' she said. 'How d'you like our Father Murphy?'

'*Who?*' I asked. That was the name of the chaplain at our school. He must have been almost dead by now. He was pensionable then.

'Father Raymond Murphy,' she repeated. She looked smug, as if she'd just discovered penicillin, without benefit of Fleming.

'You mean . . .'

'Well, I know he hides his dog collar, but he's a holy anointed priest, just the same.'

'A *priest*!' I almost shouted. My breakfast sat up and kicked me in the gut. 'He *can't* be. Priests don't wear cords with holes in.'

'Oh, but they *do*, dear. You're out of touch. Priests wear anything these days – overalls and anoraks, running shoes and T-shirts, tatty jeans. I even saw one in a flying-suit.'

'But he put *marmalade* on his sausages, I saw him. And he . . .'

'Priests have stomachs, Thea. Even Our Blessed Lord had a stomach. Don't you remember the Marriage Feast at Cana? The loaves and fishes?'

'Yes, but . . .' I felt furious, betrayed. Ray had barged into my room, bluffed his way into my confidence, let me think he was a student or a whiz with wickerwork. I'd blurted out all sorts of things I'd never have admitted had I known he was a priest. He'd turned our friendly little breakfast into a forced confession, and I hadn't even noticed. Traps again, like oily Dr Davies.

One thing I hated was pop priests. They'd exploded in the sixties when I was just a kid, but even now they were still bursting out of their boiler-suits, running youth clubs and roaring around on motorbikes and using your Christian name before they'd even met you. It was all a trick to knock you off your guard. They lulled you into saying things like 'shagged' or 'shitty' and then whispered 'pray' or 'Lord' as their own four-letter words. Or tried to pretend they didn't believe in miracles, only to appear in a cloud of white light when they'd finished shining up their Kawasakis. They turned church into a disco and hymns into folk-songs, and once they'd conned you into whistling the chorus, they'd slip religion in like the pill in the sugar. It wasn't even *real religion*. They took out all the mystery and the backbone and the sin, and left a bland, bed-sit Jesus who played lead guitar and ate in health-food restaurants. At least the collared and the cassocked ones had the decency to play it straight. *They* still believed in Hell and rubric and solemnity, and didn't bleat and sneak into your room like sheep in wolf's clothing.

The mustard spoon had slipped down between the sheets. I picked it up and hurled it on the tray.

'If you don't mind, Sister Ursula,' I said, 'I don't want to see any more priests at all.'

I snatched up St Bernadette and opened her at the thirteenth apparition – the one which had caused her all the problems with the parish priest. I felt a surge of fellow feeling. We'd both had trouble enough with clergymen.

'Get out!' the Abbé Peyramale had shouted, as she stood trembling in his presence with her aunts.

'Get out,' I whispered myself. I was addressing it to all of them. To Ray, to Father Sullivan, to the doctor and the dentist, to Josie Rutherford, even to my sacred, hated Leo.

'Get *out*!'

eleven

I stuck with St Bernadette the rest of the day. Nuns and cleaners and paper boys barged in and out of my room, but I was kneeling in ecstasy in front of radiant white ladies, or relaying Our Lady's instructions to open-mouthed French priests, or tending my sheep on the mountain slopes at Bartres. I said we had lots in common, but the differences between us were also pretty great. Bernadette had grown up in a dozy country town, grinding grain and minding lambs, while I was a child of a sprawling suburb, familiar only with petrol pumps and supermarkets. She'd had a father – a down-at-heel, out-of-work one who'd lost his job and an eye at more or less the same time, but a big, bony, doting man who supported her against all the opposition. She'd lived among brothers and sisters, cousins and aunts, whereas I was an only child with a mother who kept the blinds drawn down. Bernadette was a saint. She didn't swear or nick things. She wouldn't even take an apple when it was offered to her as a gift. She'd never had sex and I doubt if she'd even masturbated. She prayed for poor depraved sinners like myself.

I felt, though, she *could* have been a sinner. In different circumstances, perhaps, or with different parents. She had pride and verve, strong passions, even if she kept them under wraps. She answered back the priests and stood up to the Imperial Procurator. She laughed and teased and played practical jokes on people. She'd never had a proper job. Her Mother Superior said the only thing she was good for was grating carrots. I liked her even better after I'd read that.

She was fourteen years and one month when she first saw the Blessed Virgin. I was fourteen and two months when my crowing classmates first visited the town she'd built from nothing. Father Murphy (old style) had accompanied them, and another priest who actually looked like a man and could be called handsome if you didn't peer too closely, and at least six or seven of our nuns, including a withered, shrunken little sister who had Bright's disease and was going for a miracle. I was left behind. While they breakfasted on Christ's body and blood in some sublime basilica reeling with the scent of lilies, I wept into my Weetabix in a cut-price guest-house eight hundred miles away, where the only devotions were homage to the lap-dog or community singing on the radio. It was bad enough being odd one out among three hundred girls, but Lourdes received more than three million visitors a year. I was one in three million – the only outcast, the single unbaptized pariah.

I vowed I would get there somehow – more than that – I would make my First Communion in that very same basilica, even if I had to wait till I left school. I wouldn't defy my mother – that would put a stain on it – but once I was eighteen, I would be free to go my own way. I would join the church and on Easter Sunday of my nineteenth year, I would travel to Lourdes in the company of cripples, lepers and untouchables, and receive the Body of Christ among the lilies, with the Holy Ghost perching on my shoulder and a thousand angels shouting out Hosanna.

Two years later, I left convent school for the local F. E. College and swapped nuns and lilies for bummers and the weed. I still wore Our Lady's blue, but in skin-tight Levis rather than limp gym-slips. Lourdes began to fade. The following year, Adrian came to teach there part-time – history and general studies on Thursday afternoons. A year after that, he asked me to marry him. There weren't any angels present. He was helping me with George III and the American War of Independence, and he slipped in the proposal between the Boston Tea Party and the Surrender at Yorktown. I said 'yes' partly out of gratitude and partly out of shock. On Easter Sunday of my nineteenth year, I was lying in Guy's Hospital, bequeathing them their foetus. If it had been a girl, I might have called it Bernadette. I still remembered, see. But Adrian chose the names. We tried again, almost every day for five years, but there were no more foetuses until Janet's came along. She achieved in five minutes what I failed to do in five years. And didn't even interrupt her education.

Bernadette's mother, Madame Soubirous, had done still better. She'd had nine. Though five of them had died. Five little Soubirous pickled in jars. Perhaps that's why she looked so worn and grim. I'd borrowed a second book from the hospital library, one with photographs and maps, and stared at the photo of this stoic super-mother. She had a heavy peasant jowl and a resigned expression in her eyes. She was nothing like my own ma who had mini-lifts at the local beauty parlour and wasn't resigned to anything. I wondered what it would be like to undergo nine pregnancies. Your body swelling out and sanctifying, then subsiding, spitting you out a trophy, leaving you weaker and distended, every infant disfiguring you a little. Was Janet slackened and distended? Had she got stretch marks now and saggy breasts? Stitches in her cunt? Did she wince with pain when Adrian screwed her? Would they try again?

I slammed the photo upside down. I was sick of babies. Thank goodness Bernadette had none. Ray had hinted that she was wasted as a nun, but it was so much *safer*. She'd missed the divorces and the infidelities, the double shame of abortion and infertility, the broken vows, the broken vases. I was living like a nun myself – the white, the rules, the timetable. I had been lulled into the quiet, prayerful rhythm of the Sisters, restricted as they were, enclosed within four walls. I had almost taken their vows of poverty, chastity and obedience. I'd left my worldly goods behind and both sex and rebellion were impossible. Strange how it suited me. Early morning tea followed temperature-taking, and breakfast followed that; then bath, mouthwash, prayers in the chapel, chat with the nuns, reading, dozing, doctor, lunch. I felt as if I'd been there all my life instead of four short days. I didn't want to leave. I missed Leo fiercely, but I knew it was safer here without him. Everything was safer. I was part of some slow, white routine which God Himself had set in motion and which blocked out the splintered, fraying, random world outside.

There was a tap on the door. It would be afternoon tea, or the dentist with the most recent batch of X-rays, or the cosy cleaning lady who'd promised to lend me one of her daughter's night-gowns.

'Come in,' I called. I prayed it wouldn't be one of those frilly polyester nighties, with trailing lace and horrid little bows.

It was Adrian. I was so surprised, I just sat and stared. I hadn't been in touch with him – I hadn't dared to somehow, now that he was In Mourning – so how in God's name had he found me? He was hardly likely to have been exchanging news with Leo.

He was gazing at my face, looking almost numb with shock and fury, like when they assassinated Lord Mountbatten, or sacked the school caretaker for interfering with a second former. I'd almost forgotten how gruesome I appeared. After Father Sullivan, I'd made a point of avoiding mirrors. They only exaggerated.

'Thea, *darling* . . .'

I took the darling like a bunch of flowers. He had brought flowers too – well, one – a sturdy yellow primula in a pot. Adrian regarded cut flowers as an extravagance. Pot plants could be resited in the garden. Five years previously, he'd brought me something similar for Lucian, and when they discharged me with my weeping uterus and deflating breasts, he'd picked up the pot along with my suitcase and transferred it to our sixteenth of an acre. For all I knew, it could be still there. Or perhaps he'd dug it up again and presented it to Janet for the funeral. (Did you have funerals for foetuses?)

'How did you know I was here?' I asked.

He kissed me very gently on the cheek. He couldn't stop staring at my face. He looked as if he'd like to march me back to my manufacturer and complain about the breakage; storm and blame until we were granted compensation.

'A Dr Davies wrote to me. He thought we were still married.'

He would, of course. I'd written it on the form, and anyway, since I was posing as a Catholic, then I couldn't be divorced.

'Look, Thea, I *know* what happened. I've been to see Davies and he told me.'

'He doesn't know,' I said. I leaned across and sniffed the primula, but someone had already nabbed the smell – Janet, I suppose.

'Thea, darling, you *must* leave Leo. Davies is worried that he'll . . .'

In the pause, I could see clenched fists and hurtling paperweights. I suddenly felt frightened.

'Can I come back and live with *you?*'

He looked different, somehow. He was no longer Janetized, deodorized. There was a small brown stain on his tie – gravy, perhaps, or shoe polish. A button was missing from his shirt, and there were creases in the collar. Janet must be still in hospital, or convalescing somewhere. Now she was out of his house and hair, it seemed stupid not to take advantage of it.

'*Please*,' I murmured. I shut my mouth, so I didn't look too monstrous. I was glad the light was fading. Some of the bruising might even look like shadow.

Adrian's broad shoulders were caving in like cardboard. He seemed so upset, I opened my mouth again to make it easier for him. No one would want to live with a toothless hag.

'OK,' I shrugged. 'It doesn't matter. I can easily stay here. I rather like it, actually. Apart from the blancmange. If you wait until seven o'clock, you can sample the blancmange. It's pink on Wednesdays.

In fact, it's *always* pink. Except on Sundays when we have ice-cream.'

'Look, Thea, darling,' (another darling – my face had obviously impressed him) 'you *can't* stay here. That's really what I came about. Leo filled in some form when he brought you here. Guaranteeing to pay the fees. Except that he filled it in all wrong – on purpose, I suspect. The hospital got on to me, so I phoned him straight away. He's refusing to pay, Thea. Says he can't. Or won't. It's costing £120 a day.'

'A *day*!' I almost shouted. 'For pink blancmange?'

'I'll help, you know I will. But, private medicine on a teacher's salary, it's simply out of the question. *Janet's* in the ordinary NHS place.'

I felt a little dart of triumph. She'd have semi-qualified students peering up her cunt and low-grade agency nurses grumbling about their pay.

'Why aren't I, then? I didn't *ask* to come here.'

'God alone knows. Leo's got half a dozen hospitals more or less on his doorstep and he drags you down to Surrey! He said the nearest casualty was closed, which sounds suspicious, anyway. They told him to take you to St Mary's, Harrow Road. But apparently he'd been there as a patient once himself. I don't know – perhaps he got scared about publicity, or being blamed or questioned, or meeting someone he knew. He wouldn't say much about it. Frankly, I suspect he panicked – bolted out of London, if you like, so he could hush up what he'd done.'

I stared at Adrian. He never lied – he was too literal and unimaginative for that. But Leo didn't panic or bolt or hush things up. Adrian made him sound like a petty criminal.

I took a sip of water. Adrian was sitting on my foot. It hurt a bit, but I almost welcomed it. A lesser pain was a distraction from my mouth.

'There was some other chap involved – Otto, I think he said. That's how he heard of this place.'

'*Otto!*' I gasped.

'Yes, weird name, isn't it? The whole thing sounded odd. Apparently, this Otto character's got an aunt who's one of the nursing nuns here. Sister Robert, I think he said – or was it Roland? – something with an R. Anyway, he knows the place quite well, so he phoned the Reverend Mother there and then, even though it was the middle of the night, jabbered on about an emergency, and thirty minutes later you were carried through the door.'

'Otto,' I repeated. I felt I was unravelling, little pieces flaking off me and crumbling to the floor. Otto had seen me bleeding and distorted, Otto had manhandled me, tossed me in a blanket and dumped me in his car. I knew that car – a snub-nosed, low-slung brute which liked nothing better than to swallow Leo into its second seat and roar away with him, leaving me numb and powerless on the pavement. Except this time, I'd gone with them. They must have done a ton to arrive in thirty minutes. Otto risking my life to save his friend – stop the gossip, preserve Leo's reputation. I wondered if my blood had stained his car. It was red already, a shameless scarlet jade with two seats and a boot. I preferred not to ask who had travelled in the boot. It wouldn't have been Leo.

I could feel scarlet shouting through the room. My mouth was bleeding again, everything too bright. The primula was blazing like a sun. Even Adrian looked too gaudy. His navy-blue sweater and rust-coloured trousers were colliding with each other. I wished he'd go away. I didn't want upheavals and hypotheses, personal history lessons, textbook explanations. Better to remain unconscious, as I had been – mercifully – when Otto bundled me up and threw me in his car.

I picked up the packet of custard creams and tore the wrappings off. It still upset me that Leo had brought me biscuits which I could no more eat than concrete. I'd tried one earlier – a ginger-nut – and my mouth had bled with it. But at least Adrian could enjoy them.

'Have a biscuit,' I urged. 'They're nice.'

Safer if we stuck to simple things like afternoon tea in the country. With any luck, Sister would bring the tray in, and after all the fuss and clatter of teacups and hot-water jugs, Adrian might forget what he'd been saying. Even without the tray, I could still provide refreshments à la carte. I didn't want to think beyond refreshments. If I worked out how I got here, I came face to face with dangerous things like paperweights and Leo's fears and Louis de Gonzague, and if I looked the other way, they were trying to turf me out.

I couldn't bear to leave. Everything was white and safe and holy at St Maur's. It was like being a little girl again, returning to the nuns. Thea Wildman – that was my maiden name. My mother had always distrusted it. 'With a headstrong name like that, I should have *known*

I'd be in trouble.' When my father proved her right by disappearing, she reverted to her own name which was Elliott. ('Two l's and two t's, if you *don't* mind' – Ma always clung on to her every right and asset, even if they were only consonants.) I suppose Elliott is a harmless sort of name, but to me it sounded harsh and unforgiving, full of grudge and spite. I tried to stick to Wildman, which wasn't easy with my mother pouncing on it and introducing deed-polls. Marrying Adrian at least solved something for me. I could turn my back on both Elliott and Wildman, and be simple Mrs Morton – my third official name in only eighteen years.

But if they forced me out of hospital, then who should I be, and where? I was Morton and married on their records, but once outside, the divorce took grip again. I could hardly revert to my maiden name when my father was a stranger and there was nothing left of the maiden, and Elliott I out and out refused. Safer to stay where I was and be simply Thea. Children and nuns and invalids need only a Christian name.

I stole a glance at Adrian. He hadn't touched the biscuits and looked coiled up like a spring. I was scared he was going to return to dangerous subjects. 'Look,' I said quickly. 'If you don't like custard creams, I've got some other sorts. Or there's Lucozade if you're thirsty. They may bring tea in soon, but if you're too parched to wait, you'll find a glass in that . . .'

'Thea, I'm here to discuss your *Future*.'

I hate the word future, especially with a capital F. Adrian always gave it one, which made it sound terribly solemn and dreary, as if life was a form which went on and on for ever, with little spaces for boring things like pensions or insurances or Forward Planning.

'How's school?' I asked.

'Fine . . . Look, darling, you can't stay here any longer. I'm sorry to sound harsh, but I *must* make you understand.'

I tried to plug my terror with a biscuit. My hands were trembling, but I rammed the concrete rectangle hard against my gums. At least pain was a distraction. 'Have they replaced the Art Master – you know, the one you said everyone was . . . ?

'Thea, you've *got* to concentrate. Every day you stay here means another hundred and twenty pounds. And that's just basic. All your drugs and X-rays are charged as extra and every doctor you see sends in his own separate account. Just try adding that lot up!'

I *didn't* try. It's useful sometimes being bad at maths. 'I can't leave, anyway,' I muttered. 'I've got to have an operation.'

'I know, darling.' I was awash in darlings, but even they were dangerous – brightly-coloured bribes to tempt me out. I wanted pale, safe, undemanding darlings which would leave me where I was. Adrian's voice fretted me like a nutmeg-grater. 'Dr Davies told me. But they're not going to do it yet. Not until all that swelling's settled down. Anyway, they want to fix your front teeth first. The dentist here can do it on the National Health. I've already spoken to Sister Ursula about it. So long as you see him in his surgery, he's willing to take you on as a . . .'

'I'm ill,' I whimpered. I was. Everything was slowly festering – hands, legs, lips, arms – turning septic, dropping off. 'I'm not well enough to go to surgeries.'

'I'll take you, Thea, you know that.'

'I've got to have a lump cut out. There's a sort of growth in my gum where a bit of tooth got embedded. They can't do *that* in a surgery. *And* they're doing something to my upper jaw. The dentist told me. He saw it on the X-rays. He says he can't dig out the bits of broken root unless he removes a piece of the jawbone first.'

'That's *later*, darling. They're going to do it all at once, so you'll only need one anaesthetic. Sister's just explained it to me. It's far too swollen for them to touch it now. Anyway, Dr Davies thinks you're still in a state of shock. He suggested you had a little convalescence. We've been discussing it together. What about going down to Tom and Maggie's? You like it there. It's quiet.'

Tom had been best man at our wedding. I didn't see them any more. Adrian had taken Janet there instead. They'd probably conceived their baby in Tom and Maggie's double bed.

'No,' I said. 'I hate Barnstaple.' Barnstaple was Devonshire and Devonshire was where Janet had grown up. 'I'd rather convalesce here. It's just as quiet.'

'Thea, it's *impossible*, I've told you at least five times.' He was getting impatient now, like he did when the Upper Fourth confused the Peasants' Revolt with Cade's Rebellion. 'Anyway, they need the bed. Sister Ursula said they're very short of rooms. Apparently, they're closing half of the . . .'

'Don't shout,' I said. 'It hurts my mouth.' I felt betrayed. So it was the bed they wanted, was it? I was just a lump in it, like a piece of embedded tooth, something to be cut out and thrown away. I wasn't a person any more, just a hulk on a mattress who had out-stayed her time. People weren't important, only beds. Patients were just transitory objects which came and left, were born and died, conceived and murdered.

I lurched out of bed and groped over to the window. I wouldn't stay where I wasn't wanted. I had avoided windows up to now – they were too like mirrors. For the first time, I looked out. I couldn't see much of the building since it was mostly underneath me, and anyway, the light was fading, but there was a crew-cut lawn and some manicured rhododendrons and a statue of Christ who had just undergone open-heart surgery and was pointing proudly to His scar. I could also see the bottom of my tree. It wasn't the soaring slender beauty I'd imagined, but a gnarled and misshapen thing, its trunk twisted and its bark mottled. Even the one last leaf had fallen now.

'All right,' I said. 'I'll go to Leo's.'

'*No.*' Adrian almost spat. He had joined me by the window and laid his arm across my shoulders. It felt heavy like a dead branch.

'But all my *things* are there,' I said. 'I belong there.' I didn't, but I belonged even less at Tom and Maggie's, or in some gimcrack convalescent home constructed on the cheap. I knew what such places were like – bare and dreary and tinny like that row of breech-born hospital maisonettes I could see at the far end of the lawn. They were obviously a new addition and looked brashly out of character with their more elegant surroundings.

Adrian swung back from the window and rammed his fist so hard against the sill, the crucifix twitched and rattled on the wall. 'I simply don't understand how you can bring yourself even to mention that . . . that bastard's name. After what he's *done* to you. For Christ's sake, Thea, you should be feeling absolutely *murderous* towards him.'

'Murderous?' I tried to bury the word. Leo had only hit me because I'd murdered Janet's baby first. It was justice of a sort. No, I didn't kill the baby. It fell on stone.

'I mean, has he said he's *sorry*? Offered some restitution? He should have gone down on his knees to you instead of making a fuss about the bill.'

I tried to see Leo on his knees. All I could see were his tensed, weeping hands, clenching and unclenching. His hands had made restitution, his eyes had. The custard creams were his way of saying sorry. All the same, I wished he'd said it outright. Apologies were special. If he'd said sorry, he might have gone on to saying other things. I love you, for example.

'He brought me lots of . . . presents,' I faltered.

'What, *this* trash?' Adrian gestured towards my locker as if he had found its contents on a rubbish dump. 'Sister told me you hadn't even got a nightdress.'

'I'm borrowing one.'

'Borrowing! It's absolutely *monstrous* that you should . . .'

'I'm afraid you'll have to go now, Mr Morton.'

It was Sister Robert, slinking through the door. I had never liked her and now I knew why. She was bloody aunt to Louis de Gonzague. Her fingers on my bed were sharp as swords.

'No!' I said, grabbing the bit of Adrian nearest me. He was tidying away the biscuits, picking up both St Bernadettes who had fallen on the floor, putting their jackets straight. It was like a last, desperate effort to straighten up my life.

'That's *our* job, thank you, Mr Morton.'

The carnage had seeped even into Sister Robert's bloodshot eyes. She shut the door on Adrian. At least she hadn't turfed me out as well. I still had the bed and the room and my supper on a tray. I didn't touch the supper. You never knew, meals might be charged as extras, and a hundred and twenty pounds was bad enough for Leo.

It was difficult to sleep that night. Every time a nun walked by, I thought she was coming in to strip my sheets and slip another patient into the bed. Leo hadn't visited. He hadn't even phoned. How did I know he'd even have me back? He hadn't bought the Chinese vase because it was too expensive. And he couldn't afford the fees. It was almost like a choice between me and the *feng huang*. Perhaps he couldn't choose. I felt like a smashed, devalued thing myself, lying on the floor in smithereens, with no one rich or concerned enough to restore me. I felt I had lost my place in Leo's drawing-room. I'd been banished to the cellar, thrown out with the junk.

Hadn't St Bernadette felt much the same? She'd compared herself to a broom, once, which had been used by the Blessed Virgin to sweep the floor, then stuck back in its corner. I lay on my back and floated off to Lourdes. You didn't need cash to get round Madame Soubirous. She took me in exactly as I was, made me one of the family. It solved the problem of my job, my digs and my convalescence, all in one. I was lying next to Bernadette in her little wooden truckle bed (they were too poor and cramped for separate sleeping quarters), and though she was saying her rosary and refused to chat, at least it was warm and safe and comfortable. Père Soubirous brought us maize porridge on a tray and tucked us in. It was nice to have a father. He even smelt of Capstan Navy Cut. By the time the moon came up across the Pyrenees, Bernadette and I were fast asleep.

twelve

Ray arrived, next day, in time for lunch.

'You're a *priest*,' I said accusingly.

He nodded.

'I thought you were an occupational therapist.'

'They're pretty much the same, sometimes. They shouldn't be, of course. But a lot of priests spend half their time on church bazaars and bingo.'

'So what do *you* do? Apart from eating people's meals in hospitals?' I knew that wasn't fair. He had hardly touched his food again, and they'd brought us Raspberry Ripple in his honour, instead of the blancmange.

'I'm a Franciscan, Thea.'

I almost sniggered. A Franciscan was even more unlikely than a priest. Adrian knew all about Franciscans. They were thirteenth-century freaks who wore brown robes and dusty sandals and went about chatting up the wildlife.

'Friars live in friaries,' I retorted.

'Not always.'

'Friars wear dresses.'

'Sometimes.'

He had the same clothes on as yesterday, only the hole in his elbow was slightly larger now, and he had gym shoes on instead of moccasins.

'Where's yours, then?'

'In a carrier bag, in my suitcase.'

'Why? Are you ashamed of it?'

'No, not ashamed. But those robes are expensive, Thea. They take nine yards of cloth per friar. Ten for the really tall ones. And it's *good* cloth. They're more or less impossible to wash. That means more expense – dry-cleaning bills and so on.'

He was sounding worse than Adrian. Adrian had drawn a chart up once, proving how much I cost him if I left the lights on all night or used the washing-machine for only half a load.

'I thought monks had *pots* of money. I mean, all those acres of land

and fancy chapels and stained glass windows and vintage ports and . . .'

'But we're *not* monks, Thea. That's the whole point. We're not *meant* to own things or shut ourselves away. St Francis didn't want that. He went out into the world and wore ordinary ragged clothes like the peasants he saw around him.'

Christ! This was worse than pop priests. Ray sounded like some half-baked revolutionary. I'd almost rather he strummed a guitar than jawed on about Lady Poverty. Adrian had written a paper on St Francis once, examining his credentials as the first real Communist.

'So you beg in the streets, I s'pose?'

'I sometimes think we ought to.' He was grinning, but I could see he really meant it. His face had lit up. He was so thin and pale and scraggy, he looked almost under-nourished. He probably lived on bread and water, when he wasn't toying with Sister Anselm's soup. (I had eaten *both* the shepherd's pies.) 'Life's far too comfortable, even in the friaries. Three meals a day and full central heating. In my community, we've got stately corridors and a stereo cassette-player and Dunlopillo mattresses and lime trees in the garden with lawns and rose beds. We must have more than fifty square feet per friar, while bang next door there's a school with five hundred kids squashed together in a tiny tarmac playground, and their mums and dads slumming it in grotty little semis with sooty cabbage patches and outside toilets.'

I was impressed, despite myself. Father Murphy at school had eaten steak and claret in the parlour, and even Father Sullivan had quite a belly on him. Most priests had cars and housekeepers and quartz digital watches and holidays abroad. You often saw them in the theatre in the front stalls, quaffing whisky in the interval. I'd even spotted two or three at Ascot. Ray would have been *banned* from Ascot, except as a hot-dog seller or a man who picked up litter from the stands. It seemed strange to hear him talking like a worker priest.

'St Francis would have *hated* us living soft like that. Do you know, Thea, they tried to build him a house once, a proper one made of stones and mortar, instead of his mud hut or pigsty or whatever it was he lived in, and he was so upset, he shinned up on to the roof and started flinging all the roof tiles down.'

I tried to smile, but I was beginning to feel a bit uncomfortable.

Here I was, queening it in a private hospital, with *five* meals a day if you counted tea and elevenses, and extensive grounds outside, and people waiting on me hand and foot. I didn't want to give it up. I'd skip the meals, make my own bed, turn off the central heating – anything – so long as they let me stay there. It wasn't the frills I craved, but the sanctuary. Ray had power. Nuns go crackers over any priest, even one with holes and dotty principles. He could use that power to help me keep my bed.

'Listen, Ray,' I said. 'They're making me leave this place.'

'Yes, I know.' How could he sound so calm about it? The stern white life of the hospital had hardened round me like a shell, and I was safe inside it. World population had shrunk to a flock of nuns, a doctor and dentist; nature was just a yellow primula and the top part of a tree; wildlife the flash of wings past my window or a caterpillar in my salad. Seas and rivers were reduced to a bottle of mouthwash. I preferred this smaller world.

'I don't *want* to leave, Ray.'

'It *is* tough, isn't it?'

I rather liked the way he didn't contradict me. Everyone else was always telling me what was good for me, or what I ought to think, or why what I *did* think was totally misguided.

'Adrian wants me to go to Tom and Maggie's. But that's where Janet conceived the baby.'

He nodded. He seemed to understand. Adrian tripped himself up over what he called my *non sequiturs* and lectured me about logical connections and coherent narrative. Leo rarely listened. But Ray popped in and out of all my culs-de-sac and didn't say boring things like 'Who's Tom? or 'Why Janet?' He was rather like a brother. I never had a brother and my mother certainly wouldn't have produced one who looked anything like Ray. I wondered if the Soubirous would have room for him as well. He could help in the fields or at the mill. With him as a brother and Bernadette as sister, I'd have some handhold on the world.

'Convalescence might be *fun*,' he said. 'I mean, if you chose a place you fancy. What about the seaside?'

'No,' I said. The sea was too big to tackle on my own. *Any*where on my own is usually too big.

'The thing is, Ray, I don't want to go alone.'

'Of course you don't.' We had reached the ice-cream now. Or *I* had.

I doubt if St Francis approved of Raspberry Ripple. It cost 54p for the small size. Ray was sipping water.

'What about a relative? Somebody you really like. Or an old school friend? You've got to go somewhere you feel *good* about. A nice fat cosy aunt with flour up to her elbows, or a place where you were happy as a child.'

He understood exactly. The trouble was, I didn't have floury aunts and as a child I hadn't gone anywhere exciting. We either went to places where the air was good for asthma, or we stayed at home and saved my mother's money for what she called a decent education, which meant speaking like Lord Harewood and using butter-knives.

'There must be some place you fancy. Somewhere you've read about, or . . .'

'No,' I repeated. I wished he'd let me off. They wanted the bed, that's all, and had ordered him to come and turf me out of it. He'd be renouncing his Raspberry Ripple to somebody else next week. It was simply part of the service. Father Sullivan for conventional, conforming Catholics and Father Murphy for the murderers and the fornicators.

'Yes,' I shouted, suddenly. 'There *is*!'

He squeezed my hand. 'Well?'

'Lourdes!' I whispered, kicking Bernadette in the shin and begging her to support me. 'I want to go and convalesce in Lourdes.'

Ray didn't even put his tumbler down. Adrian would have said 'impossible' and started lecturing me on the commercialization of peasant superstition: Leo would have muttered '*where?*' and gone on with his *Listener*, and my mother would have closed the conversation with a shudder.

Ray just wiped his mouth and said, 'What a *good* idea. Funnily enough, I'm going there myself.'

I was so astounded, I dropped my spoon and splattered the sheets with raspberry. Though I suppose it wasn't that surprising – all priests land up at Lourdes. But I kept forgetting Ray was God's Anointed, especially when he was mopping up icecream.

'*When?*' I stuttered. It would probably be next year. I'd be dead by then, or unable to get time off from my job as a receptionist. Receptionists never go to Lourdes in any case, only Acapulco.

'Early April,' he said. 'It's glorious then. All the blossom out and the buds unfurling. I'll be there for Easter Day.'

I pushed my bowl away. I was so light and white and radiant inside. I didn't need icecream. I'd always planned to go to Lourdes at Easter. That was the date of my First Communion. It wouldn't be my nineteenth year, but not really that far off it, and anyway, I doubt if God bothers with a calendar. I could receive the host from Ray's own hands. A Ray dressed not in gym shoes, but in snowy alb and golden chasuble.

'But that's three months off,' he was saying. 'Far too late for you. You need your convalescence right away, if it's to do you any good.'

'No,' I said. 'I *must* go to Lourdes and I want to go with you.'

'I'm afraid that won't be possible, Thea dear. I'm taking a group of handicapped boys who need a lot of looking after. Sometimes, I don't get off till after midnight.'

I frowned. There wasn't room for boys. I wanted to be alone with him, holding his hand in the Grotto, sharing his poverty, mending his holes.

'I still want to go when you're there.'

'But it won't be convalescence, then.'

'I don't care. You can't go to Lourdes in January, anyway. It's freezing cold and all shut up.' The girls at school had told me that. They'd always been in August, but it was very crowded then. Easter would be better. Easter was the time of the Resurrection and I needed resurrecting.

Ray was looking worried. 'Yes, I suppose it is. I hadn't really thought about the weather.'

'*Every*where's freezing cold in January. Except ritzy places like Barbados. And if I had the cash to zip off there, then I could afford to stay in the hospital and wouldn't *need* any stupid convalescence.'

'Weymouth's quite warm in winter. I've got a cousin there who might . . .'

'Weymouth *stinks*.'

'Or there's a convalescent home in Bath. Really nice. It's even got a squash court.'

'I don't *play* squash.'

'Well, how about your mother?'

'She doesn't play, either.'

'No, I thought perhaps . . .'

'I want to go away with *you*, Ray, not my bloody mother.'

'Look, Thea, I'd love to take you with me, but priests can't just rush off on holiday with beautiful young girls.'

'I'm not beautiful. I'm *hideous*. That's why I want to go to Lourdes, with all the other wrecks and write-offs. And I want to go at Easter.'

'But Easter's thirteen weeks away. Even if you came with me, there's still the problem of what you're going to do meanwhile.'

'I'll go back to Leo's, where I live.'

'But that's not convalescence.'

'It *could* be . . .'

'But do you think you *should*? I mean, aren't you worried that . . .'

'Look, Ray, if I *know* I'm going to Lourdes, then everything feels different. It's something to look forward to. Something special. I've wanted to go there ever since I was thirteen. I had a sort of thing about it. The whole school went except me – every year in our summer holidays. I begged and prayed to be included, but I was always left behind. My mother said she simply couldn't afford it.' (I didn't tell him what she *really* said. After all, he assumed my mother and I were good conventional Catholics like the rest.) 'That's why I've *got* to go now, Ray. Don't you see, it's the first real chance I've ever had. I know I'll get better if you let me go. I don't care when it is, or how, but I *must* be there when you're there.'

'Look, Thea, dear, I don't want to be a spoilsport, but it really isn't on. Once I get to Lourdes, I'll hardly have time to turn round. It's a full-time job. The boys take all my time. They have to – they're sick and disabled. Some of them can't even feed themselves. I'd *love* to be with you, but it's just not possible. I'm even on call at night.'

'That's OK,' I shrugged. It wasn't. The last thing I wanted was a gang of greedy boys devouring all of Ray, but I didn't intend to lose Lourdes altogether. Not when I'd got this far. 'Then I'll go on my own,' I said. Once we'd both arrived there, I could always fiddle his timetable.

'You can't go alone, my girl. That's no fun. Why don't you ask one of your mates to go with you? Then you'd have some company.'

I almost said, 'I haven't got any mates', but I didn't want to ruin everything, not after that 'my girl'. I'd never been called that by a priest before. It was the sort of thing Père Soubirous would have called me, fatherly and caring.

'Good idea,' I said. 'I'll ask Patricia Jane.'

'Is she nice? I mean, will she look after your mouth and not let you do too much, and be willing to sit around and eat the odd icecream in between the services?'

'Oh yes,' I lied. 'She's terribly kind and very sort of sensible. She used to be a nurse.' I didn't even know her, but I suspect she was the daughter my mother should have had. She was the least of my problems. There were more serious things like cash to be considered. If I couldn't afford the hospital, then how could I pay my way to the very bottom bit of France? Ray's famous poverty didn't seem to stop him travelling halfway across Europe.

'There is one slight problem, Ray. I mean Patricia's *loaded*, but I'm – well . . .'

'Yes, I'd thought of that.' Ray put his glass of water down, as if even that must be rationed. 'I'm working on it. Have you any savings at all?'

I didn't know whether to rival Patricia's riches and buy up my share of Lourdes, or come clean and admit I didn't own a tin-tack. 'I've . . . er . . . got a little in the Abbey National,' I said.

'I may be able to help. There's various funds and things for deserving cases.'

'I'm not deserving.'

'Of *course* you are. I think the best thing to do is to book you on a package tour. Some of them are pretty cheap and have guides and couriers and a proper daily programme. You even get your own priest.'

Priests were becoming as common in my life as pain-killers. Once, they'd been rare and elusive; now they came cut-price in a package.

'In fact, there's one company I've got a bit of sway with. You might be able to fly with them and then book your own accommodation. That sometimes works out cheaper. Especially if you don't mind slumming it a bit. Would Patricia Jane object?'

Too bad if she did. I shrugged her off. 'Is that what *you're* doing?' I asked.

Ray grinned. 'I *have* done – many times – bed-bugs and all! I can't do it with the boys, though. We're staying at a special place which can cope with wheelchairs and stretcher cases.'

I stared. He seemed to be turning into a cross between Florence Nightingale and Albert Schweitzer, and I wasn't sure I could keep up with him.

'Can't I stay there too, then?'

'Not possible, I'm afraid. There's hardly room for the helpers, as it is.'

'Well, can't *I* be a helper?'

He took my hand. 'That's a very lovely thought, Thea. A very *holy* one, in fact, but I don't think you're quite well enough, just yet.'

'I'll be well enough by Easter.'

'I'm *sure* you will. But I'm afraid all our helpers are already booked by now. It's quite a business, you know – forms and references and things. But we're bound to see each other down at the Grotto, or at the Blessing of the Sick, or the processions. Lourdes is a very friendly place. It's crowded, of course, but every group has banners or badges to distinguish them. The children wear little woollen hats, different colours for all the different groups. You'll find us, Thea. We've got a banner big enough to be seen from the other end of France! Just come over and say hallo. Then you can help a little, unofficially. Even talking to the lads is a tremendous service. Sometimes, they feel no one has time to really bother with them.'

I didn't answer. Disabled people make me nervous. I'm always scared they're judging me or envying me, or may suddenly make a grab at me, or weep or shriek or leak.

'And I'll tell you what, Thea.'

'What?'

'You and Pat could come up to our house in Lourdes and give us a hand – just sort of casually.'

'Pat?' I frowned.

'Your friend. Patricia Jane.'

'Oh, I *see*.' I'd already ditched her, especially if Ray was on such familiar terms. My mother would never have stood for Pats.

'We can always do with an extra pair of hands, even if it's only washing dishes. That's holy work, you know.'

I *loathe* washing up, but somehow the way he said 'holy work' made me burn to be a Schweitzer or a Nightingale, to labour and serve like he did, don a Franciscan's robe and devote myself to lepers. I would go to Lourdes and become a stretcher-bearer, a *brancardier*, as they were called. My schoolfriends had shown me photographs of those dedicated, self-sacrificing men who carried the sick and led the blind and were the unofficial gods and saints of Lourdes. I lay back on the pillows. I could see myself walking shoulder to shoulder with Ray, dividing the stretcher's weight between us.

'What's the exact date you're going?' I asked. I wanted to pin him down, turn fantasy into tidy concrete fact.

'Easter Saturday. Well, that's when we arrive. We leave on the Friday on a special coach. Most of the package tours fly from Saturday to Saturday.'

'So we could arrive on the same day?'

'Mmmm.' He still didn't sound too rapturous about it.

'And I'll see you in the meantime?'

'If you want to, Thea, of course. But look, we still haven't decided about your convalescence.'

I waved it away. 'Where do I find you?' I asked. 'I mean, what's the address of your monastery?'

'It's not a monastery.'

'Well, friary, then, or whatever you call it.'

'Well, I'm not exactly *there* at the moment.'

'You mean, you ran *away*?'

He laughed. 'No. Look, my girl, I've got to go now. Don't worry, I'll make sure you have my address before you leave. I'll pop in and see you again tomorrow. OK?'

'OK,' I said. He was probably stalling. There were always tricks in things. But at least I was his girl again.

When he'd gone, I masturbated. I felt so excited about Lourdes and my First Communion and my service to the sick, I had to calm down somehow. There was a little icecream left in the second bowl. I daubed it on my fingers and smeared it between my legs. Although it had melted, it still felt cold because I was burning hot down there. I kept remembering the way he'd squeezed my hand and said 'holy thought' and 'holy work'. I *ached* to be holy. While I rubbed myself, I thought of lepers and spastics and multiple sclerosis. I came so hard, I cried.

Sister Aidan popped in later on, to take my tray away. She seemed a bit of a simpleton – only good for carrying trays and washing dishes. She had a wide moon face and white eyelashes. You could always get things out of her when the other nuns clammed up.

'You know Father Murphy,' I said.

'Yes, dear.' She was removing half a bread roll from the bed. Out in the world, she'd have been a failure and a fool; safe in the convent, she was the radiant Bride of Christ.

'Where does he live?'

'Well, actually he's living here at the moment.'

'*Here?*'

'Yes, in one of the hospital maisonettes. Only for a week or two. He's normally up at the hostel with his handicapped boys. But they had a little fire there. Nothing serious. But everything got soaked. He said the Fire Brigade made more mess than the fire itself. So while they're mopping up, we offered him a bed.'

'Is he living alone?' I asked. If we were going to share the stretchers, then I ought to find out all I could about him.

'Well, he hasn't got a housekeeper, if that's what you mean. He doesn't really need one. He still has most of his meals up at the hostel. The kitchen part escaped.'

'Do you think he gets lonely?'

'Oh *no*, dear. You're never lonely with God.' I think she really believed it. She carried God around inside her like a pregnant woman with an embryo. 'Anyway, he hasn't time. He works with those boys seven days a week. *And* half the nights. They're terrible cases, some of them. Someone told me he hardly sleeps at all. He's quite a holy man, I would imagine.'

I felt excited when she called him holy. The word was a sort of turn-on, like those magazines you see on Soho bookstalls. But instead of naked-breasted slave-girls wearing nothing but their chains, it was saints I saw, in tatty cords and gym shoes.

'I didn't know Franciscans were allowed to do work like that. I mean, I thought they wore robes and preached to birds.'

'Well, he does have rabbits, dear. Now, move those books, I want to tidy you up.'

'*Rabbits?*'

'Yes, up at the hostel. It was his own idea. He thought his boys should have something to look after. A pet of their own, to love. He was up at half-past five the other morning, collecting dandelions. I almost fell over him on my way to the wards.'

I could see Ray creeping through the dew, praising Sister Dawn and Brother Sun, tugging up handfuls of rabbit fodder, while flocks of birds warbled and followed in his wake. He could well be another St Francis in our midst. I suddenly burned to follow him, to renounce sex and take up sanctity. I could see myself like Mary Magdalene, washing his feet with my tears, drying them on the soft towel of my hair. Sanctity seemed not only safer and more wholesome, it also made sense of suffering. My mouth would no longer be the wrecked result of lust and jealousy, but a Cross to be Borne, a holy martyrdom. St

Francis himself had received the Stigmata, the five wounds of Christ imprinted on his hands and feet and side. My swollen head and battered teeth were my own Stigmata, the marks of God's dazzling hands across my face. Leo hadn't bashed me, only Christ.

Even St Bernadette had likened herself to Christ crucified. It all tied up. St Francis was her favourite saint, she was mine, and all of us had suffered in God's cause. I would rise above my suffering and use it to succour other people's pain. Ray and I would venture out together and salve the world. I shut my eyes and lay back against the pillows.

'I don't want my pills,' I murmured. 'The pain doesn't matter any more.'

'You've already had them, dear. Now up you get. I can't make that bed with you in it. Anyway, Sister Ursula wants you to have a little exercise, stretch your legs and see they haven't rusted.'

'No,' I said. I hadn't time for exercise. I had a Mission now.

'It's bad for you to lie here all the time. You'll be getting bedsores next. Sister said you're to take a little walk in the hospital grounds.'

'No,' I said. 'It's cold.'

'Nice fresh air, it'll do you good. Put some colour in your cheeks.'

'I don't *want* colour in them. Anyway, I can't go out – I haven't any clothes.'

'Yes, you have, dear. Mr Rzevski brought some for you this morning.'

'Mr *Rzevski*?'

'He's your uncle, isn't he? A Jew.' She said 'Jew' as if it were an illness.

'Yes,' I said, then 'No.' Leo wasn't either. 'You mean he was here this *morning*? Leo?'

'Yes, dear. You were sleeping and he said particularly not to wake you. He's coming back first thing tomorrow morning with a suitcase, and he'll take you home.'

'Home?' I stuttered. This was home. I had just decided on my new career, on holiness and lepers. Leo wasn't holy. I couldn't renounce sex if I was going back with him, and lepers would be impossible. Leo hated sickness. He believed in euthanasia for anything more serious than 'flu.

Sister Aidan had eased me out of bed into the chair. 'I met your husband yesterday. He's the fair one, isn't he? I suppose he's busy tomorrow.'

She always got things wrong. Surely Leo hadn't called this morning. What had he come for? Why hadn't he left a note? How had he even got there? Had Otto brought him in the car? Had they jeered at me together, while I lay there dozing? Was he angry, dragging all that way and then finding me asleep?

Sister Aidan hadn't turned the bed down. I could see I was still banned from it.

'Didn't he leave a note?'

'Who, dear?'

'My . . . er . . . uncle.'

'No. He seemed to be in a rush. Now, where did they put your clothes?'

'Sister . . .'

'Yes, dear.'

'Let me off. *Please*. I don't feel well. I'll go out later, I promise.'

'Look, if you're not well, I'd better call Sister Ursula. She's the one who . . .'

'*No*. There's nothing she can do. It's probably the Stigmata.'

'*What* did you say, Thea?'

'Nothing.'

While she tidied my locker, I sneaked back into bed. It felt cold inside, like a coffin. Sister Aidan was mumbling to herself, or maybe asking God's advice. He must have been on my side, because after a tiny pause, she tucked me up and even drew the curtains. 'All right, have a little sleep, then, and I'll be back in half an hour.'

Thirty minutes later, when she popped her head in, I was achingly awake, but I shammed a cross between a trance and a coma, and she tiptoed off, convinced. It was impossible to sleep. Words like home and holy and Leo and lust were all muddled up and shouting contradictions. How could I go home? I was still in pain, still on pills, still had no front teeth. Anyway, I hadn't any home, not really. Why hadn't Leo woken me when he called this morning? Was it just a friendly visit (or a *guilty* one?), or had he come to say it was all over? Perhaps he'd left a secret letter hidden in my clothes, and stupid Sister Aidan had mislaid them both. It could even have been a *love* letter, or the apology he couldn't say in person. 'Sorry' shining on the page in his bold black handwriting. Leo always used a fountain pen. He despised biros, like he despised people who landed themselves in hospital and then refused to wake up when he'd made the effort to visit them. Perhaps it wasn't a love letter at all, but a notice to quit.

I shivered. I was meant to be convalescing, but you couldn't convalesce in Notting Hill. Even if I returned there, Leo wouldn't want some weak and hideous woman draped across his bed. With Ray, it didn't matter. He seemed to see your inside rather than your outside, but Ray was tied up with rabbits, and even Lourdes and Easter were still thirteen weeks away. I might be *dead* by then.

I pretended to be dead. I shut my eyes and kept them shut through tea, and then through prayers and visiting hour. They woke me up for supper, but I pushed the tray away and went on feigning sleep until pills and my late-night drink. I kept thinking last Ovaltine, last supper, last night in my safe white cell. I was terrified of leaving. They'd found my clothes and I'd shaken them out and searched through all the pockets, but all I'd discovered was a bus ticket. I held it up to the light in case it had 'sorry' written on it, but all it said was 'not transferable'. Even the clothes were wrong – white cotton jeans and a T-shirt, when it was bitter January. At least he'd remembered the sheepskin. I had it snuggled across my hospital counterpane, so that I could imagine Leo was lying there on top of me. I sniffed the edge of it. It smelt of him and me combined. I suddenly felt frightened. Clothes meant a return to the world, to strength and health and jobs and dinner parties. I didn't want any of those things. I sat up in bed. I'd promised Sister Aidan I'd go out later on. She hadn't meant this much later, but I couldn't break a promise, not on my last night. I didn't fancy getting dressed, so I just pulled the sheepskin over the cleaner's daughter's nightie (which had turned out blue with little cap sleeves and ruching), and slunk along the passage, past the bathroom and the dispensary and down the stairs. I knew I was safe enough. There was an Emergency at the other end of the corridor, and all the night staff were fawning on the doctor and scuttling about with syringes and masks. The garden door was bolted, but only from the inside. The bolts were kind. They hardly sighed as I eased them down, but the cold was so cruel, it slashed across my face like a scalpel. It was as if someone had ripped out all my stitches and left my mouth raw and pulped again. My tongue was a trip-wire, my teeth were blood and ice.

I ran across the lawn, trying to move my sensations lower down, to concentrate only on the damp shivering grass squelching under my feet. They were almost numb as I stumbled on to the path which skirted the row of hospital maisonettes. There were six of them – four in darkness and two with their lights still on – all more or less as ugly as each other, except for the front gardens. Some had gnomes and forced crocuses in whimsy little rockeries, others had crazy paving and bare shrubs. Only one came complete with dandelions, so I guessed that must be Ray's.

Staring in at other people's houses is very demoralizing. They have the hearth and the fireside, the steaming Horlicks and the double bed, while you're shut out in the cold, like a pariah, with only the puddles and the privet hedge, the dog shit and the shivers. A woman from one of the lighted houses got up when she saw me and drew her curtains almost in my face. It was like being slapped or ostracized. The curtains were of cheap, unlined cotton with yellow squiggles on them. I glared at a thousand putrid squiggles which glowered back – and won.

A man was spying on me from an upstairs window, and a dog howled, sort of hungrily. I'd either have to knock or go away. I turned to go. In front of me, the hospital loomed up again. It was the first time I had seen it from outside. I'd been cooped up like a hermit in one of its smallest rooms, without realizing how elegant it was – the sort of building Adrian would have visited with a notebook and a sketch-pad, or local Historical Associations had on their conservation list. It was old and ornate and gracious like a stately home, with tall majestic pillars and a marble portico. No wonder the fees were so high. I was doubly depressed that I couldn't afford to stay there. I had never before lived anywhere so posh. I tried to locate my room, but all I could see were rows and rows of shuttered blinds and drawn curtains. It was as if they had locked me out. I couldn't pay, so I had no rights as a patient any longer, that's what they were saying.

I turned back to the maisonettes. There, I was equally excluded. I had no trim front garden, no friendly gnome to display my house-name proudly on a placard. The yellow squiggles were still sticking their tongues out at me. I could see blurred shapes passing back and forth in front of them; whole, healthy people with teeth and jobs and children. They even had winter jasmine blooming in their garden. I snapped a piece off. It smelt of cold and nothing. Little drops of water fell from the blossoms and wept between my hands. I crept along the privet hedge to the house with the dandelions, and tiptoed up the path. The front door was brown and flaking, and had a number five on it which had come loose on its screw and lurched to the right as if it was fainting. The lights had gone off by now, but the curtains downstairs were still undrawn. I peered in through the window and saw a bare, peaky room, almost devoid of furniture. If Ray was living there, then it must be with Lady Poverty. Or perhaps Sister Aidan had got it wrong (again) and he was back at the hostel, tucking up his rabbits.

I felt like a dead-headed rose or a fallen leaf, brown and tired and broken. 'Ask and you shall receive,' I muttered. 'Knock and it shall be opened unto you.'

I drew in my breath and knocked.

thirteen

About half a century passed and I got colder and colder, before I heard footsteps coming down the hall. I wondered if it would be some furious nurse or matron, who'd been up three nights already and was trying to catch up on her sleep, or a man with a ravening Alsatian, or even Father Sullivan.

It was Ray. He came to the door in blue-striped pyjamas and grubby anorak. I almost kissed him. Not just because he wasn't an Alsatian or a matron, but because we matched – both in our blue nightwear with bare feet and our outdoor coats on top. He wasn't wearing his glasses and he sort of groped and peered in my direction. I tried to smile. I thought for one sinking moment he was going to ask who I was, or say, 'No, thanks, I don't buy from the door.'

'I brought you this,' I mumbled, before he could, holding out the jasmine. He took it as if it were very precious and very heavy. I could imagine him holding the host like that in the basilica at Lourdes. Holy.

'Come on in,' he said. You could worship someone just because they didn't ask 'What are you doing?' or 'Why are you wearing your nightdress?' or 'Shouldn't you be in bed?'

There was only one chair in the room, which he offered me. He sat on a packing-case beside me, cradling the jasmine as if it were a sleeping child.

'You're cold,' he said. 'How about a drink?' He sounded as calm as if it were only six p.m. and he'd invited me in for cocktails.

I tried to stop shivering and nodded. He went out into the kitchen and I heard him filling a kettle and banging about with tea-cups. When he returned, it wasn't cups, but glasses, with something strong and steaming in them. I could smell lemon, honey and whisky – mostly whisky. Mine was fuller than his. He had brought a towelling tea-cloth with him and he wrapped my feet in it and wiped the grass stains off. It was sort of Mary Magdalene in reverse. I noticed his hands were scratched. It could have been the rabbits, or maybe he'd been inflicting some penance on himself. They were holy hands, red and lined and chastened, as if they were always put upon. Holiness lay thick on everything, like dust. I glanced around the room. There was no television, no radio, no books or ornaments, no comforts or concessions. I thought of Leo's house, the baroque clutter, his fanfare of possessions. I yearned to strip myself, renounce things, live in a cell, even cut my hair. My own hands looked too pale and cosseted.

'I want to be a Franciscan,' I said. He didn't laugh. He had his spectacles back on, and the eyes behind them were the colour of the river at Victoria Embankment, sort of mud and slime combined. But gentle slime.

'I shouldn't!' He took the first sip from his glass. It was lighter than mine in colour. I could see he wasn't a whisky man. I banged mine down on his packing-case.

'I'm not holy enough, is that it? I suppose Father Sullivan told you I'm a murderer.'

'No.' The 'no' was gentle and matched his eyes. I felt stupid, almost cheap.

'He wouldn't give me absolution, Ray.'

'Do you want it?' He made it sound like a chocolate bar or a packet of salted peanuts, something he could fetch from the kitchen and offer me on a plate.

'Not particularly,' I lied. 'Anyway, I'm too wicked to receive it, according to precious Father Sullivan.'

'No one's too wicked, Thea. And apart from playing truant from the hospital and eating double shepherd's pie, I don't think you're wicked at all.'

'But how can you *tell*? You don't know what I've done.'

'What *have* you done?'

I wondered if this was Confession, and if so, whether it was valid when the priest was sitting on a packing-case wearing his pyjamas. I could feel my thighs nudging each other underneath the sheepskin, and something feverish happening in between them.

'Well, to start with,' I said, 'I've had it away with forty-seven men.' (It was really only thirty-one, but everyone exaggerates.)

'And you think that's forty-seven mortal sins?'

'It could be three *thousand* and forty-seven. I didn't do it only once with each of them.'

Ray rubbed at one of the scratches on his hand. 'I don't think God's much good at arithmetic. He doesn't count like that. He may not count at all. Sleeping with all and sundry isn't very wise, Thea, but it's not necessarily wicked. I think you're simply using it to keep away from God.'

He sounded so cool, we could have been discussing the Sunday trading laws or the rules of Scrabble. I wasn't cool at all. Confession was an aphrodisiac as far as I was concerned, even confession in a grotty sitting-room with whisky on my breath instead of holy water on my brow.

'Even if you're screwing around, you can still be OK with God. Oh, I know a lot of priests would disagree with me, but it's the motive that matters. You've got a lot of love in you, Thea, even holiness.'

I was half-glowing, half-shocked. I'd never met a priest before who used phrases like 'screwing around', nor one who shrugged off three thousand and forty-seven fucks as if they were dropped stitches. (I was secretly annoyed he wasn't more impressed. Even thirty-one men isn't *bad*.) I squirmed at the way he said ikky things like 'OK with God', as if he and the Almighty ran their own cosy little Abbey National, with a branch in heaven and a branch down here on earth. ('Store up Your Treasure in Heaven. It's OK with God'.) Yet words like love and holiness were a genuine turn-on. They made me hot and damp and throbbing, as if he'd said 'soixante-neuf' or 'suck me off'. I had longed to be holy, and now it seemed I was. I didn't even have to renounce the sex. The trouble was I wanted it with Ray. His pyjama bottoms were fastened with a cord which the anorak didn't quite cover. There was a little gap where his groin was, and if I moved my head a fraction, I could see coarse reddish hairs poking through the space, and a coil of soft pink flesh. I tried to look down at the carpet, but his feet were there and even they aroused me; broad and white, and obscenely bare.

'Have *you* ever had it, Ray?' I inquired.

'No,' he said briefly. He didn't ask 'what?' or blush or stall or tell me to shut up. He could have been refusing a second drink.

I was astounded, really. Leo had started at thirteen-and-a-half, and even Adrian had attempted his first fumble before he'd reached sixteen. Ray was almost thirty. True, he was plain and shy, and may not have had many opportunities, but a total, untried virgin was still a creature like a unicorn, rare and white and holy. I'd never met a virgin (or a unicorn). I felt it was a challenge. We could swap expertise. Ray could teach me how to grow in holiness, while I worked lower down. I didn't want to sully him, just make him more aware.

'Do you ever *want* it?' I asked.

He paused. For the first time he looked embarrassed. I could feel the chair growing moister under me, my breasts reaching for him through the nightie.

He muttered something which sounded more like no than yes.

'That's a *lie*,' I snapped. '*Every*body wants it.'

Now the no sounded yes-ish, though both had been indistinct. He was staring doggedly at a grease stain on the carpet, the nails of one red hand biting into the palm.

'Why can't you be *honest*, Ray?'

He fumbled for his spectacles and dragged them off. He looked exposed now, almost shamed. The tiny stain seemed to be spreading like a lake. 'I want not to want it,' he said at last.

'Do you *think* about it?'

'Sometimes.'

'How often?'

'Look, Thea, I don't really see . . .'

'Do you ever touch yourself?'

'*No.*'

The 'no' was so emphatic, I knew he wasn't lying. That was even more remarkable. He was a genuine immaculate, like St Bernadette.

'*I* do. Often. Four or five times a day, sometimes. Is *that* a sin?'

I'd got him there. If he said 'yes' he'd be contradicting what he'd said before; if he said 'no', he'd be encouraging me to frig myself all the way to hell. I knew he cared about my soul. It touched me, somehow. Any man could care about your body. Souls took more.

'Is this Confession?' I asked.

'It can be, Thea, if you want.'

'I *do* want, but I don't fancy telling all my sins again. All it did with Father Sullivan was make him run away.'

'*I* shan't run away.'

I could have hugged him. Though, I must admit, I wondered if my father had ever said that to my mother, or God to *His* mother. Even gods break promises.

'Promise?' I said.

'Promise. You don't have to tell your sins, in any case. You've given me the gist – that's enough. Remember that bit in the gospel, Thea, where Jesus met the man sick of the palsy? He went straight up to him and said, "Your sins are forgiven you." The chap didn't have to spell them out, or rack his brains, or poke his conscience with a stick. Christ forgave the man, not the individual sins – wiped out the whole lot in a sort of general package deal. *And* He called him "son".'

When he talked like a priest, I felt faint and burning with the poetry of it. 'Your sins are forgiven you' was like the touch of God's finger on my cunt. Even the word palsy had a strange old-fashioned stir about it. As a child, I had always wondered what it meant. It was like those other phrases you found in the gospels – Pharisees and bushels, motes in eyes, issues of blood, fatted calves, paschal lambs – words which twisted through your mind and startled it. 'Son' was a word like that. Christ had used it quite a lot. *And* 'daughter'.

I struggled out of my sheepskin. The nightie underneath was semi-transparent and my nipples showed through like two dark blobs. I pushed the ruching down. One half-breast oozed slowly over the top. I took Ray's hand and guided it towards me.

'Do you want not to want it *now*?' I asked.

'Thea, get dressed!'

'I *am* dressed.' The nipple was still concealed, the second breast completely covered.

'Look, if that coat's too hot, I'll fetch you a sweater or something.'

'I don't *want* a sweater. I'm boiling as it is.' I wriggled my shoulder a bit, so more of the breast slipped bare.

'I'll open a window, then.' Ray had turned his back on me and was struggling up from the packing-case.

'No.' I dragged him down again, pushed up the sleeve of his anorak and ran the tips of my fingers very lightly along his wrist and up towards the elbow. Leo had taught me that. Then I placed his hand just above the ruching, where my neck ended and my breasts began.

'Thea, *no*.'

'Why not? You just said screwing didn't matter, so why all this fuss about one small breast?'

'I *didn't* say that, Thea. What I meant was that so long as you strive for good, then the sex is less serious. The important thing is to want God rather than the screwing.'

I could see he was aiming to get us back to God again. I tried to help. 'I want to screw God,' I said.

'Well, at least you *want* Him. That's the only way you know how to love at the moment, so God accepts it.'

I was disappointed, really. That was one of my best lines and he hadn't even gagged at it. 'Then why can't *you* accept it? I mean, why shouldn't you . . .'

'I'm a *priest*, Thea.'

'You're a man as well.'

'Alas, yes.'

I liked that 'Alas'. It was a sort of admission he was tempted. I scooped out the other breast and left it hanging. 'I know they're only small,' I said. 'But at least they don't flop. One of my lovers told me they were the perfect shape – somewhere between a paw-paw and a pomegranate. Mind you, he was so short-sighted, I doubt if he could see! Do you like them, Ray?'

Ray was blushing. His face was as red as his hands now. I'd trapped him a second time. He couldn't say 'no' without insulting me, yet if he said 'yes', he could hardly cling on to his status as a priest. He mumbled something indecipherable. I took it for a 'yes'.

'Well, go on, touch them, if you fancy them.'

'Thea, *please*, you're making this very difficult.'

'It's difficult for *me*. First you say sex is OK and God doesn't give a shit about it. Then you change your mind and . . .'

'You're not *listening*, Thea. That's *not* what I . . .'

'It's OK – I don't give a shit about it, either. I *want* sex not to matter, like you said. But you're contradicting yourself. If you get in such a state about a mingy little breast, then you're *making* it important. Look, just put your finger on it, just one finger – just for a second – and I'll prove to you it doesn't mean a thing, not to either of us.'

'But it *would* mean something to me, Thea. That's the point.'

'*Would* it?' I was watching the gap in his pyjamas. Something was twitching in it – stretching it a little wider. I felt triumphant. Tiny drops of sweat were gasping on his hairline, slinking down his neck. 'Well, it would to me, too, I s'pose, but only something *spiritual*. That's why I want it, Ray. To make my confession real. If you touch me, it makes it a proper sacrament. You know, like a sort of laying on of hands.'

'That's done on *heads*, Thea, not on breasts, and it's Confirmation, not Confession.'

'Christ! You're worse than Adrian. And even *he's* not such a prude. What's the point of giving me all that crap about love and forgiveness, if you won't even come *near* me? *God* would touch my breasts if He was here. Well, *wouldn't* He? He *made* the bloody things, for heaven's sake.'

Ray had crossed his legs. To camouflage the twitching, I suppose. Even his hands were tightly clamped together, as if to keep them safe. It was time for a little blackmail.

'Look, Ray, I haven't been to confession for more than eleven years.' (That was true, at least – I'd never been at all.) 'It's very important to me. You said yourself sex kept me away from God. That's right, but now *you*'re keeping me away from Him. If you mess up this confession, I'll never go again.' Slowly, his hands unclasped, the fingers trembling. I could see him trying to juggle my immortal soul against his own damnation.

'Look, I'll hold your *hand*, Thea. *Both* hands if you like. But not the . . . er . . . other. I doubt if I could even *concentrate* if . . .'

I almost pushed him off. 'Forget it! I told you I was too vile for absolution. Well, I don't even *want* it now. You priests are all the same. You're so damned scared of everything. You spew out all that stuff about being Christ's representative on earth, but *Christ* wasn't so damned fussy about touching people. He even touched *lepers*, didn't He? And your precious St Francis leapt down off his horse and *kissed* a leper. You told me that yourself. Well, I'm not a leper, and I haven't asked you to kiss me. All I've asked is . . . Oh, I disgust you, don't I? Or you just don't trust me, which is worse. If *you* don't trust me, God won't.'

'Thea – please – you *know* it's not like that. Of course you're not a leper. It's *myself* I don't trust . . .'

That was an advance. I stopped shouting and peered down at his pyjamas. The gap had disappeared. All I could see was a piece of the white cord and one clenched hand trembling on his knee.

'*I* trust you, Ray. I only want you to touch me sort of *symbolically*, like Christ would. Look, let me show you what I mean. Just . . .'

I took his hand. He had closed his eyes, as if not to witness what the hand was doing. Slowly, agonizingly, it groped towards my chest. I helped it there, felt his palm fall damp and heavy like a steam iron on my breasts. They steamed. That clumsy, clammy hand was holy proof of his virginity. He had no idea how to touch a woman. I was his first breast. I was throbbing with the rare and strange excitement of it. I burned to teach him everything, romp and grapple on the floor, pluck his virginity from him like a fat pink flower. I closed my hand over his. I could feel my right breast swooning under his fingers, the left one whimpering for him. I knew he was excited. I could almost feel the twitching now, though his legs were so bent and twisted round the packing-case, he must have been in torment. His fingers had strayed towards my nipple. He touched it very gingerly, as if it were a switch which might set off a hidden cache of dynamite.

'They *are* beautiful,' he whispered.

I bowed my head, joined my hands. Now it was a valid sacrament. I struggled to sit still, to collect my thoughts and remember the words of the act of contrition which we'd learnt at school.

'For these and all other sins of my past life, I beg pardon and absolution from you, my heavenly father.'

Suddenly, I was crying. The words were so beautiful, I couldn't bear to mock them. 'Heavenly father' took me straight back to my birthday party. I could almost taste the marzipan rancid on my lips, smell Capstan Navy Cut.

'I want to confess my *real* sins, Ray,' I sobbed.

'There's no *need*, Thea. God has forgiven you already.' I don't think he could cope with any more sins. My breasts were almost more than he could handle.

'I want to, Ray, I must. I've never told anyone before. I don't mean all the sex and screwing and things. You're right – they're nothing. It's worse than that. Far worse. I've . . .'

Ray had removed the tea-towel from my feet and was mopping up my tears with it. 'Hush, Thea, don't cry. There's nothing so bad that . . .'

'But there *is*, Ray, there is. Listen, for fifteen years I prayed that Josie Rutherford would die. I *hated* her. Nothing was too bad for her. I wanted her boiled in oil and thrown to sharks and scraped off motorways. But then she *did* die, Ray. I killed her. I *keep* on killing people. I hate them first and then they die. Look at Janet's baby! It would have lived, if it hadn't been for me.'

'No, Thea, that's not true.'

'How do *you* know? You weren't even . . .'

'Look, my girl, about one in ten first pregnancies ends in miscarriage. That's an awful lot of babies for you to have killed.'

'It *wasn't* a miscarriage – she lost it at nine months. Even the doctors don't call it miscarriage when it's *that* far on. Anyway, you're laughing at me . . .'

'I'm *not* laughing, Thea. It's just that I'm pretty damned certain you're not a murderer.'

'Oh yes, I am. What about Josie Rutherford?'

'Thea, dear, who *is* Josie Rutherford?'

'*Was.*'

'Was, then.'

'Oh, some . . . bitch my father ran away with.'

'I see. And when did she die?'

'Eighteen months ago.'

'Oh, recently. How old was she then?'

'I've no idea. *His* age, I suppose.'

'Well, how old was *he*?'

'Don't know!'

'You told me last time your father married late, and had *you* even later. So he can't be young.'

'Well, he's not old.'

'Sixty-ish?'

'*No!* Well . . . yes . . . maybe.'

'So his . . . er . . . woman was at least sixty when she died?'

'Mmmm.'

'And already had a good part of her life. Was it a *happy* life?'

'She had my *father*, didn't she? For nearly twenty years. I only had him for *four*.'

'Happy, then. What did she die of, Thea? I mean, it wasn't boiling oil, or sharks, was it?'

'No-o.'

'Well, what?'

'She had a chest infection, followed by pneumonia. It didn't kill her, actually, but she had a relapse. They were living in Saskatchewan at the time, and she insisted on swimming in some sub-zero lake when she was meant to be convalescing.'

'You mean, you *made* her swim in it.'

'I *didn't*! Hell, I wasn't even *there*, Ray. I was living in a cul-de-sac in Twickenham.'

'Exactly. It was nothing to do with you at all. She died of natural causes, Thea. Life and death belong to God and nature. Even *you*'re not powerful enough to murder people six thousand miles away.'

'You're mocking me again, Ray. I thought this was meant to be Confession.'

'It *is* Confession and I never mock. I'm speaking to you as God would. You may have hated, but you've never killed. God will forgive the hate.'

'You mean . . . you could give me absolution?'

'Of course I could.'

'Even though I hate her? Still.'

'You can't really hate the dead, Thea.'

'You *can*.'

'Well, you must want not to *want* to hate her.' He grinned. 'Could you manage that?'

'Yes, but . . . supposing she hates *me*? Well, perhaps not her – not now – but *other* people. Janet, for example. Or my mother. Or Leo, even. I'm *frightened* of that hate, Ray.'

'You don't even know it's *there*, my girl. It's only your *own* hate reflected in a mirror.'

'Well, my own hate's even worse. That's why I want to stay here. There's no hate in the hospital. And even my own I can hide away from here. Everybody's kind and decent here – well, all except Sister Robert, they are. I mean, the whole thing only exists to be loving and caring and . . .'

'You can take that *with* you, Thea, all that love and decency, set it up inside you. That's what absolution does. Gets rid of the hate, so you can put something better in its place. Look, remember that man sick of the palsy?'

'What *is* palsy, Ray, exactly?'

'Paralysis. The poor chap couldn't walk or move his limbs. But I've always suspected it was a sort of *hysterical* paralysis – you know, psychological, psychosomatic – all those long words which mean his mind knocked his body for six. You see, Thea, his sins so weighed him down, he was literally *crippled* by them. Christ realized that. That's why the first thing He said was, "Your sins are forgiven you." It was *enough*, you see. It healed him, soul *and* body. Maybe it's a bit the same with you. All that hate and stuff has been dragging you down for years, Thea. Even fear is a sort of paralysis. Once we get rid of it, you won't *need* hospitals. Oh, of course you'll have to get your teeth fixed, and rest and recuperate and take things easy for a while, but the real, essential Thea will be strong and healed and . . .'

'But supposing there *isn't* a real, essential Thea? I mean what if I'm a *fraud*? Even now, I'm not really sure I'm not deceiving you. A bit of me still wants to . . . Oh, I know it's crazy, Ray, but the more you talk like a priest and go on about Christ and cripples and miracles and things, the more I want to sort of . . . *paw* you.'

He grinned and touched my hand. 'I don't think that matters much, do you? I mean, we're all a bit of a mess, clinging on to heaven with our fingertips, while our toes trail in the mud.'

'But I think I *prefer* the mud.'

'That's only because you're so used to it. It's like people who've been in prison for years. They're scared to come out, in case the sunlight blinds them. It *won't*, Thea. In fact, I think you need some sun. Look, shut your eyes and we'll say the prayers together.'

'But supposing I'm not sorry?'

'You've made two confessions in three days. Isn't that *proof* you're sorry?'

'Not necessarily. I might just be trapping you. I *was*, in the beginning.'

'Look, Thea, you said you trusted me. Well, can't you trust me enough to know when a penitent's genuine, and when she's shamming?'

'But, you're so *simple*, Ray. You don't even see *through* me. Hell! I only said I trusted you because I wanted you to touch me. Don't you see, the whole thing turns me on? It's as if all your prayers and gospels and things were a sort of Kama Sutra . . .' How could I go on? Tell him his words were lapping against my cunt, probing it like a long dark velvet finger?

'That's OK, Thea. The gospels *are* a kind of love story and they *should* turn you on.'

'But not like *that*! You're so damned saintly, Ray, you don't even see what I'm getting at.'

'Oh yes, I do. But I think you make too much of it. Sex is your special subject, so to speak, so you keep on going back to it. It's understandable – you don't want it devalued because it's all you've got in your life at the moment.'

I drained my glass, more to hide my face than anything. Ray had put his finger, not on my cunt, but on something just as sensitive. I had so few achievements, I *needed* those forty-seven men. They were like my O-levels or my testimonials, and I didn't want him knocking them. Yet, wasn't he offering me a life-escape, a way to soar beyond them? I was still confused. I longed for absolution, but . . .

'Supposing it's all a *game*, Ray. I mean, just my way of grabbing another man? Or two, if you count God. I mean, I'm *always* playing games with people. Sometimes I don't even know I'm doing it.'

'Oh, so your tears were just a game, were they? And Josie Rutherford was a game and . . .'

'Well, *no*, Ray, but . . .'

'And you *don't* want absolution?'

'Yes, yes, I *do*.'

'Well, why don't we *finish* the game? I know you think I'm simple, Thea – perhaps I am. But sometimes it pays to be simple. Shall we try? Even the rules of this game are very simple. All you have to do is shut your eyes, listen to the words of absolution, and try and tell God you're sorry, OK?'

Holy. Sorry. Simple. Words I had never trusted up till now. Christ was probably simple. He may have had rough red hands and shy myopic eyes.

'OK.'

I shut my eyes. The night was so dark, it came roaring into my head. All I could hear, at first, was the scowl of rain fretting outside the window. Then, something like a nudge of moonlight trembled on my neck. I squinted through my eyelids. I could see Ray's hand trailing across my shoulder, returning to my breasts. A holy hand. Not pawing me, but shielding, sanctifying. I felt his fingers fall against the nipple. A great sob shook my body.

'God the Father of Mercies,' Ray began. He was saying the words in English, but even the flat Manchester vowels couldn't hide the glory in them. Hate and shame and murder were drowning in the dark waters of the Saskatchewan lake. The narrow, messy cul-de-sac which had been my past now had a wide free-flowing channel cutting through it, flushing out the debris, roaring to the sea. Healing waves were breaking over my head, grace streaming from my soul, my cunt, my eyes. Ray had reached the climax now. We were both trembling, both triumphant.

'And I absolve you from your sins in the name of the Father and of the Son and of the Holy Spirit . . .'

He made the Sign of the Cross with his other hand. The right one never wavered from its homage at my breast. I sat stone still. I could feel the Holy Spirit scudding through my body, sluicing down my thighs.

Ray was still praying. 'May whatever suffering you endure, heal your sins and help you grow in holiness.'

I swooped on the word suffering and clasped it to my chest. There was purpose in my pain now, as I had wanted all along. My mangled mouth was sanctified.

'Amen,' I stuttered. 'Amen.'

Love and light were flooding into me. I was a sun, a flame, a meteor. The humble room was a glowing golden palace, Ray's packing-case a throne. Even the stains on the carpet had turned into spinning stars. I hardly noticed when Ray took his hand away. He had put the sheepskin back around my shoulders. It felt warm like the breath of God.

We sat staring at each other. Whatever was said now could only be an anti-climax, so we left the silence stretching up to heaven. I dived in it and swam. Ray, I think, was praying. I could feel myself lapped in his soft white prayer, like sheepskin.

At last he got up and fumbled with the tumblers. 'Look, I don't want to rush you, Thea, but . . .'

'It's all right, Ray, I know I've got to go.' I was radiant now, and strong.

'Would you like a snack before you leave? There's not much here, but I could probably unearth a tin of soup or something.'

I knew he was trying to bridge that awkward, nervous gap between earth and heaven. I shook my head. I didn't need it bridged. If I still had a stomach, then grace was plugging all the gaps in it. There wasn't room for soup.

'Well, at least let me see you safely back to your bed.'

'No,' I whispered. I wanted to be alone. Or rather not alone. As Ray closed the door, I glimpsed the floor of heaven glinting through the clouds. I was walking out into a night so full of angels, the dense black sky was streaked and creamy with them. I was absolved, forgiven, one with the whole eternal, living church. I had made my First Confession, so now I was a true, authentic Catholic, joined to the eight hundred million others in the world. Every Catholic church from Walsingham to Warsaw was *my* church now, every priest my priest. God himself had been sitting in the room with me, sharing Ray's packing-case. I could still feel His fingers burning on my breasts, His grace leaking out between my legs. I lay down on the grass and tried to keep it there; stared up at the sky. Joy and rain were falling in my eyes. I was

God-sized now. All the swanking stars were only soft blossoms tangling in my hair; the soaring cedars sprigs in my buttonhole. I could feel God ravishing me, his strong limbs pressing hot against my nightdress. My forty-eighth man and still no sin in it. No sin anywhere. Even Josie Rutherford was over. Ray had wiped her out and cancelled her. She hadn't even left a stain. No stains. My soul was white and shimmering like the white beard on a wave. I *was* a wave. Breaking and pounding on the shore of heaven.

The grass was freezing, but I hardly felt it. How could I be cold with God's breath against my neck? I wasn't lonely. I was joined now with the whole singing chain of earth and heaven, with all three hundred girls at school, with all three million visitors to Lourdes. Soon I would be one of them. And at Lourdes I would creep even closer into God. I would swallow Him, store Him in my stomach, feel Him flooding through my bloodstream. This was only Confession; Communion would be as wonderful again as a constellation to a single star.

I closed my eyes. I had still to say my penance. Ray had asked me to say an Our Father. Just one Our Father for a lifetime of sin, a backlog of screwing. God wasn't insisting on His pound of flesh. I lay straighter on the grass, clasped my hands together, closed my legs. The rain had turned my nightie into a penitential garment, damp and dark and clinging, but I was so white and light and radiant, it felt like a bridal gown.

'Our Father,' I began. Then stopped. The words were so beautiful, I kept repeating them over and over again. Our Father, father, father, father, father. I could feel His rough beard prickling against my breasts, His strong arms swinging me round and round the sky; I could smell the lure of His tobacco lingering on all the trees, their brown bark stained with it. I didn't want lovers any more, only fathers. Forty-seven fathers, three thousand and forty-seven.

'Our Father,' I whispered. *My* father. I wasn't going to share Him. 'My father who art in heaven.' (I could never be an Anglican because they used to say '*which* art' and so turned fathers into things). 'Hallowed be thy name.' It was already hallowed. Father – no name more sacred or more special. And *I* was hallowed on account of it. I was made of starlight now, of lilies, snow, ambrosia – no longer a dingy thing of dust and slime.

'Give us this day our daily bread,' I continued. I think I'd missed out something in between, but God wouldn't mind. He wasn't a fusspot like Adrian, ruler-rapping your knuckles, pedantic finger pointing to the text.

Daily bread. Soft white food which couldn't hurt my gums. No aubergines, no purples, no blancmange. God providing goodies like titbits on a birdtable, sons and daughters feeding from His hand. No need to struggle to pay the grocery bills, or fake a face to convince the Burton Bureau. Just sit at home and God would pop the loaf in through the open window. Bread and jam. Bread and peanut butter . . .

'Forgive us our trespasses . . .' Another strange word that, like Pharisees and prodigal and palsy. I'd first seen it written up at school. The path beyond the lake said, 'Private, no trespassing', so when we chanted, 'Forgive us our trespasses', I'd always thought we were asking God to forgive us our secret walks beyond the water, through the thicket, over the stepping stones. But it was other thickets He'd forgiven. I was virgin now, like Ray; pink and white instead of stained and sallow. I could almost revert to my maiden name. Maiden meant celibate and unspotted. No man had ever had me, except my father. God had wiped out Elliott and Morton, rooting and rutting, marriage and divorce. He'd even forgiven murder. Josie Rutherford no longer glowered at me from the Other Side. I could feel her like a flower now, dead perhaps, but only because it was winter. She must have been flower-like if my father loved her. But flowers never lasted long. (That's why Adrian bought pot plants. Josie wasn't a primula. Only a brief, frail, fading, insubstantial weed.)

I returned to the Our Father. 'As we forgive them,' I prayed, 'Who trespass against us.' That meant Leo and there was nothing to forgive. My mouth was holy now – part of my penance, even. I wasn't hideous. Ray had told me I was beautiful.

There was also Janet to forgive. I had washed away the hate for her, but what about the envy? That was less important, now she hadn't got her baby. Janet with an empty womb and a sore, stitched cunt and her perm growing out, was easy to forgive. True, she still had Adrian, but I had Ray and God.

'And lead us not into temptation . . .'

No more pricks and park-keepers, ravening sharks, jars of boiling oil. God holding me by the hand now, guiding me from the cliff's edge, the black hole, the murderer's cell.

'But deliver us from evil.' The clenched fist, the shattered vase, the bleeding bortsch, the choking cul-de-sac.

'Amen,' I shouted. 'Amen.'

I could hear the sky roaring out 'amen' with me, the whole earth humming it as it spun and dazzled around the sun. I sprang to my feet. I was still so tall, my hair kept catching in the stars; so strong, I could have picked up the whole hospital and pinned it on my lapel like a brooch. I knew I could leave it now. Or take it with me. I had my own white walls inside me, as Ray had said. Just one more night, then Leo would come with my suitcase, and in it I would cram all the grace and strength and healing which Ray had promised me, and which the nuns stored in their light white rustling souls.

Softly, I opened the little side door of the hospital and padded along the passage and up the stairs. No one had missed me. I slipped into bed and stretched out my arms to God the Father. My own fond, returned, and doting Heavenly father who would stay with me now for ever and ever amen.

'Put out your pipe,' I whispered. 'And kiss my breasts.'

fourteen

It was still raining in the morning and God had returned to heaven with all His angels. The earth looked drab and damp without them and I had caught a cold. It hurt to blow my nose, so I dabbed and sniffed instead. It wasn't slops for breakfast, but hard toast and burnt bacon. I took that as a Sign – my time for being cosseted was over. Today was Departure Day.

A nun stripped my bed and left it stripped. The mattress was covered with a cold white mackintosh cover, like a baby's cot. I kept wondering who would be lolling on it tomorrow and whether Ray would visit them and hold their hands. Leo hadn't come. I had washed and dressed (I must have lost weight because my jeans drooped) and collected all my things together and said goodbye to Sister Ursula who kissed me, and Sister Aidan who told me it was a beautiful day outside. When I pointed out that it was pouring, she said it was God's own rain and good for the crops. There aren't any crops in January, but I didn't press the point. She was simple, like Ray – which meant holy. I wished Leo was more simple, the sort of simple person who came when he said he would and left notes and said sorry.

I sat and waited. I refused the mid-morning Ovaltine and biscuits in case they charged me for another day. It was getting close to lunchtime and I was starving. God had fed me last night with manna and ambrosia, full to overflowing, but He'd crept away at dawn and left no one on the Day Shift.

I stole down the passage to the bathroom with the mirror in it. Perhaps Leo had changed his mind about collecting me. He'd seen me yesterday, asleep, and I didn't look too fancy. Leo lived with *objets d'art*, not rejects. I didn't dare confront the mirror head-on, but darted furtive little glances in it, sideways. I think I kept hoping that somehow my teeth would have been returned to me and my old face stuck back on. It wasn't. All that had changed was the colour of the bruising which was now yellowish-purple instead of purplish-yellow. There was a brown scaly residue on the outside of my lips and a sort of pussy gunge inside them. My nose was running again. I sniffed and shook my hair around my face, to try and hide the worst bits.

As I walked back to the room, I forced a smile in case Leo had arrived. My legs were wobbly with the sheer fear and lust and longing of seeing him again. I think I was suffering Leo withdrawal symptoms. Ray and God and the Sisters had filled his place to some extent, but there was some dark, strong, violent part of him which no one else could offer.

He wasn't there, but someone else was – a small greasy man in a black leather jacket, displaying a mass of chest hair with two silver medals entangled in it. Another priest, I guessed. Their disguises were getting better all the time. This one was even armed with one of Leo's suitcases.

'Mrs Thea Morton?' he inquired. His accent was Suffolk crossed with Bethnal Green. But he couldn't be a pop priest – not if I was Mrs.

'Yes,' I said. 'That's me.' Actually, I didn't feel like anyone. Everything was crumbling. My soft white bed had turned into glaring mackintosh, and Leo into a Cockney spiv with bracelets.

'I suppose you're going to tell me you're a Dominican?' I added.

'No. Fleetway Taxi Service. Instructions to pick up a Mrs Morton and take her to W.II.' He tossed the suitcase on to the mattress and lit a cigarette. 'OK?' (You weren't allowed to smoke.)

'Er . . . yes . . . OK.' It could have been worse, I suppose. At least it wasn't Otto. Perhaps Leo had an auction or a deadline, or had fallen foul of Sister Aidan yesterday.

I opened the case. Inside was a piece of paper with a kiss on it – just one large kiss in Leo's bold black writing with a florid 'L' underneath. The fountain pen had leaked and one leg of the kiss looked as if it were bleeding or deformed. Leo couldn't come himself, but he had sent me a spiv, a taxi, and a crippled kiss.

I stuffed the paper in my pocket and my possessions in the suitcase. I had nicked the books on Bernadette. I couldn't bear to leave her in that fusty hospital library – she was my sister now, so she had to go where I went. I also packed the tiny cereal packets. There were three of them – my babies. One of the girls I'd worked with once had given birth to triplets last October. I'd read it in the *Daily Mail*.

'Kept you hungry, did they?' The driver had seen the chocolates and the custard creams follow the Sugar Puffs. He was standing in front of the window, blocking the view, so I couldn't say goodbye to my tree. Even the nuns had disappeared. It was Angelus time, so they'd all be in the chapel. A cleaner and an orderly were holding the floor with the first lay nurse I'd seen there. It seemed odd that she should come complete with legs and hair and breasts, when the nuns had managed perfectly well without them. Sister Aidan had hinted they were short of nuns. Not enough vocations.

'I'm . . . er . . . leaving now,' I mumbled.

The greyish curls and tinted spectacles barely wavered from their paperwork. 'Mrs Morton isn't it? Got your drugs?'

'Yes,' I said to both. Perhaps that's why Leo hadn't come. If I was Mrs Morton, then he was an adulterer. Wildman had disappeared again. And I'd never be Mrs Rzevski. It was a name which no one could ever spell or share.

I was still lingering by the desk. It seemed wrong to leave with so little send-off, especially after yesterday. I felt there should have been a heavenly guard of honour handing me not my penicillin, but chunks of light and love. Instead, I picked my way round mops and buckets, followed by a whistling taxi driver scattering a trail of ash. He was a fairly professional whistler, but every time he hit a high note, the noise caught on my mouth and ripped it. I hoped the cleaners wouldn't assume he was my husband. He had long black hairs protruding from his nostrils and gold bits on his shoes. Sister Aidan would have really been confused. Another Jewish uncle, she'd assume, but from a less favoured tribe of Israel. We trailed through the drizzle to the car park. I wondered what the car would be – not, I prayed, a sneering scarlet snob like Otto's. It was a green Granada Ghia with fake fur on the seats and a pink plastic girlie doll dangling naked over the driving mirror. The driver helped me in, banged the doors, flung his fag-end out of the window and lit another.

'Smoke?' he offered, as we cruised round the corner and on to the main road.

'No thanks.'

'Your bloke been bashing you up, then?'

I tried to laugh, but it came out like a gasp. Was he just joking or had he seen my case notes? Perhaps the crowd he mixed with all beat their women up, like those articles you read on battered wives or women's refuges. I'd never thought about them much. Violence was like sex – it went on all the time, but no one talked about it. Now I was a statistic, I suppose, an entry in Erin Pizzey's guest book.

'No,' I stuttered. 'I . . . had an accident.'

'Nasty,' he said and switched the radio on. So that was that. He'd dismissed the whole thing in a couple of syllables. I felt a little better. I tried to listen to the programme which was a record request thing where people called Cheryl, Val and Les were sending love to Brenda and the twins, or the Best Mum In The World. There were four Best Mums before we'd even got to Richmond. Everyone *belonged*. Stacey had six aunts and eleven cousins and wanted each one mentioned individually, and Gavin from Grimsby said goodbye to all his old workmates and hallo to all his new ones, and not forgetting Gran up in Glasgow and Mum (Best?) down in Kent.

I had only ex's. One ex-husband, one ex-baby and one almost ex-mother. She'd moved to Jersey for the climate, so she said, but I suspected it was more to avoid the burden of having me as a daughter, instead of Patricia Jane. I wondered if I should request a record for her. Thea (*who?*) Morton sends greetings to the Best Ex-Mum In The World and to her workmates at the Mayfair office where she was recently receptionist, and love to all the ex-Franciscans posing as tramps and taxi-drivers, and please tell Leo she hopes he isn't ex, and she can't wait for him to come and fetch her home from hospital.

The driver turned Gavin down and removed his cigarette. 'Can't get on with nuns,' he said, racing an amber light. 'I mean, it's not natural, is it, shutting themselves away like that, with no blokes?'

I'd yearned to be a nun all the years I'd been at the convent school. We *all* had. Who wanted blokes, when God was on offer?

'Men aren't *every*thing,' I said. I wondered if Leo would be in. If he wasn't, I couldn't even pay the cab. Perhaps he'd take a Chinese vase in lieu of, or a hand-painted jardinière.

'They go to bed in all them robes, you know. Never take 'em off. Not allowed to see their own bodies. Unhealthy, in 't?'

He flicked a long grey chrysalis of ash against the dashboard. We were crawling through the fag-end of London now, dingy, noisy, choked. The world beyond the hospital looked stained and tarnished. God had disappeared, become another ex. I wasn't sure in which world I belonged. Ray would be busy with his boys now, Sister Aidan tidying somebody else's bed. I pulled the piece of paper out of my pocket. The ink had blurred beneath my fingers and the kiss and the 'L' looked more like small black insects. I tried not to sniff in case the driver caught my cold. I wondered if he had a girl, one with ankle-chains and peroxided pubic hair.

'Who's this geezer, then?' he asked. 'The one who booked the cab?'

'Oh . . . an uncle. Uncle Les from Grimsby. He's Jewish. I've got eleven Jewish uncles.'

'*Blimey!*' He was silent for a while. Shock, I suppose.

I wiped my nose on a piece of the toilet-roll I'd pinched from the hospital and watched the traffic thicken and the shoppers crowd and tangle on the pavements. No one was alone. It was like the record request programme – mums everywhere; older ones with carbon-copy daughters; younger ones with pregnancies and prams. Boys kissed girls in doorways, friends linked arms with friends. I felt like a piece of shopping abandoned in a trolley. No one seemed to own me.

We were turning into Shepherd's Bush Road now. It could only be minutes before we reached the house. We dawdled through a hold-up, swung right, then left, then right. I glimpsed the name-plate on Leo's street. Two of the letters had been blanked out, which made it look dyslexic.

The driver was crawling now, checking the numbers on the houses. 'Nine, eleven, fifteen – right, there you are, seventeen.'

I shut my eyes. I felt dizzy and light-headed. Part of me wanted to rush inside and throw myself on Leo, the other part to double back to the hospital and never leave my bed again. I remembered those films where the Mistress returns and all the servants line up in the front hall, and step out and curtsey when they hear the crunch of gravel under wheels. No one stepped out except the driver, but I could hear Karma barking before I'd even opened the car door. The driver left me to walk up the path by myself. He leant against the bonnet with the engine still running, waiting for his fee, and whistling. I knocked. Karma's barking was a black pain in my head. As Leo opened the door, the dog darted towards me, growling, and with his ears laid back as if I were an enemy or a stranger. He had never growled at me before. All right, he didn't like me much, but he'd always accepted me as Leo's mate. Things were different now, so Karma said. Leo's face looked grey and brave and strained, almost holy, like one of those paintings of martyrs embracing God and the stake. His eyes had burnt holes through his charred and flaking skin and there were ashes on his lips. He took my hand and held it very tightly. We were both aware of the driver just outside, and of Karma's low, threatening snarl.

'Quiet, Karma. *Down!*'

'Savage brute you got there.' The driver had sidled up the path. I think he was keen to see a Grimsby Jew. Leo pulled a sheaf of bank-notes from his wallet and handed them over. I felt almost guilty costing him so much. When he'd shut the door, Karma went on growling, the hackles on his neck standing up and his whole body crouched and menacing, as if he were about to spring. Leo took me in his arms and held me against his soft healing sweater. I could smell his smell again. Juniper berries crushed up with Old Russia and back numbers of the *Listener*. He held me so long, everything went purple. Karma's growl had changed now to a note of mocking, savage jealousy. I'd almost hoped Karma might have gone – in reparation for my mouth. I'd imagined Leo sacrificing him like Abraham did Isaac, but without the providential ram.

Leo took the suitcase and my sheepskin and led me to the drawing-room. The house looked strange, almost wounded. I realized he had cleaned and tidied it. Even his music was sorted into piles on the bureau, instead of strewn on the floor. The piano had been dusted, and was draped with a long, fringed sort of cover thing with roses woven into it. There were more roses – stiff, forced, unnatural ones – standing to attention in a Ch'ien-lung vase. Their scent was trapped in the room like a prisoner and the thorns were almost bigger than the blooms. Leo laid me on the sofa like some new acquisition he had bought from the auction rooms, a chipped and broken object which needed restoration. I felt shamed, almost frightened. He was trying to say sorry. It was such a simple word, yet he couldn't get it out. He offered me everything else instead. He had swept and shopped and tidied, shrouded his piano, bought out-of-season nectarines. He was wearing the sweater I'd bought him which he hated. He'd even banished Karma to the far end of the room, where he was crouching underneath the window seat, watching us with angry scornful eyes.

Leo excused himself a moment and went down into the kitchen. He returned with lunch on a tray which he must have had all prepared, because he was only gone two minutes. I had never known him wait on me before – lunch exactly timed, everything laid out, silver salt and pepper set, damask napkin folded on my plate. He looked wrong with a tray in his hands, undignified, like those animals in zoos which are forced to play at tea-parties.

He had made me blinis stuffed with cream cheese. The batter had hardened slightly round the edges, but I forced it down more roughly than I needed to. I felt I ought to suffer in return for all his efforts. He had even put a rose on my tray, an elegant, decapitated bloom drowning in a brandy glass. There were too many blinis and they tasted now of pain and labour rather than cream cheese. But I dared not leave them. They were part of Leo's sacrifice, the careful rose-trimmed, thorn-crowned ritual he was laying at my feet. He didn't eat himself, just sat on a stiff-necked chair, twisting my unused napkin through his fingers. It was too much like the hospital again.

'Have a mouthful,' I offered. I wanted us to break bread together, share a Eucharist.

'I'm not hungry.'

'They're good, really good.' I forced the last one down.

'Leave some room, Thea – there's lemon sorbet after.' He brought it to me in a small silver goblet, like a chalice. The sorbet was white and cold and very insubstantial like frozen air or grated bits of cloud. He squatted on the floor beside me and fed me like a child. It wasn't sisterly like Ray, but sacred. Almost worth having lost a face, a tooth or two, to have this new, tender, chastened Leo abasing himself in front of me. I had suffered for it, paid the blood-price, and this was my reward and compensation. The sorbet was finished, the dish scraped, but Leo still crouched there, dark and solemn like an icon. I hardly knew what to say to him. We never just sat together. Either he was out, or working, or we slept or fought or screwed. All I needed now was for him to reach out a hand and say, 'I'm sorry', to make the ink-and-paper kiss a real one. The whole room was screwed up and waiting for it, even the walls had moved a fraction inwards as if to catch his words.

We had both forgotten how to speak. It was as if we were total strangers, or members of a different race. Leo just sat there, frowning into the silence, the heavy silver salt cellar cradled in his hands. I suddenly felt frightened. I'd never noticed it before, but the room was full of dangerous things. Bronze statuettes with jutting plinths, metal photo-frames with cruel, sharp-edged angles, foursquare ashtrays in glass and alabaster, a lump of crystal, a hunk of malachite. These objects were quiet now, heads-on-their-paws and watching us like Karma, but the slightest stir, the tiniest disturbance, could send them crashing through the air, ripping apart the dentist's slow, careful, patient handiwork. Everywhere I looked was danger. Karma's white-trap teeth unsheathed like swords, Leo's hands weighing up the salt cellar, a vicious fruit-knife gloating on the tray. I shut my eyes. I could hear the room drawing in its breath as if to strike or pounce . . .

I started counting. I'd read some article about it being a good idea to count in dangerous situations since it soothed the nerves. I fixed my gaze on the wallpaper which was covered with dark, swirly, dragony things swallowing their own tails. I counted every second tail. 'Two, four, six . . .' I began.

A clock began to mutter through the silence. I suppose it must have been ticking all along, but I hadn't noticed it. Now it grew slowly louder and more insistent, taking over everything. Our breathing was geared to it, the pulsing of our blood. It even upset my counting. At twenty-four, the tails turned into ticks, so I changed to counting ticks.

'Fifty-eight, fifty-nine, sixty-one . . .' I think I'd missed a few – it was impossible to concentrate. I wanted to choke that clock, stifle it, stuff it under a cushion. How could Leo ever say, 'I'm sorry', with that pitiless thing drumming him down? I *needed* him to say it. It wasn't just a salve to my pride, or a sop to Adrian, or a bow to convention. Those five short letters could stick me back together. I had never heard Leo apologize to anyone before, so it would make me special, safe, beloved.

'Much traffic?' Leo asked.

The words were so soft, the clock had already swallowed them. All the same, I jumped.

'Er . . . no . . .' I said. Small talk was even worse than silence. Leo was hardly there. He seemed to be growing darker with every tick, merging into the background as if he were a splodge on the carpet or the shadow of a piece of furniture. His face was just a blur now. How could he apologize if he hadn't any lips? Perhaps neither of us would ever speak again, just sit there for ever, dark and stiff and separate, running down like clocks. I could hear my own breathing rasping through my head, too loud and raw and snuffly because I had a cold. Leo hated colds.

'Two hundred and twenty-three,' I muttered under my breath. 'Two hundred and twenty-four . . .'

I longed for the phone to ring, or for Karma to go skidding down the hall and bark at an intruder, anything to break that heavy-breathing silence, that endless counting.

All the time I'd been in hospital, I'd tried not to think about how I'd landed up there. Safer to anaesthetize it. But now I could see clenched fists in every corner of the room, closing in on me, snarling at my face. One false move and a thousand paperweights would explode between my lips.

Suddenly, Leo shifted. He was rising to his feet, standing square in front of me. His shadow was scarlet now like bruised and bleeding peonies, decapitated flowers. He took a step towards me, hands still clenched around the salt cellar. I could see the glint of silver in his eyes.

'No!' I shouted, covering up my mouth. 'No, Leo, NO!'

He flinched, as if he had been struck himself. His face shut up like a jeweller pulling a metal blind down over a window. He was stumbling away from me, tail down like Karma's, kicked into a corner, banished and betrayed.

I realized now he had only been trying to say something, offer me that sorry, stick me back together. His fists were clenched simply because it was the most frightening word he'd ever had to struggle with. And all I had done was pick up his fear and fling it back at him, smash the moment, abort the words.

'Leo, look, I didn't realize . . . I mean, I wasn't really thinking. I'm just a bit on edge, you see. I only . . .'

He didn't seem to hear. He was standing by the window staring out at the dead grey afternoon, the snivelling rain. I had spurned him, humiliated him, turned his 'sorry' into fury. I would have to make amends.

I lay back on the sofa and unzipped my jeans. 'Leo . . .' I whispered. 'Come back over here.'

He didn't move. I peeled off my tee-shirt. I had nothing on underneath. It seemed strange to be naked in his drawing-room, a normal room where everything else was over-dressed – tables carved and inlaid, ceiling stuccoed, curtains tasselled and swathed. Even the people in his portraits wore wigs and ruffs and bows. They were staring down at me, blushing at my nerve. We had never done it in that room before.

I went up behind him and pressed my bare breasts against his cashmere back.

'I want you, Leo,' I murmured. It wasn't quite the truth. My face was still so battered, it flinched at the thought of his pressed-steel body slamming into mine. Sex with Leo was always sort of *desperate*. His thing was a pillar, a piston, a battering ram. I had worshipped it like that, yet now I was frightened of it. I was like a broken vase, only held together by a couple of rivets and a dab of glue. If he rammed too hard, I might crack up again. I had to be handled gently, screwed only by God or E. H. Leatherstone.

Leo turned towards me, pushed me almost roughly on to the sofa. He pulled off his own clothes, then knelt down and kissed my naked belly since he couldn't kiss my mouth. His chin felt rough and barbed.

'Leo,' I whispered.

'Mmm?'

'Be . . . gentle.'

He nodded. His naked body seemed thinner and more threatening than I had ever seen it. He was like the room, full of dark, dangerous angles.

Slowly, he moved a hand towards my breasts. I waited for it to grab, to twist my arms behind my back, to bridle me with my hair. Instead, it hovered over me, uncertain almost, touching down like the slow, shy antennae of a moth. I could hardly believe it was still Leo's hand. He had taken all the teeth out of it. It was fawning on me, begging instead of brazening. My mouth relaxed. We couldn't kiss, but Leo turned his fingers into lips and tongue, whispering over my body, finding little dips and niches to trickle in and out of. There was no danger now. He had taken off his armour, laid his weapons down. We weren't even separate people any more. Our bodies were merging in a peace treaty, arms entwined, thighs overlapping, my long hair binding us together. He was using his tongue across my nipples, his lips behind my knees. The light in the room was fading, as if it were almost embarrassed to watch this new submissive Leo. Even my cold seemed better. I no longer had to sniff or cough or rasp. It was as if he had healed me simply by the laying on of hands.

My own hands were stroking up and down his back, across his chest, in and out of all the shadowed hollows of his body. Normally, he never gave me time. He was in me, on top of me, before I had barely touched him, forcing me to buck, jump, thrust, gasp, plunge. But now, I ran long, slow, teasing circles around his thighs, moving my hand in closer, closer, and then idling it away again, back to his belly – taunting him, abandoning him – making him think I'd never quite get there.

My face was hidden against his neck, my eyes closed. I wanted to savour this new, slow, coaxing ritual. Leo fidgeted. He seemed restive, almost nervous. Or perhaps he was just impatient with so long a build-up. I moved my hand in closer. He had indulged me long enough. It was time for him to thrust and slam again, bang into me like one of those hard wooden shapes which children hammer into holes. Through my closed lids, I saw a fist again, a man's brute powerful fist, rammed right inside me, punching in and out between my legs. I realized, suddenly, all penises were fists, smashing into women, pummelling blow after blow on to bruised and flinching cunts. I wanted to sneak away, melt into nothing, sticky-tape my hole. I was too raw, too weak, too small, too scared, for any man to barge and trample into – Leo, least of all.

Yet how could I refuse him? It would be a second, worse rejection, a total act of war. All I could say was, 'Careful', and open my legs as slowly as I dared.

I reached out my hand and trailed my fingers down, still lingering, still teasing, as if to show him what I meant by careful. I dawdled through his pubic hair, caressing it a little, then back between his thighs. Another inch, another centimetre. I was almost, almost there. I felt him tense. My hand moved in, ready to snap around him like a bracelet. The fingers closed on air. There was nothing there, no clenched and hammering fist, no brutal weapon. Leo was limp.

He was *never* limp. We never screwed without him looming up and overpowering me. He was often stiff when we weren't even thinking about it – stiff in the kitchen, stiff in the auction rooms. I shifted my head a fraction and peered down. Instead of the fist, the cudgel, the battering ram, was a soft pink cringing thing, coiled in on itself like an embryo. I longed to scoop it up and put it in an incubator on a bed of cotton wool, and then feed and nurture it until it grew again. It didn't look like Leo – it was too small and shy for that. It was a child's thing, a baby's, weak and gentle and vulnerable. I felt an almost power. I had tamed and softened Leo, turned force into flower.

'Bloody sodding hell.'

I jumped. Leo was lying rigid now, arms across his body, eyes shut, dead below the navel. I had to resurrect him. I stopped teasing and used my hands more boldly – both hands – every way I knew. Nothing happened. I turned the other way and rubbed my breasts against it, the pressure of my nipples. I wound it in my hair. Still nothing – except Leo grew more tense. He couldn't even look at me. His eyes were blind, his mouth a thin sharp line.

He pushed me off, and started to rub himself, almost savagely, as if he were punishing a disobedient child. He was bawling at it, forcing it up, commanding it to stand when it couldn't even crawl.

'*Gently*, Leo . . . you'll hurt yourself. Look, it doesn't matter.'

'It *does* matter, for Christ's sake.'

I think he blamed me for ever having used words like gentle and careful. By begging for mercy, I had somehow crippled and unmanned him. He was either steel or nothing, and I had made him nothing. I must build him up again, turn him back to steel. Fingers weren't enough. I would have to use my mouth.

I didn't have a mouth, only a wounded, flinching thing, wrapped in cotton wool. For almost a week, it had been cherished and cosseted. No one had asked anything of it except to rest and heal. Nuns' hands had tiptoed over it, dentists' probes apologized for any pain they might have caused it. But now that was over and it had work to do. It must stop being an invalid and turn into a whore.

Slowly, I moved my head down to his thighs, flicked my tongue across his tip, forced my lips to forget they were stitched and bruised, and slipped them slowly round it. He was so soft, he didn't even hurt. He was only a mouthful of petals, a spoonful of pink blancmange. I tried to use my tongue, even the pressure of my gums. It *did* hurt now. Tiny black rockets of pain were exploding in my ears and through my head. I wanted to stop, to slip into bed and have my mouth pampered and coddled again, to be cordoned off by nuns. But Leo's need was greater. He was out-of-action, invalided. I tried everything I could. I used my fingers and my hair at the same time as my lips, teeth and tongue. I cupped his balls and licked them. I tongued a path from his navel to his tip; down, then up again between his buttocks. I made little coaxing noises. I remembered the Russian peasant words which always turned him on, and whispered them between his thighs.

Nothing happened. If anything, he was even smaller now. The flower had shrunk into a bud, the embryo into a single-celled amoeba. My mouth was screaming out with pain. It was as if it had been bashed again, gums bleeding, lips torn, the whole thing throbbing and unravelling. My cold had come streaming back. My nose was red and puffy, my throat scratched like wire wool. I sat up and mopped my face. Tears of pain and shame and failure were streaming down my cheeks. I often cried when we made love, but always with the exultation of it. Leo's comes were the sort that *made* you cry. A friend once told me all men's orgasms were more or less the same, but she hadn't slept with Leo. He wasn't like the rest – just a gasp, a spurt, a shudder, followed by a 'thanks, love' and eight hours' slumped and snoring sleep. Leo's comes started slowly, somewhere deep down in his feet, and spread up, up, and out, as if there was some huge, dark, lashing animal trapped and raging in his body, fighting to get out. All those tired clichés about seas and earthquakes and volcanoes had never made any sense till Leo screwed me. I'd always assumed they were invented by frustrated virgins whose only sex life was Mills and Boon. But Leo *was* the sea, thwacking and pounding into me, sweeping away whole continents, snapping ships in half. When he came, I understood how the earth was formed a billion trillion years ago, life and flame leaping out of slime, God's finger shuddering into man's.

Not now. There was only slime now, his thing wet and sticky from my mouth, and a cold, clammy fury creeping through the room like the filling in the blinis, settling damp and sour on everything. Even the clock was limping – missing ticks, hiccuping on others. I could hear walls fidgeting and yawning, Karma jeering at our double impotence.

Leo suddenly turned over and punched his fist against the pile of cushions. 'Stupid sodding bloody useless thing . . .'

His adjectives were scattering like the cushions. I suddenly wanted to laugh. We were both so sort of *tragic*. Men always take their pricks too seriously, and Leo was worse than any. He was rampaging about the room now, like something in a Greek tragedy, rending his garments and plucking out his eyes merely because six inches had shrunk to one. I felt we had mourned enough. It was time to see the funny side, shrug it off, even change the subject. We could always try again this evening. Perhaps if I made tea, offered him a let-out . . .

I got up, took a step towards him – stopped. In front of me were the broken remnants of the phoenix vase, lying on the bureau holding down some music. It wasn't mended, it wasn't even a *feng huang* any more, just a few random pieces of weeping porcelain, doing duty as a paperweight.

I backed away. The room had looked so smug and sleek before, but now I could see the cracks. Leo was right – of course it wasn't funny. I realized, now, I might never have a mouth again, just some flimsy milksop gutless cringing thing, unable to kiss or bite with any real force or passion, wailing always, 'careful, gentle,' seeing fists instead of pricks. And that in turn would render Leo powerless – had already.

Some terrible justice had descended and disarmed him, so that by maiming me, he had somehow maimed himself. He was dragging on his clothes, as if to hide the damage. His body looked smaller, almost scraggy. He stormed across to the piano, opened it up, flung the cover off.

I waited for the crash of chords, the furious stampeding down the keyboard. This was his revenge. I had smashed his strength, his sex, his golden age, and now he would make me suffer. The room would quake and shudder, the piano roar. My mouth was already flinching with the assault of it. I tried to sink into the sofa, steel myself against this new bombardment.

Through the stretched darkness, I heard slow white notes fall like flakes of sorbet. The music was so frail, so unbearably sad and unassuming, it was like the print of a bird's foot quivering on my hand. It was the moment when a leaf falls, or a chrysalis stirs in sleep. It was fields greying, trees bending, things growing old and wise and wounded before they turned young and gold again. It was white healing sound, like nuns' fingers laid upon my mouth. Pain stopped and bruising faded. London crept away, and outside were only wisps of cloud and drifts of smoke and thin mists weeping into slow white rivers. It was so simple, it was child's music. Leo was the child he had never been, small and quiet and gentle, dwarfed by his own piano, practising for his second grade exam, with God and his parents smiling down at him.

The piece ended, faded. There were no rude chords, no crashing furious finales. Just a sigh, a ripple, a last ghost petal drifting to the floor. Not once had Leo stormed and raged, used his piano to deafen or outshout me or shriek his potency. I got up and stood beside his shoulder. His hands were on his knees, his back bowed. He could have been praying to some old white smiling God.

As usual, I had no idea what he had been playing, but this time it didn't matter. It was enough that he had made the piano sigh instead of scream. He had ground the music down for me until it was only a soft white purée gentle enough for my mouth, cut off the gristle, taken out the stones. I could hear the notes still whispering through the room, returning me to the same white simple world of Ray and Sister Aidan, lilies and ambrosia. And now he himself was part of it.

I kissed his neck. He turned round on the piano stool and laid his face against me, hiding it as if he were ashamed. He was still limp – I could see that from his jeans. I suddenly knew it was me who should say sorry. If Leo could play like that, he was a god, a seer, a conjurer, and had no need to make amends. I was the one who had inflicted all the damage – wounded his pride, disabled his prick, turned my knife in his limping self-esteem. I fell on my knees in front of the piano, paying homage to them both.

'I'm sorry, Leo,' I sobbed.

fifteen

'Ladies and gentlemen, Captain Lineham and his crew welcome you on board this BAC III. Will you kindly fasten your seat-belts and observe the no-smoking sign . . .'

I almost burst with joy. We were just two minutes from take-off! In one hour, twenty minutes, we would be touching down at Lourdes, and in less than one short day, I would be making my First Communion in the largest Catholic basilica in the world, with my new Catholic family thronging and rejoicing all around me. Thirteen weeks had drifted away like feathers. The Christmas holidays had merged into the Easter ones, winter into spring. Blood-red holly berries had given way to bridal almond blossom. My soul was no longer bleak and bruised and purple, but shining singing white.

The plane blazed into action as if someone had set a match to it. I sat and burned. I could feel the engines throbbing through my body, as it slowly turned, paused, inched, stopped, and then suddenly, astoundingly, roared along the runway – fast, faster, faster, the tarmac under it only a streak of grey hurtling speed. My stomach somersaulted, my ears screamed, as the runway wrenched itself away from us and dropped down, down, and all around was space, nothing, shock. We were up. We were flying. *I* was flying – not that heavy, lumbering, overloaded plane. It was my own joy and power which had lifted us off, flung us fifteen thousand feet into the air and kept us soaring, soaring through dazzling banks of cloud.

I turned to the man beside me. I wanted to fling my arms around his neck, tell him I loved him, show him my huge shining wings. Unfortunately, he was a Ukrainian with no English except, 'Yes, 'allo', which he'd already said three times. Now we stuck to smiles.

I smiled and smiled. He was part of my elation. The fact that even Ukrainians should journey to Lourdes only proved to me what a fabled spot it was. I'd read books and books about the place since leaving hospital. I knew, now, that a hundred different nations paid their homage to it. I wasn't sure whether that included the Ukraine, or whether the man beside me was a vital new statistic. There were five of his fellow countrymen flying with us, as well as Poles, Cypriots, Scots, a large contingent of Irish, and even two Japanese. Two or three package tours were sharing the same aircraft. Ours were the ones with the blue and white striped labels on our baggage and the blue badges of Our Lady pinned to our coats. Pax Pilgrims, we were called. I'd have chosen the tour from the name alone, which I remembered from school meant 'Peace'. But Ray also knew the man who owned the company, so they were allowing me to fly with them at a special rate, and yet arrange my own (cheaper) lodgings instead of staying at one of their block-booked hotels. Ray had cut through all the difficulties. He'd even approached some (Catholic) Lady Bountiful who raised money for things like Threatened Species, and although I wasn't a blue whale, she'd rustled up some cash.

There were fifty-two other Pax Pilgrims, fifty-two mothers, fathers, uncles, cousins, aunts – my new Catholic family – all of us wearing identical blue badges, united by the same faith, travelling to the same destination. We had already mixed and chatted in the departure lounge. It wasn't like an ordinary package tour – the badges seemed to break down barriers. A lady who introduced herself as Bridie had called me 'darlin'' twenty-seven times before our flight was even called. I was one of the youngest in the group, bar a sprinkling of children. Most of them were middle-aged or over, and three-quarters of them women. The outnumbered males looked grey and rather sheepish and wore chain-store raincoats over sticky nylon shirts. The women had tried harder. There were a lot of new crispy perms and white vinyl handbags, but the general effect was a wash of pastel crimplene enlivened here and there by a splash of poppies on some large floral bottom.

I felt slim and almost exotic in comparison. I'd washed my hair in henna and it hung dark and thick and coppery to my waist. I was wearing black velvet jeans which I'd bought in a good-as-new shop at a special rate. I'd chosen black because it was still a time of penitence. Although the Lenten fast was over and today was Easter Saturday, I'd decided to continue my own penances until the actual moment of my Communion on Resurrection Sunday. I'd been reading up about the sacraments as well as about Lourdes and I knew you needed to prepare yourself. Ray had taught me about mortifying the flesh. I'd seen him only half a dozen times since leaving hospital, but on every occasion he'd been shabby, sleepless, serving, burning and obviously half-starved. During Lent, he'd almost wasted away. He never made a song and dance about it – he was holy with a small 'h'.

'Ladies and gentlemen, this is Captain Lineham speaking. We have now reached our cruising height of twenty-five thousand feet and are passing over the English Channel. To the right, you can see . . .'

I grinned to myself. I knew he'd got it wrong. We were far far higher than twenty-five thousand feet and his so-called English Channel was simply one of the paddling pools in heaven. I could see tiny toy boats chuntering across it and God trailing his fingers in the water, leaving little lines of foam. Some of the clouds had fallen in, or were floating just on top like white waterlilies. The English Channel was another world away. Ray would have crossed it yesterday, holding the heads of his retching handicapped. He'd never held my head, but he'd gripped my hands for *hours* while I'd sat quaking in the dentist's waiting-room, a month or two ago. He'd taken me to the surgery himself for all the major onslaughts on my mouth, which was just as well, since the dentist's gentleness and courtesy stopped abruptly with his private bills. On the NHS, it was a brusque, 'Open wide', or a stream of idle chatter to his blonde dental nurse across my slumped and wincing form.

At least I had two new teeth. They were only temporary fixtures until the final operation on the adjoining two, but they made me look normal, even quite appealing, instead of like a witch. Mind you, I hated wearing that slimy foreign contraption in my mouth which skidded about and couldn't cope with apples. But Ray had helped again. He'd given me a point and purpose in my life, so that things like cut-price dentures and supercilious surgeons shunted into second place. We were both preparing for Lourdes. He didn't know, of course, about my intended First Communion. He must have assumed I'd made it twenty years ago, as a tot at my mother's knee. But he'd helped get me back into spiritual training, so to speak, and on top of his lists of prayers to say, and books to skim and sudden eccentric little sermons on God or Love or Lepers, I'd added my own private religious instruction as a second secret subject. I'd mugged up saints and sacraments and refreshed my memory on all the rules and rubric of the Church I'd known at school. Then I had stood outside it, nose pressed greedily against the window. Now I was already almost in the sweet-shop, and tomorrow God Himself would lay the bonbon on my tongue.

For the first time in my life, I had a true vocation, something which kept me busy and fulfilled. There wasn't time for boring Burton Bureau jobs like Mayfair receptionist now that I had a spiritual career, not to mention check-ups from a social worker and calls from the GP. The whole world seemed to know about my mouth. Busy professional people had me on their worksheets, in their case-notes, on their consciences. I began to feel important.

I was even learning French. (I'd tried out my first few words on the air hostess when I stepped aboard the plane, but unfortunately she answered me in South Thames English.) There were also all the Lies, which, like the French, took time and preparation. I'd had to lie to Adrian who kept worrying about me not having a Future and travelling on my own; and to Leo who was angry and suspicious when I turned his house into a chapel and spent his money on books called *Lourdes, a Modern Miracle*, and even to Ray who would keep harping back to Patricia Jane, when I'd long since packed her off to hospital with a badly fractured femur. Then there were the lies about my spending money. I had raised it, actually, by selling one of Leo's Victorian prints. It was only a mingy one with a besotted nymph and shepherd on it, and Leo was so preoccupied, he didn't even notice. Anyway, it wasn't really stealing, because one of the new, vital reasons I was going to Lourdes at all, was to bring him back a miracle. He needed one. In twelve weeks, he still hadn't got it up. He had refused to even try on more than three or four occasions. Each failure made him so desperate and humiliated, he dared not risk another. I knew I was responsible. By hitting me, he'd somehow disabled himself. Sometimes I felt a horrifying little dart of satisfaction, even pride, but most of the time I just felt anguished for him. He'd developed blinding headaches and dermatitis on his hands. He was rusting, ageing, while I lolled about on sofas reciting the Prayers Before Communion in French and *blooming*.

In fact, Leo did go out a lot, striding down the street with Karma trotting on one side and Otto on the other, or blazing off in Otto's haughty car. I hated that, but at least the house was less tense and agonized without him. He'd tried ginseng and a hypnotist, and when neither worked, he wrapped his headaches around him and made the whole place glower.

At first, I missed sex. I felt so desperate sometimes, I almost went up to total strangers in the street and begged them to be so kind as to rape me. Then I realized that perhaps it was a Sign. If I were meant to be a Catholic, then I shouldn't be screwing anyway, whatever Ray might say. I wanted to make my First Communion in a state of virgin purity like his, so I accepted Leo's limpness as a sort of extra Trial. I even stopped my masturbating. It made me feel odd at first, as if there was a great tall flashing lighthouse stuck inside me, shuddering on and off. I decided later, that was Sanctity.

I could feel it now, throbbing through my thighs with the motion of the plane. I stared out of my little port-hole window (God or Lady Bountiful had even wangled me a window-seat) and there were yards and *yards* of sanctity swirling just outside the plane, trailing from the lower rungs of heaven. I watched the whole dazzling cloudscape shift and merge, higher clouds rippling into lower ones, foam breaking on to foam. I had left the earth behind and turned into a bird, a star, a soul. There was no sea or land or cities any more, nothing to hurt, want, stain, roar, die. Just light and space, radiance and God. I touched the Ukrainian's hand. I wanted to share it with him.

'Yes, 'allo,' he said. The conversation ended. I wished, now, I'd learnt a little Ukrainian as well as French. And yet it didn't matter. It was enough just to waft my joy in his direction, spread it over everyone, like grace. I gazed around the plane at the rows of heads. Half the lips were moving as they recited the rosary, some of the mouths gaped open as their owners snored. Leo would have disowned the lot of them. Adrian would have enrolled them in an adult education class on 'Agnosticism, a Rational Approach'. I *loved* them.

It was the first time I'd flown without Adrian beside me, lecturing me on the geographical features we were flying over, or the cultural treats we were about to sample on our trip. He'd be lecturing now – to Janet. He'd taken her to Poitiers to convalesce, but I suspect it was really an excuse to study the Romanesque churches in the region. I could see him marching her up and down those endless naves, marvelling at the proportions, pointing out the symbolism in worn and crumbling carvings. She'd be bored, baffled, blistered. Adrian wouldn't notice. I'd had diarrhoea in Delphi and laryngitis in Crete, but we'd still done all the ruins. I'd lost my voice completely for three whole days, but with Adrian doing the talking, it hardly mattered. I wasn't even missing him. I'd never travelled on my own before. I'd gone straight from my mother and the F.E. College to Adrian, and from Adrian to Leo. Now, I suppose, I'd jumped the gulf to God, which meant I wasn't alone at all.

With five priests on the plane, God seemed even closer. Two of them were ours, a dark stocky Dubliner and a grey ethereal wraith from Chorley Wood who looked as if he had prayed himself away and was already in the Next World. It seemed strange, almost magical, to have priests in the family, wearing the same badge as mine. I could see their black shoulders sticking up among the froth of grey perms. And the sixth priest, my own priest, would be meeting me tonight. Ray had promised he would be in the underground basilica for the Easter Vigil, which was the opening ceremony of both our pilgrimages. He'd be accompanied by all his boys, of course, but we were bound to find some chance to be alone. He'd been so busy and committed these last three months, he needed and deserved a break.

The woman in the row in front of me suddenly turned round. We were so squashed together on the plane that my knees had been almost sticking in her bottom. I thought she was going to complain, but she only smiled and said, 'Praise be to God, they're serving lunch at last! I'm ravenous, aren't you?'

I shook my head. Several rows in front of us, two stewardesses were manoeuvring a huge metal trolley along the aisle, doling out trays and snapping open bottles. As they swayed and clattered nearer, I could feel my stomach screaming out for permission to end its fast.

'No,' I told it firmly. I was determined not to eat a single crumb for two whole days. Good Friday had been the first – all good Catholics starve themselves on *that* day – but I was going one better. My First Communion would be all the more glorious for having suffered for it. Anyway, I had to pay for Leo's miracle. I couldn't expect a return to a full six or seven inches, without first punishing the flesh.

I took my tray and stared at it. There were four little plastic niches filled with food. One cradled a rubbery boiled egg, split apart and crouching on a mattress of cold cooked peas and carrots, blanketed with mayonnaise, the next a slimy slice of ham, hiding a salad so insubstantial it looked like one of Janet's 'garnishes', the third held a roll and cheese, both unnaturally pale, and in the fourth, wet glacé cherries bled into whipped cream trifle. All these offerings were tightly covered with a layer of cellophane, stretched taut like a Durex. The Ukrainian ripped his off and started on the trifle, which I think he must have mistaken for some sort of Russian *hors d'oeuvre*. I could see shiny mandarins and fat wet sponge quivering on his teaspoon. He left both his cherries till last, and then ate them slowly, rapturously, with a dollop of the cream. I turned away, to try and distract myself, but there was more whipped cream outside, a whole skyful of it, piped in rosettes all the way to heaven. God was the cherry on my own cream trifle. I would swallow Him on Sunday. Who needed mortal food?

When I looked back again, the Ukrainian had his paper napkin tucked around his neck and was biting into his cheese. I could see a line of large uneven teethmarks trampled over the square of processed Cheddar. I glanced at his teeth to see if they matched the marks. Since my accident I was obsessed by teeth. Before, they'd just been part of people, like nails or hair or necks, something you took for granted and hardly even noticed, but now I saw them everywhere – teeth grinning from posters or leaping out of magazines, bared teeth greeting you before you knew their owners' names. I gave people marks for their teeth – ten out of ten for white, bright even ones, seven out of ten if they had their own at all. The Ukrainian got seven.

The stewardess brought coffee, which I decided to drink – since the cups were too small, it hardly counted anyway. There were two little paper sachets, one of sugar and one of something called creamer which looked like powdered soul. I ignored them both, as black bitter coffee was more of a penance. The Ukrainian had two sugars and a double Cognac and then started on his roll. I was quite relieved when they took the trays away.

I was so empty, the coffee had gone right through me, so I squeezed past his knees and walked along to the toilet at the far end of the plane, passing half my family on the way. Several of them smiled and nodded, and the Irish priest called, 'How's it going, Thea?' which *thrilled* me, because I'd only half mumbled my name to him and it can't have been an easy one when most of his flock were called Mary. The seventh Mary in our group also remembered me and said, 'Nearly there now, darlin',' and I stood in the queue for the toilet and felt a wave of whipped-cream joy surge over me, I was a darlin', a daughter, a member of a large and happy family, not just a tourist wasting time and squandering money, but a pilgrim with a purpose in my life.

The loo was so small and smelly, I decided to count it as another penance. I stared at my face in the mirror above the wash-basin. It was almost beautiful. My scars were fading and I'd covered my forehead with a special camouflage cream I'd got from the doctor. My teeth looked white and at least three-quarters normal. My eyes shone with the glory of my new religion. I sat on the toilet seat and *glowed*. Through the door, I could hear an announcement crackling over the intercom: *'Ladies and gentlemen, in a few minutes we will be arriving at Lourdes. Would you please return to your seats, fasten your seat-belts and extinguish all cigarettes.'*

I almost ran back up the aisle. I mustn't miss a moment of this glorious, unique descent, the goal I'd longed for since the Upper Fourth. I could already see the land – little patchwork fields tipping sideways and still tangled up with cloud, brown ribbon roads suddenly changing direction as the plane did. Closer now – furrows on the fields, dark splodges of forest, the bowed heads of poplars dodging down from the roar of the engines.

I gripped my seat. We were lurching, tipping, out of control. Clouds shot away from us, fields swooped up to thwack us and then dived off again. Something had gone wildly, blindly wrong. We were about to crash. Any minute now, the plane would hurtle on to the runway, land sickeningly on its head and roll over, over, over . . .

I shut my eyes. It didn't matter really. Even if we were all smashed to pieces, what more glorious end than to perish in the town of Bernadette? To lie in the peace of the basilica, surrounded by fifty-two dead family, with a hundred priests weeping out a requiem.

I only hoped my mother wouldn't ruin everything by demanding my ashes back. She wouldn't really *want* them – it would be just convention, or a final attempt to circumscribe me. She'd stopper me into a neat, no-nonsense urn and stand me on her mantelpiece, between the drooping Dresden shepherdess and the coldly correct clock which pounced on every second. I almost screamed in protest. I wanted to lie full-length on my back, tangled up with earth and flowers and nature, and all Bernadette's townsmen trampling and jostling over my bare body.

The plane lurched so wildly, I was almost disinterred. We fell five rungs of a ladder in as many seconds. I had already lost my stomach and my heart. Only moments now until all my other organs were just pulp on the tarmac. I sent up a silent plea to Bernadette.

'Please,' I prayed. 'Let me be buried in Lourdes.'

sixteen

We didn't crash and it wasn't Lourdes. The airport was sited six miles north, at Tarbes. They couldn't put it any nearer – there wasn't room with all the souvenirs. Tarbes had tricky runways lying north to south when the Pyrenees ran east to west – hence the turbulence. It was the sort of thing Adrian would have told me, but I had to wait for Bridie who'd been to Lourdes twenty-three times and said they often had descents like that, especially if the pilot was C. of E.

We were still a drive away from the town of Bernadette – six enchanted miles in which our three motor coaches played follow-my-leader along small winding roads edged with mincing poplars, and slowly the mountains in the distance moved closer and closer in, until they were standing up all around us, shouting out a welcome.

I was sitting next to Doris who came every year at Easter in thanksgiving for her husband's holy death. She nudged me suddenly in the middle of their last night together, when three priests and two doctors were joining in the *Requiem aeternum*. I wasn't listening, really. I was too engrossed in watching the fields dwindle and the urban sprawl begin.

'Look, Thea, we're coming into Lourdes! See the sign.'

I looked. It said 'Lourdes', just as it might have said Luton or Southend. Surely the name should have been surrounded with a halo or picked out in fairy lights. The streets were grey, the shops busy. Buildings squashed against each other on both sides of the street. It was a town – just a town – an ordinary, bustling, crowded sort of no-man's land, with petrol fumes and litter bins on the lamp-posts, and women in headscarves, and big lumbering coaches. I had expected a village, a tiny white hamlet with a cloud of holiness curling up from it like smoke. Oh, I know I'd read all the books, pored over statistics about growth and expansion, swelling tourist figures, problems of traffic circulation. I knew that even since my schooldays, another million visitors had been added to the annual total. But somehow, I'd never quite believed it. I still saw Lourdes in terms of my school-friends' photographs – mysterious and sacred and very sort of rural, with all my classmates standing in blue cloaks and white veils against soaring churches or banks of lighted candles, flanked by priests and nuns. Now there wasn't a church or priest in sight, just more and more stalls and shops choked with souvenirs, more and more cheap hotels. It could have been the Costa Brava, without the Costa.

'But where's the *Grotto?*' I asked. 'And the basilicas? The place where Our Lady actually appeared?'

'Oh, way away yet, dear. This is just the commercial part. Lourdes sprawls a bit, you see.'

I nodded. No point being disappointed. After all, it was really a proof of Bernadette's power that she had transformed a tiny hamlet into this great metropolis, brought more pilgrims here than journeyed even to Mecca and Jerusalem. All important places had their commercial side. There'd probably be souvenir stalls outside heaven, selling plastic St Peters and spun-sugar angels. It didn't matter really. Anyway, the Grotto would be different. Ray had told me they didn't allow any shops or new development on what they called Our Lady's Domain, a whole thirty acres, set apart like a sanctuary for baths and basilicas, Masses and processions. That was the real, essential Lourdes, the nucleus, the holiness. These were just the wrappings, the outer layer, the twopenny-ha'penny sideshows outside the Great Top.

I turned away from a window display of pink and purple rosaries, dangling over wooden plaques with plaster roses on them and inscriptions saying, '*J'ai prié pour vous à la Grotte.*' I would pray for Leo at the *Grotte*, bring him back not a pink and purple rosary, but a new resplendent prick. All would be well. Even the rosaries were holy testimony to how many pious people were praying here, that God and His Mother were the chief tourist attractions, instead of heated pools or sun-drenched sands. We even had the sun, still weak perhaps, but smiling from a blue sky, whereas back in London there was fog and drizzle.

'Which hotel are *you* at?' asked Doris, as we crawled past a pâtisserie and I closed my eyes against the lure and sacrilege of strawberry tarts. 'I'm in the *Notre Dame de* what-d'you-call-it. I should have booked the *Astoria*. Edie's just told me it's got the cheapest booze in Lourdes.'

I was almost shocked. Most of our group had already bought gin and whisky on the plane, but I'd assumed it was to take back home with them, along with the Holy Water.

'I'm . . . er . . . not at a hotel,' I said.

'You must be. All our lot are either in the *Notre Dame* or the *Astoria*. Except for a few toffs who can afford the *de la Grotte*. That's four-star and frogs' legs.'

'No, I'm staying with a Madame Simonneaux.'

'Madame *who*?'

'Well, I don't quite know how you pronounce it, but she takes in lodgers, cheap. She's very vaguely related to Bernadette. Her uncle's father's niece's sister was . . .'

Doris looked at me with new respect. 'You mean, you actually know a relative of St Bernadette?'

'Well, not exactly *know*, but . . .'

We had already stopped at the first hotel which was pinioned between two larger ones, but had a shop on its ground floor with souvenirs encroaching right across the pavement. We had reached the centre of the newer, lower town and the streets were really crowded now, hotels all but bumping into each other, and traffic-logged drivers swearing on their horns.

'Right, this is us,' said Doris, collecting up her bags. 'Hey, Mary, listen to this – Thea here's staying with one of St Bernadette's family. Mind you get her to pray for you. She's got the right connections.'

Mary looked as if she was about to ask me to bless her rosary, but the driver shooed her <u>off</u>. She and all the other Marys were collecting up their bags and struggling down the steps. At least two thirds of my new Pax family had already turned their backs. Only one or two of them had even stopped to wave.

Next stop was the *Astoria*. The last of my aunts and mothers clambered off, along with the courier and both the priests. There was just me and the driver left. At least he spoke a sort of English.

'Sorry Mam'selle,' he said. 'Is walking now.'

'What?' I said. I couldn't remember learning the French for 'what', though I suppose it should have been the first word in the phrase book.

'Walking. *Marcher. Aller à pied*. How d'you say? Foot, feet . . .'

'Oh, I *see*. Look, it's a bit much, isn't it? I mean, expecting me to get out and walk when I don't even know where I'm going and I've got a *case* and everything.'

'You want case, Mam'selle?' He pushed me down the steps,

extracted the last piece of luggage from the underbelly of the coach and almost threw it into my arms. 'Here is case, Mam'selle. *Voilà.*' Then he squeezed past me to the driving seat, closed the automatic doors, and accelerated off. I stared at the blue and white striped label with the tall blue Virgin on it. I could see twenty identical blue Virgins disappearing through the glass doors of the *Astoria*. I almost dashed after them, begged them to find room for me, just a crust and a corner would do, so long as they didn't leave me on my own. Then I remembered Ray. I wasn't alone at all. I would be meeting the Pax brigade again in just a few short hours, processing down to the great basilica with them, where God and Ray and Bernadette would all be waiting for me. It was only natural to feel a little low today. Any good Catholic would and should, when our Boss had just been crucified and was still lying in His tomb. The whole church was poised and waiting for the Resurrection, and until He soared shining up to heaven, it was only fitting we should mourn.

I picked up my case and studied the little sketch map Ray had drawn for me. It wasn't easy, especially with the streets so crowded and wheelchairs to avoid. Actually there weren't as many sick as I'd imagined – it was still early in the season. Most of the pilgrims looked neither well nor ill, but sort of grey and shabby and droopy, as if they suffered not from dramatic diseases shouting out for miracles, but minor ailments like piles and prolapses and acid indigestion. I don't suppose you bother Our Lady with things like haemorrhoids when she's busy with cancer of the bowel. I must admit I was a little disappointed. I had somehow expected the place to be littered with men sick of the palsy, who would suddenly leap to their feet and fling away their stretchers, shouting out, 'A miracle, a miracle!'

Give them time, I thought. Wait till tomorrow, wait for the Resurrection. Anything could happen by tomorrow. Today they were simply tired or hungry or jet-lagged, or had even lost their lodgings like I had.

After two culs-de-sac and three wrong turnings, I eventually asked for directions in a shop. It said 'English spoke' on a notice over the counter, but was mostly full of Italians exclaiming over a shelf display of white plastic Virgins. The statues were all identical, but ranged in height from midget to monumental, so that they looked like the slope of a white plastic mountain beetling upwards. I counted seventy-five before I got dizzy and gave up. Seventy-five gleaming gilt halos reaching higher and higher up to heaven, one hundred and fifty blank blue eyes tracing a graph from shelf to ceiling. The miraculous medals were even more impressive. There were so many, they'd been tipped into a sort of dustbin like a lucky dip, and were more or less uncountable. Ray had told me some of the shops ordered thirty thousand dozen at a time. I bought one to pay for the directions. It *must* have been miraculous, because Ray's map made sense for the first time since I'd studied it, and in just three minutes I was standing outside the house in the street he'd marked.

I stopped a moment before daring to go in. It must have been one of the narrowest streets in Lourdes. The houses on one side tried to reach out and touch their fellows on the other, and then gave up and sulked. Number six was very tall and angular, squashed between a butcher's shop and a seedy *pension*. Its stained and flaking stucco was criss-crossed with a tangle of electric wires, and a metal balcony dripped rust like sour brown tears. Two dustbins crouched outside it with the first flies of the season crawling over them.

I tried not to look at the butcher's, which was open to the street and festooned with great bloody haunches of cow and pig, some still with fur and bristles and only missing their tongues, livers and intestines, which were piled on trays in front of them. A large man in what had once been a white apron before the massacre, was grinning and gesturing at me from the counter. I decided Madame Simonneaux was the lesser of two evils, so I walked up the steps and rang the bell.

She was a long time coming, but when she did, she wasn't evil at all, just tired and shabby. She was wearing an overall and bedroom slippers and had three young children clinging to her skirts. Another case of prolapse, I suspected.

I handed over the little card which Ray had typed for me, with my name on it and how long I was staying. She didn't seem impressed. I could have been Morton, Jones, O'Reilly, or Lady Bountiful herself, so long as I paid my bill. She asked for the money before she'd even said hallo. Even my French could tell the difference between '*Bonjour, Madame*', and 'Seven hundred francs in cash, please.' Once I'd handed over the notes, she relaxed a bit, and led me up the stairs which were dark and narrow and covered with several different offcuts of lino, so that the patterns changed every three or four steps. I began to feel dizzy. Madame stopped and panted every few minutes (I added anaemia to prolapse). She had left the children down below and I could hear them quarrelling and grumbling. I'd have liked to have made some kind remark about their ages or achievements, or even dropped in a word or two about the weather – anything to break the rather oppressive silence. But the only French I could recall was, '*Où va cet autobus?*' which I didn't feel was relevant.

My room was at the very top and looked as if it had crawled on its side in order to squeeze into the space beneath the roof. The walls were painted a sort of blotchy brown and there were three separate sections of some scratchy stuff on the floor, with gaps where they didn't meet. A narrow iron bed took up most of the floorspace, and opposite, a rail with two broken wooden hangers on it, which I suppose was the French for wardrobe. In the corner was a screen only half-concealing a stained and cracked washbasin, and a bidet with a notice pinned above it saying, 'Forbidden to urine'.

I sat on the bed (which sank and shrank away from me) and counted my blessings. I had a room to myself with real running water. I had a chair with three legs. I had a picture of St Bernadette – a real photograph, in fact, just above my head, smiling and encouraging me, reminding me that she had shared a room far worse than this with a whole sweaty, noisy family. I even had a window. I walked over to it, pushed aside the rusty iron-mesh blind, and tugged it open.

I gasped. I was so high up, the dingy streets had dropped away, and I was staring up at a narrow tunnel of sky with a portion of the majestic Pyrenees embedded in it, pointing its craggy finger up to heaven. I leaned out further. The flanks of the mountains were swathed in the last golden light of the fading afternoon, their foreheads streaked with snow. The grey of the streets had changed to green and white and gold. I had only to lift up my eyes to see the glory of the place. So far, I had been rooting around the pavements, snuffling in the gutters, so no wonder I had missed it. Lourdes *was* only a village when seen against its surroundings – a tiny toy-town tipped into a green valley, with great grown-up mountains towering over it. Through it rushed the headstrong River Gave, tossing and frothing from the mountain peaks, until it bowed its head by the holy shrine itself. I couldn't see the Grotto, but I glimpsed the tall silver spire of the Basilica of the Immaculate Conception glittering against a golden sky. This was the Lourdes I had come for – it was all there, all waiting. How could my room be cramped when a spire soared just outside it, or dingy, when those mountains ringed it round?

Anyway, I'd turned my back on comforts. If I was following Ray, I should *rejoice* that there was only one grubby sheet, and that brackish-brown water coughed and grumbled out of the taps when I tried to turn them on. I could pile penance on privation until tomorrow glorious morning when Christ rose shining from the tomb.

Meanwhile, I'd join Him on His back. I was exhausted from the journey and it was still several hours until the Easter Vigil which began at nine o'clock. There was no evening meal to mop up one or two of them. Not only was I fasting, but I had agreed with Ray that I would pay just for breakfast at Madame's. He was hoping to wangle me in to some of the meals at his hostel, and the rest of the time I'd buy bread and oranges and eat them in my room.

I fell back on the bed. I longed to see the Grotto, but I'd decided to save it until Ray was at my side. It was the high point of the pilgrimage and I wanted his hand in mine when I first set foot upon that spot where Bernadette had knelt before Our Lady. We would go tonight, together, when the Vigil was over. Meanwhile, I must prepare. I threw the pillow on the floor, kicked the duvet off. Christ had no comforts in the grave and I must follow Him. I closed my eyes, took His hand. While my fellow pilgrims guzzled veal and chips in the *Astoria*, I would spirit myself to my own tomb – that great underground basilica, from which tonight I would arise triumphantly a Catholic.

seventeen

Five hours later, I entered the basilica, not in dreams this time. I gasped. It *was* like the tomb. I was groping my way through a huge mausoleum in almost total darkness.

Nothing had quite prepared me for the size and strangeness of the place. I'd seen pictures of it, of course; knew it was one of the largest underground buildings in the world, with wide sloping ramps leading down to it and huge concrete ribs straining up to the pre-stressed concrete roof. People had compared it to a massive underground car-park or an aircraft hangar. It reminded me more of a giants' air-raid shelter, but perhaps that was just the dark and all the scurrying people jostling for a place. Easy to have been lost, swept aside by all those thronging crowds, trampled underfoot. I huddled close to Bridie, kept my eye on our two Pax priests who were shepherding us through the gloom to the section where the English pilgrims sat. We were all arranged by nation – Belgians next to English, across from them the Germans, then Spanish, Poles, Italians, Austrians, French. The place held twenty-five thousand worshippers. My family had swollen now to twenty-five thousand relatives, pressing and milling all around me, each of us grasping an unlighted candle, symbol of our spiritual darkness. Slowly, their bodies began to take shape and substance in the gloom. I even made out features – fifty thousand eyes, a hundred thousand arms and legs, give or take a few for the blind and handicapped. I could see rows and rows of wheelchairs banked round the altar, stretchers, crutches, trolley-beds, with their nurses and attendants. Ray would be among them. I couldn't see him, of course – the faces were only blurs – but I could almost feel his prayers breaking over me.

Suddenly, the whole congregation sort of rippled as if a wind had sprung up across it and set up little waves. Bridie nudged me in the ribs. 'Here they come!' she whispered. I looked where she was pointing, saw a stream of white-robed figures frothing into the basilica like a white wake behind the dark hulk of a ship. Never before had I seen so many priests. At school we were lucky to have our one scrawny

Father Murphy and perhaps a visiting chaplain on high days and Holy Days; at Westminster Cathedral I'd seen up to half a dozen at the altar, with two or three more patrolling the aisles. But here were two *hundred*. Two hundred radiant white seraphim dispersing the gloom, two hundred representatives of God on earth. There was even a bishop. Some of my swankier schoolfriends had been introduced to bishops, kissed their rings, curtseyed to them, begged them to bless a prayer-book or a rosary. They had told me this with the same hushed awe and pride my mother reserved for Rothschilds. Yet here was my own tame bishop, parading up the aisle for me, welcoming me into his fold, resplendent in his snow-white chasuble and gold-encrusted mitre, and carrying a gleaming crosier. I had never seen a crosier before. I knew it was the pastoral staff, the shepherd's crook. Christ was the shepherd, we His lambs. It felt safe and warm and sacred to be a lamb.

The priests had reached the altar now, and the entire congregation (handicapped excepted) risen to its feet. There was no sound except the shuffling. The massive organ was dumb, the choir silent. And yet the hush was so tense, so expectant, it was more like a stifled scream. Muffled coughs choked through it, a sudden groan from an invalid or gasp from an idiot sliced it in half. Hopes, fears, prayers, longings, clogged and stained that winding-sheet of silence.

Suddenly a tiny point of light sprang through the shadows, a pinprick in a huge lowering cave. The weak flame flickered, wavered, almost went out. Twenty-five thousand people held their breaths. This was the paschal candle which would illuminate the world, the flame which would pierce the sin and death and darkness of the Lenten night.

The flame shuddered, sagged, and then miraculously revived, flared higher, almost sang. Every eye was on it as slowly it tipped sideways to light a second candle, a third, a fourth, a fifth, and suddenly there were five, six, seven quivering tongues of light. Every candle lit another candle, priest illuminating priest, until there was a circle of golden flame around the altar, two hundred candles holding hands. The first candle moved outwards now, bobbing down towards the altar-rails, reaching out to the darkness all around it, until every pilgrim, every nation, was lighting its candle from the next. The whole gigantic basilica and its throbbing congregation were coming alive, coming alight, as little by little, one by one, twenty-five thousand candles turned from cold wax to leaping flame. Rock-hard pillars seemed to move and tremble. The solid roof dissolved into shadows. Eyes, medals, buttons, buckles, glinted in the gloom. Faces thawed from blank stares into rippling, flickering surfaces, candle flames were trapped in every eye. We had all left the base element of earth behind and been transmuted into fire.

We were one. Each individual candle flame was swallowed up in the total glare and roar of light. Mine was one of them. It was impossible to be an outcast any more. My candle had been lit by Bridie's and hers by Paddy's and his by a swarthy woman in the Belgian group, and hers by a nun's and the nun's by a child on crutches and the child's by a priest, and the priest was God on earth, so my candle had been lit by God Himself. I stood clutching it in front of me, watching the huge, saw-toothed shadows of the Easter palms fling themselves across the altar, knowing my own light had helped to banish the darkness of the world. I was fiery, radiant, as strong as one of the gigantic thrusting pillars supporting the heaviest concrete roof in Christendom. I belonged. Not only to my own Pax family but to all the nations shimmering around me, all the billion million Catholics who had ever lived since Christ and now sat smiling on their fat white clouds.

'Alleluia, alleluia,' sang the chief celebrant, his voice leaping like a hawk to heaven.

'Alleluia, alleluia!' thundered the whole church in response, and the sea of lighted candles swept up, up, as if twenty-five thousand puppet masters had all pulled their strings at the same instant. I, too, had lifted my candle high above my head. I wasn't even a Catholic, yet I was following the ritual. It was like dancing when you don't know the steps. If your partner is skilled enough, you go along with him, never stumbling, never treading on his feet. My partner was God, so every time I had to kneel or stand or sit or raise my candle, I did it exactly as I should. If there are angels (which Leo doubts and Adrian classes under 'Paranormal'), then they had all flocked here to join us. I could sense them filling all the empty spaces in the church, their soft white wings brushing the rough grey concrete of the walls.

My brain had been kindled as well as my candle, because slowly, gropingly, I began to understand lines and fragments of the service. I recognized the Latin from my schooldays, but there were other languages alternating with it and I realized now that every nation was allowed a share of the prayers and readings in its own tongue. Adrian would have understood them all. I could make out odd words here and there, different accents, different intonations. And then suddenly, the high electric voice of the English priest cut through the congregation like a saw on stone. Every word he said was addressed to me:

'This is the night when Christ
broke the bonds of death
and rose triumphant from the grave . . .'

I had broken the bonds of sin and death myself. This was my own glorious baptism. I knew from all my homework that the early Christian catechumens were baptized on this Easter Saturday night, before they received the Body and Blood of Christ. I was following their example. I loved the word catechumen. It sounded mysterious and special. It *was* special – I was the only catechumen in that whole thronging congregation. All the others were cradle Catholics who had been baptized long ago, so in a sense, the entire ceremony was for my benefit alone. All those thousands had only gathered there to witness my admission to the Church. They would renew the baptismal promises made for them as babies, as a symbol and an echo of my own vows. My years of schoolgirl prayers would at last be answered, as the outcast was admitted, the leper made clean.

Latin, Italian, German, French, washed over me. Incense soared to the ceiling like the soft smoky wings of the Holy Ghost. They had switched on all the lights now, and the church blazed with splendour. The English priest was standing at the lectern, directly facing me, his eyes piercing down almost into mine. I recognized the lines from Genesis.

'And God created man in His own image. In the image of God He created him, male and female both. And He blessed them, saying, "Increase and multiply and fill the earth."'

I knelt. The hard stone floor bit into my knees. I knew now that this was the time to pray for Leo's miracle. The priest had just declared sex holy and therefore Leo's prick was holy. I prayed that it would swell and harden like a paschal candle and that he and I would increase and multiply and fill the earth. That had been God's first command to man, therefore my life was sacred. All I had been doing with my forty-seven men was seeking to procreate. My record was poor as yet – only one four-month foetus pickled in a jar, but after these rituals of fire and water, I would pour out sons upon the earth. Janet would be shamed as Leo's sallow features were reproduced a score of times between my loins. The English priest was already prophesying it:

'The time is coming when every plant and tree in the land shall swell and be fruitful . . .'

The organ was resounding now, shrills and squawks of sound echoing round the walls, the whole congregation roaring out Hosanna. I rose from my knees, whispered some excuse to Bridie, and crept out through the swarming, singing thousands. Everyone made way for me. It was like the Red Sea parting so that I could pass. My heart was so full, I dared not stay a moment longer, in case I dissolved into flame or turned into a disembodied spirit before I had made my First Communion. The catechumens would have made it there and then, on the same night as their baptism. I preferred to wait till morning, when Ray could lay that first host on my tongue. He would be acting priest then, one of the two hundred sanctified, robed in shining vestments instead of just a helper with his handicapped. He had told me already he planned to concelebrate the Easter Mass.

I walked up the wide ramp to the exit. The crowds had spilled over even here, and were kneeling on the concrete, peering over the balcony, praying, singing, taking part. I flung them a handful of smiles, then pushed my way to the shivering night outside. The sky looked dark and very far away, the stars more scarce and grudging than the wealth of dazzling candles in the church. But the air was so clean and cold, I gulped down greedy mouthfuls of it. My stomach was fainting for some substance. I almost took a bite out of the moon, it looked so fat and full and creamy. But this was the great Domain where everything was holy. I could see the other two basilicas, one built above the other, soaring up to heaven, blazing with floodlights, haloed by stars. I could almost hear Christ rising from His tomb. The breeze in the plane trees sounded like the swish and rustle of His garments.

I stood against the railings which ringed the ghostly white statue of the Crowned Virgin, where Ray had arranged to meet me after the Vigil. It was the Number One Rendezvous in Lourdes, like the lions in Trafalgar Square or the Juice Bar at Harrods. It was almost deserted now. Ray and all the rest were still coffined in the tomb of the underground basilica. I had risen early, prematurely. I sat down on the cold stone step to wait for him. Stuck all round the railings were bouquets of fresh spring flowers left there by Our Lady's fans. I pulled one free. I would present it to Ray as soon as he appeared for our assignation. He had given me a faith, a purpose, and a Resurrection – the least I could do was pay him back with flowers.

Almost absent-mindedly, I broke off one of the blossoms. It was a round sort of daisy thing with small white petals. I sniffed it, but it didn't smell. I could hear my stomach rumbling and complaining. It was difficult to keep my thoughts on heaven, when my belly gasped for food. I remembered my father feeding me at my birthday party ('She's far too old for *that*,' my mother had snapped), cutting the cake into easy little fingers, his own hands huge against my lips.

'One for Daddy,' he'd said. 'One for all the poor sick people in the world.'

Strange he'd said that, when here I was in Lourdes surrounded by the sick and poor. It was almost like a Sign.

I plucked off a daisy petal and placed it on my tongue. Flowers didn't count as food. 'One for Daddy,' I whispered.

eighteen

'Hi!' said Ray. He was still in jeans on Resurrection night and pushing a wheelchair. The quiet, deserted square had suddenly turned into Piccadilly Circus, as all the crowds streamed out of the basilica, staining the night with their bright, raucous voices. Ray had his own mini-crowd in tow, three-quarters of them male and crippled, but at least a quarter blatantly female, with long hair and longer legs, frothing and giggling all around him. When I saw them, I chucked away my flowers. I didn't want to turn into a laughing-stock.

'Hi!' I said, trying to exclude them from my greeting and fix only on Ray's face, which looked paler and more haggard than I'd remembered it.

He came forward and kissed me on both cheeks. It was such a brief, formal gesture, I didn't count it as a kiss. I wanted him to crush me in his arms, lift me high above the people, and set me down somewhere soft and sheltered, where there were only the two of us.

'This is John,' he said, turning to the boy in the wheelchair. I say 'boy', but he looked like a full-grown man, with huge shoulders and stubble on his chin. When Ray had talked about his boys, I'd always imagined *little* fellows, strapped into push-chairs and playing with their rabbits. Most of these were giants.

John stared at me, not rudely, just stolidly, as if I were a new cow in his field. His mouth was a broken hinge, gaping open as if it were waiting for repair. He had one good hand, strong and almost beautiful, and one left claw, limp and curving inwards, missing two of its fingers. Ray was buttoning up his coat for him. I turned away, but there were other boys, crowding all around us. Half of them were in wheelchairs, two or three in callipers and one lying horizontal on a trolley-bed. That one jeered and pointed at me, the smallest picked his nose.

'I'd like you all to meet Thea,' Ray said. 'Mrs Thea Morton, a friend of mine from London.'

There was a sort of awkward silence, made worse by the babbling murmur in the square. I wished my name was Mary and that he hadn't called me Mrs. Perhaps that was to protect himself, so that they wouldn't guess he'd ever touched my breasts. John was still staring at me, the lad beside him making strange convulsive gestures with his head.

One of the girls came forward and shook my hand.

'Hi!' she said. 'I'm Cammie. Short for Camilla. Wasn't the service *great*? Bit long I thought, but then they always are. So you're a friend of Ray's.' Ray had turned away again and was busy with the horizontal boy. A younger girl with ginger pigtails was holding on to his arm as if she owned it. I noticed, now, there were more male helpers than female, but somehow the girls loomed larger. 'He's really great, isn't he?' said Cammie, lowering her voice as if she were in the confessional. 'I mean you'd never guess he was a priest. He's so sort of relaxed. Are you a nurse?'

I mumbled something indecipherable.

'Great!' said Cammie. 'Mary-Lou and me are both nurses. And Val's a speech therapist. That's Val, over there. And wait till you meet our doctor. He's a scream! Dr Norman Bradbury. We just call him Fatso. He's trying to lose a stone. Where did you do your training, by the way?'

'Er . . . Guy's,' I said. I tried to edge out of her way and move closer to Ray who was standing beside a tall sulky boy of about seventeen.

'This is Lionel,' said Ray. 'He's deaf and dumb, but he likes it if you smile.'

I smiled. Lionel looked more normal than the rest. All his limbs and features were in their proper places and he was walking on his own legs. He was even beautiful, with dark thick hair and full wet red fat lips. I smiled so hard, my face ached. Ray had said 'deaf and dumb' so matter-of-factly, he might have been saying left-handed or blue-eyed.

'Ray,' I whispered. '*Listen.*' I'd never be ill enough to keep him for myself. You had to lose your tongue and your ears for that, or at least a couple of fingers. But he was my priest, too, and I ached to be alone with him, if only for half an hour. I needed him to take me to the Grotto, to light a candle with me.

'Ray,' I tried again. He wasn't even looking at me, but fussing over a boy in a bib who was dribbling in a wheelchair and had a huge head lolling on top of a shrunken pygmy body, as if someone had muddled up the parts of two separate people.

'And we mustn't forget Jimmy, must we. Say hallo to Thea, Jim.'

Jimmy dribbled in my direction, grinned at his own wasted, twisted legs, and said 'Hallo Jim.'

I backed away. 'Look, Ray, there's something I want to . . .'

'And this is Mike, who comes from Wales. He can even talk a bit of Welsh, can't you, kid? And that's Barry there beside him. Barry's a whiz with a football.'

I stared at Barry. There was only a hollow blanket where his football legs should have been.

'Hi,' I said. 'Ray, I think it might be better if . . .'

'And these are all our helpers. Sam's the tall one there, Desmond next to him, Alan, Eddie . . . Oh, and this is Mary-Lou. She's a midwife. Though we're hoping not to need her in *that* capacity!'

They all laughed. I hated her at once. Midwives have privileges enough, without being beautiful on top of it. She had hair as long as mine, but fairer, and the sort of breasts which make tee-shirts look obscene. Ray went over to her.

'Do you think the group would mind if Thea came up to the house with us? She's on her own, you see. Her friend broke a leg and couldn't come.'

'Oh, bad luck! Yes, of course, Thea, do join us. It's John's birthday and we're going to have some wine and stuff.'

'Look, I don't really think . . .' I started. I didn't want to join them. I hadn't even seen the Grotto yet, and I hated the thought of being granted permission by a 'group' I clearly didn't belong to; made into an outsider again when all the rest were midwives, helpers, priests. I hadn't even the distinction of being handicapped. A gammy tooth or two couldn't compare with *these* cases.

'Great!' said Cammie. 'We'll squeeze you on the bus. Can you sing, by the way?'

'No.'

'Pity. We'd planned to have a sing-song and we need a few more female voices. We girls are rather heavily outnumbered. We have to be careful with all these lady-killers around! Especially Jimmy, there. You're a terror, aren't you, Jim?'

Jimmy grinned and dribbled. I wondered if he wore his bib when he killed the ladies. I made one last attempt to prise Ray away from the group. 'Listen, Ray, I know you're busy, but I thought perhaps . . .'

He took my hand and squeezed it. 'Not now, Thea, my girl. It's the lads' time now. But you come along with us – they'd like that. In fact, if you push John, I can go on ahead and find our bus.'

That 'my girl' was the only thing he'd given me. He'd more or less ignored every word I'd said, and now he'd disappeared into the crowds. *Why* was it the lads' time? They'd had him now for two solid days, not to mention all the months before. He *lived* with them, for God's sake.

I'd never pushed a wheelchair in my life. I was terrified I'd do it wrong or tip John out or something. He kept turning round and staring at me. Lionel tagged behind, pulling at my arm and making strange soundless movements with his lips. I felt deaf and dumb myself. I'd always kept well away from the disabled. Even back in London, when Ray had suggested that I meet his boys, I'd totally refused. But now they were surrounding me, jostling me, touching me, and Ray himself was not even there to help.

John had turned round again. I could see his lips moving, his broken mouth struggling to get a word out.

'I beg your pardon?' I said.

The noise he made bore no relation to normal speech. I had no idea whether to smile or frown or answer yes or no, or whether he'd understand me anyway. I'd seen a television programme once, about a brilliant mathematician in a wheelchair – thick glasses, stunted limbs, the lot – yet he had a mind as sharp as Einstein's. John could be like that. Or a moron with a mental age of six. The mouth was still struggling, the sounds just strange zoo noises.

'I'm sorry,' I muttered. 'I don't quite follow.'

'He's saying, "isn't it cold?"' That was Mary-Lou, chief translator.

'Oh, I *see*. Yes, it *is* cold. Well, I suppose it isn't really. I mean, back in London . . . Oh hell!'

How did Mary-Lou know, anyway? Just because she was a midwife, it didn't mean she had the Gift of Tongues. John might have been gasping out a new formula for relativity, or the fourth law of thermo-dynamics, for all she knew.

I was glad when we reached the gates. The bus was waiting just outside, but it took over half an hour to load everybody in. The wheelchairs were folded and the boys lifted up like sacks. There was a subtle difference, though. The helpers handled them like sacks of coal, Ray like sacks of diamonds.

Everybody laughed and joked and told stupid stories about shaggy dogs and Irishmen, and generally carried on as if they were Adrian's First Year on a school spree. Ray tried to include me in the camaraderie, but it didn't work. They had travelled eight hundred miles together, slept and sung together, fed and toileted each other, were wearing the same grey and orange badge. Mine was an alien blue badge. I belonged to Pax, but had lost my peace along with my family.

Ray drove the bus himself. I'd never imagined him doing things like driving. He seemed too vague and holy and unmechanical to be messing about with gears and carburettors. When we'd gone to the dentist together, we'd always caught an eighty-eight and sat on the top like schoolkids, telling our fortunes with the numbers on the bus tickets.

I stared out of the window. It was almost midnight now, and swirly dark outside. The bus was climbing, but the mountains climbed still higher, so they were always taller, always ahead of us. We stopped too soon. At least the noise of the bus had prevented any need for conversation. We were parked in a sort of clearing, outside a long, low ruin of a house which had once been painted white. A man came out to greet us. He must have been forty-five at least, but was wearing tight faded denims, a checked cowboy shirt which barely concealed his paunch, and a little cap with 'Elvis' printed on it.

'Hi Boss!' he called to Ray.

'Hi Doc!'

So that was their famous doctor, flaunting his mufti and trying to pretend he was just the caretaker, or a guitarist in a rock band, when he probably had strings of letters after his name and three or four degrees and had written books on Paroxysmal Tachycardia. It was part of the whole jolly, matey, social-worker thing. We're all equal, kid, even though I've got a First from Cambridge and you've lost your eyes or your brain or the odd limb or two. It was almost worse than pop priests. Clerics should stick to their dog-collars and doctors their white coats; midwives should be plain and spinsterish and wear their hair short, and cripples and dribblers should stay shut up in their hospitals.

'Right, everybody out and in the Rumpus Room,' called Sam. That took an hour, by the time they'd all been washed and brushed and put their things away and been taken to the toilet. One of the boys had even wet his trousers. No one minded. The helpers made a joke of everything, even pissed pants. 'If you do it again, I'll put you in my nightdress,' Val giggled.

'I'll go to bed with Father, then.'

Everybody screamed with laughter. I just stood by the door, cracking my thumbs. I'd noticed that several of the boys called Ray 'Father', though he answered to anything – you, boss, mister, Four-Eyes, Murph. He was somehow the star and centre of them all. He didn't say a lot, but everyone deferred to him, even the doctor. I noticed how he spread gentleness on everything, like jam.

Cammie was setting out the glasses. There was beer, wine, Pepsi and an assortment of crisps and biscuits brought from England. It should have been cosy – all those Chocolate Crunch and Golden Wonder reminding me of home – but I just felt more and more an alien. Mary-Lou had baked a huge cake with 'Happy birthday, John. Deo Gratias' piped on it in pink and white icing. I wondered what the Deo Gratias was for. Were we thanking God that John had six fingers rather than just three, or that he was alive at all to celebrate his birthday? Ray had told me one of the boys had died just three weeks before he was due to come to Lourdes. Aged fifteen and a half.

Val moved the cake in front of John who was sitting in his wheelchair in the place of honour. Ray sprawled on the floor sur-rounded by his harem, and I slumped in a corner. It was a shabby cheerless room, with lino on the floor and broken sofas, but no one seemed to notice. They were far too busy singing 'Happy birthday, dear Jo—ohn' and linking arms and stamping feet and wolf-whistling each other. The whole thing was like a midnight feast in a dormitory. Half of them were even wearing their pyjamas and Jim had changed his bib for one with a clown on.

The singing was the worst bit. I've always hated sing-songs – they remind me of guide camps and drunken soccer crowds – but when half the party have speech deficiencies and can't even get the words out, the results are shuddersome. Sam kept trying to organize us all, which only made it worse. Jimmy got the giggles in the middle of 'Lead Kindly Light', and Cammie crowed 'Great, oh absolutely great!' after every number, even the ones which foundered. We covered every-thing from 'Ten Green Bottles' to 'Faith of Our Fathers' (which I always thought had been banned, on account of its being unecumeni-cal). Actually, it was the only one I liked. I even joined in the chorus:

> Faith of our fathers, holy faith,
> We will be true to thee till death.

At school it had made me feel excluded, because if it wasn't *my* faith, how could I be true to it, let alone till death? But now I Belonged. I only wished I could be alone with Ray to dwell on Spiritual Things, rather than thumping out 'Irish Eyes Are Smilin'' with a roomful of cripples. Ray cut himself into twenty pieces and threw us all a morsel. Mary-Lou got the most. It was her hair, I suppose, and those valiant tits jutting through her tee-shirt. Though I had to admit she was marvellous with the boys. Things like piss and dribble or missing bits of people hardly bothered her. One lad didn't even have a neck. His head sort of sprouted off his shoulders, but she stuffed it with biscuits or trickled cider down it, and then wiped its mouth and grinned at it, as if necks were merely optional.

They didn't leave me out. My paper plate was piled with crisps and gingernuts (which I couldn't eat), and one of the boys kept jabbing me in the leg, and another repeated my name over and over (even through the singing) as if it were stuck in his throat and he was trying to dislodge it. Lionel, the deaf and dumb boy, wouldn't leave my side. He had squeezed in the corner beside me and was clutching my hand in his own hot clammy one. He had a list of words printed on a card in big black capitals – things like DRINK, TOILET, SLEEP, BREAD – with little pictures underneath them, and a stick to point to the one he wanted. I could have made my own list – RAY, KISS, GOD, GROTTO, MIRACLE, or (less ambitiously) HOME, BED, PEACE, MEAL, QUIET.

At least the singing had ended. Everyone was talking now, or lying about and drinking. All except me, that was. I'd even refused a Pepsi. I couldn't break my fast until the morning, although it could only be a matter of hours now to the Easter Mass. I should really be preparing for it. I shut my eyes and tried to remember the Prayers Before Communion.

'So who's your guru?' joked the doctor.

I jumped. He had joined me on the floor, his cowboy shirt open to the navel. 'I hear you're a nurse,' he said. He was drinking rough red wine out of a Snoopy mug.

'Well . . . er . . . not exactly *now*,' I muttered. 'I mean, I was, but I've . . . been ill.'

'Oh? Seriously?'

'A sort of . . . accident.'

'Make sure you get to the baths, then. That Lourdes water's *amazing*. Filthy dirty half the time, and full of microbes, but I've actually seen people limp and stagger into it and scamper out like three-year-olds.'

'I expect that's just the *shock*,' giggled Val. 'I mean it's fearfully cold. *I* sprinted last time, just to stop them pushing me right under.'

'You're just a coward! Val only comes here for the thrills, Thea. All these lads, you know. We can't keep her and Jim apart.'

Jim gurgled with delight. He obviously thrived on being thought a Don Juan rather than a dribbler with no legs.

'Oh *shut* up, Fatso. We all know why *you* didn't come to the service tonight. He's a boozer, Thea. He *said* he stayed behind simply to keep an eye on Derek's drip, but Ron's just told me the only bottle he was monitoring was the Châteauneuf-du-Pape!'

'Liar!' He punched her in the stomach and they laughed and wrestled on the lino.

They were all so relentlessly *jolly*, even in the midst of missing limbs and broken bodies. Only Lionel stayed subdued. He was still in his corner, but had pressed closer to my body, as if he wanted to merge with it. He was like a child clinging to its mother, a six-foot son with neither ears nor tongue. Perhaps Lucian, had he lived, would have been like that. I shuddered. I didn't really want to be a mother. Safer to cling myself. I looked across at Ray, but he was still common property, spreading himself so thin that everyone got only a smear of him. Back in London, he'd been strictly rationed, but at least when I was with him I had always gulped him whole.

He was the centre of attention now, lighting the candles on the birthday cake. He had turned the lights down so they'd make a better show, and his long haggard shadow leaned across and almost touched my own. There was silence, suddenly, as everybody stared at the tiny flickering match. It was like the Vigil again – light leaping out of darkness. I stared around the room. Everyone looked so *hideous*. Even in the gloom I could see the twisted limbs, the twitches, the fat flabby cheeks, the dead eyes. Mike had his shoes and socks off and even his toes were crooked. One boy was hiccuping, another smearing sucked and soggy biscuit on his face. The room itself was disabled – shabby, squalid, badly put together. How could God have created it all? That great glorious God of the basilicas who lived among gold and alabaster, who smelt of lilies, whose back garden was the sky. Could these shambling rejects spring from grace and light and fire?

'Well, are we going to *eat* the cake or simply sit and look at it?' That was Desmond, drunk on Double Diamond.

'Eat it, fathead. But we've got to let the candles burn down first. They cost 2p each, those candles, and I refuse to waste them.' Val sounded almost worse than Janet.

'I'll eat *them* if you like. I'm starving! It's hours since supper, and I didn't think much of that spam stuff, anyway.'

'It *was*n't spam, I'll have you know. It was best tinned ham in peach sauce.'

'Oh, *peach*, I see. *Now* she tells me!'

Val waved the knife in his direction. 'Right, if you insult the cook, you don't get any cake. Sorry, mate, not a crumb! Pity, because I'm just about to cut it. Here we go – John first. You get the best piece, John – OK? Some for you, Ray?'

'Just a finger.'

'Thea?'

'No thanks.' I wasn't even hungry any more. One of the boys was lapping his cake straight off the plate like a dog. Another smashed his up and dropped it on the floor. Lionel kept pushing his slice towards me. He seemed to want to give me things. He had already handed me a bent franc and a piece of crumpled paper from his pocket. I smiled at every offering. If he hadn't been deaf and dumb, he might have been a pop star. He was the only boy there who was beautiful.

Sam had changed places with the doctor and was squatting at my feet. 'D'you realize, Thea, Lionel's really taken a fancy to you? That's rare for Lionel. He keeps himself to himself most of the time. Even Mary-Lou can't charm him. I don't know how you do it! You'd better stay up here and be a helper.'

All I wanted to be at the moment was a stretcher-case. I was so tired, I was dropping. I wouldn't stand a chance as a helper, anyway. Mary-Lou was universal favourite and there were two other girls both younger and prettier than I was. Even the men, who were mostly older and plainer, had degrees or doctorates or driving licences, or had spent years being busy and important, or could at least mend a fuse.

I felt very spare and stupid. All my Lourdes elation had somehow drained away. It was partly anti-climax. I'd looked forward to Lourdes so long and avidly, I couldn't really square its breezy wretchedness with my high-flown fairyland. Or maybe I could have done if I'd kept away from the hostel. It was the helpers who had really ruined things.

They were so smug and pious and jolly, they made me feel a sham. They were all cocky crowing Catholics like the Irish, locked in their special relationship with God. I was just a novice and a new girl, not even a communicant yet, let alone a saint or ministering angel. They were doing their A-levels while I was still at nursery school. And their syllabus included Ray, of course. I'd come to claim him for a measly hour or two, and found they'd grabbed the whole of him as their guru and their Pope. They belonged to him in a way I never could – fawned on him at Masses, lapped him up at meal-times, shared his dormitory. I was simply the intruder and the dunce.

I stared across at him. Even now he was totally preoccupied, feeding John his cake. I was wrong about the lad. He wasn't another Einstein. Even his so-called normal hand seemed to be more or less inoperative. It just lay on his lap, as if it had been cut off and left there by mistake. He had a tea-towel knotted round his neck so that he looked like a huge stubbly baby in his high chair. Ray was crumbling the cake into pieces, dipping each morsel into his glass of water to soften it, then slipping it gently between the boy's lips. John just sat there with his mouth open, a dumb fledgling cuckoo waiting for the next worm. Ray ate nothing himself, just took the odd sip of water from the glass, which was cloudy now and full of cake crumbs. He fed John with a sort of reverence, slowly, graciously, as if it were a privilege instead of a chore. I had stopped existing. I had legs and fingers, so why should the Blessed Raymond bother with *me*?

I sprang up. I couldn't bear to watch him any more. I excused myself, muttering something about going to the bathroom. In fact, I trailed into the kitchen, a glaring, cluttered room, which smelt of cats and cooking oil. The sink was piled with dirty dishes. No one had touched the washing-up. Holy work, Ray had called it, hadn't he?

I rolled up my sleeves, plunged my hands into the filthy lukewarm water, and fished out a saucepan ruffed with cold scrambled egg.

'Oh, you *are* a brick,' said Mary-Lou. She was standing at the door with a tray of glasses. 'I was just coming out to have a go at it myself. You don't mind a wee bit more, do you?' She offloaded her glasses on to the draining-board and tipped a pile of ashtrays into the sink.

'Lionel was quite upset when you got up, you know. We're all amazed at how he's taken to you. He's usually quite sullen.'

I suspected she was only sucking up. I liked her even less now she was standing next to me, swishing her hair about and making mine look mousy. She kept jabbering on about what *wonderful* work it was helping the handicapped, and didn't I prefer it to ordinary nursing, and wasn't Ray *fabulous*, and how long was I staying.

'I'm *not* staying,' I snapped. Actually, if you cut off her hair, she'd look quite ordinary. Her eyes were too close together and a boring shade of blue.

'Well, how d'you plan to get back then? It's nearly two o'clock. I'd take you myself, but I'm not allowed to drive the bus. It's not insured for all of us.'

'Ray'll take me,' I said, sort of airily.

'*Ray?* Come off it, Thea, I don't think that's really fair. Ray's needed *here*. Mike won't go to sleep unless he reads to him. And then he always says the rosary with us when the boys are all in bed. He's dead tired, anyway. He didn't sleep a wink last night. You could always *walk*, you know – it's not that far. The doc'll go with you. He needs some exercise.'

I banged a plate down on the draining-board. Mary-Lou was a stupid sort of name. Hyphenated people are always trouble-makers. Leo had a friend called Matthew-John. He actually had the hyphen on his birth certificate. Of course he turned out gay. Mary-Lou looked all too heterosexual. I could just imagine her and Ray saying the rosary – the Glorious Mysteries of course, never the Sorrowful. I dunked the last glass in the clogged and smelly water, wiped my hands on my jeans, and walked out. I'd done my stint of Domestic Holiness – now I wanted the real sort. I'd go and find Ray and more or less insist he drove me home, with a detour to the Grotto on the way. Mike would have to read to himself for once.

I marched along the passage which was empty. Most of the group had already moved upstairs and I could hear them giggling and talking in the dormitories. Lourdes was meant to be a place of miracles. I'd clearly need one to get Ray on his own.

There was a step behind me. I swung round. It wasn't a miracle, only the deaf and dumb boy holding out a broken piece of biscuit wrapped in an empty crisp bag. This time, I didn't smile. OK, I was flattered that he fancied me, but I'd had enough of him, of all of them. Just because they were dumb or deprived or crippled, everyone had to be so fucking nice. You couldn't say 'piss off' or 'drop dead' like you might to a normal person. That would be discrimination or mean you were a Nazi. Lionel was pointing to something on his list. I wished I had my own list and could show him the words bore, nuisance, and pain in the arse.

The word he'd chosen was TOILET. Christ Almighty, surely he wasn't suggesting I should accompany him *there*. He had legs, didn't he, and could walk? Anyway, what were all the helpers doing? That was *their* job, wasn't it? I had no intention of taking some six-foot mute to the lavatory and showing him how to crap or pee in sign language.

All the same, I didn't like to simply walk away. It would be different if I could say something – 'Must dash', or 'Train to catch', or 'Babysitter waiting'. All he'd hear was silence and rejection. After all, I was the only one he'd ever responded to. Hadn't they all said that? It was quite an achievement, really – better than mending fuses. Perhaps I could ask Ray's help and that would give me my chance to be alone with my private confessor. It wouldn't be too romantic, holding our spiritual communion in a toilet, with Lionel peeing and trickling in the background, but at least it would be a start.

I peered at his card to see if it said RAY on it, or even PRIEST. It didn't. If I shouted for Ray, the doc might come instead, or worse still, Mary-Lou. I dithered. Lionel was standing absolutely still. He was like a huge dark wounded animal. A lion. I realized suddenly, he had the same name as Leo, more or less. They were both lions – Lionel and Leo – a young lion and a Latin one. I smiled. His whole face lit up, as if I had handed him a jewel. He was like Karma, crushed if his master said, 'Down Sir', exultant if he fondled him.

He was staring at me with his dark worshipping eyes. I had a sudden nervous feeling that maybe he could see right into my mind. I'd read somewhere that the deaf and dumb have strange uncanny powers, to compensate. Perhaps he knew I'd been contemplating euthanasia for people who couldn't speak or had claws instead of hands, or had even seen my private mental picture of rows and rows of little jars like Lucian's, each one holding a tiny pickled boy. Lionel was too big to fit into a jar. Far too big to be taken to the toilet.

'No,' I said, firmly. '*Ray* take you.' I wondered if he could lip-read, or even knew who Ray was.

He moved a little closer. I could see the faint down glistening on his cheek. He hardly needed to shave. He was smooth like Leo. Two smooth and wounded lions. He took my hand. It didn't feel so limp and clammy now, but fierce, almost urgent. Perhaps he was simply desperate for a pee. At least I should take him to the toilet door. That couldn't do much harm. Worse if he wet his pants. If only I could say, 'What d'you want *me* for?' or, 'Why can't you go yourself?' It seemed incredible that the world was silent for him, his entire life's conversation just twelve short words on a two-dimensional card. I smiled at him, more in pity now.

'Look,' I said. 'I'll just take you to the door . . .'

Suddenly, he grabbed me. I could smell cider on his breath, feel his fat red lips groping along my neck, his arms around my own.

I tried to pull away. 'Ray,' I shouted. 'Ray!' But then I realized, almost triumphantly, I *wasn't* shouting. I was whispering, and his hands were on my breasts.

nineteen

Madame Simonneaux had long since gone to bed. We stood on the dark shadowy landing, trying to grope our way up the last flight of stairs. I tripped on a loose piece of lino, almost fell.

'Steady, Thea. It's treacherous up here. Is it far now? We must have climbed almost up to heaven!'

'No, this is it. Here – take a look – my suite at the Savoy! Luxurious, isn't it?' I struggled with the door-handle.

'I've seen worse,' said Ray, peering in. I could tell he was embarrassed. He didn't feel he should waltz into a lady's bedroom and yet he knew he couldn't leave me. I tried to look more desperate than I was. I'd been practising all the way from the hostel, slumped against him in the front of the bus and almost sobbing. I'm good at almost sobbing.

'Thea, look, about this . . . Lionel business. I just don't know what to . . . I mean, I'd no *idea* the boy'd do a thing like that.'

I shrugged. 'It's OK,' I said. I tried to look brave and sort of poignant. I needed courage. My room looked even worse in artificial light – if you could call it light. The bulb was weak and wavering and had no shade. Dingy shadows stalked in all the corners, things jumped out at us. A cloud of small black insects buzzed around the ceiling. I'd left the window open and the damp night air had seeped in like black mud. We were both still standing just outside the door. The handle was half off, and Ray was trying to screw it back again.

'No, it's *not* OK,' he said. 'I know how upset you are. I'm upset *myself*, for heaven's sake. I feel I should never have taken you up there in the first place. On the other hand, I had absolutely no reason to suspect that . . .'

'Oh, really? So why did you all keep saying Lionel fancied me? You were almost gloating over it. God! If I'd realized you meant it *sexually*, I'd never have . . .'

'Of *course* we didn't, Thea. How could you think we'd encourage a thing like that? Oh, it *happens* – I can't deny it. One boy we even had to send away. He was continually pestering the cleaning ladies. But Lionel, *never*. I mean, that's why I'm so shocked. Are you absolutely certain, Thea, he did what you said he did? I know you're upset, but . . .'

'Oh, so you're calling me a liar, now, are you?' I marched into the room, straight over to the window, and slammed it shut. 'Christ, I've done my best not to make a fuss so you wouldn't feel responsible, and the only thanks I get is for you to turn round and say it never bloody happened.'

He looked more desperate than I did now, but at least I'd lured him into the bedroom. He'd even got the handle back and shut the door behind us. 'I'm *not* saying that, Thea, of course I'm not. It's always a problem with the handicapped. They do have all the normal . . . well . . . *urges*, but there's not much they can do about them, so they get frustrated. On the other hand, we must be fair to the lad. You were holding his hand half the evening and he probably thought . . .'

I kicked my suitcase out of the way. There was no proper storage space, so it was doubling as a cupboard. 'Hell, Ray, I didn't *want* to hold his rotten clammy hand. I was only trying to be decent. Your precious Mary-Lou told me it was most important never to let the boys feel rejected. So all I did was sort of mother him a bit. I never thought I'd more or less get raped for it.'

'Try and calm down now, Thea. What's happened, happened, and at least he *did*n't rape you. Oh, I know it was bad enough. Don't think I'm whitewashing him – I'm not – but he didn't *mean* it. He's not really responsible, you see.'

'Like *hell* he's not! Want to see the marks?' I showed him a nick Karma had given me the day before. Karma liked me less and less these days. Something to do with Leo's impotence, I reckon.

'Nasty. You sit down and rest a bit. Is there anything I can get you?'

I wondered what he had in mind. There wasn't even a decent chair to sit on.

'How about a glass of water?' He was already at the basin. I think he'd have offered me water even if we were camping in a vineyard or guests at Château-Lafite.

'I need something stronger than *that*, Ray. Don't worry, I've got some brandy somewhere. I bought it for Leo on the plane, but I can always get him another.' I pretended to be searching in my suitcase, and with a little sleight of hand, produced a bottle which had been secreted under my sheepskin. I'd pinched it from the hostel. It was the doctor's, actually, but it didn't count as stealing, simply takeaway.

After all, I'd refused all their beer and Pepsi, so this was just instead of. Anyway, it was Ray I'd nicked it for. Somehow, I had to get it down him. I poured a tooth-mug full.

'Stay and have one with me,' I urged. 'Please. It'll help calm me down. There's only one glass, I'm afraid, so we'll have to share it.'

I took a swig, then pushed the mug towards him. 'God, I do feel lousy. If you don't mind, I think I'll put myself to bed.'

'Good idea!' I could see the relief even in his body. He'd been standing all hunched up before. Now he relaxed his shoulders. 'You get a good night's sleep, Thea, and I'll come and see you in the morning, after Mass. I ought to get back now, you see – if you're quite sure you're all right.'

I banged the brandy bottle down. 'I'm *not* all right. I just told you, Ray, I feel *bloody*. Lionel's six foot tall, you know, and extremely strong. Of course, I suppose you've *got* to defend him, haven't you? It wouldn't sound too good if people heard that one of your precious handicapped went around raping people.'

'Thea, he *did*n't rape you.'

'As good as. Oh, I don't care. You just walk out. Block your ears to anything unpleasant.'

'Thea, girl, do be reasonable. It was *you* who said you didn't want to talk about it.'

'Well, I do now.'

'OK, we'll talk.' He was still standing by the window, as far away from me as he could get in an eight-foot room.

'How *can* we talk, with you all stiff and fidgety and us both buttoned up in our outdoor gear as if we're about to rush off for a ten-mile hike? Look, Ray, I'm going to lie down. I feel rotten. And I want you to take your coat off and come and sit beside me, and just bloody *listen* for five minutes. Is that too much to ask?'

'No, it's not.' He didn't move, though. He looked so tired, all the stuffing seemed to have trickled out of him. He was drooping against the window-sill like an empty sack. I felt sorry for him, really. I think he was torn between us – me and Lionel. That's why I had to tread so carefully. The slightest thing could frighten him away, back to his darling boys. If I started unzipping things, he'd run a mile. On the other hand, I didn't really fancy climbing into bed in a sheep-skin.

'Look,' I said, grabbing my nightie and a sponge-bag. 'I'll just get changed in the bathroom. OK? Don't go away, Ray, will you? I'm not well enough to be left here on my own.'

There wasn't a bathroom, but I didn't tell him that. I ran two floors down, locked myself in the cramped and smelly loo and struggled out of my clothes. The nightie smelt sort of musty. I'd bought it from the Oxfam shop to double as an evening dress. It was their prize exhibit, black satin slashed from thigh to ankle, like something out of an MGM spectacular. I feared it might be more than Ray could cope with, so I threw the sheepskin back across my shoulders like a cape, had a quick pee, a quicker comb, then panted back upstairs.

Ray hadn't touched the brandy. He was standing by the window exactly as before, but with his eyes closed now. He might have been praying or simply half-asleep. He jumped when I came in.

'Sit down,' I said.

He inched a little nearer, looked around the room. 'There doesn't seem to be a . . .'

'Sit *here*,' I said, patting the bed. I realized he was trying not to look at me, or at least not at the nightie.

'OK, but just for a minute, Thea. They need me at the hostel. I promised I'd be straight back. You see, Mike gets difficult when I'm not there. And the doctor's waiting up for me. I said I'd go over the schedule for tomorrow with him.' He was using words as blinkers to save him from the satin. 'I'm sorry, my girl, but I did try to warn you I'd be busy once I got here. And then there's . . .'

'You didn't warn me half your boys would be raving sexual maniacs. Or that they'd try and rip my clothes off and rape me in a filthy lavatory, or . . .' I stopped. He was actually sitting down now, though so close to the edge of the bed, he was in danger of sliding off again.

'Look, Thea, I don't like you to keep using the word rape. It's not really fair to Lionel. You'd better tell me exactly what happened for the lad's sake, as well as yours.' He shifted a fraction further towards me.

I think he'd have defended Jack the Ripper if he'd been living at his hostel. But at least we were both on the bed and one of us undressed. I pushed the duvet back a little, shrugged the sheepskin off. That nightie had cost me one pound twenty-five and all Ray could see was the first five penn'orth of it.

'Sit *nearer*,' I whispered. I was freezing cold, but it was worth it.

He moved quarter of a centimetre. I was glad the lights were low. It made it more romantic, or at least disguised the stains on the carpet, the dirty, crumbling patches on the wall. 'Well,' I said, 'first he sort of stopped me in the passage and pointed to the word toilet – you know, on that card thing.' I've learnt from experience that lies work better if you graft them on to truth. 'I didn't know what to *do*, Ray. There was nobody downstairs and I wasn't sure whether women helpers were *meant* to take boys to the loo. I mean, I never suspected for a moment that it was just a ploy. Anyway, while I was dithering, Lionel suddenly dragged me along the passage, right into the toilet, locked the door, and stood with his back against it so I couldn't escape. Then . . . Oh, Christ, Ray, I . . . I don't think I *can* tell you – it brings it all back. You see, I *tried* to stop him, I almost fought with him, but . . .'

Ray was staring at me with that mixture of fascination and revulsion priests always reserve for sex. It's amazing, really, what stories the clergy swallow. I suppose the old guard are so ignorant, and the pop priests so determined to be 'with-it', that either way they go along with you. If I massed all my fiercest fantasies together and multiplied them by ten, most priests would still believe I'd done the lot in a single session.

Victim of rape was quite an appealing role to play, especially now I was lying on my back with Ray bending over me. I only wished I had a cleavage. My breasts tend to disappear when I lie down flat. Mary-Lou's would have formed a second bolster.

'Look, Thea, you've had a shock – I can see that. And of course you're still upset – it's only natural. I don't really think I should leave you here on your own. Why don't you come back with me? To the hostel, I mean. There's not much room up there, but . . .'

'No *fear*! I wouldn't dare close my eyes with all those dangerous louts around. They're bad enough fully dressed, let alone in their pyjamas.'

'Come off it, Thea, don't exaggerate. You'll be perfectly all right. Mary-Lou will look after you. We can fix you up a sleeping-bag in the girls' dormitory.'

That wasn't what I had in mind at all. 'It's OK, Ray, I feel better, actually – now I'm lying down. Just give me a minute and I'll . . .'

'You see, I've got to get back my*self*, Thea. If you came with me, the doc could give you something to help you sleep.'

I didn't *want* to sleep – that's not what I'd bought the nightie for. 'No, really, Ray, I'm OK. Honestly. Just stay here beside me and . . .'

He shifted a little. I could see his eyes burning through the spectacles. He had brought the holiness with him, even here. 'Look, Thea, I want to try and understand. Lionel didn't *intend* it as an attack. In fact, you could almost say it was a compliment. Oh, I know that sounds insulting, but the lad was obviously quite dazzled by you. He's a handsome fellow himself, but completely cut off from all the normal boy/girl things. He can't even *talk* about his feelings. Then he meets an attractive girl like you, someone who seems to take an interest in him, and he reacts in the wrong way. To *him* it probably seemed more like a sort of . . . tribute to you.'

I shut my eyes. I could see Lionel's full red lips pressing on to mine. He had kissed me exactly twice and touched my breasts for a full five seconds. Finish. *I* was the one who'd tried to take it further. Lionel seemed so surprised, disgusted even, he'd simply walked away. We hadn't even made it to the toilet. It was just a quick grope in a draughty corridor, then the getaway. Hardly a tribute to be rejected by a deaf-mute.

'Hold my hand,' I said. '*Please.*'

He didn't. 'Thea, I . . .'

'Lionel *hurt* me,' I whimpered.

'Look, come back to the hostel with me and I'll get Doc to . . .'

'All right, *don't* hold it. But stay here. Please. Just a few minutes more. You don't have to do anything. Just talk. You never talk to me. I mean never about your*self*. It's always me moaning on about me.'

He grinned. 'You're more interesting.'

'No, I'm not. I'm boring. I want to hear about *you*.'

'There's nothing to hear.'

'Christ, there's *every*thing! I mean, what made you become a friar in the first place? Tell me that.'

He looked embarrassed as if I'd asked him about his bowel habits. 'I suppose I liked the uniform.' He laughed – the first time I'd heard him laugh all evening. I felt we were getting somewhere. It was probably better to play interested companion, than crumbling invalid.

'But you don't *wear* it,' I said.

'No. Not now. I used to.'

'I can't quite see you in skirts. Were they prickly?'

'A bit.'

'What did you wear underneath?'

'Not a hair shirt, if that's what you're getting at.'

'No, I mean, was it – you know – like a kilt?'

'Of *course* not, goose. Just ordinary underpants. And trousers too, unless it was a heat-wave – rolled up to the calf, so they didn't show.'

I couldn't imagine God's Anointed in rolled-up trousers like those men on comic postcards at the seaside, or wearing white interlock pants from M & S. Golden singlets would have been more suitable, or loincloths embroidered with lilies.

'And what did you *do* all day?'

'Oh . . . things.'

'What *sort* of things?'

'Parish work.'

'What's that?'

'You know, priestly stuff. Masses, confessions, sick calls, death-beds . . .'

'Sounds exciting.'

'Not always. I was only the office boy, so to speak. The other two priests were older and more experienced, so a lot of the time I was just . . . Look, Thea, you don't want to hear all this.'

'Yes I do. Go *on*. I mean, you couldn't have had death-beds all *day*. What else did you do?'

'Prayed. Dug the garden. Ran the youth club. Prayed some more. Visited old ladies.'

'Did you like it?'

He didn't answer. He didn't even look as if he'd heard. I think he was still worrying about the time and the boys and being in a woman's bedroom.

'You're not drinking,' I said.

'No.'

'Did you take a vow of poverty?'

'Yes.'

'Does that include brandy?'

'I suppose strictly speaking, yes. But if it's offered to us, no.'

'You mean you can have *any*thing you're offered?'

'Well, not quite *any*thing, but it's a general Franciscan principle to take what we're given and be glad of it.'

'Why don't you *do* it then?' It wasn't just the drink I meant.

It was hopeless, really. Even now, he was more interested in his watch. He was trying to peer at it without me noticing. I tugged at his sleeve. He'd no right to be worrying about the time, when I was offering myself, body, soul and satin nightie to him.

208

'Look, Thea, you seem much more relaxed now. Why don't you try and get some sleep?'

'Just another minute, Ray. *Please*. I'm only relaxed because you're talking. Don't you see? You're taking my mind off things.'

'Well, at least I'd better telephone. I mean, they'll all be wondering where on earth I am.'

'*Telephone?* At three a.m.! Madame will go mad. You'll wake all her children up. The phone's downstairs in her part. Anyway, the bloody thing's deranged.'

'*Deranged?*'

'Yes, I passed it this evening on my way to the Vigil, and there was a notice on it saying "*téléphone en dérangement*". Something like that. Anything'd be deranged in *this* hole.'

'Damn!'

That was the nearest he'd ever got to swearing. He was obviously loosening up. I moved the duvet down another inch. 'Tell me some more about when you were a friar.'

'I'm *still* a friar, Thea, I keep telling you.'

'So why did you leave the friary? I mean, what are you doing living with cripples instead of with your Brothers.'

'I . . . er . . . had my reasons.'

Silence. I watched a tiny insect scurry down the wall. Ray was frowning. His face looked shifting and uneven in the shadows, sort of pitted like a building site.

'Look, Thea, I'm sorry, truly I am, but if I can't phone, I'll have to go. They'll be getting frantic, imagining I've had an accident or something. Mike's the one I'm worried about. He gets these panic attacks – you know, can't breathe, starts to choke. I am *here* for the boys, you see. I told you that.'

I sat up in bed and punched my fist down on to the pillow. 'For God's sake, Ray,' I shouted. 'I've just been more or less assaulted by one of those boys, and all you can rabbit on about is them. Christ Almighty, they've already got a score of helpers and a dozen midwives pandering to them. I've got no one. I've tried to be reasonable, not to make a fuss. Hell! Some girls would have *reported* the bloody boy, kicked up a stink about it. I'm not even *complaining*, Ray. All I've asked is for you to stay a few lousy minutes and try and take my mind off it. And what do you do? Keep bleating on about getting back to bed!'

'Not *bed*, Thea – that's not what I'm . . .'

'You don't even take me seriously. Everything I ask, you shrug off or wave away. I've told you every fucking thing about *me*. Poured out my sins, explained about Adrian and Leo and . . . but if I want to know a single thing about you, it's jokes or evasions or "I had my reasons." OK, I realize you're used to dealing with morons half the time, but I'm not one of them. You're like *all* bloody priests. You've got to be superior, haven't you? I mean, you can't even have a drink with me. You said yourself you're meant to take what's offered, but you haven't had a *sip*. Didn't it strike you that it might be holier actually to *share* the stuff, instead of leaving me to swig it on my own and feel like some drunken boozer? If you ask me, all that bread and water lark is simply showing off. Even *Christ* didn't do it. He changed the bloody water into wine. You'd change it back again, wouldn't you, just to go one better? No wonder people puke at priests. It's not just vows of poverty, it's vows of secrecy, vows of superiority, vows of shutting people out, walking out on women when they've just been raped, vows of . . . Oh, never *mind*!'

There was silence so thick and trembly I could feel it hanging between us like a frayed black curtain. One of the insects was slipping down the wall just above my head, struggling desperately to right itself, its tiny black legs slithering and flailing. Ray took off his glasses and wiped them with his handkerchief. 'I'm sorry, Thea,' he said.

He spoke so softly, so simply, with such obvious penitence, I went wet between the legs. The silence had shifted slightly. Now I could hear the grumble of a car outside, the jagged yelp of a night bird. He picked up the tooth-mug and took his first swig of brandy – quite a long one.

'You're right, Thea. I *have* been secretive. It's difficult, you know. In a way, we're almost *trained* to be a bit detached from people. I suppose we're frightened of letting our hair down, or committing sins of self-indulgence – perhaps even giving scandal. You see, what may start as a confidence could turn out like a criticism.'

His voice was so soft, I could feel it whispering up and down my body like a moth. It didn't really matter what he said. For the first time I'd got his full attention, and every word was like an antenna on my breasts. He was the penitent now, begging for forgiveness. He still had his glasses off and his face looked defenceless without them, as if anyone could have marched in through his eyes to the interior of his skull and annexed all the squashy bits inside. He moved a little further up the bed – he even took my hand. I suppose it was the brandy. He was so unused to drinking, even half a mugful could have made him rash.

I leaned out of bed and filled the mug again, passed it to him. He gulped it. I think he was only programmed to deal with water and didn't know how to sip. I felt his fingers relax into mine. The silence between us was paler now and milder, almost companionable.

'You can trust me,' I whispered. 'I mean, if you *want* to talk.'

'It's late, Thea.'

'So?'

'Well, I mean, I hardly know what to say. There's . . .'

This time, I left the silence there. I felt wise, powerful, almost like his confessor. I looked around the room – dirt and shadows mixed, the rusty metal blind at the window, the oilcloth on the broken screen. We were sharing our poverty, our holiness.

Ray had his eyes shut now, the brandy mug clasped against his chest. He seemed to be groping for something, stretching out towards me with his soul.

'You see, Thea, a year or so ago, I . . . had a sort of . . . crisis. Oh, I know all priests are *expected* to feel like that from time to time – doubts, restlessness, the Dark Night of the Soul – it's almost textbook stuff. The Eight-Year Itch, if you like. But real, Thea – bloody real.'

I jumped. He'd moved from 'damn' to 'bloody' in the space of just ten minutes, in less than the time it took to down his second glass of brandy. I wriggled the duvet almost off. He wasn't looking at me, just staring at his hands.

'Maybe it sounds naive, Thea, but I seemed to be battling with all the issues I'd agonized about as a novice – you know, was I really following St Francis? Could I do more good elsewhere? Was I meant to be a priest at all? The religious life still seemed far too cosy.'

'*Cosy!*' I exclaimed. Vows of chastity, digging vegetable gardens, playing second lead in death-bed scenes . . .

'Yes. We might preach poverty, but in fact, we never wanted for anything. I told you in the hospital, remember? How comfortable it was – a nice plush, regular existence which many less privileged folk would have jumped at. Before I joined the order, I worked with thalidomide kids. Some of them were just *stumps*, Thea. Stumps with souls. Mealtimes were a nightmare. There weren't enough hands to go round, to start with. We only had two each, and most of them had none. They all had vocal cords, though. The noise was like a monkey-house! Yet there I was, six months later, lolling in the novices' refectory, listening to a little gentle reading from the Life of Our Holy Founder, while I toyed with my prime pork chops and fresh fruit flummery. Sometimes, we even had *wine*, for heaven's sake, and coffee in the lounge to follow, and a chance to put our feet up. Hell! With the thalidomides, we were lucky if we even got a mouthful down, and then it would be meat stew without the meat, dolloped on to enamel plates with pieces bitten out of them. But – oh no! – not as novices. That was *civilized*. Decent china and easy chairs. We didn't even have the problems of a normal family – toddlers in tantrums or cross incontinent old parents spitting out their teeth. I *know*, Thea – I was one of seven kids, with two sets of parents all squashed together in a terraced house. And yet all I heard at meals now was, 'Father, could I bother you for the cream?' or, 'I must tell Brother Cook to use more seasoning', or readings from the Life of St Francis, our thirteenth-century nutcase who was quaint enough to believe in poverty – ha ha!'

I took a swig of brandy. Ray had drained the mug again, so I gulped it from the bottle. I needed courage. I wasn't sure I liked this new ranting Luther. I'd asked him to talk, but only because I thought he wouldn't. In all the time I'd known him, he'd never said more than three or four sentences in succession. It was mostly monosyllables, or little nods and smiles while *I* held the stage. Now he seemed to have forgotten I was there.

'We had no real responsibilities except for our own freshly laundered souls. Oh, I know I said I did parish work, but *paperwork* would be a more accurate description. I spent most of my time writing begging letters for bingo prizes, or getting estimates for roof repairs or trying to balance the books of the Parish Club. The older priests made all the big decisions, married people, manned the death-beds. All I manned was the cake-stall at the church bazaar. None of us seemed to *reach* people – not even the older friars. We were the *priests*, you see, which meant we were too important to be shown the muck. Even in the poorest homes, we were ushered into the front parlour and given the cup and saucer with the roses on, or the cake they'd been saving all week. Then, when we'd taken all they'd got and offered them some half-baked little homily in return, back we waltzed to our fricassee of veal and potted plants, our early bed and wool-and-mohair blankets.

'Oh, there *were* problems – of course there were. Wife-bashing and incest, gangs of coloured youths beating up old ladies ... But we weren't *part* of them, not really. We might meddle in them, pray for them, but basically we were just the Friar Tucks, quaint cosy little brothers who lived in the Big House and hid behind our education and our middle-class manners, warm and dry and safe and civilized in our picturesque brown robes, a thousand years away from the spirit of our founder.'

I lay utterly silent, like one of the trembling feathers in the duvet. I'd never heard Ray storm and rave like this – it scared me. I didn't *want* him to have problems – that was my prerogative. He'd never talked before or boozed before, and now the barriers were falling all around us. I hugged the duvet close against my breasts.

'I grew up in Preston, Thea. In a slum. A Roman Catholic slum. The church was at the top of the street, a fancy sort of building with a dome and pillars. All around it were mean little terraced houses with communal lavatories and tiny cramped back-yards. The priests' garden was the only piece of green in a three-mile radius. Quite sizeable it was, too. Apple trees and flowerbeds – even a rustic garden seat. The only time I ever got to sit on it was when Father O'Leary caught me trespassing and tanned my bare bottom over the slats.

'Twenty years later, I went back there for a wedding. One of the lads in the street made good and married a local magistrate's daughter. Both Catholics. They got married in that church and held the reception in the garden. I was standing there, all dressed up in some fancy suit I'd borrowed and watching two little boys rolling down the slope, stuffing grass down one another's necks, tearing up the daisies. I realized, suddenly, that was the very first time I'd ever seen kids playing in that garden. I felt a sort of *rage*. None of our parents had owned so much as a blade of grass, and there were those priests sitting on three-quarters of an acre. I remember, once, they caught me stealing an apple. I hadn't even picked it. It had been lying on the grass, half-mouldy, yet for all the fuss they made, you'd have thought it was a chalice.

'I don't want a church like that, Thea. That's why I joined the Franciscans. They don't shut themselves off, cultivate their gardens for their own private pleasure, put up signs saying PLEBS AND LAITY KEEP OUT. Or at least I *thought* they didn't. After eight years as one, I wasn't so sure.'

I coughed and fidgeted, but he didn't so much as glance at me. I

213

wanted to cling on to him and shout, 'I'm here, I'm here!' before he totally forgot. He was burying me in words. I was just a tiny face at the bottom of a hole and he was flinging earth on top of me, tearing up that priests' garden. He'd even stopped worrying about his boys. When *I* had problems, it was, 'Sorry Thea, poor little Mike can't breathe'; now he was deep in his own, Mike could have choked to death for all he cared. All he could see was that community of friars.

'About nine months ago, I went on a call to see a Mrs O'Leary. She was new to the parish. No one knew much about her, but she'd had a win on the pools and wanted to donate some of the money to the church. I was sent to fix up all the details – you know, covenants and interest rates and tax exemption clauses. I was hoping to persuade her to use the cash on some of the real grinding problems of the parish. She refused. She wanted to give us something tangible, a hideous plaster statue of the Sacred Heart or some fancy altar-rails with her name and virtue splashed all over them. We sat in the front parlour drinking tea out of rose-patterned cups again, nibbling on dainty little almond cakes and discussing perms and Lit-Plans and score-draws and dividends.

'When we'd finished the money side, I tried to get her to talk about herself – you know, any problems she might have – spiritual matters, personal. She wouldn't. It was just, "Everything's *fine*, Father, now we've had the win."

'It was only later I found out she had a thalidomide son. A bad case – no lower limbs at all and mentally retarded. He was living with her at the time. In fact, he must have been somewhere in that house the day I called. But she didn't choose to mention him. We'd talked about her *daughter*. She was marrying well – a computer operator, I think she said the bloke was. I guess the pools win helped. But the son, no. He was too squalid for the front parlour. No roses on him, I suppose. Or perhaps he couldn't be trusted with an almond cake. She didn't want to *spoil* things by bringing out a cripple. Or embarrass the good priest.

'Later, he landed up in a home like the one I used to work at. They were desperately short of cash, of course, yet his own mother had just squandered hers on a new gilded statue of St Francis the Poor and a hand-embroidered chasuble. That did it. I don't know why, exactly, but somehow it brought all my doubts and disillusions to a head. I realized I'd been doing more good as a school-leaver, slaving night and day for my thalidomides, dressed in an old pair of denims and grabbing a sandwich when I could, than I ever did now in all my sackcloth finery with a time-table which included three meals a day and seven hours' sleep and formal recreation hours.'

'Why didn't you *leave*, then?' I whispered. I could have almost wept with disappointment. There I was, sitting up in bed in MGM's most stunning rig-out, with a naked body underneath it and only half a duvet between us, and all Ray could talk about was sackcloth.

'If I hadn't been a priest, I might have done. But seven years' training seemed to have left me almost . . . paralysed. There was nothing left, no impulses, no certainties. I'd analysed them all away. I got so I couldn't make a single decision – not the simplest one. I was just a brain and a soul, with nothing solid else. No gut, no centre. I couldn't even *pray*. Too many things had always been decided for us – all the small details of our lives – when we got up, what we wore, what we ate for breakfast. It was like a great high wall, keeping out the bogies, the free choices, the decisions, but also shutting out the light, the thalidomides, the real crippling poverty of the world. Franciscans don't *have* walls, Thea – we pride ourselves on that. Our houses are meant to be accessible. But our *vows* are walls, cutting us off from all the real human problems and responsibilities, from sex, from parenthood, from . . . You've just said that yourself, Thea. You *saw* it, you see. That's why I've tried to explain things. I wanted you to understand, to realize that . . .'

God, how I wished I'd never said a word. I didn't *want* Ray breaking out. If he smashed his walls, the débris would fall on both of us. I wasn't his confessor. He was a priest himself, for heaven's sake, and the joy of priests is they don't have problems of their own. If he'd been anyone else, I could have felt sorry for him – pitied his squalid childhood, understood his anger. I *did* feel sorry for him. But I also felt horribly confused. I'd often imagined his background as a spoiled and only child, with a saintly mum and a pipe-and-tweedy father who called him 'son' and bought him electric train-sets. I didn't want slums and communal lavatories. I needed Ray to be strong and safe and stormproof, not racked by rage and anguish with a shop-soiled family swearing and scrapping on the sidelines. All that did was make him a *mortal* man.

And a mortal man who didn't even desire me. I'd just been spurned by Lionel, Leo couldn't even get it up for me, and here was Ray more interested in his soul than in my body. I must be really hideous to turn everybody off. Mary-Lou could have seduced an entire seminary or a boys' school, single-handed, and even Cammie would be gasping 'Great!' by now.

I kicked both girls out of the room. I didn't want to think of them. It was the hostel which had upset me in the first place. And even now I'd escaped from it, with Ray as my stolen goods, his priestly shine was already tarnishing. His face was flushed and fretful, not pious pale. He'd had more to drink than I had. The famous holiness had cracked like a cut-price halo. His hair was tousled, his hands sweaty. Even his voice had changed. There was less of Surrey in it now, and more of Preston. To tell the truth, I didn't really fancy him as a man – spectacles never turn me on. Of all the forty-seven (thirty-one) men I'd had, only three wore glasses, and those three were unquestionably the worst in bed. It was the priest I craved – not the mortal – the friar, the confessor, the Father. They were still there, underneath the flush. Looks hardly matter when you're God's Anointed. Christ Himself may well have been plain and scrawny with thinning hair and hammer toes. Artists always flatter Him, but no one really *knows*. It was Ray's soul and sanctity I lusted after – the robes, the vows, the rituals; the fact that bishops had breathed on him, altar boys and acolytes haloed him with incense and hemmed him in with prayers, the Paraclete perched crowing on his shoulder. His hands had touched the flesh of God – now they must touch my own flesh; his lips which had said, 'I absolve you', must say it to my cunt.

He mopped his forehead, wiped his mouth. I yearned for him to fall on his knees and remember his vocation, but all he did was go rambling on again.

'Well, finally, I went to see the Guardian. He's head of our community, like your Reverend Mother. We talked. He didn't understand. How could he? He'd been stuck in the system fifty years or more and couldn't even see it straight. In the end, he sent me to the Provincial – that's our really big boss – who granted me a year out. Meaning out in the world. The very fact we call it "the world" shows we're not part of it. The earth spins on its axis, and we, the religious, sit aloof from it, on our own cosy little planet, refusing to look further than our holy Roman noses.

'He suggested I work with prisoners down in Southampton. I was quite attracted by that, I must admit, but I knew my real vocation was with the handicapped. I told him so. We had quite a long discussion.

The thalidomide home I'd worked in had been recently closed down – lack of cash, of course – but eventually he found me this job in London with my boys. And', he shrugged, 'that's what I'm doing now. I'm still under vows of course. I'm still a priest.'

'You're *not*,' I almost shouted. 'You're just a flimsy, limping layman, threatening my religion, upsetting all my plans.'

Once he'd been as solid as St Peter's Rock, sanctified and sinless, his foundations as sturdy as one of Adrian's Romanesque cathedrals. That was how I wanted him, not crumbling away in dribbling little doubts. I glanced at him, standing with his back to me, still clutching the empty tooth-mug, a most unpriestly gap between his sweater and his jeans, one foot twisted round the other. Was that my priest, my rock, my comforter? I could almost feel the room unravelling. It was my duty to shore him up again, return him to his calling. I didn't want my First Communion from a rebel or a social worker. I had to turn him back to God's Anointed. I had no intention of arguing, of taking up his points like Adrian would, and starting a debate. We'd talked enough, for heaven's sake. We needed some action now, some drama.

I got out of bed and marched over to the bidet, pulled my nightie up. I didn't bother closing the screen around me. I just peed, noisily, in the bowl, leaving the nightdress looped across my arm so that it was displaying half my thighs.

'Finished?' I asked, mincing back towards him. I made my voice half-angry, half-voluptuous.

He didn't answer. He was turned towards me now and staring at my thighs, hands trembling on the tooth-mug.

I fell back on the bed with my legs apart, nightie still rucked up. 'Come over here,' I whispered.

'No, Thea, I . . . er . . .'

'Look, I'm tired. Absolutely pooped. D'you know how long you've been talking?'

'I'm *sorry*. Hell, I got sort of carried away. I must have . . .'

'Sit down.' I patted the duvet, parted my legs another inch or two.

'Look, if you don't mind, Thea, I think I'll just . . .'

'Sit *down*.'

He stumbled over to the bed, perched on the end of it. He was trying not to look at me.

'Nearer.'

He edged up almost to the pillows and leant against the wall. Either he was drunk or shagged, or so embarrassed by his outburst, he was willing to submit to anything. His face looked shuttered, barred, like a shop which had stopped trading.

'It's *my* turn to talk now, see? And I want you to listen, Ray.'

He nodded.

'I'm going to tell you exactly what Lionel did to me. OK?'

'OK.' His voice was slurred, sleepy, furred.

'Well, first he kissed me. Right? Not a brotherly kiss, not a *friar's* kiss. Oh no – it was more like *this*.' I grabbed him by the shoulders and demonstrated. I could smell the brandy on his breath. It tasted sour and almost blasphemous.

'Thea, *no*.'

'That's what *I* said, Ray. But Lionel didn't choose to understand. In fact, he moved down further. Shall I show you?'

'*No*, Thea. Look, you said you were tired. I really ought to leave now, so you can get some sleep . . .'

'You didn't care how tired I was when *you* were talking. You didn't even mention leaving. I *had* to listen, didn't I? Well, now it's *your* turn.'

I took his hand and shoved it on my breasts. 'Lionel wasn't gentle, Ray. Why should he be? He more or less *pummelled* me – like this.' I rammed his palm hard against my nipples.

'Don't.' He sounded strangled, almost scared. He could easily have stopped me. Leo would have grabbed my wrists, pinioned them behind me.

'Lionel's *strong*,' I whispered. 'He twisted my arms behind my back and kept them there. D'you want to know what it felt like?'

I seized his arms and dragged them up and back. They were feeble, puny, almost unresisting. He was probably feeble further down as well – limp, like Leo was – like Lionel. I'd pressed against Lionel's trousers when he kissed me, and there was nothing there. He was deaf and dumb between the legs, a lion without a mane – *two* lions. Perhaps I made *all* men limp. Since the blow, I'd lost my power. I was so shit-scared of fists now, all I got was eunuchs.

I released Ray's arms, flung them back to him, as if they were little twigs. 'Listen, Ray, you've got to understand. It's not just Lionel, it's Leo. He doesn't want me any more. Since he hit me, he hasn't come *near* me, hasn't even mentioned it. I think I must disgust him now. I mean, people just don't *fancy* girls with false teeth. You don't yourself. Look at you – you're not exactly slavering over me, are you? All you want to do is leave. Oh, I don't blame you. I wouldn't want to kiss myself. Of course I'd choose a girl who hadn't been bashed up. That's why I'm so upset about Lionel. It was the very first sex I've had since leaving the hospital, and it had to be like . . . *that*. I suppose nobody normal will ever want me now, only cripples and deaf mutes. I'm just a reject like your handicapped.'

'Thea, *nobody*'s a reject. Anyway, you're *beautiful*, you're . . .' Oh, he was trying to be holy again now, was he, sucking up to me, telling me my soul was radiant in God's sight?

'He came in my *face*, Ray. Did I tell you that? Spurted it all over me? Smeared it on my clothes. No, I suppose I *did*n't tell you. There wasn't time, really, was there? I mean, we had to deal with *your* problems.'

'Oh, *God*, I'm sorry, Thea. I . . .'

'No, it doesn't matter. Of course it doesn't. You're still here. You're still a priest – you told me so. Well, you can make me clean then, can't you? I feel *polluted* by Lionel, but you can undo that if you hold me. It's OK, I won't take advantage of you. We've been over all that before – at your place. You touched me then, didn't you, and nothing happened. I told you you could trust me, and you could. Well, touch me now. Put your arms around me.'

'I . . . I *can't*, Thea.'

'Christ, you're selfish! You've just been giving me all that spiel about doing some good in the world, going out and really *reaching* people instead of being shut off by your vows. And yet the very first chance you get to put it into practice, you run a mile.'

'I'm *not* running, Thea. I'm here. I'm sitting right beside you.' He was speaking slowly now, sort of fumbling for the words. I think he was still befuddled by the brandy. It was best VSOP cognac – wasted on him, really.

'Well, hold me, then. I'm a human being, not a whore.'

He stroked one nervous hand along my shoulder. 'Well, just for a moment, then. Just a hug, Thea – nothing more.'

'Yes,' I murmured. 'Just a hug,' and pulled him down towards me.

He struggled at first, but I eased myself underneath him and sort of *pressed*, and suddenly he was lying there on top of me, his whole body slumped against mine, only the silky black skin of the nightie like a chaperone between us. I clung to him. It was the first time I had been warm all evening. He smelt of the hostel; the boys' cigarette smoke still lingered in his hair and something bitter besides – the smell of poverty, of handicap. His body felt too heavy. He had collapsed on me like a sack. I could feel months and years of exhaustion spilling over me like coal-dust. He wasn't holding me, but flattening me. This was the first female body he'd ever had beneath him, and he was using it as a mattress or a crash-out pad.

'You're heavy, Ray,' I whimpered. 'You're hurting me.'

He didn't answer. He was lying almost like a corpse. I remembered those stories of medieval saints who shared their beds with naked virgins merely to prove their own strength against temptation. I *wasn't* naked – perhaps that was the trouble. I wriggled out from underneath him and ripped off the black satin. This time I lay on top of him. He still had all his clothes on, but I had rolled him over and was fumbling with his belt.

'No,' he said, almost irritably. 'I've told you, Thea, not that.'

'Shssh,' I murmured.

I took his hand and moved it slowly down between my legs, squeezed my thighs around it.

'No,' he said again, less certainly. He didn't move the hand, didn't even seem to know what to do with it. He wasn't looking at me, just sprawled there with his eyes shut. He might have been praying, drunk, dead. Maybe he was even wrestling with some new spiritual crisis in his life. Should he switch to the Dominicans, or become an Anglican? He'd given God eight solid years of his existence. Couldn't he spare me half an hour?

I flung the hand away from me, kneed him in the stomach. 'Get *off*!'

'What's wrong?' he mumbled. 'What's the matter?' He sounded like some small bad-tempered rodent disturbed in hibernation.

'Get *off*, I said.'

He stumbled to his feet, tripped, stood trembling against the wall. Standing straight and unsupported was a skill he'd lost that evening. Hell – other men could drink *bottle*fuls of brandy and still seduce a woman.

'I don't *care* if Lionel hurt me. In fact, I'm *glad* he did. I'd rather have that any day, than you and Leo just lying there like *sacks*. Christ! I take every last stitch off and all you can do is agonize about which *order* you'll join next. Go back to your lousy friary – you're safer there.'

I fought with the duvet until I was lying half on top of it, jammed my legs apart, licked a finger and stuck it up me.

'I tried to follow your example – give up sex, turn to higher things.

But what's the point? That's not sanctity – that's bloody impotence. You've conned me. You never gave up women – you simply ran away from them because you couldn't handle them. You called it holiness to save your face, that's all, so people wouldn't despise you. *Look* at you! You're all fucked up, for heaven's sake. No impulses, no certainties – you told me so yourself. You're not even a real priest. If you could only *bring* yourself to screw a girl or wank in bed at night, you might be more damn use.'

I was rubbing myself so hard, it was hurting. But at least the pain was no longer in my head. There was a rhythm now, a movement. Something else was taking over. I didn't even need to jeer at him any more. My taunts had turned into noises. Simple gasping noises. The whole room was joining in, as I rocked and hammered on the duvet. Three months of false frigidity were over, and I could feel the relief roaring through the room, throbbing between my thighs. I was coming like Leo came, a great wild violent noisy come. I was sobbing like he did, not with anger now, but with joy, glory, exultation.

'Leo,' I panted, 'Leo, Leo, Leo Leo Leo . . .'

All the doubts, fears, scruples, sins, were pouring out of me, leaving me shining and unburdened. I was sheet metal now, gold ingot, not damp cotton wool like Ray was. He had forced me to join the wrong order, but now at last, I had jumped the wall. My body was restored to me. It felt real, right, solid, soaring, free.

I lay on my bed, recovering. My eyes were still tight shut, but I could see fireworks exploding underneath the lids. I touched my body, stretched my arms. I knew I was beautiful. Leo once said that someone ought to sketch me at the moment of my come – lying there, flushed and panting, wet between the legs, nipples hard, cunt swollen and red-hot. He fancied me like that. If Ray rejected me, who cared? That was *his* problem. I didn't even need him now. I squinted through my eyelids, ready to face his disapproving mouth, his averted eyes, the saintly spoilsport grimace matching the shabby, fly-blown room.

His eyes *were*n't averted, but staring full frontally at my naked body. It wasn't a friar's stare, a priest's stare, but a lecher's. The nuns had always used the word 'lascivious', and for the first time now I understood what it meant – that flushed furtive urgent sort of *hunger*, those wild guilty greedy grabbing eyes.

He was fumbling with his zipper. There was something underneath it, something moving and alive. I almost laughed. A friar with an erection!

'You're a *friar*,' I mocked. 'Remember? You told me so. Still a priest. Still under vows.'

'No,' he muttered. 'No, not now.'

So he was throwing away his priesthood, his high-flown principles, his seven years' training, his vows of chastity, for no more reason than that a slut with false teeth had frigged herself in front of him.

He slunk towards the bed. He had dropped his trousers, but still had a sweater on and a pair of gym-shoes over green nylon socks. His legs were thin, white, veiny. He didn't know how to put it in. He was fumbling, missing, sliding out again. I didn't help him.

After three false starts, he got it right. I shuddered as he slithered in. He felt small, slimy, apologetic almost, and yet that look was still all over him. Lascivious. It wasn't how I wanted it. I had imagined him screwing me purely as a pastoral duty, undoing the stain and shame of Lionel, his prick like a bishop's crosier, proud and tall and sacred. I'd dreamed of divine passion, not this furtive cringing lust.

He didn't even seem to be enjoying it. I was his first woman and yet it was an agony, a penance for him. His face was anguished, his eyes screwed up. I might have been just a bolster he was clinging to, a hankie he was sobbing into. He wasn't even moving. Somehow, I had to make it better – not just for him, for me as well. After all, he *was* a priest. It was still a triumph that he had entered me at all. If I shut my eyes, I could give him back his dignity, his sanctity. I could even have my crosier, turn him into a bishop if I wished, a cardinal, a pope.

'Wait,' I murmured. He was just beginning to shudder. I wanted to soar to Rome, to do it in the Vatican. Pope Leo was inside me now, robed in white and gold, the crusted embroidery on his silken cope scratching against my thighs. The spectacles had gone and been replaced by a papal tiara. A second pontiff slipped into place beside him, a third and fourth, a fifth. A dozen popes, all worshipping at my body, backed by a hundred cardinals, two hundred priests. I heard the organ swell, the choir thunder. It was sacred now, a ritual, a sacrament. I rubbed myself slowly, solemnly, against Pope Leo's thighs.

Suddenly, the Holy Father collapsed. There was a little shudder, a tiny mewling cry.

'God,' he yelped. 'Oh God!' He might have been repeating the responses to some divine service, a gabbled slipshod service that had lasted only two seconds, a Mass without the Communion, with no oratory, no build-up. Back in the Vatican, we were only at the start. The clergy had just come in, the congregation ready, primed, rapt, expecting a solemn ceremony which would last an hour or so at least.

I opened my eyes. The pontiffs slunk away. Only one thin sweaty friar was left – slumped across my stomach, his straggly pubic hair wet with his own semen, his thing already shrunk and sort of wizened. He was lying as if dead, feet tangled in the duvet, face turned away from me. He was panting, out of breath. I'd no idea what he had to pant about. Two seconds isn't really exercise. Two seconds isn't really *any*thing. He struggled up. His face looked so pained, so tortured, I felt like Eve. I was Sin for him, Satan, shame, the serpent. Even his voice was sliding away from him, tripping and stumbling in his throat.

'Thea, I'm so . . . Christ! I don't know *how* I . . . Oh *God*, I can't . . .'

Yes, it was God he was talking to, not me. He was almost on his knees to Him. His spine had turned to foam-rubber – he couldn't stand up straight. He was falling over himself, trying to drag his trousers on, find his belt, apologize, make acts of contrition, all at the same time. His voice was broken into bits. He was almost crying. We'd only *coupled*, for heaven's sake, and only for two seconds. The way he was going on, he might have murdered half a million Jews.

'I'm *sorry*, Thea. I mean, I just can't tell you . . . God! I . . .'

People only really apologize for the harm they do themselves. Ray had lost his virginity, stained the virtue which for him was wealth and power. I was *furious* with him. I'd never really intended him to submit. I'd wanted to tempt and tempt him until he had *proved* to me his sanctity, shamed me with his unwavering vows of chastity. Or if he *did* give in, he would do it sacredly, deliberately, as a willing sacrifice, renouncing to me his celibacy, the greatest treasure any priest could give. But what in fact had happened? Just a grope, a poke, a two-second, shame-faced fumble. He wasn't a noble Vestal, just a premature ejaculator. My forty-eighth man, last not only in number, but in order of achievement. Even the park-keeper had kept it up for two *minutes*. Dribbling Jimmy could have done it better, or the boy with no neck. Rather no neck than no prick.

'Thea, I'm *sorry*. I simply don't know how to . . .'

If he said sorry once more, I think I'd have whipped out a knife and cut it off. He'd hardly have missed it, anyway.

'Get out,' I shouted. 'Get *out*!'

He picked up his coat, dropped it, knocked into the broken chair, swore, apologized, turned away, came back again. He didn't even know how to leave. He was backing towards the door, stuttering and stumbling, shedding 'sorrys' like dandruff.

When he'd gone, I wept for half an hour. I knew I wouldn't be granted Leo's miracle – not now. Ray had ruined everything. He'd broken my vow of chastity, scotched my First Communion, slipped from being a priest into a man, and then lapsed further into a eunuch. I stuffed the nightie in my case and struggled into a tee-shirt. I sat on the bidet and slapped myself so hard with soap and flannel, I almost cried out in pain. I crouched there a moment, just staring at the wall. More of the little black insects were scurrying and slithering up and down the cracks. I flung the towel at them and squashed a score. Another hundred or so were still buzzing round the lamp.

I trailed back into bed, lay on my back and scrubbed at my sore red eyes. Just above me, on the wall, was the photo of St Bernadette. She'd been there all the time, but I'd been too involved to notice her. She wasn't frowning. She didn't look shocked or cross or even disappointed. In fact, she was smiling at me, a friendly, open, understanding sort of smile. I remembered the prodigal son, the bit in the gospels about all the angels of heaven rejoicing over one reformed sinner. I'd almost forgotten this was the church of sinners, the church of second chances, of forgiveness. Of *course* I could make my Communion. I'd just had a little relapse, that was all – been thrown by the shock of Lionel, tempted by a priest. Two seconds hardly counted anyway – it was too short to be a sin. After all, I was only a new Catholic, a babe in arms squealing from my baptism, still wet behind the ears. Babies had to *learn*. I *needed* my First Communion to make me stronger, help me grow up, turn me into a pro. Meantime, broken vows could always be renewed. Hell, it was almost easier to pledge myself to chastity after the farce of Ray. Who *wanted* sex in socks? Anyway, I knew I had to save myself for Leo. That's what God had been trying to tell me all along. All I had to do was wait for my miracle and then return to London and present it to a man who knew what to do with it.

I stood on the bed and unhooked the photo from its nail. I stared at the large brown eyes, the pale oval face with its heavy jaw and generous mouth, the tiny indentation above the upper lip, the bulky peasant clothes.

'Bernadette,' I whispered.

I laid her on the pillow, her face almost touching mine. Although she was poor, she had made her First Communion in a showy white dress and cape, like a richer child. Someone had lent them to her, pulled her out of her poverty to receive her pauper God. She would do the same for me, stuff the rags and tatters of my sin into my suitcase, and dress me as a shining virgin bride.

I shut my eyes and smiled. It was only four-and-a-half hours till Easter Mass.

twenty

The light woke me – the light of Easter morning, streaming in and turning the duvet golden. I bounced to the window and gazed out across the shining new-born world. The Pyrenees were shouting and soaring in a semicircle round the town, sun on their flanks, snow on their topknots, the first buds snapping open, a faint green glaze of life fringing the trees. The air was cold, clean, pure; the sky white and newly hoovered. I could almost *smell* the Resurrection, a scent of cows and almond blossom, fresh-ground coffee, rabbit stew, and the raw, randy tang of cut grass. Only the first week of April and they were already cutting grass! It made everything seem lush, fertile, ripe.

I turned back, stepped on a handkerchief, a grubby chequered one in blue and beige. Ray must have dropped it from his trouser pocket. It looked limp and knackered as he had. But that was last night, and since then, the whole world had resurrected.

Easter had always been important to the world. Even before the Christian Resurrection, the pagans had celebrated the return of light and spring, the death of dark and evil. In fact, Adrian had told me that the Christians simply pinched the pagan ceremonies, but gave them different meaning. Even the rituals were the same – symbolic light and cleansing fire. He'd written a paper on it once, about the god Adonis who died and rose again, and some bitch called Eostre who was the goddess of spring and gave her name to Easter. I'd hardly listened then, but now I could see those new-hatched deities sitting smiling on the mountain peaks, thawing the snow into white spring flowers, making all the centuries join hands, uniting all religions.

Ray would be changed this morning, transfigured, reordained. No more green nylon socks and semen-spotted denim, but sacred white petticoats to symbolize his rebirth as a priest.

I knew I had to match him. I opened my suitcase and took out a pair of dazzling white jeans which I'd washed three times in biological detergent and the frilly white shirt I'd borrowed from a shop. It was the nearest I could get to a dress and veil. This was my marriage to Christ, as well as my Communion day. I'd never had a proper wedding – not one with a showy gown and six tulle bridesmaids and a car with flowing ribbons. Adrian had insisted on Richmond Registry Office in a plain suit. I didn't even carry flowers. I suppose I could have clutched one of Adrian's famous potted primulas, but he hadn't offered me so much as a buttonhole. (He was saving up for a second-hand set of the *Encyclopaedia Britannica*.) The registrar was bald with a flat South London accent. When he said, 'I pronounce you man and wife', I was thinking of my father and how I might have strutted down the aisle clinging proudly to his arm. My mother would never have stood for it. Even without him there, she was wearing her most put-upon expression and the navy hat she reserved for funerals.

Today would be different. It had been raining at Richmond, whereas now the sun was shining. All the first shy mountain flowers were opening for me, the trees breaking into leaf. The Pyrenees were bridesmaids, the registrar was Ray. I was fusing Christian and pagan in one ceremony, marrying Christ on one level and Leo on another, uniting all my men. Leo, with his miracle, would be my dead and risen Adonis. Ray would set the seal on it by administering the sacrament. And even Adrian, with his plain suit and *Encyclopaedia Britannica*, could be regarded as a sort of official herald or precursor, like St John the Baptist.

I dressed myself solemnly, as if my clothes were vestments and the robing was a ritual. I left my sheepskin off – that belonged to yesterday, to sin and cold and winter. I brushed my hair a hundred times and wound a wide white ribbon in it. There was no mirror, but I knew already I looked beautiful.

I opened the door and fell over my breakfast tray. I was now so used to being hungry, I'd almost forgotten meals. I stared at the cup of already tepid coffee, the hunk of coarse greyish bread. There wasn't any butter, just a dab of orange jellyish stuff which looked like gum. I didn't want it, anyway. God was about to leap into my stomach – it would be sacrilege to mix Him up with cheap bread and jam. On the other hand, meals cost money, and with a dab of liver sausage or a sliver of cheese, breakfast could be transformed into lunch. I picked up the bread and the two crumbling sugar-lumps, wrapped them in a face-towel and hid them in my suitcase.

As I walked downstairs, the noise of a normal human morning grabbed me by the ears. Madame was quarrelling with another woman and their two shrill voices were rising higher and higher up the house;

two of the children were wailing, and a man was shouting what sounded like Algerian obscenities. Various machines like hoovers and coffee-grinders filled in any gaps. I smiled at the happy family and stepped out on to the pavement. At street level, the sun, the spring and the mountains had all disappeared. I shivered. A cat with no tail was sitting in the gutter scratching, two little boys were raiding the dustbins, and a woman two floors up was stringing wet nappies across her balcony. I smiled at all of them. This was Easter, the day of universal brotherhood, of joy, of peace, of hope.

I turned the corner and started running towards the Rue de la Grotte which led down to the old bridge and then on further to the basilicas. I was late. Pax Pilgrims would already be sitting expectant in the church. It seemed a hundred years since I had seen them. If you don't live with your family, you soon lose touch. They'd have their own cosy little notice-boards posted in the two hotels, their representatives, their couriers, their nightly cocoa parties. I was just a step-child once again.

The town was crowded, the souvenir shops already open, despite the holy day. Soon I was tangled in a mass of pilgrims, some storming the counters, others making for the Grotto. Nobody else wore white. The colours were predominantly sombre – men in stern grey suits, peasant women dressed all in black except for their ashen faces, navy-blue nurses, sin-black nuns, married couples beige all over. Even the streets were grey, the bridge, the walls, the water. Yet the whole rejuvenated world should have been clad in white, or daubed with singing colour.

The crowds and I surged across the street, through the great gates of St Joseph, and down the slope to the underground basilica. It looked different in the light – heavy, grey again, crouching almost sullen and oppressive, its huge concrete ribs no longer soaring, but pressing down, down, on all the heads. I felt dwarfed as I entered it, lost and insignificant. There were so many throngs of people crowded in the nave and jostling all the entrances, it was impossible to find the English group, let alone Pax Pilgrims. I inched down the ramp into the body of the church and squeezed myself on to an empty scrap of bench at the end of a pew. The fat woman next to me shifted and grumbled a bit, otherwise no one seemed to notice me. I was a refugee here, with no family, no nation. The service had already started, but I had no idea what was happening. It seemed nothing like the Masses we had had at school. The priest was speaking a language I had never heard before. I was further away from the altar than I had been yesterday, so all the priests looked smaller and somehow less impressive. They seemed to be short of vestments. I had imagined all two hundred dressed in richly embroidered gold and silver chasubles, but half of them wore dingy white nightshirts with their grey or navy turn-ups showing underneath. I couldn't spot Ray immediately, but I was almost relieved by that. After last night, it was probably less embarrassing to leave him as a blur.

There was still no colour in the place – apart from the flags of the different nations grouped around the altar. The nations themselves were dressed in mourning. I had pictured the church piled high with Easter flowers, their scent choking through the nave, blending with the incense, but there were only five sparse lilies standing stiffly in a vase. Five lilies for twenty thousand people. I'd be lucky if I got a stamen.

Suddenly, the organ pealed out, and the chief celebrant lifted up his hands to heaven and thundered forth *'Credo in Unum Deum'*. The entire congregation rose to its feet and joined in. Awe and excitement pierced me like silver arrows as the great bellow of sound hurled itself up to God. Now, at last, I knew where we were up to – the Creed – that great love song to the Catholic faith. *Credo* is my favourite word. *I believe.* I yearned to believe in everything, not only in the mysteries and marvels the congregation were crooning (the Holy Ghost, the remission of sin, the resurrection of the dead), but also in peace, in joy, in sons, in fathers, in Leo's miracle and Ray's spring-clean.

It was almost an anti-climax to sit down again and listen to some long, fidgety sermon in a foreign language. I knew I should be concentrating, preparing myself for First Communion, but somehow, when the dramatic bits were over, I kept getting distracted by the crowds. I consoled myself by the thought that the First Communicants at school had also been inattentive. Sometimes they got so nervous before the ceremony, they even wet themselves and had to change their dresses. I was always jealous of those dresses, the snowy frills, the petticoats, the wreaths of roses on their heads, the tiny golden crosses. Every year I knelt there, sick with envy, watching the new batch of seven-year-olds flow up to the altar-rails, tip back their heads, join their hands. The priest would approach with golden vestments, blazing eyes, the soft-lipped organ throbbing out the *Pange Lingua*, the nuns exultant. Seven-year-olds! I'd been fifteen, for heaven's sake, and still banned from that table.

Not now. The ban was lifted now and, any moment, I would receive the sacred host from Ray's own hands. The only problem was I still hadn't spotted him. True, I was some distance from the altar and there were even more priests than yesterday – all of them looking more or less the same – but even so, flame-red hair is difficult to hide. I counted thirty-three fair heads, eighty grey or thinning, and every variety of brown from mouse to burnt almond. Nothing carroty. Next I tried the footwear. In all those rows and rows of shiny black toecaps, moccasins or sneakers would shout out loud, even at that distance. The only unconventional shoes I saw were a pair of ox-blood slip-ons, but they belonged to a six-foot-six Nigerian. There was one small priest who had the same build as Ray, and even wore dirty shoes, but when I looked higher, he was completely shiny bald. It struck me for a second that Ray might perhaps have shaved off all his hair as a penance for the sex, but then I realized he wasn't wearing spectacles. Even Ray wouldn't renounce his glasses as a second penance. He was so short-sighted, he'd have bumped into the altar.

So he wasn't there, wasn't redeemed, reborn, and dressed in shining white. Maybe he was still slumped on his bed in dirty denims, sleeping off the brandy. No, Mary-Lou would have brought him Alka-Seltzer and no one could have slept through early morning with Cammie's 'greats!' and all the jokes and clatter of the boys. Something else had happened – something worse. He was in mortal sin and all two hundred priests had refused him absolution. Franciscans' sins were probably trickier to forgive than mine. He'd told me, once, St Francis had rolled in the snow to cool his lust, and that was merely for *thinking* of a woman. Perhaps Ray had been banished to the highest snow-capped peak of the Pyrenees to shiver away his lechery. I felt a tiny plume of pride. My body had the power to banish a priest, to bar him from the Communion table, to send him like the Emperor to Canossa. I was truly Eve – the first woman, the first sinner, but also the mother of the human race. Eve was in every art gallery in the world. Leo even had a picture of her in his lavatory, a pale deep-breasted hussy with the serpent in her hair. Christ had *died* for Eve.

All the same, I wished Ray would return. His absence was a deep sharp nagging pain underneath my ribs. He might still come in, of course – late or sick or flinching pale from his confession. He *had* to.

For three long months I'd planned to receive Communion from his hands. No other priest would do. He was my private confessor, my book-skipper, my dental nurse, my Adam.

Maybe he was even in the church, sitting somewhere in the congregation, still tending to his boys. Maybe Mike had choked or Lionel vomited up my kiss. I gazed around. The huge basilica was oval-shaped, with the altar in the middle, so wherever you looked there were banks of people, rows of heads. I'd never find him there. I'd simply have to trust him, keep sending up my own private credo until he stepped radiant up the altar steps. Meanwhile, I'd try to pray.

It wasn't easy. A man had oozed into the last six inches of bench and was shunting me up against the fat woman's overflow. The boy in front was cleaning his ears out with his little finger. People were shuffling and fidgeting all around. Some even strolled about as if they were in Selfridges. Others took photographs with flashlights, or jiggled babies on their knees, or offered drinks to the sick and handicapped. Someone seemed to be offering *me* a drink. A sort of jug on a long handle was suddenly shoved beneath my nose. I wasn't sure whether it was a loving cup, or holy water to sprinkle on myself. It looked, in fact, like one of those bottles men pee into in hospitals. Everyone was digging in their pockets. It was only then I realized it was their version of the collection plate. The woman beside me dropped a fifty-franc note into the jug. I almost fished it out again. Fifty francs would have kept me for a week. I struck a bargain with God. 'Look,' I said, 'I'll leave it there, if you send Ray back in time for my Communion.'

I only wished he'd hurry. I was so tense now, I could feel the sweat prickling between my breasts. There were great gaps and silences in the service, when the priests just sat or stood about or mumbled things or passed each other various bits of silverware. When they *did* say something, it was largely double Dutch, though occasionally they tossed us a morsel of English, or a word like 'amen' which I suppose is universal. I think I must have been sitting with the Germans. The man beside me smelt of garlic sausage and he had one of those small green feathers in his hat you see in commercials for Kronenberg.

Suddenly he shook my hand. I almost pushed him off. I'd had trouble enough with Ray, and didn't want a Kraut on top of it. Then I realized that *all* the congregation were shaking hands. This was the famous Kiss of Peace. It had been a *real* kiss in the early days, a sign of affection and commitment to each other. But then the Church had lost its nerve. Kiss is a four-letter word for bishops, so they'd pared it down to a handshake. In one English diocese, they'd tried even to forbid that, on the grounds that any physical contact whatsoever might incite dangerous and uncontrollable passions. But this was France, not England, so I turned to my other neighbour and shook her warmly by the arm. She was dressed in a sort of damask tablecloth with a medal round her neck. She took my hand very gingerly, as if she feared I hadn't washed it. I yearned for the whole vast congregation to *really* kiss and cuddle, to cast aside all barriers, lie down on the concrete floor and unite in true affection. Why was the church so *terrified* of passion, the slightest stirrings and twitchings condemned immediately as sin? I thought of Ray – outlawed from that band of priests merely because he'd fitted one bit of his anatomy into a slot in mine and kept it there two seconds. I closed my eyes. I could see twenty thousand worshippers rolling naked in the aisles, nuns and priests included, humping and thrusting in their paschal joy. Only last night God had requested us to increase and multiply. What better place to do it than in His own temple which had floorspace enough for everyone and even an organ.

The German tablecloth was trying to retrieve her arm. I'd been pumping it for a good two minutes. My vision faded. I was aware only of Ray's absence now. The huge crowded church was empty because he wasn't there. 'Credo,' I whispered. 'I believe.' He could still slip in, late but fervent, a newly-shriven sinner with all the angels of heaven rejoicing in his wake. Everyone was kneeling now, as if they were expecting him – twenty thousand people on their knees in relief and gratitude because my Ray had come. The English priest was speaking:

'Lord Jesus Christ,
I eat your body and drink your blood.
Let it not bring me condemnation,
but health in mind and body.'

We had reached the Communion! Christ had exploded from a wafer into living, breathing flesh and I hadn't even noticed. He was there, now, in our midst, waiting to slip inside me. This was the moment I had longed and prayed for since the age of thirteen. I ached to share it. The girls at school had always had their parents present. I remember the mums looking brightly dressed and almost blasphemous among the chaste black nuns. The fathers were more sober, but still too broad and booming for that quiet cramped convent chapel.

Vast hairy hands spreadeagled on flimsy prayer-books, resounding baritones making the ceiling flinch. My only parents now were a fat Bavarian *Hausfrau* on one side, and a man with garlic breath on the other. My real father was an out-of-focus snapshot tucked inside my soul, and my mother would have no more gone to Lourdes than to Sing Sing. Even my priest was missing still. Or hiding.

I was suddenly pushed almost off the bench. Everyone was surging and milling past me like a football crowd. Some forty or fifty priests were processing down the aisles, each preceded by a deacon with a lighted candle, each with his chalice full of God, ready to dispense Communion from a dozen different sections of the church. I could hear my stomach rumbling, crying out for Christ. I felt a wild, tearing hunger as if I were standing in a bakery surrounded by fresh-baked loaves, or touring a chocolate factory with rows and rows of candies chugging past. I longed to cram God in my mouth, grow fat and glossy on Him, swallow Him a hundred thousand times. It was all I could do not to rush up to those fifty priests in turn, receive the host from each of them, then double back and beg a second helping, a third, a fourth, a fifth. I wondered how many times you could receive Communion at a single Mass. Could you even attend all the different Masses through-out the day and keep on and on receiving it, glut yourself on God?

No, that was forbidden. Greed was a sin – even greed for God. One single host would be a banquet, as long as Ray had laid it on my tongue.

Where was he? My heart was thumping with fear and hope and longing. He might have just slipped in, arrived that very second, or be round the other side. The trouble was, it was more or less impossible to see. The entire basilica was a tangled mass of bodies, people converging from every aisle and angle, those returning bumping into those still fighting their way towards the priests. I jumped up on the bench and scanned the whole swarming space. I had to have my Communion from Ray. Only then could last night be cancelled and Ray restored to his priesthood. Even without last night, I knew it was essential. My faith and Ray were totally entangled. Even the fact that his surname was the same as our school chaplain's somehow mattered to me. I had knelt in that convent chapel every day, watching a Father Murphy dispense Communion to everyone else but me. Now at last I could receive mine from a Murphy. No other name could really compensate. I jumped off the bench and struggled round to the far side of the altar. Perhaps Ray was hidden there or about to burst in from the other door. 'Oh, *please*,' I murmured. 'Please.'

The crowds were returning now with God in their mouths. They still looked grey, grim, dyspeptic, grudging – jostling and obstructing one another, treading on each other's feet. There was no harmony, no order, not even any Communion rails. The crowds just stampeded towards the priests, who might well have been mobbed or injured, had the *brancardiers* not linked arms to keep them back. The organ was almost sobbing, the choir singing something sad and spiky which sounded as if it had been stolen from a funeral service. Christ was in twenty thousand stomachs and there was still no jubilation.

By now I had panted and elbowed my way round the entire basilica. Ray simply wasn't there. If I dithered any longer, Communion would be over and I'd have to wait another twenty years. I wouldn't get so much as a morsel or a *crumb* of Christ, let alone a blow-out. Swiftly, I scanned the three priests nearest me, chose the one who looked most like Leo, a dark skinny fellow who could have been Bulgarian. I joined the dregs of the queue, feeble old wrecks who had been pushed aside by the young and strong. A crone with one eye stood just in front of me. She received the host in her hand as if it were a government hand-out, peered at it almost in disappointment, and crammed it in her mouth.

Now it was my turn. Someone in the queue behind me was shoving me almost into the hard golden rim of the ciborium. I opened my mouth, tipped back my head. I only hoped my tongue looked pink and healthy, not furred by my long fast. Bad breath is always a problem with lovers – I'd never really thought of it in the context of Holy Communion. I wished I'd chewed an Amplex now, or gargled with Listerine. Hours seemed to ache and hobble by. My neck hurt, my tongue lolled out, but there was still nothing on it – except a sour and prickly fear. Perhaps the priest had guessed I wasn't a normal cradle Catholic, or Ray had reported me immediately and every priest in Lourdes now knew I'd profaned their profession. Would God send down a thunderbolt, or the entire basilica come crashing down in ruins? Already the organ had stopped crying and started threatening, the choir taken up an angry battle cry.

I squinted through my eyelids. The priest had his back towards me, but it wasn't disapproval. He'd merely run out of hosts and was being refilled from a huge ciborium borne by a younger deacon. Behind their heads I could see the stern white trumpets of the Easter lilies. I

closed my eyes again. Relief had made me dizzy. I tried to concentrate.
I had been nervous and distracted almost all the Mass – this was my
last chance. I remembered the great Prayer of St Bonaventure which
the nuns had always recited in the chapel:

'Be thou alone ever my hope and my whole confidence, my riches, my delight, my
pleasure and my joy; my rest and tranquillity; my peace, my sweetness and my
fragrance; my sweet saviour; my food and refreshment; my refuge and my help; my
wisdom, my portion, my possession and my treasure, in whom may my mind and
my heart be ever fixed and firm, and rooted immovably. Amen.'

It was so beautiful, I almost wept. I had tried with *all* my men to make
them my riches, my pleasure, my food, my refuge, my portion, yet I
was lucky if I even went six weeks without a bust-up or a broken vase.
I'd never met a man called Bonaventure. If I had, maybe things would
have worked out differently. Now I was meeting God. I tensed. The
priest had turned towards me again and I could feel the host falling on
my tongue. It was bigger than I'd imagined, with rough scratchy edges
which hurt my convalescing mouth. I couldn't swallow it. There was
no wine, not even any of Ray's famous water, to wash it down. I had
been pushed away from my place in front of the priest, and the old man
behind me was already gulping down his slice of God. I waited for the
miracle to fizz and froth inside me. The host tasted slightly fusty like
my mother's biscuits which she bought in bulk to save money, and
then rationed to three a week to save still more.

I still couldn't get God down. I knew it would be blasphemy to chew
Him. You didn't use teeth on Christ. The girls always told me the host
simply dissolved away, but this one seemed indissoluble, an invader,
an intruder, pressing against my still sore and sensitive gums. My
mouth was completely dry with no saliva to lubricate God's body. It
was like being frigid with a new, important man. I was also terrified of
choking. If I spat out God, it would be proof of my unworthiness. I
remembered those books in the convent library about schismatics and
apostates swallowing the host in mortal sin, and then being punished
with racking pains or terminal diseases.

I bumped into a pillar. I had lost my bearings. Even the German
tablecloth had disappeared. I was walking straight towards a bank of
wheelchairs. A girl with no arms leered and blinked at me. I swung
away. The host was still looming in my throat. In panic, I called on St

Bonaventure, St Maur, on St Bernadette, even on St Raymond, if there was one. I squeezed beside a posse of French nurses who were kneeling on the concrete floor. If I choked to death, at least I could be sure of medical attention.

Slowly, agonizingly, the host scratched down – past my throat, down my gullet, slipping lumpenly into my stomach. I had triumphed. I had swallowed it, I had made my First Communion.

I had eaten God. His arms and legs, His torso and His bowels, were all inside me, His prick and His balls, the crease between His bum. I had eaten a man like Leo who sobbed and thundered when He came, who burst out of His grave clothes, who absolved the world. It didn't feel like that. Once I got Him down, He just melted into nothing. I could hear my stomach rumbling and grumbling louder than before, crying out for something with more substance. It was like impotence again, or premature ejaculation. There was no sense of being filled or satisfied, no mutual orgasm. I was more aware of the pain in my knees from the concrete floor than the hosanna in my stomach.

I couldn't even concentrate. One of the nurses was whispering, another stifling a yawn. The priests had all returned to the altar now and were doing the washing-up. I tried to pray, but all I could think of was breakfast. I hadn't had a banquet, I'd hardly had a mouthful. Blasphemous pictures of huge squidgy croissants, hot crusty rolls, were rearing and steaming in my head. I'd almost rather God had changed into bread than the other way round. I wondered how long He *stayed* God, before He crumbled into chemicals, or became pulp in the bloodstream and finally clogged into a turd. I was already bunged up. Without my branflakes, things were worse than usual. Perhaps if you were constipated, God remained with you longer. Had the medieval theologians debated things like that, or was it only angels on a pin?

The service was over now. The long tide of clergy (still no Ray) was processing out, the organ playing strong conclusive music full of amens and underlinings. I wanted to race after them, tug at their nightshirts, yell, 'Don't go yet. Please don't go!' I hadn't prayed, I hadn't concentrated. I craved a second chance, a second Communion, a God who would explode like a rocket in my gut, fill me up like a whole fresh fragrant loaf.

I dashed up the ramp so that I could see them better, watched them disappear into the sacristy. Two hundred priests now dwindled to six or seven strays! Those straggledy few were already disrobing in full view of the congregation, snatching off their albs and girdles, and revealing creased shirts and baggy trousers underneath. They were no longer Reverends or Divines, set apart by trailing skirts or ritual vestments, but shabby commoners bundling their sacred garments into tatty plastic bags or canvas hold-alls, sloping off for a pee or a smoke or even forty winks. It was the same with the choirboys. One minute ruffed and snowy angels, the next wrangling urchins in short pants and runny noses.

I turned my back. I couldn't bear to look at them, to see coarse humanity swilling and grunting beneath the sacred packaging. The crowds were bad enough, pushing me from every side towards the exit. I had no choice but to join them, a piece of litter swept along by blind and trampling feet. Everyone was buttoning up coats, turning up collars, fumbling for umbrellas. The rain was stinging, sheeting down outside.

I stood at the exit cringing at the cold cruel Lenten air. I was dressed for spring, but the new-born Easter sun was already dead. Christ had risen and God was in my stomach and all He could do was steal my priest away and turn two hundred others into soggy, dripping seculars.

twenty-one

'Happy Easter!' said a voice, and a black umbrella poked almost in my eye. I stopped in my tracks, ready to welcome Doris, Cammie, anyone – but it was a nun in an anorak greeting another nun. I had never seen nuns in anoraks. These two even had their hair – thin wispy stuff – hardly hidden beneath their short, immodest veils. I glowered at them. The only English people I'd spotted in the entire square and they couldn't even wear the proper uniform. If they were truly religious, they'd give me their umbrella. St Francis would have done.

I didn't want to think about St Francis. He only reminded me of Ray, and that set the pain off in my ribs. It was bad enough being freezing cold and soaking wet and the only person on my own in the whole of Lourdes. Everybody else was in couples, groups or hordes – flurries of nuns, coach-parties of school-children, fat Italian families arm in arm and gabbling, lovers under shared umbrellas, nurses with their invalids, helpers with their wheelchairs. I'd have been grateful to have glimpsed even Lionel – at least he would have smiled. Pax Pilgrims were nowhere to be seen. Maybe they were already tripping up the hill towards their cosy communal breakfast, their shared Easter eggs and Irish jokes, their unpolluted priests.

At school, there had always been a special gala breakfast for the First Communicants. I'd never gone, of course, but my friends had told me how Reverend Mother poured the tea herself and there were saucers of sugared almonds on the table and little pats of butter with Easter crosses on them. I had a hunk of bread back in my room. I could always mark a cross on it with the orange gluey stuff. Or go up to Ray's hostel and try and seek him out, share a bowl of porridge with dribbling Jimmy. I stood a moment, trying to decide. The daisies in the grass outside the basilica had closed up their petals, their undersides stained pink as if somebody had grazed them. Even the chestnut trees had furled their buds in tighter. Everything looked as if it were flinching from a blow.

Breakfast could wait – it was the Grotto I must go to, that sacred spot where Our Lady had appeared to Bernadette. It was a place of miracles, the very heart and nucleus of Lourdes, the reason for it all. I had planned to visit it with Ray, but now he was missing, it was a miracle I needed. Everything was crumbling and disintegrating. I would go to the Grotto and beg St Bernadette to put joy and Ray back into Easter. After that, I'd eat.

I crossed the square, passed the other two basilicas, one perched above the other, and walked through the huge stone archways to the river bank. There was no need to ask the way – the crowds were surging there in thousands – gabbling and jostling as if they were about to visit a circus or a zoo. A notice said 'Silence' in a score of languages, but no one took much notice. One man was munching a banana and I saw several people chewing gum. My shoes were already squelching, my pure white jeans wet and muddy round the hems. One of the miracles of Lourdes was that it never rained – at least, that's what the girls at school had told me. In all their photographs, the sky was always smiley blue and sparkling. Nothing sparkled now, except the puddles.

All the same, I couldn't help but be excited. I was approaching the very spot where Bernadette had knelt before the Mother of God, the dazzling Queen of Heaven! I could almost see the fierce rushing river which she had feared to cross, the spreading meadows, the browsing flocks of sheep. The grass should be damp and cool beneath my feet, the air rich with the scent of flowers and lambs and miracles. All I could smell was wax. They were selling candles, the largest I had ever seen, huge phallic flagstaffs stacked in what looked like coal bunkers. The cheapest cost five francs. Five francs would buy two bread-and-salami meals a day. Bernadette would be *furious*. She'd continuously told the townsfolk not to turn the shrine into a corner shop. Actually, I couldn't see the shrine – not yet. I had only reached the water taps. I stopped and stared at them. So this was their famous Holy Water – twenty taps, each with a long queue snailing behind it, like check-outs at a supermarket. Bossy women with shopping baskets full of empty bottles were shoving each other out of the way, as if they were fighting for bargains in the sales. A paunchy Frenchman had stripped to the waist and was splashing holy water on a chest already drenched with rain. Every face showed greedy self-absorption. One woman had a ten-gallon plastic jar which she was filling slowly to the brim, while the man behind her swore and grumbled about the delay. Another was struggling with twelve Pepsi bottles, emptying out the dregs and replacing them with cola-flavoured water. Most people used the hollow plastic virgins sold everywhere in Lourdes, which were both statues and receptacles in one. You filled one Lady up to her neck with water, then screwed her crown on as a stopper. A group of Germans were swigging mouthfuls out of Mary's head. It looked strange and almost blasphemous to see a dozen Virgins dangling upside down with their feet in the air, while their owners gulped and swilled.

I watched, appalled. It wasn't just the jostling and the guzzling, it was the lack of all result. That tide of miraculous water should have washed the last germ and microbe off the earth, restored mankind to his Garden of Eden. Yet all I could see was sin, disease and shabbiness. Even the able-bodied had their varicose veins and acne, their warts and squints and eczemas, their scuffed shoes and blistered feet, their dandruff and their head-colds. Those in the wheelchairs were too weak and crippled even to approach the taps. Bernadette's water had gushed out from a holy spring and dashed laughing down a hillside. This was grudging, godless water trickling sullenly from some municipal plumbing system to splat out into a dirty gutter which looked all too like a urinal. Where was the hillside and the holiness, the pure healing torrent, the open countryside?

Bernadette had called the place her paradise. She wouldn't even recognize it now. Nature and beauty had been banned from it. True, the river still rushed and rippled on, but a tamed and castrated river, its banks pushed back, its meadows besieged and overrun. The trees were docked and pollarded; flowers and shrubs had turned into cold iron railings.

I took a few steps forward. Now I was at the very threshold of the shrine. I only had to lift my eyes up higher and I would see the famous statue of the Virgin. I hardly dared. I stared first at the pilgrims kneeling in the puddles, rapt faces upturned to God and His driving rain. Slowly, I looked higher. Saw the candlestands, the altar, the outline of the cave, the faithful trooping round it, the rock worn smooth where a million million lips had kissed it. I turned my eyes to the left, where a row of rusty crutches dangled over the rock-face, abandoned by their owners who had leapt to health and strength. At last – and tremblingly – I flung back my head and gazed at the focus of it all, the statue of the Immaculate Conception.

It was hideous. Bernadette had been rare unearthly beauty in a small young simple shining girl. The sculptor had made her a taller, older, simpering, Gothic matron with a pious smirk and dead marble eyes. Yet everyone was gazing at her, worshipping her almost, as if she were the Blessed Virgin come to life again, standing there in person.

The candles lit below her had almost all been extinguished by the rain. In the books and photographs you always saw them burning. Our Lady herself had asked St Bernadette to bring a lighted candle to the spot, and ever afterwards the tourists copied her. Yet here were only damp black wicks, spluttering stumps, grotesquely spastic wax. The light in the sky had also been extinguished. The clouds were the colour of dirty handkerchiefs, the rain had slowed to a mean grizzling drizzle. It could have been Scunthorpe on a November evening, instead of Easter morning in the most holy place on earth. There *was*n't any holiness, not even any joy – only a sort of total poverty. A boy in a wheelchair was tearing a piece of paper into tiny useless scraps, stuffing them in his mouth, then spitting them out again. A little girl with burn scars on her face crouched down by the railings and peed on her new shoes. A thin nun in mufti snapped at a fat one in black robes. I ached for angels, for miracles, even for some hushed sacred centre of it all.

If this was the Grotto, you could almost have passed it by. It was just a dingy cave on a weeping stretch of concrete, mobbed by greedy grousing bargain-hunters in their drenched and shabby clothes. How could the Queen of Heaven step on earth and leave behind only drizzle, litter, and the smell of steamy humans in their plastic pack-amacs? One of the proofs of the existence of God was the beauty of the world He'd made. What beauty? Had He created those pinched pasty faces, those mouths drooping at the corners, that sulky sky? Would God Himself turn out to be a bald man with a hernia and age spots on his hands?

I turned away. If I got my miracle, it would be halfway up a mountain or in a meadow full of cowbells, not in this tarmac wasteland. I trudged back across the square, through the gates, up towards the town. I was soaked and shivering, my clothes sticking to me, my hair in seaweed strands. The shops were in full commercial swing now. I stopped for a moment, tempted by a rack of warm fuzzy scarves marked 'Local Pyrenean Wool'. When I looked closer, I saw they had labels on them saying 'Made in Hong Kong. 100% acrylic'. I almost knocked the stand down. Bernadette had said 'no profits', and here was filthy lucre built on lies.

I stormed into a chemist. At least there were no plastic virgins there, just toothbrushes and Tampax. My phrase-book French was limited to things like, 'My big end has gone' and, 'Where is the municipal art gallery?' so I asked rather nervously for *l'aspirin* and *le laxative* and was amazed when the woman understood. I suppose the words must be the same in both languages. Someone like Adrian could write a thesis on French and English words which are identical – amen, alleluia, sex(e), revolution, laxative, orgasm, Communion. But not God or sin or father.

I was so exhausted when I reached my lodgings, I could hardly crawl upstairs – a combination, I suppose, of hunger, four hours' sleep and disillusion. I tried not to smell the almost taunting reek of roast lamb which followed me up all five floors. My room looked different, somehow – cleaner but sort of barer. Someone had made my bed which pleased me and nicked the bread from my suitcase which did not. I almost marched downstairs again and demanded it back. But breakfast words are not the same in French. Bread, jam, thief, snooper, spoilsport, all sound hopelessly Anglo-Saxon. I rummaged through the case. I knew Madame had done her own private rummaging an hour or two before, because she'd put the things back different-ly. Apart from the bread (which was mine by rights in any case), she must have been impressed by my devotion. There were far more books on Bernadette than clothes. I opened the largest and turned to the picture of the Grotto as it was in 1858 – a natural cave springing out of the wild rugged countryside around it, the Savy stream frothing and rippling round its entrance, a sturdy sheep-track leading up to the lush green grass beyond.

Perhaps I was being unfair or too romantic. After all, four million visitors couldn't really fight their way over stepping-stones and sheep-tracks. Lourdes was an industry now, or an idyll. I closed the book, measured out three spoonfuls of the laxative, and made a sort of porridge by mixing it with three crumbled aspirins. That was break-fast, now the bread had gone. The instructions were in French, so I'd guessed the dose, then doubled it. In less than half an hour the griping pains began. I had to dash along the passage and down the stairs to the poky little lavatory three times in just ten minutes. In the end I stayed there, leaning my head against the damp flaking wall and feeling like an empty paper bag blown up by a jeering schoolboy and then burst between his hands. I shat the last dregs of God into the toilet bowl.

Even He could never have withstood that total flush-out. I felt better, almost, to be rid of my Communion. The whole thing was a cheat and an illusion. God only came as dove or lamb to His own Chosen People. To outcasts and pretenders He sat in the stomach like a stone or roared through the intestines like a tiger.

It was still Easter Day. The smell of new-baked Easter biscuits had joined the *agneau* and was now creeping up the stairs. I was *starving*. It was almost sixty hours since I had eaten and the laxative had cleared out all my reserves, so that I was a completely empty larder. I could always cadge a free lunch at the hostel, but I hardly dared set foot there. If Ray was still missing, I would feel guilty and responsible, and if he weren't, I would have to face his fury at my having made him a sinner. I could stroll down to the café and buy a French Welsh rarebit. But cheese on toast cost money. It would be cheaper to buy plain bread and eat it in my room. I hadn't seen a food shop anywhere. I felt too weak to face the stairs and rain and crowds again, and maybe, even then not find a loaf. The only thing left was bed. I'd read somewhere that the body burns up fewest calories when sleeping, so I peeled off my soggy clothes and climbed in under the duvet.

I fell asleep in minutes and dreamed I was Janet making her First Communion in a black priest's cassock and a white tiara. When they laid the host upon my tongue, it was in the shape of a tiny baby, dead, yet somehow struggling.

I could hear myself screaming and choking in my sleep.

twenty-two

When I woke, it was dark. I think the laxative must have contained a sedative because I'd slept eleven and a quarter hours and that in daytime. Easter Day had simply vanished off the calendar. Ordinary people had been eating spring lamb and simnel cake, sampling their Easter eggs, picking pussy-willow in the woods. Back in London, funfairs were grinding and jangling on Hampstead Heath and Clapham Common, the first tulips and the first tourists admiring each other at Hampton Court. And I'd been unconscious through it all, lying in my shroud on the day of resurrection. I grinned. It pleased me somehow. I wasn't a proper sanctioned Catholic, so why should I celebrate their sham? Now that everyone else was going to bed, I'd get up and out.

My stomach felt as if some great wild beast had trampled through it, leaving jagged clawmarks. The room smelt stuffy and airless. I pushed open the window and cold black air rushed in and almost raped me. The moon had dwindled to a sliver as if it, too, had been fasting, and had now wasted away to almost nothing.

I put on my thickest cords and two sweaters under the sheepskin, and crept downstairs. The streets were almost deserted except for the tailless cat, who was crouching under a van licking out the last dregs of oil from a sardine tin. All the shops were shuttered, the pilgrims had disappeared, and even the cafés were closing up. Lourdes doesn't have a night life. The only drinkers are the holy water addicts, the only strippers those who take the baths. There were a few odd youths roaring around on motor-bikes and the odd tourist trailing home. The streets were still pot-holed with puddles but at least it wasn't raining. The night smelt clear and fresh and a soft glow from the street-lamps prettied up the pavements. Lourdes looked almost appealing in the dark. Maybe even the Grotto would seem holy and impressive without the rabble and the rain.

I hardly knew why I was going there, except that all the roads in Lourdes lead down to it. The natural flow of traffic is always west-wards towards the river and the shrine. All the cars, all the pilgrims, turn in that direction as if magnetized. Almost unthinkable to go any other way, to climb uphill instead of down, or turn your back on Mary. Anyway, it would be a peaceful spot at night, a safe one, like a sort of sanctuary, and I needed somewhere quiet where I could think. I had glooms enough, for heaven's sake. My stomach was still an empty bag, Ray was incommunicado and might be angry, revengeful or even plain despairing, and my First Communion had turned out a disaster. And yet I wasn't gloomy. I stopped at the bridge for a moment and tried to work it out.

There was a swirling feeling in my head, almost like relief. I felt like a nun who realizes she hasn't got a vocation after all, and has just ripped off her habit and rolled naked down a grassy slope. I knew now I didn't want religion in the form Ray had offered it. Why should holiness mean a grumbling belly and a padlocked cunt? He couldn't keep his *own* vows, so why inflict them on a girl whose ma had flung God in the waste-bin along with joy and love, and whose father had only gone to church to chat up all the hats? My true vocation was a worldly one. I was needed back with Leo to be a mistress and a mother – a calling no less holy, but requiring a high-protein diet of substantial meals and even more substantial sex. Now I thought about it, Leo's impotence had probably only been caused by my religion. He had sensed it like an alien cloak around me and feared to sully it. Once I returned without that thick nun's habit clinging to my body, his loins would spring to life and power again. *That* would be our miracle.

I stared down at the water slapping black and glossy against the river bank. The stars had fallen into it and were frothing like effervescent pills. I felt light and frothy myself. Perhaps it was nothing to do with religion or Leo or miracles, but simply that I was no longer constipated. Constipation itself is a type of impotence. Adrian had a book on Martin Luther which attributed most of his doubts and ragings to a lazy bowel. Odd to think the entire Reformation might have been prevented had Luther had his branflakes. Maybe that was all Ray needed – more bulk, or senna pods. I wondered what he was doing at that moment. Was he asleep, or on his knees in prayer, or ministering to his handicapped? Did he feel bitter towards me, or simply embarrassed or ashamed? I shivered suddenly, sprinted across the bridge and ran down the Avenue Bernadette-Soubirous. It was too cold to hang about.

Strange to see the streets so empty, when they'd been thronged and jostling only hours before. Now there was just a little knot of nurses standing on the corner and one lonely waiter cycling home. I felt I almost owned the town. The pilgrims had soiled and crowded it all through Easter Day; now it was mine to stretch my soul in. I crossed the road which skirted the Domain and stared around me. Something was different. Not just the peace, the lack of crowds, the hushed black muslin sky, but something else: the huge iron gates of St Joseph were locked and barred.

The nuns had told us the gates were always open, ready to admit the sinner and the pilgrim at any hour of day or night. Perhaps it was just another lie. Childhood is probably only bearable because it's built on lies. Growing up is finding the scrawny shreds and scraps of truth between them. I pressed my whole body against the gates, but they didn't yield. A gendarme shouted something at me, so I moved away. I didn't want trouble, not after midnight on my own. I walked up the hill to the Chapel of Reconciliations (which sounds like a place where quarrelling couples sort out their grievances, but is really a sort of gigantic confessional with forty-seven separate boxes. Just one lone box is enough to turn me on, so forty-seven was more or less an orgy). I tried the door, but it was also locked. Even confessions were restricted to a timetable. You couldn't sin after midnight – only from eight a.m. till noon, or from two p.m. till ten. The times were posted on the door, plus a sort of chart showing all the different languages. Adrian would have loved it. There were also other notices – details of the services, Easter treats and music. I had slept through all the highlights – the Blessing of the Sick, the Torchlight Procession. I didn't care. I could always catch up with them tomorrow.

I crossed the road again and stood a moment in the shadows, listening to the faint plop-plop of raindrops falling from wet trees. I could see the stars tangled in their branches, seeming to bend a little nearer as I gazed at them. I must have been standing right above the Grotto. Ray had told me there was a little zig-zag path winding down to it, which a lot of pilgrims didn't even know existed. I groped my way along the wall and found the gate. It wasn't locked. I pushed it open and stared down through banks of massed trees and tangled ever-greens to a blaze of lighted candles gleaming at the bottom. The flames made their own bright pathway through the trees, flinging grotesquely spindly shadows across my own. A notice said 'Silence' in three languages, but the river was ignoring it, shouting and singing on its way to the Atlantic. I longed to sing myself. Nobody at Lourdes showed any *joy*. All the crowds were chastened, gloomy, grey. No one ran or jumped or yelled with laughter. Even their hymns were dirges. It was like the nuns at school. They'd always insisted that we slink and creep and whisper. Running was unladylike, shouting was a sin.

Suddenly I ran. Round and round, down and down, zig-zagging faster and faster as trees pushed past me and the disobedient river called and encouraged from the bottom. I stood panting by its banks, gazing at the water frothing white and feverish over the tumbled stones, the same water as that which flowed so sluggishly beneath the old bridge, but now quickened and transformed. I could smell hot wax, wet leaves, the lush rangy smell of damp meadows oozing in the dark. I turned towards the Grotto. The harsh concrete was glistening now with gold. The three basilicas were floodlit and poured their million-watt bounty over the surrounding arc of earth and sky. No wonder the moon looked cheated – weak and anorexic against their dazzling light. Above me, the glittering fortress soared like a magic castle in a fairy story. Beyond me, a line of shivering poplars stared at their trembling faces in the river. Nature and beauty had come rushing, whooping back.

I knelt before the shrine. The candles were alight now, leaping and flickering in the breeze. The rock itself seemed to writhe and ripple as the tiny flames reached out their fingers to it. I stretched out my own arms at shoulder level on either side, as I had seen the more devout of the pilgrims doing. I felt like a bird, a huge broad-winged, proud-beaked phoenix which had been mended and restored and which could now fly a thousand thousand miles above the grief and pain of Lourdes. I gazed up at the statue hoping it would look less ugly in the shadows.

It wasn't there.

I gasped and rubbed my eyes, pinched myself, stood up, peered nearer. No, I was not mistaken. The niche where it had stood that morning was only a black and empty hole. The statue had completely disappeared. Impossible! It had been installed in 1864 and had stood there ever since, the focus of the entire Catholic world. Candles were lit before it, pleading letters dropped in the hollow beneath its feet, prayers and novenas addressed to it, donations left in front of it, endless photos taken of it, and a million million copies of it made in plastic, plaster, wood, stone and wax.

And it wasn't there.

I closed my eyes a moment. Maybe it was just some trick of the shifting light. When I opened them again, the statue would be back in place. I'd probably had a blackout for a second, some side-effect of the laxative, perhaps, or I'd lost my balance and my bearings by stretching out my arms. I stood completely still now, breathing deeply, and holding on to a bench to steady myself. I counted to ten, then to twenty, then to a hundred, before I dared look back again. I wanted to be sure I was strong and sane and completely calm.

At a hundred and one, I opened my eyes. There was still no statue, but in its place was a short plumpish girl with a broad oval face (no cheekbones) and a pale rather blemished skin like mine when I have my period. Her eyebrows were heavy, her dark hair almost hidden beneath a coloured kerchief. She had a full, generous mouth, with a tiny indentation above the upper lip. She was wearing the local old-fashioned Pyrenean dress of coarse striped cotton with an apron and a heavy patterned shawl. The clothes were bulky and voluminous, but even so, she looked no more than a child. It was only the expression on her face which made me realize she was older, the suffering in those great dark glowing pleading eyes.

'Bernadette!' I said.

It was impossible to mistake her. I had seen her picture in a dozen books, slept with her photograph, adopted her as my sister, devoured everything I could about her for the last three months. Even without all that, she stared from every shop and hotel and hoarding in the town – giant-sized on posters, thumb-sized on bookmarks, three-dimensional in statues, even lifelike in wax-works. She didn't look quite as attractive in reality. Her figure was shapeless, her clothes unflattering, and that sallow, almost liverish complexion had obviously been tinted and retouched in all the photographs. It was the eyes that were beautiful, eyes almost black, but then changing their mind to brown again, with deep glowing lights flecked and sparkling in them, and a brilliance which cut through all the shadows.

She smiled. An honest, open, friendly sort of smile. I noticed her teeth, of course. They were small and fairly even, but not as white as they could have been. Everything I had read about her was seething and churning in my mind. Today was April the seventh, the very day that Bernadette herself had had her seventeenth apparition, the last one to be witnessed by the crowds. I'd read the story more than twenty times – how the flame of a lighted candle burned between her palms for a full ten minutes without leaving so much as a blister. Thousands were convinced by that, including Dr Dozous, a rational man of science who had been a sceptic up till then, and like Adrian suspected so-called miracles.

I tried to peer at her hands to check the story, but she was wearing those woolly half-mitts bus conductors use. I seized a candle from the giant candelabra burning in front of her and held it in my joined hands. I made sure the flame was safely clear of them. I couldn't rely on miracles myself. But at least I must seem reverent and prepared. I felt something was expected of me, some gesture or salutation. I remembered Bernadette herself had always made the sign of the cross when Our Lady had appeared to her. I tried to copy her.

She smiled again. 'No need for that,' she said. Her voice was soft, but very clear and high. I was surprised I understood her, for she was speaking a language I had never heard before. I replaced the candle in the stand. The flame had gone out, in any case. I just stood there looking flustered and confused, wondering whether to pray or kneel or simply greet her as a friend.

There wasn't time for greetings. She was speaking herself, solemnly, emphatically.

'Thea,' she said. 'I want you to help me, please.'

I was instantly on my guard. I know from experience that when people ask your help, it's often something dodgy or even dangerous which they shrink from doing themselves. I tried to avoid her urgent, searching gaze.

'I'm afraid it won't be easy,' she was saying. She sounded awkward, almost embarrassed, as if she were apologizing to me in advance.

I knew the Blessed Virgin had asked outrageous things of her – commanded her to eat grass and scrabble in the dirt and daub mud and water on her face. I was terrified she'd ask the same of me. I'd had enough of penance. Hadn't I just decided my own way to religion was through joy and sex and fulfilment, not grovelling and self-abasement?

'You'll need strength, Thea, courage.'

'Look . . . I . . . I *have*n't much strength. I've been fasting for the last three days. I'm weak and empty and . . .' I stopped. I could hardly tell her that, when she and her family had been more or less *permanently* hungry. I remembered the coarse maize porridge, the watery cabbage soup eked out among too many grabbing hands. I almost regretted now that I'd wormed my way into her family. Fine to have her as a sister so long as she stayed flat and two-dimensional, made no trouble or demands. She was there to help *me*, for heaven's sake, not the other way round.

'Well, what? What is it? What d'you want me to *do?*' I was shivering now. The night had turned colder, and a fine white mist was creeping from the meadow, closing round me like a shroud.

Bernadette had moved forward to the very edge of the niche. Her eyes were so dark and sharp and brilliant, they seemed to pierce my skull. 'Are you listening, Thea?'

God Almighty! I didn't have much choice. Even the river had gagged itself so that her voice could reach me better.

I nodded. A tiny dart of terror scuttled down my back like a rat. I didn't *want* to eat grass or be burdened with some pointless, joyless penance. The mist tasted cold and phlegmy on my tongue. I stared at Bernadette. Her lips were moving again.

'Thea,' they said, slowly, solemnly. 'It wasn't Our Lady who appeared to me.'

I collapsed back suddenly on to a bench. I knew now why the river was so silent. Its roar had got trapped inside my head and was pounding and surging through my ears.

'Wh . . . what?' I stuttered.

'I didn't see the Blessed Virgin. It was somebody else, but not her.'

'But . . .' I gazed around at the altar with its flowers and candlesticks, the dangling crutches – witness to Our Lady's miracles, the pavement where the thousands knelt in prayer to her, the rock worn smooth by a million million lips.

'Yes, I know it must be quite a shock for you. It was for *me*. But I've come to ask if you could help to put it right.'

'You've come to do *what?*' I murmured, aghast.

'I want you to tell people that it wasn't Our Lady.'

'*Tell* people?' I felt like a fool repeating all her words, but somehow I just couldn't take it in. 'Tell *who?*' I muttered. Who in heaven's name would listen? People yawned and fidgeted if I even tried to tell them who I was, or finish a funny story at a dinner party.

'Everybody. The priests first, and then the public.'

'But why *me?*' I almost shouted. 'You don't think they'd *believe* me, do you? Look, I'm not even a proper Catholic. Even my First Communion went wrong. They'd just assume it was sour grapes or revenge or something. Anyway, I don't *know* any priests. Well, only one and he's in mortal sin.'

I don't think she was listening. She'd caught her shawl on a rough place in the rock and was trying to work it free. She had taken off the mitts. I couldn't see any burn scars, but her hands were peasant hands, rough and chapped, with short stubby fingers. Leo hated peasant types. He always went for pale slender hands, as much like his own as possible. He wouldn't approve of me hobnobbing with a low, illiterate shepherdess. OK – I know I'd accepted favours from her family – Ma Soubirous fishing me out the best bits from her stockpot, her father carrying me triumphant on his back, but that was only safe in bed at night. For Bernadette to burst out of that flat, sheltered, picture-postcard world and make her presence real, to change my vague, soothing comforts into her harsh and impossible demands, was something like a sick joke. Except it wasn't funny, only terrifying.

I jabbed my foot against the base of the marble altar. Lourdes was *full* of marble – bronze, mosaics, silver, gold – precious, dazzling things in honour of the dazzling Queen of Heaven, who had not, in fact, appeared.

'Look,' I faltered. 'I don't understand. I . . .'

'You don't *need* to understand, Thea. All you have to do is pass on my message to the world.'

'The *world*?' Things were getting worse now. I had no proper friends and almost no family, no connections, no sway with anyone, and here was Bernadette commanding me to make a universal broadcast, to undo over a hundred years of history, to shatter marble, trample gold.

'Ask someone *else*,' I pleaded. 'Please don't mix me up in it. I've got troubles enough of my own. I don't feel well. My mouth's still sore. I've got to have my teeth fixed. I'm starving. I haven't got a penny. I'm no one. I'm nothing. I . . .'

My voice was petering out. Bernadette had been a nobody herself, an invalid with asthma and a delicate stomach, a peasant's child who hadn't owned a sou. Yet she'd never said, 'Why me?'

A pity she hadn't, in the circumstances. If it wasn't the Blessed Virgin, then who the hell *was* it who showed up eighteen times and sent all those impertinent instructions? Adrian would have demanded all the facts, drawn up a dossier, worked out a chart. I longed to have his vigorous, ordered mind. There were probably things I should be checking on – dates and records, fingerprints, questions to be asked and answered, evidence to be amassed. Yet I was simply standing there, shivering and trembling, my brain crumbling like a biscuit.

'Look, Bernadette, who . . . er . . . *did* you see then? I mean, if it wasn't Mary.'

'I'm sorry, Thea, I can't say.'

What sort of answer was that? She sounded worse than Ray hedging about his life and habits at the friary.

'Could it have been the devil, perhaps?' I tried to pump her – anything to get more information.

'Oh no, no. No one *evil*.'

'A holy soul in purgatory?' That's what some of Bernadette's contemporaries had thought. Even her mother had first assumed it was the soul of a dead relative come back to beg for prayers.

'No-o.'

'Well *who*?'

'It's not easy to explain, Thea, and even if I tried, I doubt if . . .'

'You mean I'm too damned stupid to understand, is that it?'

'No, Thea, of course I don't mean that.'

'Look, you *must* tell me. Everyone will ask. They're bound to. You see, Adrian says I never get the facts and . . .'

'I'm sorry, Thea, but I'm afraid I have to leave now. Please don't get upset. It won't be easy, but I know you can do it for me. Just tell the priests and people that it wasn't the Mother of God. Make sure they understand. I trust you, Thea.' And she disappeared.

Oh, I know it sounds ridiculous. People don't vanish into thin air, except in fairy tales. But Bernadette *did*. I didn't imagine it, I know I didn't. I've said already it wasn't even dark. The candles and the floodlighting saw to that. I was stunned, of course I was, but absolutely sane. I tried out little tests on myself to prove it. I ran through the alphabet backwards and then forwards. I added and subtracted figures. I repeated the words of the Credo, in English first and then in Latin. I could tell my mind was working, was razor sharp, in fact.

'Bernadette,' I called. 'Bernadette!' I had to get her back, ask more questions, insist she told me everything.

No answer. Only the river swallowing up my words, the hollow cry of an owl, jeering at me, jeering. I had no information, nothing solid or convincing. Bernadette had given me no reasons to change a story which stuck like a limpet to the town which had spawned it, no sharp, lucid facts to use as bulldozers. My mind felt like Bank Holiday on Brighton beach. There were so many thoughts and fears and speculations jostling and crowding through it, it was almost trampled into pulp. If Bernadette's Lady hadn't been the Blessed Virgin, then the whole of Lourdes was one gigantic sham. All those priests and bishops, doctors and magistrates who had worn themselves into a frazzle trying to confirm the facts, now looked like fools or charlatans. Even so, it wasn't simple. What about the miracles, for instance – each one so slowly and nit-pickingly tested to outlaw fraud or chance? Or Bernadette's own cross-examination at the time – a real out-and-out relentless grilling, in which they had *tried* to find her out?

Even the statistics of the place itself were something of a miracle. Four hundred plus hotels in a town of only eighteen thousand permanent inhabitants; four thousand seasonal workers with a language laboratory built especially for their benefit; a post office handling six and a half million postcards every year; an International Medical Committee with posh professors from a score of different countries; a municipal tourist office with a crazy annual total of three hundred thousand documents; a ton of candles churned out every day from the local wax factory. All this – and more – had sprung from Bernadette. I'd read it in a score of trumpeting books. She'd turned a sleepy one-horse village into a pulsing commercial centre, built three soaring churches where there was only a piddling mill-stream. And now she had commanded me to overturn it.

Me, Thea Morton, of no fixed address, scarred, sick, starving and divorced, with neither permanent teeth nor temporary job, was expected to stand up to the entire Catholic world and tell them their shrine, their Mecca, their international centre for both miracles and money-making was a lie, a fraud, a stupid little error. They wouldn't even listen. They'd lock me up, label me a madman, send me to another Dr Davies.

Yet, I couldn't help remembering it had been no less difficult for Bernadette herself. She, too, had been laughed to scorn, accused of lying, madness, even obscenity. At least I was middle-class and could read and write. I'd been married to a teacher and mixed with professional people who could do at least three-quarters of the *Times* crossword, and wrote self-important letters to the *Guardian*, and were Friends of Covent Garden. Bernadette's father was a casual labourer when he wasn't unemployed or in prison. Her mother took in other people's washing and scrubbed it on the riverbank. My ma used a high-class laundry service and throw-away handkerchiefs. She'd no more enter a launderette than a bordello. If a peasant girl whose only skills were darning socks and herding sheep could build a new Jerusalem on the dregs of a peasant village, then was it really so impossible for me to pull it down again?

The trouble was, nobody *wanted* it pulled down. In Bernadette's day, people had craved for signs and miracles. Maybe that explained how she herself was gulled. Visions were all the rage in the 1850s, Blessed Virgins spotted up and down the land like UFOs a century later. Easy for a highly-strung and groggy child to imagine she'd seen another. The crowds were equally eager to believe her. There was no National Health Service, no wonder drugs or equal opportunities, so holy springs and miracles were the only hope they had. If Bernadette had been conned, then the whole panting town had gone willingly along with her, preferring mumbo-jumbo to a deaf, uncaring God. And now the thing had mushroomed. It wasn't just miracles they wanted, but booming business, full employment, a hundred different layers.

Who was I to block and deny the lot of them, empty their crowded shops and packed hotels, muddy their million-dollar water? And for what purpose? Merely to establish truth. People didn't *want* truth. They'd far rather cling to the belief that Mary had appeared there and made them and their city special. It suited everyone – pious peasants and greedy speculators, busy nurses, bustling restaurants – all thrived on the apparitions. Adrian's brand of pseuds like Keats and Blake and Socrates might rave on about Truth with a capital T, but ordinary folk have never gone for it. It's too uncomfortable.

Anyway, what *was* the truth? If I told the world it wasn't the Blessed Virgin, I still had to explain who the hell it *was*. It might have been another saint, of course. If that was so, I could still save Lourdes. They'd have to re-make all the statues, change the inscriptions and the prayers, but there'd still be a shrine and focus, a reason for it all. But if it were merely an illusion, the result of Bernadette's hunger or illness or over-active imagination, or even a hallucination caused by that fungus stuff Ray had mentioned once, then things were much more serious. My 'announcement' might perhaps bring still more fame and uproar to the town – at least in the beginning. Four million tourists could even swell to six. Perhaps Thea Morton's photograph would smirk from all the hoardings, sharing the billings with the Mother of God herself. I must admit I was tempted. Adrian would find me immediately more interesting once I was an historical phenomenon with *dates*. Leo loved fame in any form and even Ray would get a certain spiritual *frisson* from a girl who was chosen as Bernadette's confidante.

Had I *really* seen her? The first tiny serpent of doubt flickered across my mind. After all, I was weak and starving myself, and though I hadn't eaten fungus, there could have been something in the laxative. I looked around. There were hardly any witnesses – just an old man slumped on a bench and a woman walking further down by the bath-house.

No – even without witnesses, I was absolutely certain. I had noticed all the tiny details, the heavy eyebrows which a Mayfair receptionist would have long since plucked, the sallow skin with blackheads round the nose, the high smooth forehead, the little indentation above the upper lip exactly like the one in my photograph. I'd even spotted a darn in her shawl, neatly worked, but in a slightly different colour, so it showed. You wouldn't see things like darns and blackheads if you were hallucinating. The Bernadette I'd seen was a peasant girl of flesh and blood with dark rings underneath her eyes and a slack chin, not a ghost or a visionary who spoke in tongues or arrived in a cloud of angels. Bernadette's Lady had appeared in radiant light and a gust of wind. But not Bernadette herself. She had just showed up as naturally, as matter-of-factly as Adrian might have done, or Ray, or my sister if I had one. Anyway, if I had to imagine things, why not something glorious and uplifting – Bernadette assuring me I was loved by God and destined for heaven – rather than burdening myself with the most unwelcome tale to tell since Adam's fall from paradise?

Tell everyone, she'd said. But *how*? Should I walk about the town stopping people and saying, 'Sorry, but it wasn't Mary after all. You'd better all go home'? They'd merely assume I was one of the mentally sub-normal and pray for a miracle for *me*.

'The priests first,' Bernadette had advised. She'd spoken as if I could count priests on the fingers of both hands. True, I knew more now than I ever had before, but none of them would listen. Ray would regard it as some trick to get him into bed again, and the two Pax priests would hardly be sympathetic when their whole role in life and Lourdes was to help people believe, not take away their certainties.

There was also Father Sullivan back at the hospital, but he *knew* I was a liar, and anyway, the hospital was tricky territory since I hadn't paid my bill. (There'd been endless fuss and correspondence about it. Leo was ignoring it and Adrian was querying it and the accounts office had added a threatening letter to the third demand.)

I walked slowly, wearily, up the zig-zag path again, trying to calm the turmoil in my mind. Lourdes was *packed* with clergy. Surely one of them would be kind or tolerant enough to listen. In fact, the Maison des Chapelains was only a hundred yards or so in front of me, the home of the most important priests in Lourdes and where all the visiting dignitaries were offered board and lodging.

I slipped through the gate, crossed the road, up the hill, and almost ran towards the huge barred and bolted doors. The place looked like a prison, with bars on the lower windows and a stern forbidding façade which growled, 'Get out, keep out, watch out!' I trailed away. Even if they heard my puny knock through all that stone and steel, were they really likely to admit me, knock up their bishops at the dead of night to listen to some fable? Anyway, they would be ninety per cent foreign. My feeble phrase-book gropings could hardly explain a story which, even in the most lucid and carefully chosen English, would still sound quite preposterous.

I kept on walking. I recognized the road now which led up the hill, out to the open countryside and on at last to the hostel for the handicapped. I really had no choice. Ray at least would listen, open his door to me, offer me a glass of water. Thank God I'd slept all day. I'd need my strength to endure so long a trek on an empty stomach and a rough path. The road was already narrowing, the lamp-posts dwindling. I stumbled in the shadows. Only an hour or so ago, I had decided to turn my back on all the dangers and excesses of religion. Yet now I had been chosen to play an almost religious role. To establish Truth. Bernadette could have picked almost anyone from the whole teeming universe and she had chosen me. It was a dazzling, terrifying honour. I realized suddenly that the whole thing had been *meant*. It was some sort of mysterious supernatural plan. Why else should I have crept down to the Grotto at the dead of night when everyone else was sleeping, stumble on the unlocked gate, the zig-zag path? Even the shock and muddle of my First Communion I saw now as intended. Had it been as rewarding as I'd hoped, I might have been less willing to listen to a story which threw my new religion into disarray. As it was, I had become the ideal person to pass on a message of mistake and disillusion.

I walked a little faster. The road was running steeply uphill now, the lights of Lourdes thinning out behind me. I wouldn't look back again. I would go only forward, upward. I could see the huge crouching flanks of the Pyrenees closing in around me like lumbering animals. The night was full of noises – rustlings in the trees, tiny cries from small scared creatures in the grass, the endless rushing of the river, my own gasping breath.

A damp grey fog began to grope its way towards me from the mountains, blotting out the peaks, catching in my hair, stroking cold clammy fingers down my face. A bat blundered through the darkness, a train rumbled somewhere far below. I kept on walking.

'Tell the priests,' Bernadette had said.

I mustn't be afraid. I was on my way to telling one of them.

twenty-three

I was almost crying when I arrived at the hostel – cold, blistered, limping and exhausted. Struggling halfway up a mountain when you've been starving for three whole days is hardly the most restful way of passing Easter night. The place was completely in darkness. I stood outside the door, hearing the blank black silence heaving back at me. When I knocked, the noise echoed like a stone bumping and clattering down a dry well-shaft. No one answered. I looked around me. Solid mountains had turned into shifting, swirling waves of fog. The sky was a huge black hole. I knocked again, tugged at the bell-pull, hammered with my hands. I could hear someone stumbling to the door. I prayed it would be Ray, not Mary-Lou, not Cammie, least of all not Lionel.

It was Doc, looking paunchier in pyjamas and with a lock of greyish hair falling over one bloodshot eye.

'What's up?' he asked. I wasn't even sure if he recognized me, but I could tell he was used to dealing with emergencies. He hadn't bothered with hallos, but was already revving into action, ready to seize his scalpel or his oxygen, according to my story.

I almost wished I could announce a car crash or a heart attack, make the whole thing simpler. But Bernadette seemed still to stare and plead in front of me, as vast and eternal as the sky, imploring me to speak.

'It's . . . er . . . *Ray* I really want,' I mumbled.

'What's the trouble? Can't *I* help? I mean, Father Murphy's only just got to bed. He's absolutely shattered. We've had an emergency.'

'So have I,' I said. 'I wouldn't bother him otherwise. It's a . . . *spiritual* emergency.' Those deep, dark, desperate, hurt saint's eyes were boring into me. I couldn't turn my back on them.

'No such thing!' grinned Doc. 'If it's not actually festering or haemorrhaging or hanging on a thread, best to leave it alone. OK? Look, come in and have a cup of tea or something.'

The little jokes again, the panacea teapot. I'd just seen the saint who had set up the whole of Lourdes and now ordered me to pull it down again, and here was Doc downgrading me to out-patients.

'I don't want *tea* – I want a priest.'

'Look, lass – what's your name, by the way?'

'Thea Morton. I met you yesterday. You've probably forgotten.'

'No, no. Of course not – I remember now. Look, be a dear and don't disturb Ray. He's not been too well today.'

That hardly surprised me, remembering the cognac (and its aftermath). But what were guilt and hangover compared with the shock and wonder of my vision? They were still so bogged down in trivial things – in sleep, in sex, in headaches, in jokes, in normal life. I had bumped into another century, stumbled on to Truth. The world should be shouting with it, yet all it could do was whimper excuses and go back to sleep again.

'Ray really needs his rest, my dear. We've had one heck of a day. Only been in bed an hour or so. Can't it wait till the morning?'

'No, Dr Bradbury,' I said. 'I'm afraid it can't. And if it *could* have done, I'd hardly have scrambled four miles up a sheep track in the pitch dark merely to have a cup of tea with you. There's a café where I'm staying.' I knew I sounded insolent, but if I gave up now, I might never find the guts to start again.

'All right, keep your hair on. I'll go and wake the Boss if you're absolutely sure it's urgent.' He swung round and grinned at me. 'But what about that cup of tea *first*?'

They'd offered me tea when I'd lost Lucian. I'd been crying so hard then, I couldn't even hold the cup. Tea is a sort of escape-hatch, I suppose. In times of danger, or sickness or embarrassment, people just hide behind the pot and hope you'll go away. Even a blazing vision they try to drown in Typhoo.

'Look, if you don't hurry up, I'll have to go and pull him out of bed myself. I'm sorry, but this is serious.'

'OK, OK, you win. I can see it's Casualty Department stuff. Look – *what's* your name again? Ah yes – Thea. Unusual name, isn't it? Look, Thea, why don't you go and wait in the kitchen. It's warmer there.'

I trailed into the dingy jumbled mess-room which had rusty waterpipes running down one wall and oilcloth on the tables. Mary-Lou or someone had done the washing-up, but there was still a rank, greasy odour clinging to all the surfaces. I perched myself on a fold-up chair and tried to calm down by squeezing B's (for Bernadette) out of the plastic ketchup dispenser. My mind was blazing with her – her small stocky body, the open trusting frankness of her gaze. She was a

259

wanderer from another century, yet she had seemed as real, as solid, as tangible, as Doc had done just now.

There was a long row of B's across the oilcloth and even a few smaller R's, but Ray still hadn't come. It crossed my mind that perhaps he hadn't been sleeping at all, but kneeling in the fog outside, naked except for a hair shirt, weeping for his sin, unable even to face me. Once he'd heard my message, petty things like screwing would fade into insignificance. He could join with me then, not for hopeless, joyless fumbles, but in working for the Truth.

I was almost despairing of Truth when the door opened and Ray grouched in. He was not on his knees – in fact he looked taller, somehow, and extremely dangerous. He was wearing faded green pyjamas and somebody else's dressing-gown, too short in the sleeve. His hair was tousled, his skin blotchy, but the expression on his face was that of a tiger who had been caged up in a small enclosure with neither food nor exercise for several weeks on end. If he could have eaten me alive, he would have done, bones and all.

'Look here, Thea, I don't *want* you just barging in like this, least of all at night. Do you realize what time it is?'

I cowered on my chair. I hardly recognized him. He had never used that tone before, not even to a dog. 'Well, I suppose it must be . . .'

'It's *bloody* three o'clock.'

'Yes, it . . . er . . . would be. I . . . I'm sorry. I didn't think you'd . . .'

'No, you *don't* think, do you? I told you very loud and clear that if you came to Lourdes, I wouldn't be available. I'd have thought by now you might have understood that I have to put the boys first.'

I jabbed at the R's with my finger, smeared them into each other until they were just a pool of ketchup blood. 'You didn't put them first on Saturday night,' I said.

The tiger almost sprang. I knew I had sounded petty and vindictive. The last thing I wanted was to bring the sex thing up. St Bernadette had cancelled it, had wiped out everything except the shattering shining startle of her presence. But if Ray flung me only anger and reproaches, how could I show him that the world and I were changed? He pulled out a chair and slumped on to it at the table, facing me, but staring at the floor. Silence stifled both of us like smog. I longed to speak, but I didn't have the words. Ordinary speech was too flat and constipated to deal with apparitions. If only I were a conjuror and could call up Bernadette again – flesh and blood and blackheads – or trap her voice in a seashell and send it roaring through Ray's ears. I opened my mouth and shut it. Ray sat as silent as I did, but I could feel his soul tap-tapping towards me like a blind man with a stick. At last, he groped a hand across the oilcloth and left it there, about an inch or two from mine, as if it were a present or a peace-offering. I realized with a sort of joyous shock that his hands and Bernadette's were similar. Ray's were larger, of course, but both of them had red, rough, holy, peasant hands.

'I'm . . . er . . . sorry I snapped,' he faltered. 'I'm a bit on edge. Look, I . . . I owe you an apology, I know that.'

'You *don't*, Ray – it doesn't matter. It's not that I've come about. It's . . .'

'I was *going* to come and see you, but we had a crisis here. Mike went into a coma in the middle of last night. We took him up to the hospital, of course, and I've been there with him almost ever since, but it's still touch and go. It's thrown us all. That's why I . . .'

'Gosh! I'm *sorry*, Ray. It must have been a shock. But listen – I've . . .'

'We *will* talk, Thea, but not now, if you don't mind. You see, the hospital may phone me any minute and I'll have to drop everything and go dashing up to Mike. That wouldn't be fair on you. Let me just say I behaved very badly and I deeply regret it.'

At any other time, I might have enjoyed this new hang-dog, grovelling penitent, but now I was so enslaved by Bernadette, I had no desires beyond her. I longed to entrust the whole thing to Ray's hands, to draw on his priestly strength, so I was less flimsily and frighteningly alone with the terror of my mission.

'Look, I don't *mind* about Saturday. It's something else, something far more vital. You see . . .'

Ray hardly seemed to hear me. He was crouching over the table as if he were too exhausted even to sit up straight. He had found a small stray crust of bread which he was shredding with his thumbnail. 'On the other hand, Thea, I do think you owe me an apology as well, or, more strictly speaking, you owe it to Lionel. I had a word with Sam about that . . . business. He said he was bathing Jimmy in the downstairs bathroom the entire time you and Mary-Lou were washing up. He swore to me that neither you, nor Lionel, nor anyone else ever came *near* the toilet.'

'Well, no,' I muttered. 'Actually, it *was*n't the toilet. I mean, what I said was . . .'

'You *said* the toilet, Thea, quite distinctly and more than once – I heard you. If you must lie to me, I'd rather you didn't do it about my boys. Especially one who can't even speak up in defence of himself. I can hardly credit your story now at all. I mean, if you lied about the place and the circumstances, then have I any reason to believe that Lionel even touched you?'

'He *did*, Ray, I swear he did.' I squirted the last dregs of the ketchup into an angry, lurching L. I could have wept with fury and frustration. Somehow, Bernadette had got entangled with two major but quite irrelevant other dramas. I knew why Ray was so resentful. He felt he'd lost his precious virginity on sort of false pretences. If he hadn't believed my rape-by-Lionel story, he'd never have lingered in my room, would probably never have been there in the first place. So now that he guessed the whole thing was a sham, he felt conned, trapped, seduced and doubly shamed. What was worse, he could now label me a liar and close his ears to my tale of Bernadette. It was a wretched irony, since on this occasion, I had never been more burningly sincere. The truth of her appearance was so fierce, so real, so urgent, it was tearing me up inside.

'Ray, *forget* about Lionel. He's not important any more. I mean, not compared with what's just . . .'

'Lionel *is* important, Thea, and so is his reputation. All right, I admit it doesn't excuse my own action. It was unforgivable. I used you . . . abused you even. I realize that – and you've every right to feel resentful. I should never have burdened you with my life history, let alone the . . . other. But I think we ought to leave it until we're both a bit calmer. I've said I'm sorry, Thea. I am. It was a grave sin on my part. But you'll only make things worse by pursuing me up here.'

Pursuing him? He must be crazy, blind. Couldn't he see that sex was just a bauble, now that a saint was tugging at my sleeve? Surely I must be changed, transfigured almost. Bernadette's presence had left some aura around me, some residue of heaven. I could feel it leaking from my soul, pricking behind my eyelids. The trouble was, Ray was still staring at the floor. He seemed too embarrassed to look at me at all. He was so trapped in sin and semen, he couldn't lift up his eyes and behold the gasp and glory of a world beyond our world.

I *willed* him to look up, crammed my voice with the blazing urgency Bernadette herself had used. 'Ray,' I implored. 'I'm not concerned with you or Lionel or sex or Saturday or any other mortal thing. And I'll tell you why' – I paused, trying to still the shaking of my hands. 'I've just seen Bernadette.'

'You've what?' I don't think he could have grasped it. He looked numb, dazed, almost stupid. The crust of bread was pulverized into a little pile of sawdust, which he was prodding with a finger.

'Seen – St – Bernadette,' I gave each word a supernatural charge. 'She appeared to me in the Grotto, about an hour or so ago. She told me to tell you . . .'

Ray had closed his eyes. If he looked like a tiger earlier, now he was a stone sphinx, face of flint, ears of granite, refusing even to listen.

'No, Thea, no more stories. *Please.*'

'She *did*, Ray. That's the only reason I'm here.' Christ, if only he'd lift his head, open his mind, see for himself Bernadette's footprints streaked across my soul.

'Thea, it's late. I'm tired, you're tired. It's all right. I won't send you back. I think you need some rest in any case. You can sleep here. I'll fix you up a sleeping-bag.'

'I can't sleep *any*where. I've just had the most amazing experience of my life. Look, Ray, I actually *saw* St Bernadette as clear as you are now.'

'Thea, dear, you don't have to make up fairy tales. I understand. You wanted a reason to see me, didn't you? Something dramatic which you thought I couldn't refuse. It's all right, I won't refuse you. I'm here if you need me. We'll even talk now, if that's what you want. But no more lies.'

His voice was kinder now, the sort of gentle, wary, pitying voice you use to invalids or idiots. I suppose he thought the shock of the sex had unhinged me somehow. How anyone could inflate a two-second grope to such ludicrous importance quite defeated me. Here I was, entrusted with the biggest news in Lourdes for a hundred and twenty-four years, and the very first priest I'd approached was still relating everything to his E-stream prick. I tried to keep my temper. If Bernadette had chosen me, then I mustn't let her down. Shouting and storming wouldn't help her cause.

'Thea, let me get you an aspirin. You don't look well at all. You've probably caught a bit of a chill or something.'

So he was looking at me at last, furtively, shame-facedly. And all he could see was mortal cold and cunt, not supernatural shock-waves.

'I don't *want* aspirin!' I stared at a faded pin-up of a movie star I didn't recognize. One eye was a grease-spot, and a bushy black moustache had been pencilled in above the full pouting lips. She was cheering on Manchester United who'd been ripped so roughly from a newspaper that their goalkeeper had lost his lower legs. The boys had set up quite a picture gallery on the kitchen walls. Pop stars and footballers rubbed shoulders with the Pope who in turn smiled down on a small, fuzzy reproduction of Bernadette herself, stuck up with a piece of chewing-gum. I kept my gaze firmly on her face. I had looked upon that face and must be worthy of it.

'What I *do* want, Ray,' I said, seeing again the full pleading brilliance of her eyes, 'is for you to go and tell your fellow priests.'

'Tell them what, Thea?' He was humouring me now, the way he might an infant or a loony, smiling gently at me, setting down the words like brightly coloured sweeties.

'That it wasn't the Blessed Virgin.'

'*What* wasn't?' Ray reached up for a tumbler, dodging the damp trailing washing dangling on the airer overhead. There were pants, shirts, sheets and even nappies. I wondered which of those muscly, stubbly lads were still in plastic pants. They came to Lourdes to beg Our Lady to relieve them of such miseries, to give them grown-up bladders, working tongues and hands. Could I really wrench their miraculous Lady from them, send them home still dribbling and piddling in their beds?

Ray looked as if he could use a miracle himself. His face was grey with tiredness, his movements slow and stumbling. I stared around the room where Lady Poverty had crouched so long, she had left a whispering snail-trail of rust, odours, mould. I almost weakened. If only I could simply shout out, 'April fool. April fool!', pretend the whole thing was the sort of stupid joke his own boys might have played on him. But Bernadette was counting on me. Her very last words had been, 'I trust you, Thea.' Maybe she herself was now in Purgatory, racked with pain until her story was put right. Not many people trusted me. I couldn't let her down.

'Look, Ray,' I said. 'I'll start again and keep it as simple as I can.' It was no good hoping for the gift of tongues. I would have to rely on my own slight halting powers. Bernadette was probably listening somewhere – she would help. I stretched out my hands and soul and heart and voice to Ray.

'Bernadette appeared to me,' I said. 'Down in the Grotto where the statue is. She told me it wasn't the Blessed Virgin that she saw – it was somebody else. I don't know who, I'm afraid, but she asked me to tell everyone – starting with the priests. That's why I've come to you.'

'There we are, Thea. I've given you the fizzy sort. They're easier to swallow.' He had picked out the prettiest tumbler for me, a tall fluted one with flowers tooled into the glass and Disprin frothing at the bottom. He set it down very gently and carefully, as if the slightest noise might drive me further into lunacy or raging influenza. I suppose it suited him to suppose I was a crack-pot. It made his own sin less. Either he could safely deny that the sex had ever happened – pass it off as one of my choicer illusions like seeing saints or receiving heavenly messages from people long since dead – or he could believe that I'd seduced him as a sort of crazed witch with supernatural powers. Either way, his guilt diminished. I realized to my horror that Bernadette was tainted now. Ray could only relate my story to the whole seduction thing. He was convinced I'd come to see him simply to get revenge, or play a mad scene like Ophelia, not to report a vital piece of news which would shatter every life in Lourdes. I should never have gone to him at all. He was too petty, too limited, too entangled with me personally.

'Look, Ray, if you won't believe me, at least you can help me. I want you to write down the name and address of . . .'

'What the *hell*'s going on down here?' It was Doc, shambling in in his tartan dressing-gown with a half-empty whisky bottle under one arm, and Val and Alan trailing along behind him. 'I can't sleep a wink with you two clattering about and jawing at each other. What's wrong, for heaven's sake? I thought spiritual emergencies would at least be *silent* ones. You've woken half the house.'

'Thea, you look awful. What are you *doing* here?' That was Val, bouncing across the kitchen in winceyette pyjamas and her heavy nurse's shoes.

'Hi, Thea!' grunted Alan, half asleep. 'Nice to see you again, even if it *is* the middle of the night. What's up, though? You look as if you've seen a ghost.'

'*Tea*,' said Doc. 'Definitely. If Thea doesn't need it, I do. Put the kettle on, Val, there's a dear.'

The kettle looked sick and dazed itself. It was a decrepit, dented thing with half its metal coating flaking off, and orange sticky tape wound round a broken handle.

'Any decent grub going?' Alan yawned so hugely, his face concertinaed out of shape. 'If you've *got* to wake us up at this unearthly hour, we might as well have breakfast and be done with it.'

Val peered into the fridge. 'Well, I could do you eggs,' she offered. 'Fried or poached or scrambled. We seem to have about fifty dozen here. Or – I tell you *what* – let's have a pancake party! After all, it *is* Easter Saturday night. Fancy pancakes, Doc?'

'At three a.m.? You must be joking. I'll stick to tea and Johnny Walker, if you don't mind.'

'*I*'ll have pancakes – good idea! And I'm sure Desmond won't say no. He was just complaining he was starving. I'll go and get him, shall I?' Alan ambled out again.

'Let's get *every*one.' Val was flinging cups and saucers on the table, banging cupboard doors.

'Val, *no*.' Ray looked hopeless, helpless. 'Thea's not too well. She needs some peace and quiet. She's just had a sort of . . .'

'Oh, don't be a *spoil*sport, Ray. The boys would love to see her. They'll cheer her up. She looks as if she could do with it. I've never seen anyone so sort of . . . *shattered*. What's hit you, Thea? You look white as a sheet. Look, have some tea. That'll help. I'll make it nice and strong, shall I? Fancy a pancake with it? I know the lads would! Shall I get them down? They'd be *thrilled* to see you again, I know they would. Barry kept asking about you yesterday, and John even saved you an extra bit of cake. He said you didn't eat yours. You wouldn't mind them down here, would you? They're all awake in any case, so we can't really leave them out.' She filled the teapot, crashed the lid down, sloshed milk into a jug. 'Right – tea up! I've made enough for everyone. We'll call this Party Night! Hold on a mo – I'll just get Mary-Lou to give me a hand with those scamps.'

She rocketed off. Doc groaned and rubbed his eyes. He had slumped beside me with his elbows on the table and his feet stretched out on a second chair. He was a small wiry man, with that sort of bluff, jokey veneer which people have who deal with suffering all the time, but have never bled themselves. He reached across and touched my arm. 'What's the trouble, kid?'

I glanced at his strong shoulders, his broad, coping hands. Bernadette hadn't actually said, 'Tell the doctors', but on the other hand, her own Dr Dozous had been an ally from the start, and at least Doc had never screwed me. 'It's not exactly *trouble*,' I said. 'Well, I suppose it *is*, but . . . You see, Bernadette appeared to me. Oh, I know you'll think I'm mad. It *sounds* mad, I realize that. But I'm perfectly sane, I promise you. You can do any tests you like – take my pulse, blood pressure – anything you choose. Then you can *prove* I'm . . .'

'It's not tests you need, love, it's a good strong drink and some shut-eye. That's what we *all* need. I'll be seeing Bernadette myself if I don't hit the hay soon.'

'Oh, for God's *sake*!' I almost shouted. 'I've been sleeping all day long.'

Ray stumbled on his words, he was so keen to take me up. 'It w . . . was probably a *dream*, then, Thea, don't you see? One of those very vivid frightening ones which seem so real, you can't really tell you're not asleep. That would explain it now, wouldn't it?'

'It doesn't *need* explaining,' I said. 'It's a fact – not a dream or a delusion or a joke or a . . . Look, you can all accept that *Bernadette* saw someone, can't you, so why is it so impossible to believe I saw *her*?'

Doc was pouring out the tea. 'Well, she was a bloody *saint* to start with.' He added a generous sloosh of whisky to my cup. I ignored it, like the aspirin. 'Sugar?' he asked. 'You shouldn't, you know. It's bad for the teeth.'

'No – I mean yes to the sugar, but *listen* – you've got it the wrong way round. She was only *made* a saint because she saw Our Lady. Without that, she might have married a punk or beaten up her kids or . . . anything. So if she *did*n't actually see Our Lady, well, where does that leave us?'

'Ready for our beds, I'd say,' grinned Doc. 'Here, want a snifter, Boss?'

Ray shuddered. 'No, I . . . er . . . won't, thanks.'

Doc cradled the bottle on his lap as if it were his first-born. 'Don't want to be rude, my dear,' he said. 'But why should Bernadette appear to *you*? I mean, when there's hundreds of nuns and priests available – not to mention doctors!'

I knew what he was getting at. No doubt Ray would have thought the same himself, had he ever believed my story in the first place. Why should a saint pick a common whore, a slut, a liar who even lied about the fact that she wasn't a Catholic? There were precedents, of course. Mary Magdalene was a real live prostitute who probably had crabs and clap and God alone knows what else besides, and St Augustine had made his mother *weep* for his excesses, and even St Francis himself had been a raver and a gambler before he turned to wildlife. 'Yes, I *know* it sounds ridiculous, but . . .'

'Honestly, Val, this is the second knees-up in a row, and we've only just *arrived* here. Can't we *ever* be left to sleep?'

Mary-Lou was stumbling through the door in a thigh-length nightie, with her long fair hair floating round her shoulders. She looked sulky, sleepy, irritable, and quite depressingly attractive. I was suddenly aware of my own torn and muddy clothes, shoes scuffed, hair tangled, hands scratched by thorns and brambles. No wonder they had labelled me deranged.

Val had bounced back to the stove and was starting on the pancakes. 'Shall we have savoury ones, or sweet?'

'Champagne ones, I suggest,' quipped Doc. 'We should be celebrating. Thea here's seen Bernadette.'

'Bernadette!' said Val. '*Gosh*.'

'Oh, come off it, Thea,' growled Mary-Lou. 'I'm not in the mood for jokes.'

'It's *not* a joke,' I muttered. 'I *did* see her. I went down to the Grotto about half-past twelve at night and she was . . .'

Mary-Lou had seated herself as near to Ray as possible and was tossing her hair all over him. 'The Grotto's *locked* at night,' she said smugly.

'There's a *path*, for heaven's sake. Ray told me that himself and anyway . . .' I stopped. If people wanted to believe in strange and supernatural happenings, even miracles, they'd witness them. Eyes would be opened and ears unstopped. But, equally, if they clung to the safe, the accepted, the so-called rational and normal, then nothing in the world would change their minds. All those bureaux and commissions, all that sifted evidence, was so much dross. The only thing that mattered was a person's state of mind. Leo would believe my story. He hobnobbed with sixteenth-century murderers, so a nineteenth-century shepherdess would hardly pose a problem. But the rest of the world, especially the priestly, professional, superior, well-educated world, refused to look further than their own narrow, lying, blinkered senses.

Here I was, with a friar, a doctor, a midwife and a nurse, people who had witnessed miracles all their professional lives – amazing things like organ transplants and wonder drugs, the miracle of the body itself – sex, conception, birth and death. They were all Catholics, clinging to a religion which smashed natural laws as easily as tea-cups, and which trumpeted screaming inconsistencies like Three-In-One, Life After Death, Virgin Birth, World Without End. They pinned their faith on a God who died and rose again, who floated up to heaven, walked on water, cured incurables. They attended Mass where fusty bread was changed into living flesh. How could they swallow all those bombshell paradoxes, those holy impossibilities, yet still refuse to accept one simple fact because it wasn't printed in their missals or their Gray's *Anatomy*? They hadn't even listened – just fobbed me off with tea and jokes and condescension. I was beginning to understand how Bernadette had felt. She, too, had been faced with arrogant doctors, deaf and scoffing priests.

'Look, forget it,' I said. I could feel my anger bubbling up like the butter in the frying-pan, turning black and hot and frothy. I hated them for ruining everything, for making me a laughing stock when I was a heavenly instrument, for driving me from dignity to fury. Even Ray was worse than useless. He kept hovering around me, but feebly, almost defiantly, as if he was scared I was going to burst into tears and start blabbing about the sex thing. I wouldn't say a word. All I wanted was to shut everybody out and stay only with the simple truth of Bernadette. I stuck my head in my hands, my fingers in my ears.

'Where's Thea? Where's Thea? Val says she's come to visit us. Oh, *there* she is! Hallo, Thea. Why have you woken everybody up?'

'She's crying, Thea's crying!'

'No, she's not. She's sleeping.'

'She's *not*. Shove over, Barry, will you? I can't get in if you block the door like that.'

'What are we having *breakfast* for? It's still pitch dark.'

'Pancakes! Who said pancakes?'

The tiny kitchen was filling and shrilling with them. Barry had bashed into the door-posts with his wheelchair, two boys clattering in on callipers, Sam and Cammie singing arm in arm, Desmond tickling Jim. Val was shouting above the whir and drone of the mixer, Alan clashing plates. The jokes, the chatter, the imbecilities, were all starting up again. I realized, suddenly, they were not as saintly or as special as I had first assumed. All they cared about was japes and jaunts and as many parties as they could cram into a so-called pilgrimage. Bernadette had promoted me above the lot of them. Even with all my faults and lies and frailties, it was *my* voice she had favoured to proclaim her message to the world. Doc had scoffed, 'Why *you*?', and yet Bernadette had chosen me above all the priests and helpers and doctors in the place. A lot of good they had done me, anyway. I should either have started with the simple accepting peasants like Bernadette herself, or gone right to the top and tackled a bishop or a cardinal.

'Look, I'm sorry I ever disturbed you in the first place. Just tell me one thing and then I'll leave you to your binge. Where does the nearest bishop live? *Any* bishop, so long as he speaks English.'

'Search me!' said Doc. 'I've always steered clear of Messeigneurs since the time I removed an episcopal gall bladder, only to find it was a case of simple nervous dyspepsia.'

Ray disentangled himself from Mary-Lou and came and stood beside me, stroking my hair very gently as if I were an injured pony. 'Look, Thea, my girl, I don't think you're quite well enough to go. At least, not back to those lodgings on your own. You look very strange, you know. Let me take you to St Catherine's. You'll be better there. I know the Reverend Mother and the infirmarian. They're both very kind.'

'No!' I almost shouted. I knew what St Catherine's was – a loony bin. You spoke the truth and people locked you up for it. I remembered all the brave and lonely souls who had been persecuted for nothing worse than trying to set the record straight – people I'd picked up from Leo's dinner parties or Adrian's textbooks – Socrates and Abelard, Galileo and Darwin, Jesus Christ Himself. Now I was one of them. It didn't feel noble or exhilarating, just exhausting.

'Look,' I said. 'I'm tired. I'm flaked bloody out. I've been walking for . . .'

Ray picked up my coat and put it round my shoulders. 'Of *course* you are, Thea. You need a really good night's sleep. You'll feel better in the morning, you see. They've got a lovely little guest room at St Catherine's with a real . . .'

'No, Ray, *not* St Catherine's.' I snatched my coat from him and struggled into it. 'I wouldn't set foot there if you *paid* me. I'm going back to my room.'

'Well, at least let me drive you there. It won't take a minute in the van.'

That was almost proof he thought I was delirious. Nothing else would have induced him to risk a second soul-endangering excursion to my bedroom.

Mary-Lou jumped up and forced her way between the two of us. I could see her plump pink knees dimpling under the nightdress. 'That's stupid, Ray. You must be around in case the hospital phones. Mike would never forgive you if you weren't there, when . . . if . . . Look, *I'll* take her. I know we're not insured, but just this once. She ought to have some Valium first, in any case.'

So I was 'her' now, was I? They were talking about me as if I wasn't there; doping me, even, so I wouldn't upset their cosy little house-parties. Of course they didn't want to hear my message. Mary-Lou wouldn't be able to flirt with Ray in her flagrant night attire, if there was no Lourdes left to give her the excuse for pancake parties and package tours with priests. I had to get away. I couldn't stand their pettiness, their footling, jarring noise. Someone had put the stereo on in the rumpus-room and it was blasting through the door. Sam was playing drums with a saucepan and two serving spoons, the whole hare-brained, raucous night deaf to the urgent pleading of St Bernadette.

Ray was still fluttering round me. 'Would you mind that, Thea? Mary-Lou's a very careful driver, I can vouch for that. And I tell you what – I'll come and see you first thing in the morning, shall I? I'm saying early Mass in the Grotto, and I'll call straight round afterwards. All right?'

'No, it's *not* all right,' I snapped. I had important work to do and couldn't hang around. I'd planned to go to the Grotto myself as soon as it was light. It was obviously my duty to check the place in public and in daylight. Bernadette might even reveal herself again. I prayed this time she would address the thousands, speak to the priests themselves.

'Right, first batch up!' bawled Val. 'These are plain, but I'm making cheese ones next. Get your nose out, Barry, I don't want germs all over them.'

'But you didn't *toss* them, Val. That's the whole point of pancakes. Here, let *me* do it.'

'No, love. It's too late now. They're already cooked. Oh – damn! – *now* look what you've done. Sam, get a floor-cloth, please.'

Barry hacked with laughter. 'They're dust-and-fluff pancakes now, not plain.'

'Well, you can jolly well *eat* them dusty. There were three whole eggs in that lot.'

'*I'm* not eating dust. Give them to Thea.'

A wheelchair was bearing down on me, the grimy corpse of a pancake pushed against my mouth. I blundered to the door.

'Goodbye,' I stormed. 'I'm going!'

I almost crashed into Lionel who was standing just outside the kitchen. I tried to mutter an apology, knowing already that he couldn't hear it – he was hearing something else. I stared at him in wonder. His ears were in touch with heaven, his mind in tune with mine. He wasn't smiling any longer, but gazing right inside my soul. I realized suddenly *he* knew about my vision. If he had words like 'flu or nightmare on his card, he wouldn't point to them, but only to God and Truth and Mission. The deaf and dumb are always less scared and scoffing of the supernatural than ordinary people – closer to it, perhaps. Although I had libelled the boy, he alone could see I was transformed, and was bearing silent witness to my calling.

Our eyes met and spoke for one fleeting second, and then I stumbled past him. Ray and Mary-Lou were both clucking and fretting after me, but I hardly saw them now. OK, I'd let them drive me back, but I didn't need their Valium, their Ovaltine, their good night's sleep. They were too limited, too blinkered, to realize I had been entrusted with a universal mission. But Lionel understood it. Dumbly, loyally, rapturously, he was shouting to the whole crass mob of them that there was only Thea Morton against the entire Roman Catholic world.

She hadn't time to sleep.

twenty-four

I turned my back firmly on the bed. If Ray wouldn't help me, then Adrian could. I'd follow his methods, his order, his careful pernickety scholarship, and prove to Bernadette she was right to have chosen me. It wasn't easy in a room with no desk, no proper light, a three-legged chair, and nothing to write on except a paper bag and some stolen toilet roll which felt more like sandpaper. Nor had Adrian ever tackled a major project without a good square meal inside him. I was sick, dizzy, starving, and so light-headed I found it difficult to read or write at all.

Nonetheless, I rigged up a sort of makeshift study by propping my suitcase on the bidet and squatting in front of it on a pile of books. I dared not work in bed, in case I simply fell asleep. I took each book from under me in turn, and made careful notes and jottings from it. All the pages and the frontispieces were emblazoned with the hospital library stamp – to deter pilferers, I suppose. I wondered if Sister Ursula would believe my story about seeing Bernadette. I doubted it. Once you've seen a psychiatrist, you're always suspect. Safer to label people mad than have all your own beliefs and structure overturned. That's why I had to try and build some evidence. Since Bernadette herself had given me no reasons for her sudden change of story, no background explanation, then I'd have to find my own. I knew already no one would even listen unless I was armed with what Adrian called a foolproof case.

It surprised me really that supernatural messages should be so vague and flimsy. If the Powers Above wanted something done, why couldn't they assist us mortals by supplying all the facts? Bernadette herself had been told so little, no wonder she had got it wrong. When she'd asked the apparition to identify herself back in 1858, the Lady had only smiled and categorically refused to write her name down, even when offered the local bailiff's pen and inkstand. *'N'ey pas necessári,'* she'd replied. But it *was* bloody necessary. My present dilemma and confusion only proved it.

Bernadette herself had never called her Lady the Blessed Virgin – that was a strong point in my case. She'd used the term '*Aquerò*', a neuter word in her own local dialect which meant 'that thing'. I wrote '*Aquerò*' on my toilet paper and underlined it twice. Other people had soon *assumed* it was the Virgin, but perhaps only because they hankered for some heavenly presence in the midst of poverty and illness. There was such a hunger for excitement that fifty other villagers were soon claiming to have seen Our Lady as well, plus half the local schoolkids. They were all suppressed. Now it seemed that Bernadette herself was merely number fifty-one. Certainly, she'd seen *some*thing – that was not disputed. Thousands had witnessed her ecstasies, her conversations, and she herself had told me in the Grotto that it was 'someone else'. But *who?*

At the sixteenth apparition, the Lady had introduced herself at last. 'I am the Immaculate Conception,' she told Bernadette. That was the turning point. Or so the standard biography said. Even the Dean himself felt now that such words could only come from the Blessed Virgin. Who else but Christ and His Mother could be conceived immaculate? I rubbed my eyes. It was cold in the room and the light was so dim, I could hardly see the print. I tried to think of Adrian, his concentration on the task in hand, his slow laborious reasoning. 'Immaculate Conception', I jotted down. I couldn't even spell it and I very much doubted whether Bernadette could either. She admitted herself she hadn't understood it. She knew as much theology as I knew Higher Maths. She may even have got it wrong, muddled up the words perhaps. The theologians themselves were buggered by the phrase. They felt a living person couldn't or shouldn't call herself an abstraction. That's what one of the books claimed, though I was feeling so weak and weary, even the word 'abstraction' whirled around in my head without meaning much, and the authorities seemed to contradict each other.

The whole thing struck me as fishy, anyway. If it *had* been the Blessed Virgin, then surely she'd have announced herself clearly and simply as the Mother of God or Our Lady of Lourdes, instead of using high-flown jargon to an illiterate peasant girl. After all, Mary herself had come from humble stock. She had been the wife of a carpenter. Actually, I'd never met a carpenter, but I knew our local painter's wife in Twickenham, and the only fancy words she used were the ones on the Dulux colour cards like Indigo and Persimmon. She'd even suggested Aconite for Adrian's study walls, but Immaculate Conception would really have stymied her.

I was getting off the point again. It was difficult to concentrate. The books felt hard and uncomfortable underneath my bottom, but when I tried the floor, that was harder still and scratchier. I yawned and stretched a bit, then smoothed out the paper bag and wrote on it:

'Could anyone else but Mary be conceived immaculate?

Did Bernadette mishear or mistake the phrase?

What else could it mean?'

I must admit I'd never been quite certain what it meant myself until the nuns had dinned it into me at school. It's one of the things they labour at Catholic convents, like the Cardinal Virtues, or the Dangers of Disco Dancing, or wearing your blouses loose so they don't show off your breasts. Lots of non-Catholics still misunderstand it. They think Immaculate Conception means that Mary conceived Jesus without recourse to man or prick. The Holy Ghost just hovered over her, and – presto! – she was pregnant. That's what happened, in fact, but it's called the Virgin Birth – another of those R.C. Technical Terms we spent most of our precious school time sorting out. (The nuns were so coy about the word conception that lots of the smaller girls thought it meant something hard and cold and boring like prie-dieu or ciborium.) What Immaculate Conception *really* means is that Mary was born sinless, the only human creature unstained by Original Sin (yet *another* of their terms!) from the first moment of her conception. It's nothing to do with pricks or sex and semen.

Actually, the whole subject was beginning to depress me, because words like conceive and sin reminded me of the whole mess and loss and tangle of wombs and babies and Confession and Ray and Lucian. I decided to move on, and wrote MIRACLES in large block capitals on the other side of the paper bag, and then '64' underneath it. Such a mingy figure was another point in my argument, especially with so many million invalids. If the Lady *had* been Mary, then surely she'd have acted faster and more generously. An all-powerful Queen of Heaven could have cured the whole damn lot of them just by lifting a finger. On the other hand, if she *was*n't Our Lady, then how could I explain the sixty-four, let alone all the myriad other cures, non-miraculous but still disturbing? The power of the mind, perhaps, as Ray had hinted, when we'd discussed it in the hospital – hysteria, wishful thinking, self-hypnosis. I decided to try it out myself:

'My brain is working vigorously and well,' I said slowly and out loud, in one of those doomy mysterious voices I imagine hypnotists use.

'I am warm, content and comfortable. I feel no hunger pangs.'

My stomach growled in protest, so I stuffed the end of my flannel in my mouth and chewed on it like gum. It kept my jaws busy and helped me concentrate. I pinched my leg once or twice to disperse the pins and needles, then settled back with my dossier. I tried to remember what else Ray had said on the subject of Bernadette. His priestly logic might convince the other priests.

'Bernadette not cured herself,' I scribbled. That I did remember. In fact, in her later years, she'd been something of a physical and mental wreck. I opened the book in front of me and turned to the closing chapters, underlined the phrases 'inner torment' and 'spiritual desolation', skimmed the pages where she died in agony with tears coursing down her face and proclaiming herself a sinner. Maybe she knew already that her story was built on falsehood – that would explain her anguish.

'Anguish,' I jotted, and then 'rose bush' underneath it. The rose bush had always been a stumbling block. Dean Peyramale had demanded a miracle as proof of the Lady's supernatural powers. 'Ask her to make the rose bush flower,' he'd said to Bernadette. It was a wild rose growing at the bottom of the niche where *Aquerò* always appeared. Bernadette had asked, but nothing happened. Our Lady could easily have made a rose bush bloom in early March – nothing to it, if you were Mother of God and mistress of the seasons – but someone less illustrious would have had trouble messing around with nature, coaxing summer out of early spring.

Bernadette's novice mistress had never been convinced. It wasn't just the matter of the rose bush – it seemed absurd to her that God should choose a sick and ignorant peasant child to pass on His High Commands. There I couldn't agree. After all, Bernadette herself had chosen me, and on a previous occasion God had picked out a humble artisan's wife to be His mother, a simple homely girl who hadn't an O-level to her name. Perhaps I was tackling the thing all wrong. After all, if Bernadette had wanted Adrian's methods, why hadn't she appeared to *him*, touched him on the shoulder as he sat deep in his books in Twickenham public library? It was me she'd come to, me she trusted. She hadn't wanted teachers or professionals. Maybe I should trust her in turn and rely purely on simplicity and truth.

I dragged the suitcase off the bidet, collapsed the pile of books, slowly, achingly got up and stretched my limbs. I pushed open the blind and stared out at the huge black duvet of the sky, snuggling against the town sleeping underneath it. It was still dark, but bleached and fading round the edges where the dawn was nibbling at it. A few stray feathers of mist curled against the broad bare shoulders of the mountain peaks. I marvelled that in a world so vast and magnificent, some supernatural power should knock at my shabby soul and ask me to rewrite history. I should be exultant, not exhausted. Pins and needles hardly counted when the sword of Truth had been entrusted to my hands.

I shut the window and stripped off all my clothes. It was already half-past five. I would wash and change and go down to the Grotto in time for Ray's early service. That was the perfect place to start my mission – a small congenial Mass said in English for the English, so at least I'd be understood without the need for interpreters and interme- diaries who would only muddle things; a gathering big enough to carry weight with the authorities, yet not too large to shout me down. Ray himself would be officiating and was bound to back me up, if for no other reason than to prevent me blackmailing him or blabbing out his sin. And there would be other priests around him who might know French and Bishops.

I chose the most boring of my clothes, a droopy brown skirt and matching jumper, and coiled my hair on top. Long hair and jeans tend to make people hostile before you even open your mouth. I crept downstairs and knocked at the connecting door which led to Madame's quarters. I wanted my breakfast early. I'd paid for bed- and-breakfast, yet hardly made the most of either. I could take my bread with me and eat it on the way. I knocked again. Madame was either asleep, or chose not to be disturbed. I shrugged. To tell the truth, my hunger had almost faded now. It might have been the self-hypnosis, but all I felt was a sort of empty curdled nausea.

I hurried through the streets towards the Grotto. I knew my way there almost blindfold now, yet, every time, the town looked different. Now it was suspended between night and day, the street lights still shining, but dawn reaching out and muffling them, the moon fading into a faint singe-mark in the slate-grey sky. There was litter in the gutters, rubbish-bins overflowing with tins and cardboard boxes, but the buildings themselves looked pale and clean and delicate, like invalids who had been woken early in a hospital and washed before their breakfasts. There was a hushed, brooding, expectant feeling poured gently over everything like thin milk over porridge. A few uncertain birds twittered through the gauzy greyish light. A milk van chuntered up the hill. It was a frail and private morning, newly hatched and mine alone, not yet blemished or invaded by the crowds.

St Joseph's gates were open now, and as I walked through them and down into the esplanade, the place became slowly more alive. Little knots of nuns and nurses were hurrying towards the shrine – children in wheelchairs, priests in petticoats. I turned the corner, past the candle stores, the bookshop, the holy water taps. I kept my eyes cast down. It wasn't piety, but fear. If the statue was back in place again, then who would believe my story? But how could it be gone, when all those devout and placid pilgrims were already kneeling in front of it? Slowly, I raised my eyes. It was there – as serene, as hideous as it had been for over a century. It looked smaller somehow, almost insignificant, lost in the dark shadows of the niche. I turned away. It made no difference, really. It was only a hunk of marble, a sculptor's toy. True, it might help my cause if it was seen publicly to have vanished and I could simply step forward and explain the whole mysterious story. But, knowing the authorities, they'd accuse me of larceny then, as well as lies. Best to accept what was.

I glanced at my watch. Only a few minutes to go before the service started. The sky was paling now, every object striding forward with firmer, clearer outlines, the green in the meadows slowly filling in like colour on a palette, and the huge drowsy mountains yawning and stretching in the background, shaking night and snow and sleep out of their eyes. The English pilgrims were taking up their places for the Mass. I made myself as inconspicuous as possible. I had already recognized a posse of Pax Pilgrims, with Doris jabbering in their midst. In any other circumstances, I'd have rushed across and joined them, but I felt they'd hardly welcome me as the Attila of Lourdes. Despite the early hour, there were many different groups and banners present – Birmingham and Liverpool, Killala and Pontypridd. I began to feel a little more at home, seeing all those friendly British faces, with badges I could understand and British Home Stores cardigans. They might even be proud that an English voice had been chosen to proclaim the truth.

I wormed my way towards the front. Truth would only suffer if I had to shout it from the middle of a scrum. The priests were processing in now – five of them in all, with the Irish Father from Pax in second place and Ray bringing up the rear, his rude red hair almost blasphemous above his white priest's petticoat and his golden chasuble. He hadn't slept a wink since I had seen him – that was obvious. His face looked as if it had been sent to a bad laundry and had creases ironed into it where there were none before.

'In the name of the Father and of the Son and of the Holy Ghost,' he intoned. It sounded odd, as if he had borrowed a voice from the Posh Poetry Department at Radio Three and then had trouble fusing it with his own. In different circumstances, I'd have been more or less ecstatic to see him standing there in full vestments, handling hosts and chalices as familiarly as if he were making tea. But now the magic had gone out of it. I kept imagining his limp pink prick coiled exhausted in his nylon pants, polluting all those sacred robes, and anyway, I was so preoccupied with Bernadette that priestly fantasies seemed pointless.

The Mass was going so fast, I feared they'd reach the end before I'd spoken, but suddenly there was silence, and all the priests sat down on the benches around the altar as if they were almost expecting my announcement. My heart was beating so loudly, I felt Leo could have heard it back in England. I groped to my feet, stumbled towards the altar.

Somebody was there before me. A blind girl from the Killala group was standing on the steps, strumming a guitar. I turned my back on her.

'Er . . . Bernadette . . .' I started.

A high clear soprano voice swallowed up my own embarrassed croak. It was the blind girl singing a ravishing hymn in Gaelic. I could almost see the sad proud notes swirling up to the sky like the frail white smoke from the guttering candles flickering in front of me.

'*Is maith an bhean Muire mhór,*' she sang, and suddenly the sun slit through the clouds and touched one bright finger against the gloomy rock behind her. A sparrow soared up after it, his ragged shadow dark against the gold. It was so beautiful, I couldn't speak at all. I gazed around at the gold-flecked congregation – a twelve-year-old as bald as an old man, a wailing baby swathed in bandages, a withered grandma with pink woolly bed socks peeping out from under her plastic wheelchair cover. How could I wrest their Blessed Virgin from them when they were crippled, lame and bald; break up the party, tell them to go home?

The hymn had ended, the priests were on their feet again. I had lost my chance.

'The Lord be with you,' chanted the Irish priest from Pax.

'And also with you,' I responded, almost automatically, along with the rest of the congregation.

The *Lord* – for heaven's sake – they still had Him. God Himself, the Blessed Trinity, the gospels, the mysteries of the Mass. All those consoling, gentling, Sister Aidan-ish phrases I'd heard spoken in this service would still be there to comfort them – child of God, love of God, *agnus dei*, kiss of peace, unity, eternity – *those* I wasn't spoiling. Even without a Blessed Virgin at all, would it really be such a loss? Frankly, I'd always preferred a *man* in heaven, a Father, not a Virgin. I myself had rarely prayed to Mary. She always looked a little too like Janet with that superior smile and perfect skin and everlasting baby in her arms. Everything she'd done was a put-down. Conceiving her baby via the Holy Ghost without even taking off her clothes, when I'd have insisted on a hot-blooded man and the whole works, including simultaneous orgasm. Giving birth in a stable after a rough and dangerous journey by donkey-back to Bethlehem. I hadn't even risked a bicycle and yet I'd still miscarried. All those paintings of her kneeling on the straw and *beaming*, only minutes after the birth, when I'd have been howling on my back, sore and stitched and drugged, with puerperal fever or post-natal depression, or breast-feeding problems. I couldn't identify with her at any point at all, from her immaculate conception to her deathless death. Perhaps it was because I was so involved with her Son – a sort of mother-in-law problem if you like. I'd always kept away from Adrian's mother, so I suppose I did the same with Mary.

There was a sudden wail from one of the handicapped, a creak and rustle from the congregation as they all fell to their knees. I was still standing, rambling again, my mind on Adrian's mother instead of on the service. How would I ever carry out a vital months-long mission, if I couldn't even concentrate on one mingy Mass? Ray and his fellow priests were grouped around the altar, already preparing for Communion.

'The Lord has risen and has appeared to Peter, Alleluia,' announced Ray in his new, phoney voice.

No one contradicted him. Every pilgrim present was happy to accept that a man three days dead could slip out of his winding-sheet and carry on as usual. Christ had appeared to his disciples at Emmaus – spoken to them, eaten with them, and then vanished up to heaven. One of the priests had read it to us in the gospel only five minutes previously. If dead people could appear and disappear in first-century Emmaus, then why not in twentieth-century Lourdes? My story was no more exceptional than the one they'd just swallowed, standing there fidgeting and yawning while the priest dropped phrases like 'rose from the dead' or 'vanished from their sight' as casually as if he were saying 'lovely weather' or 'mind the step'.

The priests had consecrated the bread and wine and were receiving their own Communion. I watched Ray's rough red hands clasp the silver chalice and tip it to his lips. No longer illicit brandy in a tooth-mug, but Christ's own blood steaming hot and crimson down his throat. Ray was a priest again and his sin forgiven. I could hardly take it in. The living God was crouching on that altar – God in a goblet, the world in a grain of wheat. A million million priests from the time of Peter onwards had believed it unwaveringly, and all their countless congregations through the centuries. Seeing Bernadette was nothing to that miracle. Indeed, the dead were probably all around us, supernatural powers hovering over our gas-stoves or our easy-chairs, and all we did was slam the door or spray them away with Air-fresh. People tried to make a sane and safe society, pin things down in catechisms, define them in dictionaries, cage them up in fusty encyc-lopaedias. All the rest they fled from, or unloaded on to madmen or to children. Witches, ghosts and magic they gave away like presents to their kids. Snowqueens and stepmothers were dismissed as myths or fairy tales and any remaining mysteries re-labelled 'religion' or 'phy-sics' or 'philosophy' so they didn't sound so threatening, then sternly separated, so no one went berserk trying to reconcile them all. Other societies hadn't been so blinkered. The Greeks had talked to ghosts and gods and dealt in dreams and entrails, at the same time as inventing geometry and being better at rational things like maths and medicine and astronomy than anyone before them. The Chinese allowed mystery to curl up in their souls and homes like cats. We had only science.

Maybe I should turn to science. It had often rushed in like a shining knight to slay the last expiring remnants of some religious dream. The scientific world might even *welcome* my announcement, set up a laboratory where Our Lady's statue had stood. New facts for their textbooks could flow from Thea Morton's humble message, new definitions of death or time or ghosts cluster around my name. Scientists and ESP societies might flock to Lourdes as new-style priests and pilgrims.

I had to speak – it was my duty to truth and textbooks – and I had to do it now, or as soon as the singing was over. The Liverpool mixed choir had launched into a noisy and discordant rendering of the '*Adore Te Devote*'.

'Truth itself speaks truly,' the sopranos were shrilling. 'Or there's nothing true.'

Truth, true. My head was spinning with the word. It was like that game you play as a child, where you repeat one word over and over until it loses all its meanings and disintegrates into a fraying web of empty syllables. How could so many battles have been fought for truth, so many lines written in its honour when it was only four consonants with a vowel shoved between them? And yet I had been entrusted with it, chosen to make it manifest to the entire Christian world, to change history, challenge science, to bring the ancient world nearer to our own.

The last verse wavered to an end. I sprang up on a bench so that I could address the crowds from a higher vantage point and lifted up my hands. I could see the sun rising in my honour, climbing in the sky. The mountains seemed to bow to me.

'I have a message for you . . .' I announced, cursing the shake and wobble in my voice. I stopped a moment. A train was rumbling by on the railway line high up behind me, the noisy river rushing through my words. They couldn't hear. I'd have to go up to the altar itself, where there was sure to be a hidden microphone. I clambered off the bench and pushed my way towards the priests.

'Wait your turn, can't you?' muttered an angry Liverpudlian, jostling me out of the way. I shook her off, fought my way towards the altar, then turned to face the congregation.

Christ Almighty! The whole seething, struggling crowd was surging towards me. They had somehow guessed the content of my message and were out to get my blood. They didn't want truth or science, only miracles and Masses. Heavy shoes and flailing arms were bearing down on me. I slipped through a gap in the offensive and hid behind an invalid carriage. Yet the charge continued, not towards me any longer, but still towards the altar. I stared at the tangled limbs, the shoving bodies. It was the Communion rush – nothing to do with my message. They weren't out to lynch me, just to grab their God. Mouths open, elbows jabbing, they pressed towards the priests like parched and angry tipplers shut out of the pub all week. Ray was filling mouths like tankards. Greedy lips smacked shut. I hadn't a hope of speaking. Not only would they never hear nor see me, but they were so avid for everything religious, they'd flay me alive if I trampled on their favourite shrine. What did they care for laboratories or textbooks, or for contributing to the march and clash of knowledge? All they craved were the old safe solid rituals, the comfort and luxury of hope, the Virgin they had prayed to since they were babes in arms, even if she was a fraud.

The bells of the basilica were chiming out the notes of the Lourdes hymn, before the clock struck seven. '*Ave, ave, ave Maria.*' The Aves showered across the town like advertising leaflets dropped from an aeroplane. All the streets spelled Mary here, all the shops sold her as their number-one product, even the clocks cried out her name before they told the time. The Blessed Virgin had become as huge and indestructible as the Pyrenees which ringed her round. She was imprinted on every page of Lourdes like that hospital library stamp on all my books. However much I chipped away at her, or tried to rub her out, she would still stamp and stain the town like a tattoo.

I slipped away, dodging the crowds, weaving in and out of wheel-chairs, treading on toes. More and more people were sweeping down towards the Grotto, buying candles, booking Masses. It was only early morning and yet the rush hour had begun, the whole busy ferment centred on a sham. I couldn't buy a candle, I wouldn't buy a Mass. I'd splurge my few mean francs on a decent cup of coffee and something to dip into it. I hadn't swallowed a morsel since I'd set foot in France. Christ Himself had eaten before He ascended into Heaven – hadn't we just heard it in the gospel? Right – I, too, must break my fast before I descended any further into the hell of being a heavenly messenger.

twenty-five

I entered the first café I came to which was open. It was almost empty, but the noise made up for the lack of customers. A juke-box was playing some wailing heartbreak song with extra sobs from three electric guitars; a coffee machine was whooshing and whirring on the counter; and the radio was turned up full volume so that the waiter could hear it over the clattering of his cups. Even the cafés thrived on Our Lady's presence. It was she who swelled their profits and left the tips. I felt more and more like a messenger of doom. How many cafés would I close, how many waiters would I turf out into the street?

'*Bonjour, Mam'selle!*' It was the barman come to take my order. He looked fat, almost glossy, as if starving in the gutter was a long way from his plans. '*Que prenez-vous, Mam'selle? Du café au lait? Des croissants?*'

I was ravenous. I'd assumed my hunger had faded, but now that food was all around me, I felt weak and dizzy with desire for it. A baker's boy had just walked in, staggering under a tray of fresh-baked croissants. Their scent wafted behind him like a golden vapour trail. A man at the table opposite was dunking his brioche into a mug of steaming chocolate, ruffed with a high white collar of whipped cream. Someone had left a crust and a sugar lump on a dirty plate on my table. I crammed them into my mouth, swilled the dregs from the almost empty coffee cup. The prices were appalling. Bacon and eggs cost more than I'd allowed for lunch and supper combined, let alone a paltry little breakfast. Even coffee took a chunk out of your wallet. Ray had warned me that the prices got higher the nearer you approached the Grotto, which was good business but rotten religion. I should have walked on further, but I was so famished now, I stayed where I was and ordered the two cheapest things on the menu which were hot milk and plain bread. When they arrived, I mixed them together into a sort of gruel, which made them easier to eat. Although my teeth had been temporarily fixed, the gums were shrinking slowly as they healed, so that my denture slipped a bit and couldn't be trusted to cope with things like crusts. Anyway, gruel was more comforting than plain unbuttered bread.

I felt I needed comfort. I was the only person in the whole of Lourdes who knew that it was hollow. And here in the café, I was the only woman and the only English customer. The radio spoke French, the waiters looked Algerian, and the four other breakfasters were resolutely foreign. Even the pilgrims streaming past the café window on their way to the basilicas were mostly aliens. The food itself was French. No comforting English toast and marmalade, or homely fried bread soggy with Heinz baked beans. Only swarthy strangers sipping red wine for their breakfast, or gulping pale gutless tea from smoked glass tooth-mugs with one anorexic teabag floating on a tide of lemon pips. I longed for the sizzle of bacon, the Kellogg's packet with its consoling list of vitamins, boil-in-the-bag kippers with their frozen pat of butter slowly melting into fishy yellow juice. Breakfast with Leo – branflakes and the *Listener* and peanut butter kisses. I felt weak and sick with loss. True, Leo was a foreigner, but he didn't count as one because he lived in England and bought English watercolours and proper Fortnum's tea. God Himself would be a Middle Easterner. So would His Blessed Mother, come to that. I'd always pictured her pale and smug like Janet, but in fact she'd be Jewish like some of the mothers of Adrian's private pupils, with their coiled black hair and dark eyes.

But, wait a minute – the Lady whom Bernadette had seen had *blue* eyes. I remembered that distinctly. One of the books had described them as azure, and another as forget-me-not. Wasn't that a perfect piece of evidence to back up Bernadette's words? Surely no woman of Galilee could be born with forget-me-not eyes. They belonged strictly to the West. In fact, true blue eyes are exceptionally rare. Adrian had done some research on it once, and worked out that not much more than one per cent of the world could boast blue eyes. They were a product of the gloomy north, he said, specially adapted for seeing more acutely in overcast conditions of fog and haze. Mary wouldn't need them – she was a southerner who lived with blazing sun and cloudless skies.

I picked up the menu and scribbled 'Blue eyes' on the back of it, next to the *soupe du jour*. Odd, really, that no one had puzzled about it at the time. Even odder that in another vision, a good three centuries earlier, the Madonna had had *brown* eyes. I remembered that from school. Mother Perpetua had read the story to us during our embroidery lessons. I was always pricking my finger or losing my thimble while she rattled on about the dark-eyed, dark-skinned Virgin who had appeared in Guadalupe in 1531. Surely the Blessed Virgin wouldn't keep on changing her appearance in every different century and country – a Mexican Indian one time, a blue-eyed northerner the next? It seemed neither honourable nor fair. I'd have to mug up all the other times and places Mary had appeared to people and see if she looked alike in any of them. Maybe the whole lot of them were shams. At this rate, I'd be destroying not just Lourdes, but Fátima, Knock, La Salette, Guadalupe itself – *all* the Marian shrines.

One thing was clear – I hadn't time to waste. It was already Monday, and we were due to depart on Saturday – five short days to undo centuries of falsehood. I still needed a plan of action, even more now that my task had been extended. Truth and simplicity just hadn't proved enough, science had misfired, and Ray was confusing sex with insanity. There were other priests, of course. Bernadette had commanded me to start with them. I mustn't forget her words and go gallivanting off on some vaguer, wider mission of my own. I wrote 'Priests' as the next heading underneath the sorbets and sat staring at it while I scraped out the last tepid morsels of my gruel.

Almost as if in answer to a prayer, a priest walked in. He was wearing a grubby black cassock with hobnailed boots underneath it, and a small black beret perched on top of untidy greying hair. He had dirty fingernails and a rough red complexion criss-crossed with tiny broken veins. I knew he wasn't English. English priests (bar Ray) are always posh and have pale, pasty skins and manicure sets for Christmas, and finicky housekeepers who handwash everything. He chose a seat in the furthest corner from me, but I refused to be deterred. I picked up my bill and the menu and marched across.

'*Bonjour!*' I said and seated myself beside him.

He didn't look surprised. I suppose he thought he was meant to recognize me. Priests meet so many people, they probably learn to smile at total strangers, just in case they turn out to be last night's communicant or the multi-murderer in Saturday's confessional.

'Do you speak English?' I asked. The *bonjour* had exhausted my only general French, and I didn't want to start on big ends or sparking-plugs or municipal museums.

When he nodded, I almost threw my arms around his neck. The

waiter had brought him a glass of cold colourless liquid, three croissants and a plastic pot of something called *gelée de groseilles* which sounded vaguely obscene, but looked much the same as jam.

'You like?' he asked, offering me one of the croissants already spread liberally with butter. Its fresh greasy fragrance wafted up to my nostrils, tempting me, enticing me, little golden flakes crumbling off it into the glowing pool of jam.

'No,' I said firmly. I must keep my message pure. Bernadette herself had never accepted a morsel, preferred to starve rather than risk anyone accusing her of graft. I removed my eyes from the breakfast and fixed them on a poster of the bare and starving Pyrenees. 'I have a message for you,' I told him. 'From St Bernadette.'

He smiled, but continued chewing. 'St Bernadette, yes.'

I stared at him. How could he calmly carry on with breakfast when I was about to bulldoze his life and Lourdes' at once.

'Bernadette *appeared* to me,' I said, in case he hadn't understood.

Little morsels of half-masticated croissant sprayed from his lips. His fingers were stained with nicotine, and there were grease stains down his front. 'Very good,' he murmured.

'She *spoke* to me,' I insisted, making the words as clear and distinct as possible, like the tight-arsed lady on the Linguaphone records. I only had half his attention, anyway. The other half was on his spirits glass. I wondered what it was. It looked decadent like absinthe.

'She told me to tell you it wasn't the Blessed Virgin that she saw.'

'Good,' he repeated. '*Very* good.'

'Do you *understand*?' I almost shouted. He was drinking the liquor now. It shocked me, really. First Ray with an erection and now a priest with an aphrodisiac.

'Yes, yes, I understand.' There was a little ruff of butter along his upper lip. 'The Blessed Virgin. *La Sainte Vierge*. I understand.'

'No!' I howled. '*Not* the *Sainte Vierge*.' Even my phrase-book French could cope with that. 'It *was*n't the Blessed Virgin who appeared to her.'

He smiled again and nodded. 'The Blessed Blessed Virgin. *Mère de Dieu*. *Notre Dame*. Our church in Amiens, we calls 'im *Notre Dame*. You understand?'

'Yes, but you *don't*,' I blurted out. 'Look, she *said* she was the Immaculate Conception, but that didn't mean Mary. Well, not necessarily. The priests just *assumed* it. There may have been another one. I

287

mean *anyone* could be conceived immaculate. It's up to God, I suppose. If He did it once, He could do it several times.'

I'd lost him now. The croissants were finished, but he was scooping up the last scattered crumbs with a moistened finger and cramming them into his mouth. He kept on smiling through the guzzling, but I knew he hadn't understood a word.

'You nursing?' he asked.

I glanced down at my meagre, unmaternal breasts. '*What?*' I exclaimed. Surely he couldn't think . . .

'You teaching?'

'Oh, I *see*. No, neither. Look, what I'm trying to tell you is . . .'

'*Touriste?*'

'*No!*'

He jumped when I shouted. It was simply a waste of breath. Half the clergy were imbeciles and drunkards, and the other half sexual cripples who couldn't keep their vows.

'Bishop,' I demanded. 'Where does the bishop live?'

He stopped suddenly, with his mouth open and his glass poised motionless before his face. 'You work for *bishop?*' he asked incredulously, and with new respect.

'Oh *fuck*,' I said and got up. I suppose he thought it was some sort of English *au revoir*, because he jumped to his feet and shook my hand and kept on saying, 'Bishop. Good, very good,' over and over.

A sort of damp, lumpy fury was seeping out of my body like wet sawdust. I was almost surprised he couldn't feel it sticky on my hand. All my simple joy at coming to Lourdes had crumbled into horror and frustration. Even the fact of being chosen by St Bernadette I now saw less as an honour and more as a crippling burden. Judging by my lack of results so far, I would need at least a year in Lourdes, not one paltry week – yet how could I survive on a pocketful of centimes? Truth wouldn't fill a belly.

I snatched my hand from the priest's and turned to go. Someone was blocking my way – a waiter with a three-foot silver serving platter piled high with an authentic English breakfast. *More* than authentic. There was not only bacon, eggs and sausages, but steak and chips as well. The steak itself was a good two inches thick, oozing blood and juices. It was like a miracle, an answer to my prayer. The only problem was, the waiter was setting it down in front of the priest – not me – and then besieging him with napkin, mustard, salt, coffee, bread. I stared.

Mon père had already demolished three whole croissants and a glass of booze, yet here was a full cooked breakfast (*dinner*, almost), when I was starving, hollow, weak. I sat straight down again. I wasn't leaving now – I was going to have it out with him.

'Is that *yours?*' I asked. 'I mean, who's *paying* for it? What about your Vow of Poverty? Your conscience? All those slums in Preston with communal lavatories and families of seven who can't *afford* a decent meal?'

He beamed, tucking his napkin tight beneath his chin and gesturing with his fork towards the steak. '*Bifteck*. Good. You 'ave in England, yes?'

'No, I *don't* 'ave. Can't afford. Can't even afford one mingy little croissant. You had *three* – I counted. No *wonder* you don't care about Bernadette. You're too busy with the fleshpots.'

The smile cracked a bit. His English might only be rudimentary, but bitterness sounds the same in any tongue.

'You 'ave pain?' he inquired. 'You 'ave sad?'

'Oh *no*,' I said. 'I'm only bloody starving. Don't mind me. You go ahead and eat.'

He was. He had already salted his sausages and blasted his bacon with the peppermill. He was now uncapping the mustard.

'No!' I shouted, suddenly. '*Don't* – please don't. You'll ruin it. I *loathe* mustard on my food.'

I snatched the jar away. Little flocks of *moutarde à l'estragon* sprayed across his sleeve. He was goggling at me, astonished, almost scared.

'I'm sorry,' I muttered. 'It's *not* mine, is it – it's yours. That's priests' perks, I suppose.' I remembered the huddle of faithful, queuing for Masses. Thirty-three francs a Mass cost – three pounds-fifty, English money – except it *wasn't* Mass, it was meat. Those wretched, patient, conned and simple pilgrims were buying egg and chips and absinthe, not hosts and God and prayers. 'D'you realize,' I quivered, 'they're not only sick and crippled, they're *bankrupting* themselves as well, to subsidize your fancy five-course breakfasts, your finest fillet steak.'

He was feeding his face again, munching stolidly through my monologue, egg yolk glistening on his upper lip, little threads of *bifteck* stuck between his teeth. I think he'd stopped trying to understand me, was just shrugging me off as a crackpot like Ray and the rest had done. Easy to label someone loony when they were simply crazed with hunger. Anyway, it wasn't just the food I craved – it was the sudden sight and taste of England – that same crisped and streaky bacon which we had at home, the fat familiar sausages with little uneven knobs on the end of them, the greasy 'Fred's caff' chips. I longed to cling to their safe and solid solace, to stuff myself with them until I was whole and strong again.

I almost genuflected as the priest sliced into his egg. I tried to shut out everything but that slimy viscous white quivering from his knife-blow, the rich gummy yellow spurting towards the breakwater of his sausage. If I kept my eyes fixed only on his plate, I could imagine I was sitting safe with Adrian, sharing a fry-up in our cramped and steamy kitchen, or back at school, gorging a bumper breakfast on Reverend Mother's Feast Day, with the scent of stocks outside the refectory, and the nuns' cool white voices echoing from the chapel. I watched him cut a chunk of sausage off – a plump pinkish bolster studded with tiny jewels of fat. He left it idling on his plate while he laid his knife and fork down and poured his coffee. The sausage stump was almost *speaking* to me, throbbing across the table, flinging me its smell. My entire body ached and slavered for it. I waited till the priest was blockaded by his cup, then – grap, gulp, gone. He hadn't even noticed, so I pinched the largest chip on his plate and then the second largest. I hardly dared to chew them in case he saw my lips moving, just forced them down, whole and fat and greasy. He caught me with the fourth – it was red-hot in my hand as his eyes looked up and followed it from his platter to my mouth. I didn't falter, just swallowed it unflinchingly.

'Go on,' I challenged him. 'Criticize me, tell me I'm a glutton.'

Now that he had caught me, I might as well continue. I seized a piece of bread from the piled-high wicker basket, leaned across and dipped it in his egg yolk. I almost choked as I crammed it huge and scratchy in my mouth. Tears were streaming down my face. The food was so dear and safe and beautiful, I couldn't bear to have to snatch and snarl it up like this, ram it down my gullet like an animal.

Tears splashed on to my hands. I was weeping not just for my own shock and disappointment, but for all the empty bellies in the world, the whole aching sham of Lourdes.

People were staring at me. A nun at the next table had come clucking over and passed me a large white handkerchief to dry my tears. I tied it round my neck like a napkin. The priest and I were both robed for eating now, but it was my turn for the plate. I yanked it over to my side of the table. The smell of grease, of meat, of plenty, was like incense in my nostrils. Almost reverently, I picked up the sacred implements and knifed into the steak.

'I'm sorry,' I whispered to the gawping, plundered priest. 'I know you don't understand, but I've been given a mission to the world and I can't cope with it until I've eaten. My stomach's rumbling so loudly, it blocks out all the words.'

The fork felt so heavy in my hands, it was as if the whole burden of Bernadette's message was bleeding and sobbing into it. Staunchly, I clung on – swallowed bacon, sausage, comfort, nurture, strength – the strength to continue my calling. I mustn't mewl or falter any longer. This afternoon at the Blessing of the Sick, I would take up my task again. The whole of Lourdes would be gathered together then, in the most important ceremony of all – every nation processing round the square with their sick and handicapped, their laymen and their priests. The procession didn't start till half-past four – I couldn't starve till then. Bernadette had sent this blessed breakfast to feed and fortify me, had broken my fast through the bounty of a priest.

Even so, I was still sobbing into his chips. The *relief* of food, the wonder of it, had touched me like God's finger. There were other hands on mine. The nun had joined our table and was crooning at me in a language so strangely guttural, I couldn't even guess which half of the globe it came from. Two waiters had waltzed over and were shouting and gesturing at my plate. I was terrified they'd charge me chip for chip. I shoved in another mouthful. A knot of people were gathering round me now, all jabbering, all staring. Alien words lashed at me like hail. All those different languages were almost proof that God was a muddler. Any rational, orderly deity like Adrian would have insisted on one universal tongue, with compulsory demotion for anyone claiming to be a foreigner.

Yet, here, I realized, was a captive audience. I had tried and failed at an English Mass; a French café might prove simpler. Bernadette had addressed me in a strange outlandish language I had never heard before, and made me understand it. Maybe she could do the same for them.

I untied the hankie from my chin and struggled to my feet. I stared at the swarthy faces – puzzled waiters, suspicious customers. 'Listen,' I implored them. 'Our Lady never appeared here. St Bernadette didn't see her. She thought she did, but she was wrong. I know it won't help your profits or your livelihoods, but Truth is more important, isn't it?'

Silence.

'*Isn't* it?' I repeated in a whisper.

Mutters, giggles, shrugs. A circle of blank uncomprehending faces, a sudden howl of laughter from the coffee machine. I tipped the last two inches of steak into the handkerchief and stuffed it up my sleeve. At least I wasn't starving any longer. I'd *make* them understand me. At the Blessing of the Sick, I'd win a sudden blazing breakthrough, a total revelation.

'Just wait till half-past four!' I cried, as I marched through them to the door and made them scatter out of my path. That was just a foretaste of my power.

twenty-six

Half-past four. I heard the music before I even reached the square – church bells tolling, hymns of praise and supplication in several different languages roaring through the microphones. The crowds were converging all along the esplanade, excited and expectant as if waiting for a coronation. Except this was the Blessing of the Sick, the greatest parade of the diseased and disabled anywhere in the world.

I took up my place by the steps of the Crowned Virgin, midway between the processional route and the steps of the rosary basilica where Benediction would be given. I had been resting since my breakfast and felt calmer, stronger, now, but I had no intention of joining the procession myself, walking side by side with my compatriots or holding up a banner emblazoned Notting Hill or Twickenham. I was so much an outsider, it would be a mockery to process around that concourse, singing hymns to Our Lady when I knew she had never set foot in Lourdes in all her life and hadn't even had the decency to correct the story herself.

Yet Our Lady was everywhere. In the prissy statue of the Virgin towering over me; sitting sculpted above the doorway of the rosary basilica, dressed in frills and flounces and looking cross; weeping in bronze at the foot of the cross at the far end of the esplanade. Her statue stood in all the churches, her name was woven into every hymn; her face shone on all the medals hung round necks and pinned on coats; she dangled from a thousand rosaries. She was even stamped on the holy lozenges which people sucked for sore throats or sore souls. All around me were her fans, her satellites, her suckers.

I shivered. It was colder now. The Easter sun had vanished and a grey bad-tempered sky lowered down on stoic crowds. Not that anyone cared about the weather. Every eye was turned towards the white-haired, black-robed priest at the head of the procession, holding up his placard of a suffering Christ. The sick and handicapped were lining up behind him, nurses wheeling crocks and cripples, nuns leading halt and blind, all the diseased from all the different nations flocking to his banner.

A blast of music thundered from the loudspeakers and the sort of proud, plummy voice which Leo likes announced, 'This procession is a celebration of our Faith' – and then repeated it in several languages. I could hear the capital letter echoing across the square, the same triumphant F which Adrian gave to Future. Lourdes had neither Faith nor Future now, yet no one even suspected it. They were like passengers on the Titanic, tangoing towards the iceberg.

Suddenly, the whole crowd bobbed and rippled. There was a murmur of excitement, a stir and shuffle like horses in a stable when they hear their buckets coming. People stood up straighter, joined their hands. The priest with the placard stepped forward, held his banner high above the crowds. The procession had begun.

The babies came first – pale, withered creatures whimpering in their pushchairs. Some of them would never walk at all. Their prams would be exchanged for wheelchairs or their cots for coffins. For the first time in my life, I was almost relieved Lucian had never made it past his jar. Next came the children – kids who should have been running and tumbling in the grass, strapped like sacks on to stretchers or wearing ugly metal callipers; toddlers with bumps instead of legs, teenagers with acne and no arms; a lad with a punk pink haircut pushed by a Mongol girl with a moustache. Scores and scores of children who, if they survived at all, would only join the battalion of handicapped hobbling and dribbling behind them, the mindless pushing the legless, the blind leading the blind. One huge man of fifty-five or sixty was sucking his thumb like a baby, two or three wore bibs. Some moaned or shivered or threw their hands about; others lay so pale, so still, so hopeless, they were dead in all but definition.

I watched in horror as row after row of sick passed slowly by – strange distorted creatures like rejects in a doll factory, their limbs and features twisted out of shape. Many were just old, or had been old since they first drew breath – withered – shrivelled rag-bags staring woodenly ahead. One woman was crying in a low, hopeless wail; another cackled to herself, screwing up her face and pointing at the crowds. Most were silent – a grim, resigned silence which had no more tears to shed and nothing left to laugh at.

A boy as beautiful as Lionel but without his legs, grinned at me from his stretcher-bed. Tears were streaming down my face, but I tried to smile at him. Two French nurses were pulling his bed behind them like a coal wagon, girls younger and prettier than I was, but as familiar with pain and horror as if it were their step-sister. My words would disrupt all these nurses' lives as well. Where could they bring their patients, once I'd removed Our Lady from Lourdes?

The loudspeakers were blasting out the *Lauda Sion*. Although it started in Latin, I remembered it from school and knew it was a song of praise. How could we praise a God who had created handicap on such a scale? Every sick person passing now in front of me had parents, relatives, helpers, friends, all of whom had wept and suffered with them, so that their combined grief was shouting up to heaven. Even the able-bodied looked shabby, plain and tired, trudging behind the wheelchairs, with their bunions and their heartache, their dreary faded clothes, their concrete faces. All the world's misery seemed to be concentrated in this one grey square. Not just the sick, but the lost and the defeated, the poor and the bereaved. I could almost see the broken nights, the bleeding marriages, the lost fathers, dead babies, tears, fights, deceits and disappointments. If Mary hadn't appeared here, then she bloody well should have done. She and her Son could have wiped out this weeping world and made a better one. Just one word, just a gesture even, and all that pointless suffering could be swept away.

The English contingent was shrilling the chorus now:

> 'Praise O Sion, praise your Master,
> Praise your Saviour, praise your pastor,
> In a joyous melody.'

The crowd took up the refrain in a score of different languages, praise and joy resounding all around me. I myself was dumb. I couldn't hymn the Lord, only blame Him, rail at Him, weep for His cruel and senseless world.

The next verse was swallowed in a sudden crash of thunder. In seconds, the sky had turned from grey to purple, and stinging rain lashed the bowed and shivering procession. It was as if God had added the last mocking test of faith and courage. No one failed it. Wheelchair hoods were snapped firmly into place, plastic covers patiently fastened, waterproofs put on. The singing hardly faltered – 'Praise him, praise him' – even soaked to the skin or threatened with pneumonia, they would still ring out His praises.

Umbrellas sprouted all along the esplanade, but there were still many with no shelter. Either they had come without their brollies, or they needed both their hands to push the wheelchairs. Sick and helpers alike squelched along in the pouring, drenching rain. Hair dripped, glasses steamed, clothes were splashed with mud. Rain rattled on the hoods of wheelchairs or slammed against the white sticks of the blind. Nurses' uniforms turned from blue to weeping black, nuns dragged their skirts through puddles. I had no umbrella myself, but even if I had, I would have given it away a thousand thousand times. It seemed scandalous that the well and strong should shelter, while that army of disabled limped and tottered through the downpour. Yet they kept on singing, kept on praying, lips moving, hands joined, while the rain joined in the choruses and lightning crackled through the clouds. A storm was nothing to them, because at the end of the rainbow stood the Blessed Virgin herself, ready with her miracles. How could I dethrone her? At any moment, her slim white finger might flash down from the sky, restoring sight or limbs or strength. It *had* happened. I had read the records, seen the photographs. Even if it were only psychological, merely the power of their faith or hope or longing, who was I to take that hope away? Hope and faith were more valuable than truth, more necessary. Truth would never heal them.

I watched nation after nation plod and shuffle by, all united by that one hopeless hope. Most wore black or grey. There was almost no colour, save for the bobbing umbrellas and the embroidered banners shouting Meaux, Milano, München, Deuil-La-Barre, Corbeil-Essonnes, even grand Versailles. Some of the names sounded exotic or quaint and reminded me of fairy tales, until I looked down and saw the wrecks and rejects holding them. The sad clock chimed the quarters, the hymns resounded on, and still they came, rank after rank after rank of fervent dripping faces. At last, I could see the end, the line of white-robed priests following after all the people, and, finally, the Blessed Sacrament sheltered under its golden canopy, Christ Himself caged in a gleaming monstrance, held high in front of him by a purple-skirted bishop. As he splashed and splendoured by, the first half of the procession had already doubled back again and was now streaming past me on the other side, and then forming up in rows in front of the basilica. I pressed forward. Even with my news of gloom and disillusion, some crazy spark in me still dared to hope. Hope was catching like the 'flu and all around me were desperately hoping people. This was the place, the moment when miracles occurred, and everybody knew it. I gazed around the square. The plane trees had been docked and pollarded and looked handicapped themselves, their bark blemished, their branches stunted and deformed. One or two stern marble statues stared out across the trees, too high and lonely on their plinths to care about the suffering. Thin white clouds bandaged the pointing finger of the Pyrenees which jutted behind the spire.

Everyone was waiting. Slowly, the golden canopy lurched and swayed towards them, the dazzling monstrance blazing underneath it. The crowds parted like the Red Sea as the Blessed Sacrament sailed past. Pilgrims fell to their knees in front of it, cowering on the cold hard concrete, as if pain and rain were nothing compared to the presence of their Christ. Now the blessing itself began. The bishop went to and fro along the rows of handicapped, signing them with the sign of the cross. Some of them were too sick or dotty to even know he was there. Others yawned or twitched or made strange spastic gestures, or leaned forward from their stretchers and groped out greedy hands towards the host. The prayers continued. The priests stood on the altar steps, taking it in turns to speak to their own nation in their own language. An English priest was now at the microphone, a tall dramatic-looking Titan with a great lion head and a voice dipped in fire and brimstone.

'Lord, that I may *see*,' he cried, on behalf of all the blind, all those who lived in darkness, or were blinkered, blindfold, groping.

'Lord, that I may *see*,' roared the English pilgrims after him.

I held my breath. Surely the Lord would hear them now. Even if the Lady was a sham, God was still in heaven, still had power. I gazed at a blind man with a guide dog, its harness drenched with rain, its fur dripping. 'Lord let *him* see,' I begged. 'Just him. Just one.'

Hope was so thick, you could almost see it spread on everything like honey. Maybe God was still not quite awake, still yawning and stretching after His afternoon siesta. I willed Him to get up and get a move on. I had almost forgotten my mission, my announcement. My entire attention was on these desperate sick. Far from kicking all their props away, I was praying for their miracles.

'Lord, let them see,' I mouthed, over and over again, filling in the silence, the suspense.

Nothing happened, except the rain beat faster. No one seemed surprised. The priest continued, as if he hadn't really expected much the first time.

'Lord that I may *hear*,' he tried again, now praying for the deaf, who wouldn't even be aware that he was speaking.

'Lord, that I may *hear*,' took up the crowd.

Most of them had ears, but never heard anything kind or soft or beautiful. They were praying for magic phrases like 'everlasting arms' or 'peace which surpasseth all understanding'. I was praying with them, praying to hear Leo say 'I love you', or even just 'I'm sorry'. (He still hadn't said it yet.)

I wondered if Lionel was there, his full red silent lips mumbling to a God he only saw in pictures, or knew from three barren letters on his card.

'Lord, that *he* may hear,' I implored. Just Lionel. I owed him prayers for having slandered him.

The rain was like grapeshot now, battering down on the faithful, almost drowning the priest's voice. A few people had scuttled away to seek for shelter, but most remained, enduring the weather as simply one more trial. Half of them were still on their knees, their feet in puddles, their bowed necks lashed with rain.

'Lord, that I may *walk*,' intoned the priest, louder now, so that he could be heard above the downpour.

'Lord, that I may *walk*,' bellowed the crowd.

I shut my eyes. When I opened them, every cripple would have leapt out of his wheelchair, or flung away his crutches and be dancing and cavorting in the square. No God could be deaf to such a plea. I could almost see Him rising from His throne, opening up his Box of Miracles and showering them on earth, smiling at the ease with which He did it.

I hardly dared look up. When I did, the crowd was motionless. Not a single skipping spastic or whooping stretcher-case, not one triumphant crutch waving in the air. Only bent heads, stiff legs, dead and palsied limbs. I almost jeered. Of *course* Bernadette had never seen Our Lady. What other proof was needed? How could a Mother of Mercy look upon these wretches and simply shrug?

'Lord, your word is life,' the priest was saying, *insisting* almost. Yet some of these cripples would be dead within the year.

'Lord, your word gives joy,' he chanted. But there was no scrap or shred of joy in the whole of Lourdes – only suffering, shabbiness and profiteering.

'Lord, your word is food.' I almost spat. What had I eaten other than a sham and scratchy host and a dish of over-priced gruel, followed by a stolen, tepid breakfast which I'd wrested from the clutches of a gross and oafish priest? What had *any* of them eaten in their poky, smelly, grease-bespattered dining-rooms – coarse bread, cheap chips, brackish holy water instead of sparkling wine. They weren't there for the frills. They scraped and pinched all year not for golden beaches or gourmet's fare, but for non-existent miracles and double pneumonia. They belonged to a church which kept them poor and sick and starving, and then went on to call pain noble and suffering blessed. The church got all its definitions wrong. Greed was wicked, joy was dangerous. Only poverty and penance won gold stars. I glanced around the square. Sex was life and joy itself, yet here was only crawling celibacy, mean and scared like Ray's, blushing behind its fig-leaf. Nuns and priests who cut the body off at the neck with their wimples or their dog-collars; convent girls taught that sex was sin and cunts were hell-holes; the sick and handicapped who were either too deformed to do it, or caged up in institutions which only admitted people above the waist; withered peasant women who had swapped their young-girl guilt for disgust and apathy. Swarms of people for whom sex was shame, and joy was something strictly confined to a heaven which would probably be confiscated before they ever got there.

'Hosanna, hosanna!' they were singing, which should have been translated 'misery and pain'.

I gazed up at the sky. If only I could see a *different* God – Adonis crossed with Leo, or a Father who was still young and strong and potent, a Priest-Son with an erection.

Rain fell in my eyes.

There was a sudden peal from the organ. The crowds rose to their feet, as if they were lifted up on the clouds of incense now swirling up to heaven. Everyone joined hands and then stood with arms outstretched at shoulder level. I was included in the human chain. A woman on either side of me had grasped my hands and held them high.

'*Pater noster*,' roared out the whole massed congregation. They were reciting the Lord's Prayer in Latin, the universal language, so that everyone could understand. A vast united nursery of children crying for their Father. I remembered the night of my confession –

God was present then. He had snuggled up beside me, offered me His arms. Now He was as deaf, blind and crippled as His children.

'*Panem nostrum quotidianum da nobis hodie* . . .' beseeched the throng.

I yanked my hands away, broke the chain, plunged and butted through the crowds. I didn't want a Father who soaked and drenched His children, who sent them hailstones when they begged for bread; a swarthy foreigner who spoke only a dead language, or who was deaf and dumb like Lionel; a trickster and a conman who allowed poor simple peasants to muddle up His Mother with a ghost, a fraud, a sham.

I fought my way through the ranks, the only moving creature in that great rigid, worshipping mass, the only seeing person who knew the niche was empty and the Grotto false. People frowned and muttered as I elbowed past them, the *brancardiers* tried to stop me, but now I was almost out, darting towards the huge stone ramparts and safely underneath them to the river. I raced across the bridge, pounded along the path which crossed the meadows, then on to the grass itself, feeling it damp and spongy underneath my feet. I passed the second bridge, back to the path again. On I went, beside the dark, rain-tossed water of the Gave. The ground became rough and stony. I tripped and almost fell. I could hear the prayers rising up behind me, fainter now, but chasing me, accusing me.

I threw myself down on the grass, stuffed my fingers in my ears. I could smell wet earth, rich mud, the gamy throbbing scent of spring. Golden celandines were tangled in the grass, tiny purple vetches almost hidden amongst the taller plantains. An insect struggled up a stalk, a pebble shone. The rain was faltering now. I rolled on my back and peered up at the sky. One brave bird was spiralling through the clouds – a hawk perhaps. The only birds I could recognize were sparrows, but this was something classier. Its wide raggedy wings were plunging and soaring high, high above the river. Could God be a bird? Not a Father, but a disembodied spirit, a high free happy thing, a phoenix? I almost craved a God like that. Religion should be light and fire and freedom, not a frowning headmaster with a ruler and a cane.

I couldn't do what Bernadette had asked me. I knew that, now I'd seen the sick – the babies who were simply swaddled corpses, the boys who had never kicked a ball or kissed a girl, the dying old ladies who had been dying for a hundred years, I couldn't wrest their only hope from them. They *needed* that Lady to be the Blessed Virgin. Bernadette was wrong to give them cruel fact instead of faith and fantasy.

I'd fly away. Take the first plane or train or coach I could arrange and return to England. I'd burn all my books on Bernadette, disown her as my sister, return to Leo, get a job. I'd forget the whole cruel Catholic sham, turn my back even on Ray himself, live for my body, not for my soul, further my name through Leo's kids, not through dead and dusty scientific books.

The hawk had disappeared. There was only a hole in the clouds now, a shining halo touched with gold. In my mind, I saw Bernadette's dark pleading eyes staring from the centre of it, heard her cry 'I trust you'. I sprang up from the grass. Any moment now, she might appear to me again, try and change my mind. Not likely!

I started running across the fields, away from Lourdes, towards the lowlands and the sane non-Catholic North, towards cakes and steaks and pricks and wombs and sheer crazy easy happiness. Bernadette's voice kept tripping me up, unravelling all the joy.

'It wasn't the Blessed Virgin,' she was saying. 'Tell the people, tell the priests.'

I stopped my ears, fell on my knees. 'Lord that I may not hear,' I cried. 'That I may not hear.'

twenty-seven

Rush hour at Victoria. Crowds of grey-complexioned commuters churning their way across the station. People bumping into me or my suitcase because I was dawdling at a time when all the rules said 'Rush!' Everyone else obeying – seething and surging past me with dreary gaberdines and set, sullen faces. Out-of-work pigeons chuntering high up in the roof, the odd frail feather drifting down on all the bobbing heads. Trains panting at the buffers and red raucous buses glimpsed through the exits, while a still-early morning shook and stretched itself outside. The *smell* of morning – coffee, and cold, and sudden wafts of after-shave. A porter swilling tea while all the world rushed by him.

It had taken me twenty-three hours, twenty-seven minutes to exchange Lourdes for London. (The last train had been late.) I'd tried to go by plane, fly away like the hawk that very same Monday afternoon, while the Procession of the Sick was still shambling and sobbing through my soul. But Pax Pilgrims only flew on Saturdays and were most unhelpful when I told them my grandmother was dangerously ill, and (later) that all my favourite relatives had died in a multiple car crash on the motorway. All I could do, they said, was take the ordinary scheduled airline from Toulouse or Biarritz. The only problem was, it cost a little matter of a hundred odd pounds, when I'd already paid my all-in fare with Pax. I spent so long arguing with them, I missed the last decent evening train. I packed my things (leaving the book on Bernadette as a present for Madame) and went to catch the midnight one, which was slower and stopped at all the boring little stations in between. It was only then, I discovered that even the train fare cost more than I had in the world. I was so discouraged, I trailed back to my lodgings and went to sleep in my clothes with my case still packed beside me.

First thing in the morning, I trekked up to the hostel and asked Doc for a loan. (Ray wasn't there – thank God. He was saying Mass in the hospital where Mike was dying, more or less.) At least Doc was up and semi-dressed this time. He even laughed and said, 'Why not ask St

Bernadette for a handout next time she appears to you?' When he realized I was serious, he got quite piqued and uppity, and went on about things like collateral and guarantees. I was forced to resort to tears and the grandmother saga again, and even then, he only forked out a mingy half of what I'd asked. I still had Leo's spending money which I'd hardly touched at all, and a tenner I'd earmarked for emergencies, so in the end I scraped together just enough for the basic ticket, so long as I avoided frills like meals or sleepers. Doc drove me to the station, which was just as well, since the porter was waving flags and slamming doors as we stampeded on to the platform. I made it with a second to spare, like one of those dramatic sequences in films where they build the tension by playing 'she'll-never-make-it-music' and superimposing pictures of the breathless heroine with the almost departing train. I stuck my head out of the window and waved to Doc who was still wearing his pyjama top above a pair of tartan golfing trews. The train from Amiens was in, and my last view of Lourdes was of hundreds more handicapped being lifted down like parcels in their wheelchairs, the whole sombre station blooming with blue and white nurses' caps and a new instalment of holy hope and fraud.

I knew, then, I was right to get away. Wasting fifty pounds on a train fare when I'd already paid via Pax was hardly economical, yet the thought of five more days in that weeping, bleeding, hollow, swindling town filled me with such gloom and almost panic, I think I'd have shelled out double to escape it. I realized, too, I was escaping Bernadette. I was terrified she'd appear to me again, saddle me with some new impossible instructions. I couldn't carry them out. The Blessed Virgin was more valuable to those hopeless hoping sick than all the drugs, doctors and priests put together.

I stopped for a moment in the swarming, fuggy station, leaning against the window of Victoria's Pantry, one of the British Rail buffets which was crowded with commuters and reeling with the scent of bacon. I'd travelled so long, my legs felt strange and choppy, as if there was still a jolting train or a lurching channel ferry underneath them. I'd spent the entire journey trying to undo the last three months. I'd booted Ray's religion out of the train window and flung it overboard into the seething Dover Straits. As we'd chugged through Bordeaux and Angoulême, Poitiers and Blois, past fields and cows and vineyards and the first shining splinters of spring wheat, I'd gulped down great mouthfuls of nature and fertility, prayed to a pagan god, embraced

Leo and Adonis. Every time Bernadette's sad eyes flicked into my mind, or Ray's limp prick or stricken face, I replaced it with an instant snapshot of Leo erect and radiant. *He* would be my new religion. I'd been vowing that, the very night that Bernadette appeared to me – she'd simply messed things up. True I hadn't brought his miracle, but he wouldn't need it now. It was only my religious hocus-pocus which had turned him off. All that Latin and jargon and asceticism and mugging up Masses in his bedroom must have been a put-down. Once I returned without a soul, he'd rush back to my body and respond the way he always had. Ray and the church had somehow cast a spell on him, but now I'd run away from them. I heard the train wheels singing 'Free free free', saw Leo's strong dark body soaring past in all the tree-trunks, felt his power throbbing through the rails.

I'd practised my new religion for twenty-three and a half hours. I'd sung, slept, sworn, indulged, rubbed myself sore in smelly train toilets, flirted with railway men and passengers – even managed to stuff myself, despite being skint. It was almost a holy principle now to feast instead of fast. A nun with a cheese and salami roll and a bag of macaroons had shared them with me on the first lap of the journey. When I'd changed at Paris, I'd found a half-eaten sandwich in a litter bin, and had then toured all the station bars and cafés, picking things off plates and raiding sugar bowls. On the boat, I was feeling peckish again, so I changed into my skimpiest sweater and my tightest jeans and sat around looking hungry. That always works. A sales rep from Châtillon brought me a sausage and a double gin, and was so intent on trying out his English, he left his change on the bar top. I pinched it when he wasn't looking and used it later to buy a synthetic cream *mille-feuille*.

I was almost relieved to be nicking things again. It cut me off from Bernadette, proved I couldn't be a saint. I was secretly scared that seeing Bernadette had branded me for ever, made me a seer, a guru, a visionary, someone special and elect. Supposing I had other apparitions, further messages, which flung me into chaos, tore my soul apart? Life with Leo was hardly silk and roses; it was rarely even predictable, but at least it didn't smash up natural laws. Leo didn't die and then turn up again, speak in riddles, vanish into thin air. I must return to him and cling to simple, solid things – sex and pricks and bodies, jobs and dogs and food.

I pressed my nose against the steamy window of the Victoria

cafeteria. There everything was simple – tycoons snatching breakfast, typists swilling tea. A bank clerk in a bowler hat had just attacked a doughnut. I watched the sugar sparkle on his fingers, waited for the jam to drool triumphant down his chin. I had less than a pound left in the world. I stood there dithering, trying to decide whether to splurge it on two and a quarter doughnuts or the tube fare back to Notting Hill. The tube fare won. I was far too tired to walk three miles with a suitcase, and anyway, the thought of Leo was growing more and more insistent. If there was any miracle at all, it would be the one of our reunion.

I could see him now, scowling in the hall as he heard the doorbell ring, thinking it was the postman or the man who reads the meter. Groping to the door, half-asleep and crotchety, Karma growling at his heels. His eyes kindling when he sees me, his whole body suddenly awake. He grabs my hair, pushes me against the wall, loses his mouth and face and tongue in mine. He's screwing me on the lino now, because it's nearer than the bed. Later – on the bed as well, the twenty dragons joining in, the mulberry tree shaking its hair across the window to hide us from the light. The smell of dark and pain and velvet and Leo's sperm. Everything long drawn out. No more quick splashes in bad-tempered bidets, but an hour's hot soak in pine-green water. Then lunch. Not litter bins or leftovers, but six or seven courses of hot steaming complicated things, and wine in *tumblers*. And Leo again, tasting of wine and sin and garlic now, screwing me under the table with the dirty dishes still sitting there on top of us.

I turned my back on the buffet and ran down the steps to the tube. There was a long queue for tickets which I joined. (Victoria is one of those smug, spoilsport stations where you can't slip by without paying.) I sat in the tube train and gazed around me. It was strange being in London after Lourdes. There were hardly any handicapped and no one was singing hymns or crying out to God to heal them. People had bosoms and buttocks and thighs again, whereas in Lourdes they'd done without them. The clothes were brighter (and tighter) and the women's faces lipsticked and mascara-ed instead of pious grey. There were far more men than women, while at Lourdes the females had outnumbered them by almost three to one. Even the smell was different – fug and tweed and cigarette smoke and sudden nudges of women's sharp fruity perfumes, instead of candle-wax and wet plastic wheelchair covers.

I glanced at the advertisements. There was one for brandy with a St Bernard dog sitting on the headline. I tried to avoid its eye – its name made me nervous. I'd assumed I'd run away from Bernadette, but if she could step into a different century, then eight hundred miles and a paltry channel crossing would do nothing to deter her. Apparitions don't need planes or passports. They can turn up anywhere, in the time it takes them just to think about it. Bernadette might even appear to me on this crowded lurching tube train. I tried to calm myself by reading the racing page over my neighbour's shoulder. After all, it was hardly sensible for Bernadette to waste her time in England. Half the English had never *heard* of Lourdes. When I'd told a man in the chemist I was going, he thought I'd said *Lords* and warned me the cricket season hadn't started yet. Far more practical for Bernadette to choose a fellow countryman, someone braver and better qualified than I was, preferably a business speculator who could develop Lourdes as something new and different. If Our Lady was no longer the centre-piece, then perhaps they could discover oil or wildlife or ski-runs, even a Gallic version of the Loch Ness monster – anything to give the tourists a new goal or purpose for their pilgrimages.

I arrived at Leo's station while I was still wondering whether you could turn the Grotto into a funfair and the Gave into a marina. It was good to leave the fug and dark behind and step out into light and air at street level. Notting Hill was as frowsty and frenetic as ever, but Leo's road looked as if it had dressed itself up to welcome me. It's one of the few in London with decent greenery and gardens which are more than just a drooping bay tree or a window-box. Most of the trees are planes and sycamores but there was one flowering cherry, iced with thick pink fondant clusters along its black boughs. Little splinters of white almond blossom lay in the road like the fragments of a shattered windscreen. The sky was a deep trusting blue. Strange to travel so far south and find only rain and storm, and then return north again to the sort of weather you see in holiday brochures.

I took off my sheepskin and shifted the case to the other hand. I was almost at Leo's door. He'd still be in his dressing-gown, his body naked under the rough caressing camelhair. I picked up a handful of blossom and scattered it through my hair. This was my real wedding. I was married to Leo in everything but name. Ray and God had merely been adulteries.

I pushed open the gate, passed the prickly bush whose name I never knew and the tangled plants my mother called weeds and suckers. The front door beetled up, black and heavy-featured with a brass nose which I thumped. Leo had refused to let me take my key away, since the time I'd left it on a beach and forgotten that tides come in.

I knocked again, louder. Perhaps Leo had the radio on or both bath-taps running full blast. He might even be asleep. He'd taken to sleeping later these last few weeks. He claimed it was an effect of the hypnosis, but I knew he was drinking more, to try and forget that the hypnosis wasn't working. It was whisky which was keeping him in bed when he should have been blazing to the door and melting in my arms. I tried the bell instead, kept my finger throbbing on it for a full two minutes. The house seemed to frown and mutter in disgust. It hated vulgar and unnecessary noise, like Leo did himself. I walked down the chipped stone steps to the basement door and hammered on it. Silence. Peered in through the window. Everything looked normal – coffee mugs making dirty pawmarks on a copy of the *Listener*, a score of Scriabin's 'Dance of Ecstasy' open on the table. I like the word ecstasy. You can't rush or gabble it. All those hissy consonants mean you have to spell it out. If Leo was still in bed, then I'd join him there and start on the ecstasy as soon as he opened his eyes. His bedroom's in the basement at the back, so I walked round and tried to re-connoitre. The curtains were still drawn which meant nothing, as Leo never lets the light in, even if he's been up and dressed for hours. I squinted through a gap in the velour and saw his bed unslept in, the Indian rug drawn over it, and all twenty dragons quietly dozing in a neat, unruffled line.

I swallowed a tiny shred of panic like a crumb. He'd made his bed, that's all, and gone out for an early morning stroll. Or was breakfasting with Otto in a café or a club, or had rushed to an auction room to inspect a Chinese vase. Perhaps he'd planned moussaka for lunch and was out buying aubergines, or had taken Karma for a run in Holland Park. For the first time ever, I actually longed for Karma – that hoarse throaty bark, those howls of black clotted fury which meant that Leo was there. He and his master always went in and out together.

I tried all the doors and windows at the back, but every one was locked, so I went round to the front again and waited on the step. He wouldn't be long – he never was at this time. He worked at home in the mornings and left his social and business calls for later on. I amused myself by writing his name in pebbles on the path, and then in leaves, and then in almond blossom. The woman next door came out to collect her milk. She had a white jowly chin and a pink hairnet over sparse grey curls.

'Seen Mr Rzevski?' I called.

'No,' she snapped, and slammed the door. She hated Leo. Most of his neighbours did, or they were either mad or foreign or bad-tempered, so even if I called on them, I doubted if they'd help. It would have been nice to wait in comfort in somebody's sitting-room, instead of on a doorstep.

Every few minutes, someone passed the gate. At each set of footsteps I jumped up, peered over the hedge, then sank down disappointed. After the fifth foreign student or dumpy waddling housewife, I refused to even check – just shut my eyes and prayed it would be Leo. It never was.

Forty minutes passed. I went out into the road and stretched my legs a bit. Easier there to see him coming. A child was playing on a tricycle, a cat's green eyes gleamed at me from under an abandoned car, a little knot of Indian women giggled on the corner. I started walking up and down, each time a little slower than the last, to give Leo time to return from his shopping or his brooding or his breakfast. Actually, it was nearer to elevenses, so I nicked a bottle of milk from one of the doorsteps and drank it for my breakfast and lunch combined. When Leo did return, it would line my stomach for the celebration wine.

I'd been up and down thirteen times by now. The fourteenth time, I went a little further, crossed the road and turned the corner to the public phone-box. Otto's number rang out smug and shrill. I was half relieved when no one answered it. At least Leo wasn't loitering in Otto's fringed and fancy drawing-room with his feet up on the sofa and his tea in a Yung Chêng bowl. Leo had been spending more and more time with Otto in the last few weeks. When I complained, Leo said it was business pure and simple. Otto, he claimed, had a better eye for a bargain and a sharper nose for a fake than anyone else in London. He owned certain pieces of Chinese porcelain which Leo told me were rarer than any friendship. His father had left him his collection when he died. He'd been a trader in the Far East, who spent his last years in a bare and shabby flat in Finchley. After the funeral, they found no food in the larder, nor clothes in the wardrobe, but every nook and cranny stuffed with shoe-boxes full of cracked Ming and dusty Ch'ing. Now they were Otto's shoe-boxes.

I tried to keep my mind on something safe and dreary like shoe-boxes rather than on Leo, as I trailed back to the house again and knocked. I suppose it was stupid to worry. People go out for a hundred reasons, and Leo wasn't even *expecting* me till Saturday. He might have planned a visit to a gallery, or a meeting with a dealer out of town. Except he never went out on Wednesdays – it was the day he always reserved for his accountant chap. They sat in the basement all day, going over papers.

There were other tiny things which fretted me – Leo never normally made his bed or locked the fanlights or told the milkman not to leave him milk. There were probably explanations, simple ones. Or perhaps I was only nervous because I'd chucked out my religion and turned my back on Ray and Bernadette, and now I needed Leo to fill the hole. Notting Hill without a Leo was almost as bad as Lourdes without Our Lady. Great chunks kept breaking off from my life and I had nothing to stick them back with. Anyone else would have gone to the public library, or passed an hour or two dawdling round the shops. All I could do was sit on his doorstep and slaver like a spaniel.

After another hour, I made myself get up and trudge back to the tube. I was window-shopping for one thing only – Leo. I checked all his favourite haunts and then searched the shops and bars and restaurants in between. I asked at the delicatessen and the Pakistani grocer's. Neither of them had seen him for at least four days, but they both lent me a pound. (I was down to my last 2p.) I plodded through Holland Park, covering every path and avenue five or six times over, but all the dogs were smaller and paler than Karma.

I was almost crawling when I reached the house again. I hadn't slept a wink the night before. The channel ferry had been crowded and the crossing rough. Even my double gin I'd sicked up over the side. I stood in front of the inhospitable door and prayed for it to open. Leo might well have returned by now. I listened for the sudden crash of the piano booming out the way I never liked it, proving he was there. But there wasn't so much as a *pianissimo*.

When I did knock, the echo seemed to mock me. I peered in through the letter-box, but all I could see were black and white squares of lino distorted into strange crippled shapes. I slumped down on the step again and tried to think of nothing till he came. After an hour or so, nothing got boring, and then frightening. There was a strange irrational panic gnawing at the edges of my mind, and so much space and silence in the centre of it that Bernadette's voice kept sneaking through and scaring me. I knew I'd let her down. I wondered if I'd be punished for it – some grisly penance or racking spell in Purgatory.

The light was already fading, as if to remind me of the glooms of hell. I began to feel so small and miserable, I slunk round the back again and crawled into a sort of coal-cellar-cum-dungeon which was used for storing tools and smelt of fusty things like dead moths and old rope. I cleared a space on the floor and lay down on two sacks and my sheepskin. I'd have a siesta like God did, and when I woke, Leo would be back. It was difficult to sleep and even when I did doze off, I kept starting awake again, thinking I'd heard footsteps round the front. Finally, I took the sacks and spread them on the doorstep. People might stare or assume I was a squatter or a tramp, but at least I'd be there the second he walked in.

It was turning colder now and darker. My earlier elation had subsided into flat and sour champagne. The summer skies, the smiling cherry blossom were only a half-forgotten picture on an empty chocolate box. Now the sky was overcast and cloudy, the street lights coming on, cats and children scuttling safe indoors. My hands and feet were almost numb, but I still had feeling in my middle parts. In fact, I was trying to remember how many days or weeks or months it was since I'd last had proper sex. (Ray didn't count and nor did Leo's limpings.) I'd worked it out as the night before the night before the hospital which made it ninety-nine and a half days – more than a quarter of a year, and the longest time I'd ever gone without it. I'd probably develop nervous tics or eczema or ulcers. The Victorian books said over-indulging wore the brain and body out, but now the medicos had changed their minds and claimed abstinence led to stress-induced diseases. (No wonder Ray looked haggard.) I didn't want to think of Ray. It was Leo who was shouting through my body, squeezing through all its crevices. I longed to hug him close to me, cling to him for comfort. If I concentrated on him hard enough, he might actually turn up. Things often worked like that.

I went through all our mutual history, starting with the first time he'd fucked me, which was the second time we met (our introductory meeting being taken up with tetanus injections). He'd stayed stiff and thrusting for two and three quarter hours. When I purred, he told me it was something they practised in the East. If I hadn't been so sore, I'd have knelt down there and then and worshipped him. Women talk crap about men's looks or jobs or bank accounts, but there's only one thing really – the time between in and come. The longer the interval, the more precious the man. It doesn't matter really how many noughts on his pay-slip or letters after his name, or whether his hair is thinning or his waist thickening (although Leo has both hair and waist as well as staying-power). When you see gorgeous girls slavering over four-foot-nothing little creeps, you can tell they're three-hour men. Napoleon was one, almost certainly, and Charles II probably, and Jesus might have been, if He hadn't been so busy with other sorts of miracle. Leo was my first. He was not only a stayer, but he had those amazing comes which confuse the so-called sex experts who go around measuring penises and arousal levels and reduce everything to chest flushes and dilated pupils and carpopedal spasms. Their scientific orgasms are charted only in terms of seconds and centimetres, whereas Leo's lasted *centuries*.

I spread my legs on the step, emptied my mind of everything but Leo. I could see him coming round the corner now, running down the street as he caught sight of me, unbuttoning his coat. His hands were already on my breasts, his mouth ravenous. I pressed towards him. I could feel every bone, every tiny indentation in his body. He was kissing every inch of me – fingers, spaces between fingers, the little knob at the bottom of my spine, the insides of my knees. His mouth moved swiftly, almost angrily, as if he were punishing me for all the hours and minutes that I'd been away. Then he pulled me to my feet again, seized my hair and yanked it away from my face so that he could kiss and comfort all the bits which had been hidden underneath it – ears, nape, the hollows in my neck, the dip between the shoulder-blades.

He's pushing me against the wall, still with my hair twisted up behind me. He bends me back, and goes down on my face as if he were attacking it, mouth, lips, teeth, tongue. The woman next door is peering through her curtains, muttering 'filthy slut', and the man upstairs spying through the opera glasses he bought to study wildlife. Leo hardly notices. He's dragged me to the ground now, the sacks spread underneath us, my feet hammering on his shoulders, nails clawing down his back. People are walking home from tubes and buses, passing us, peering at us, complaining, criticizing. I don't see them. I'm so wild, I can bite through bone. Leo is tearing me to pieces, stabbing me, scaring me, pain and fever and radiance all mixed up, the boundaries between them dashed and broken and singing. Even the light has crept away. Leo is so dark and violent, the day shudders and gives up. We're alone now. Only Karma sniffing at us, howling out his jealousy, his rough tongue rasping down my thighs, his teeth tearing deep inside me, his wild, black, terrifying bark crying Leo Leo Leo Leo Leo Leo . . .

No one. Only a shadow spilling from a bush, a flicker from a street light, Karma just a black branch on the ground. Even the woman next door had slammed her window shut. The day had disappeared. It was neither afternoon, nor evening; just a sick, lonely twilight. A whole working day had passed away. From nine to five, governments had debated, secretaries typed vital memoranda, shopgirls given change. All I had done was waited, waited, waited, yet it had worn me out. I was panting, weak, and sore.

I zipped up my jeans, flung the sacks on the flower-bed, and drudged back to Notting Hill. I sat in a sandwich bar between the cinema and the tube station where I could see everybody passing. Leo had been out now for over eight hours. He never did that with Karma. The dog needed meals and pees and runs, and very few of his acquaintances would allow Karma in their houses. He tore things (and people) up. I'd already phoned Otto again, let it ring for seven minutes by my watch, but there was still no answer. I tried the picture dealer's, but they'd shut up shop.

I spun my coffee out till seven o'clock. Everyone else was in couples. A man and a girl were even wearing identical duffel coats, and another two sharing a raspberry milkshake and a straw.

At 7.02 I paid the bill and left. I'd decided to ring Adrian from the tube station. As soon as I heard his voice, I felt a little comforted. He sounded like a duffel coat himself – warm and strong and practical.

'But you weren't coming back till Saturday,' he said, after the first greetings and surprise.

'Patricia Jane got ill,' I lied. 'She's OK now, but they thought she ought to travel home, just in case it developed into something. Look, Adrian, I've been at Leo's place all day, but I can't get in. He . . . doesn't seem to be there.'

'No,' he faltered. The duffel coat seemed thinner now, as if someone had shrunk and spoilt it at the cleaner's.

'What d'you mean "no"?'

'He's . . . er . . . gone away.'

'Gone *away*? But he didn't *tell* me. I mean before I went, he hadn't planned to . . .'

'No.'

'What d'you keep saying "no" for?' I jabbed my foot against the wall. 'How the hell d'*you* know Leo's plans?'

'He's . . . er . . . been in touch with me.' The duffel coat had completely vanished now. There was only a frayed and holey sweater unravelling at the seams.

'*You?*'

At that point, the pips went and I hadn't got another coin. I begged for change at the kiosk, but they said only if I bought a paper which I didn't want. I didn't want anything except that stupid lying phone-box to shatter into pieces and Leo to come sauntering through the ticket barrier and rush into my arms. I stood a moment while the whole dizzy tube station slowly somersaulted through my head, then I marched up to the window and bought a single to Waterloo. Even a frayed unravelling sweater was better than sitting naked on a doorstep.

twenty-eight

Gone away, gone away, gone away, goneaway goneaway goneaway-goneawaygoneawaygoneawaygoneaway gone a . . .

Leo never went away. He hated holidays. And he never confided in Adrian. People with semi-detacheds in suburbia and Mortgage-Protection Policies don't induce his confidence. All the way on the slow, shabby train from Waterloo to Twickenham, I tried to picture him and Adrian talking. I couldn't. I couldn't even imagine where they'd meet. Adrian would suggest half of Black Label in the saloon bar of a small hotel with racing prints on the mock-walnut walls and the barman in a maroon bow tie, wise-cracking across the rubber plants. Leo would lurk in the basement of the Ganymede Club where the bum-boys wore dark glasses and an ex-Norwegian seaman played the accordion and showed off his tattoos.

I went through all the reasons why people have to go away. Dying relatives, perhaps – but all of Leo's had conveniently died already, or if they hadn't, he didn't want to know. Business trips. Leo's work was confined to London, more or less, and when it wasn't, he persuaded someone else to do the travelling. Personal injury or accident. I saw Leo howling in a hospital, black head bleeding into glaring white bed-linen. Why assume the worst? He might simply have gone to the coast for a day or two, or abroad to visit a new superior hypnotist. The better ones probably all had addresses in Vienna, like the early Freudian analysts. All the same, why should he tell *Adrian*? Why should Adrian be involved at all? Why had . . . ?

I ran all the way from the station to Adrian's semi. My suitcase was still on Leo's doorstep, so it was easy to go fast. I was glad I'd left it there – something of mine to nestle against his house, to bring him back like a magic talisman, welcome him when he blazed in through the gate.

Adrian's door was an inch or two ajar, so I walked straight in and shouted 'Piggy!' which was what I called him when we were first married and he'd always wanted more. Unfortunately, it wasn't Piggy, but Janet wearing a sort of maternity smock, which I thought was taking things too far, considering it was three months since she'd lost the baby. Her skin was a smug complacent healthy pink all over, as if she had a hot water-bottle snuggling just inside her body where other people have hearts and lungs and things. Her cheeks looked like an advertisement for those glowing Barbara Cartland sort of people who stuff themselves full of Sanatogen or Horlicks or multi-vitamins. Her plump pink upper arms could barely squeeze themselves through the prim puffed sleeves. She made me feel sallow and sleazy and faded in comparison. It was as if she had never eaten anything but hothouse peaches and orange-blossom honey – wholesome, sun-kissed delicacies which shone through her skin and sang along her bloodstream, while my drab body groaned and heaved with husks and scraps and greasy rancid leftovers. Her hair had been newly permed and every tight little yellow sausage curled its lip and sneered at me. Her legs were bad (thank God) and she was wearing those dark brown crêpey support tights they sell for varicose veins. They were so thick, I couldn't see whether she had the veins as well. She smelt of lavender bags and halibut and self-congratulation all mixed up together. She stood in the hall blocking my way to Adrian, glowing and frowning at the same time in a manner which said, 'This is my house and my husband and you haven't a chance against the three of us.'

'Hi!' I said, trying to see what size her breasts were now, under her baggy smock. Mine had collapsed only days after they'd pickled Lucian, but hers still looked megalithic.

She pressed her lips together in what might have been a smile, had her eyes not frozen over. Janet is unfailingly polite. Even if the Nazis had forced their way into her bedroom for rape and arson, she'd have offered them a Durex or a box of matches and said, 'Let me take your coat.'

That's exactly what she did say, though when I handed over Leo's sheepskin, she shrank away from it as if it were infectious. I could see her making a mental note to wash her hands before she touched her food. They'd been sitting over supper when I barged in. It was late for Adrian. When I lived with him, he'd liked to eat at six o'clock and was starving again by ten. I suppose late dinner was part of Janet's rationing process, like no eating between meals and instant confiscation of his Creamline toffees.

'I'd have made more if I'd known you were coming,' she peeved, scraping out the remnants of a fishy (halibut?) thing in wine sauce.

There was almost nothing left of it except the garnish and the fancy French name. 'People usually phone if they plan to come for dinner.'

'It's OK,' I said. 'I'll finish up the veg. I don't like fish much, anyway.'

Adrian still looked ravenous and watched in admiration as I polished off the potatoes and shovelled in the last of the *petits pois à la française* (Birds-Eye brand with a sprinkle of herbs and a bit of soggy lettuce leaf clinging to the bottom). I felt I had to stuff and stuff, to shore me up before I heard where Leo was. *Gone away goneaway*. It was also a sort of thumbs-down to religion. Bernadette was far less likely to approach me while my mouth was crammed with Camembert and my plate piled high with Crawford's mixed cheese biscuits.

'No pudding?' I inquired. I wanted to drown everything in food – Lourdes and Ray and Leo and cold abandoned doorsteps, and proud possessing Janets.

'Adrian's *slimming*, Thea.' She made the word 'slimming' sound like some holy and high-principled form of torture, like crucifixion or the rack.

I didn't dare catch Adrian's eye. He was fiddling with his napkin, a heavy damask one with 'A' embroidered on the corner. Janet loved things with initials on. I suppose it gave her a surer sense of who other people were and who she was herself. If I'd had 'T' embroidered on my knickers, I might have had fewer problems with my lovers. Somehow I always thought of things like knickers when I was with Adrian. The only time I had any dregs of ownership left over him was when I managed to seduce him. Apart from that, he now belonged exclusively to Janet. She'd probably embroider an 'A' or a 'J' on his prick next, to ensure it didn't stray. It still seemed strange I hadn't had it for so long – with him or anyone. Janet must have abstained even longer – what with losing the baby and then the D and C and convalescence and being stitched and sore and bleeding and probably disapproving of it anyway.

She was making coffee now in a prissy jug with roses on, dribbling it into mean little cups which were so small, it was hardly worth dirtying them. The sugar was that coarse brown flinty stuff which breaks your teeth and isn't even sweet. I put so much in, the coffee overflowed like Archimedes' bath. Janet mopped it up with frowns and tuts and dishcloths, and then slipped a plastic mat beneath my cup as if I were a baby or a dog.

There were terrible, tepid silences in between our tiny sips of coffee. Adrian had been tackling the critics' reaction to the new biography of Gladstone, but it was really Leo's name which hung across the table. The longer I went on munching mixed cheese biscuits, the longer I could pretend he was just down the road at the Classic dissecting the new Buñuel, or had been given a ticket for the New York City Ballet, or was dining with the philatelist. 'Gone away' could simply mean a day trip.

'Enjoyed your holiday?' asked Janet. She was the sort of person who used words like 'holiday' in a tone of sour recrimination, as if she'd been given all your work to do while you lolled about in hopeless self-indulgence. It was the same with 'birthday' or 'pay-rise' or 'sabbatical'. Janet slaved while you blew out the candle or hogged all the icing or jetted to the sun.

'It *was*n't a holiday,' I said. I didn't add 'I went for a miracle'. She probably liked men limp. The only miracles *she* believed in were the ones in the commercials – Washing Whiter Than White, Cleaning Round The Bend, Spreading Straight From The Fridge. Adrian was staring at his plate. The silence was thick and damp and lumpy like the sauce. Even the Camembert was only a ruin now – a tangle of rinds and a shred of silver paper. I couldn't bear it any longer. The whole of south-west London seemed to be holding its breath.

I pushed my plate away and flung back my chair. 'Where's Leo, then?' I shouted.

There was the sort of hush in which hundreds of pins could have dropped and both Adrian and Janet would have rushed to pick them up, to prevent them having to answer.

Then Janet said, 'We don't . . .' and Adrian said, 'He couldn't . . .' at exactly the same moment. They both stopped and laughed rather forcedly, and Janet said, '*You* tell her' and Adrian said, 'No, no, please go on, I'm sorry', and a few more hundred thousand pins dropped and I grabbed another biscuit and held tight on to it to stop my hands from shaking.

'You see, Thea dear, he should never really have *sent* you there if he couldn't pay the bill.'

'*Would*n't pay, you mean.' Janet banged her cup down.

'Ssshh, Janet, there's no need to . . .'

'Couldn't, wouldn't . . . what difference does it make in any case? All I know is that's not *your* responsibility, Adrian, not any more, it isn't. The National Health was good enough for *me*, Thea, and I had complications. I can't think why he had to *choose* a private hospital.'

'Safer,' Adrian mumbled. 'Less publicity.'

'Oh, of *course*,' cooed Janet. 'The nuns would hush things up for him, wouldn't they?'

'What d'you *mean*?' I said. 'The casualty was closed at Hammersmith. I *had* to go to St Maur's.'

'*Had* to? At a hundred and twenty pounds a day! I suppose you *had* to have a room of your own, and four-course meals, and all the frills, and top-notch specialists. I might have said the same, Thea, but it wouldn't have got me far.'

I glanced at her cherry lips, her strawberry cheeks. She'd been eating four-course meals since the day she was weaned, even in the womb, perhaps. I nudged my denture with my tongue to make it slip a bit. 'Actually,' I said, 'I didn't have much of a mouth to eat at all.'

'I'm sorry about that, Thea. Of course I am. We *both* are.' (I hated that 'both'. I could almost see the Morton Ring of Confidence binding spouse and spouse together.) 'But it only makes Leo's behaviour all the more despicable.'

'What's he *done*, for heaven's sake? Where's he *gone*?' My biscuit was just a shattered mass of crumbs now, as Leo dwindled further and further away from me.

'Do you realize, Thea, how much that total bill was?'

'Yes,' I lied. I didn't, but I couldn't bear to see Janet purse her lips over all those accusing noughts. X-rays and stitches and Confession and Raspberry Ripple would all be charged as extras. It wasn't just Janet – it had always been the same with Adrian – totting up extravagances, nagging about waste. He'd made me keep accounts in little red-ruled cash books with carbons underneath. 'Don't buy English Cheddar. Brown eggs are a con.' Bills took all the pleasure out of life. All that soapy Irish cheese and sparrow-size anaemic eggs and slaving away at extra coaching to pay for night-storage heaters which were never hot when you wanted them, and buying dreary things like toilet rolls in bulk, so you hadn't got the cash for impulse Baskin-Robbins.

Leo didn't live like that. Leo got credit from Pakistani grocers and shopped at Fortnum's with money he owed the Inland Revenue. Leo had guts and spirit and the most expensive cheeses in London. If he avoided bills, it was only because he opposed them on principle. The hospital thing was probably just his gesture against the Catholic Church, or against the iniquities of private medicine or the sex life of the nuns.

I was feeling better all the time. It was only a matter of a paltry little bill, not the death or accident I'd dreaded. Leo was merely hiding somewhere to escape his creditors. Or maybe the nuns had forced him to get a proper full-time job. He was probably doing overtime – that's why he was out. Even if it was a residential job, he'd soon be back with the money in his hands. Janet and Adrian treated bills like some disaster – I had feared a real one.

'Don't worry,' I said airily. 'They'll sort it out between them.'

'Oh, *will* they?' Janet banged the drawer shut. 'Well, it certainly won't be any thanks to *you*, Thea. You didn't exactly help matters, by filling in the form with Adrian as your *husband*. The Accounts Department were totally confused. You shouldn't be so careless.'

I suppose she thought I muddled up my men by mistake, like all those dreary medieval kings, endless Henrys and Edwards with only their numbers to distinguish them. Oh, no! I had every right to claim Adrian as my husband. He was far more mine than hers. I'd lived with him nearly six and a quarter years, whereas she was just a beginner. Adrian and I had screwed one thousand nine hundred and fifty-three times. I grinned to myself. I doubt if Janet had ever made three figures.

'It's not *funny*, Thea.' Janet crashed the cups together and flung them on a tray. 'Adrian's got enough to worry about without getting mixed up with summonses.'

'*Summonses?*' It was a strange word like blancmange, a word you could choose as a mantra and say over and over until the world calmed down again and Leo returned from his residential job. I should have left a note for him, so he could phone me at Twickenham and meet me on the next train back again.

'Yes, I'm afraid they're suing him, Thea.' That was Adrian. He seemed smaller, somehow, when Janet took the floor. She looked as if she'd like to pile him on her tray and stack him with the cups.

'But he's got a *job*,' I objected. 'He's working overtime. He'll pay.'

'*Pay!*' brayed Janet. 'You must be joking. He's already sent the bill back twice. He said it was *nothing* to do with him at all and that he signed the form in a state of shock and under pressure, without even understanding what it meant.'

'Oh, I see . . .' Perhaps I could get a job and pay myself. Worth it, just to have him back again. I'd be his saviour then – drag him out of hiding, redeem him from the law courts.

'Look, leave it to me,' I said. 'I'll go to the Burton Bureau in the morning. They've got a job still waiting for me more or less. Receptionist in Mayfair. I owe it to Leo, really. I mean I . . .'

'*Owe* it to him? Have you *any* idea what . . . ?'

'Janet, I'd rather you . . .'

'I'm sorry, Adrian, but I think she ought to hear.'

'Yes, but not just at the moment, when she's . . .'

Janet cut him short. 'D'you know what he told the nuns, Thea? That he hardly knew you at all. He was simply an odd acquaintance who happened to be around when you fell.'

Odd acquaintance. Fell. The words crashed like a paperweight against my mouth. Janet hadn't noticed. She was shaking out the tablecloth as if it were Leo's limp and mangled body. Adrian came and sat beside me on the sofa. His whole body seemed to bend and ache towards me. I could see 'darlings' seeping out of him, but he had to dam them up again when Janet flounced and frowned.

'Where . . . is . . . he?' I whispered. I tried to get the words out straight, but my mouth was wounded again and all the syllables seemed to stick and jar together. Adrian was almost holding my hand. He had inched his fingers along the sofa until our thumbs were touching, then left them there until Janet turned her back.

'He's . . . er . . . left the country, Thea.'

'Run away,' rammed Janet. Words like holiday and birthday sounded almost friendly now, compared with the venom she squeezed into those three short syllables.

Gone away run away summonses blancmange. Nothing meant anything any more. Words were just strings of letters curdling in my head – *halibut left the country odd acquaintance fell* . . . I hadn't got a lover any more or a religion or a husband. I hadn't even got a bed or house or a shelter any more. Not even a front door key.

'Er . . . did he leave me a . . . ?'

'*No*,' pounced Janet. 'He left *nothing*. No explanation, no apology, no address, no . . .'

'So how d'you know he's gone, then?' Still hope. Still a tiny trickle of hope. He might be at the Classic. Or even at the ballet. People gave him tickets to the ballet.

'Look,' I shouted. 'He may be simply out. He's *often* out in the evenings. I *did* try Otto's, but that was earlier. He could be back there now. It's only business, actually. You see, Otto's a sort of expert on . . .'

'Otto –' Janet lingered over the name as if it were one of the germs her latest cleaner hadn't reached – 'has gone with him.'

'Oh,' I said. *Otto. Odd acquaintance*. I tried to think of shoe-boxes in Finchley. Only business. Only Chinese porcelain. They'd probably gone together to inspect a vase. It could even be a phoenix. Perhaps Leo had planned a surprise for me – another *feng huang* preening its wings in greeting as I walked in tired from Lourdes. I'd spoilt the thing by arriving back too soon, but he wouldn't have to know that. I could stay at Adrian's till Saturday and then slink back as if I'd just stepped off the plane and find him and the phoenix risen from the ashes.

Funny, though, that he'd been in touch with Janet. He'd never met her in his life. Otto didn't bother with people who knew nothing about Ming celadons or eighteenth-century monochromes or *blanc de chine* or *hua shih*. All Janet collected were twopence-off coupons cut out from *Woman's Realm* or new superior foot deodorants. I stared at her pursed lips, her podgy hands. She was lying to me, that was it. She was furious about the bill and trying to get her own back. She was probably even jealous because she'd guessed that I had wilder comes than she could. All she wanted was to scare me out of the house.

'I don't believe a *word* of it,' I yelled. 'Leo wouldn't confide in you. You haven't even met him. He'd *never* come down here. And Otto even less. Just because you're . . .'

'Hush, Thea.' Adrian inched his fingers a centimetre nearer. 'Leo *phoned*, darling. It was the day you went away yourself – the Saturday. The call was very brief. He just said . . .'

'*Brief?* Downright rude, I'd call it, if he didn't happen to be a friend of yours.' Janet was furious about that 'darling' and was trying to pay me back. She made the word 'friend' sound like the Gestapo.

'Janet, I'd rather handle this myself.'

'She's got to know *some*time, Adrian. You can't wrap her in cotton wool for ever.'

So I was 'her' now, was I, just to make it clear all further 'darlings' would be confiscated. She turned to face me, her huge breasts quivering through the smock. 'Leo simply said that he had to go abroad, so you couldn't live there any longer. No explanations. Nothing. I think he expected Adrian to take you in, there and then.

Doesn't he realize Adrian's *married*, Thea? I mean, it's a bit of a cheek, isn't it, to . . .'

'Look, why don't we leave it till the morning?' Adrian's voice sounded grey and almost wounded. One hand grasped my own, the other limped lamely after Janet. He seemed to be physically torn between the two of us. 'We'll all feel better then.'

Janet totally ignored him. 'Well, anyway, Adrian was decent enough to catch the very next train up there and try and sort things out. It was most inconvenient, in fact. We had to cancel a very long-standing . . .'

'Janet, I don't see any reason to . . .' Adrian was slumped in on himself, spine hunched and flinching like an old man's. Janet dislodged him from the sofa and sat down there herself.

'Leo wasn't in, of course. Or if he was, he wouldn't open the door. Adrian left a note and phoned at *least* six times, all through that day and the next. But not a squeak from anyone. So yesterday, up he goes again. This time, I went with him. It's not just a question of where you're going to *live*, Thea – Leo may believe in bigamy, but I'm still a bit old-fashioned, I'm afraid – it's this whole hospital business. I'm *not* having Adrian saddled with lawsuits and unpleasantnesses just because your . . . boyfriend decides to . . .'

'He's *not* my boyfriend,' I whispered. Odd acquaintance. Wildman. Lover, husband, God. Her hips were oozing into mine, her plump pink thighs edging me into the corner of the sofa. I could smell hair lacquer and Johnson's baby powder.

'Well, this time there *was* someone in, but it wasn't Leo – oh, no – it was Otto's brother, a most unsavoury chap called Jochen, wearing a sort of smock thing. He told us Leo and Otto had already left the country, if you please. He was *furious* with them himself. Otto owed him money and Leo had promised to sell some valuable pictures for him, which had simply vanished without trace. And there the two of them were, hitch-hiking to *Kashmir*, would you believe it.'

'Kashmir,' I whispered, trying out the word. It was simply a hole, a gash, a cry of pain. Words were meaning less and less every minute. I didn't even know where Kashmir was, except it was far too far. Somewhere strange and foreign and difficult, without a happy ending. So it was nothing to do with Chinese porcelain or shoe-boxes in Finchley. Nothing to do with business. More like an elopement or a tryst. I could see Otto bending over Leo's thighs in a lay-by off the autoroute. Other words were slicing through my brain – obscene, forbidden words – consummation, honeymoon.

The coffee and the Camembert were curdling with Kashmir in my stomach. I was car-sick as I sped along the motorways, sobbing and retching in the passenger seat, not daring to look round. If I squinted into the driving mirror, I could see Leo and Otto tangled up together in the back, one heaving shape beneath the car rug.

'Please,' I said. 'I'd like to go to bed.'

Janet was double wrapping the last three Crawford's biscuits. They would probably stretch to Adrian's lunch tomorrow, with half a gherkin and the cheese rinds.

'*Bed?*' she winced. She made it sound obscene. I hadn't said bed with *Adrian*, for heaven's sake. They had a spare room at the back where all their guests were segregated. Adrian and I had used it as a lumber room. We'd even screwed there sometimes, on the floor-boards.

I dared not think of screwing. It reminded me of Leo – his long, thin, open, thrusting legs, and Otto underneath them. I turned to Adrian. Janet had pushed a tiny brush-and-pan set into his hands. He was meant to be clearing the crumbs off the table with it, but he was so distressed, he was missing most of them. I closed my eyes. Leo and Otto had arrived in Istanbul and were standing thigh to thigh in a small sleazy bathroom. Otto took his shaving brush and teased it down Leo's chin, across his chest, down further to his . . .

'I don't feel well,' I faltered. 'I must lie down.'

Adrian stopped sweeping. 'Thea . . .' he murmured. I could see a 'darling' sneaking out, but he swept it strictly up again. 'You see, Janet thought it might be more . . . well . . . *convenient* if you . . .' His voice tailed off. The crumbs fell on the floor.

'Yes?' I prompted. I fixed my gaze unflinchingly on the pupil of his left eye and challenged him and Janet to turn me out. It's a trick I learnt with dogs. It intimidates even fierce Alsatians. Karma's the only dog it's never worked with. I wondered what they'd done with him. You can't take half an Afghan hound to Kashmir. I could hear him howling in my head.

Adrian had dropped the brush and was twisting his thumbs together the way he does when he has to tell a boy he's been expelled. I never heard what Janet thought, what chill little guest-house or cosy prison cell she'd booked for me, as far away from Twickenham as possible.

'Look, Jan,' he whispered. 'She'd better stay here. *Please*. Just tonight. She's shocked.'

Oh, so it was Jan, now, was it. He'd be darlinging her next, snuggling up to those double-bolster breasts while I shivered in the spare room, and Leo and Otto coupled in the back of a lorry speeding towards the border, one coat flung over their two panting bodies . . .

Adrian was still whispering. He'd never learnt to do it softly enough. 'You take her up, Jan. She looks awful.'

Janet marched me into the spare room which was cold and so square-rule tidy, it seemed to recoil from me in distaste. Everything was green and slippery. There was a green satin bedspread and a matching pond-green frill concealing the legs of the dressing-table. The walls were shiny and the ceiling glared. Even the Kleenex were green, those fancy-packaged ones meant only for admiring, not for weeping into. There was a fringed shade on the bedside light, the colour of a sick weeping willow, and green crocheted doilies smirking on the dressing-table. Everywhere I looked, Leo and Otto were whispering in corners, snuggling under blankets, slipping off their clothes. I held on to the wardrobe and tried to find my way back from Kashmir. It was cold and dark and lonely on the roads.

Janet flicked a non-existent speck of dust from the bedside table and turned the counterpane down, as if she feared I might contaminate it. I undressed in front of her. My legs were longer than hers and at least I had a waist. If she could parade her Devon-cream complexion at any hour of the day or night, and point those vast tits at me across the table, then it was time I answered back. Leo liked small breasts. More like a man, I suppose. I could see his hands caressing Otto's nipples. I stood there naked while Janet pursed her lips and stared at a picture of a vase (green) of flowers (mauve) which hung just above the bed.

'Haven't you got a nightdress?'

I didn't bother answering. She'd seen me arrive with nothing more than my sheepskin and a shoulder-bag, so, 'Haven't you got a nightdress?' meant 'Slut, whore – that Camembert was meant to last all week and why can't you choose a boyfriend who's *respectable*?'

She returned with the sort of garment they sell in mail-order catalogues for the overweight and house-bound. It had long sleeves and a high neck and was made in some school-knicker fabric in a shade they probably described as 'Dawn' or 'Oyster', but was more like puke. It even smelt of Janet, though, mercifully, I couldn't see a 'J' on it.

''Night,' I said, crawling in between the slimy nylon sheets which lapped damply at my legs.

'The bathroom's next door,' she primmed. That was Janet-esque for 'Decent people wash themselves before they get into bed.' But if she thought I was going to drag myself out again and waste their precious, budgeted, cheap-rate, cut-price water, then she was seriously mistaken. I'd been travelling for an entire day and a night, sitting on a step another day, and now my whole life and God and home had been blown to pieces, and all Janet could suggest was soap and flannel. They weren't even necessary. The way she sterilized everything, I'd probably be fumigated just by lying on her bed linen. I could feel the germs simply giving up, dropping off me in groaning little clusters as they whiffed the Ibcol on the sheets.

I couldn't sleep. I tried to count germs instead of sheep, but I kept limping after Leo, stopping in squalid cafés on roaring foreign motorways, watching Otto's soft fairish hair drip on to Leo's shoulder. They were sharing everything – coffee, curry, beds, bodies, mouths. I had driven Leo away by landing myself in hospital with a bill he couldn't pay, by being poor and dim and ill and unemployable, by messing up my looks. He had turned to a man whose soul was a piece of Sung – a flawless specimen neither cracked, nor chipped nor riveted. A man with a proper mouth whose lips were always open, and a proper four-square father who had grown up with him and played with him and had only finally died so that Otto could inherit all his Ming. A man he could get it up for, a man he didn't despise, a man he had to deceive me over because he had invested all his wealth and passion in him. There had been a hundred thousand clues and I had turned my back on all of them. The time they spent together, the way they sat so close, the Ganymede Club, the bum-boys in dark glasses, the sleazy bars they haunted, the naked greed in Otto's boiled-fish eyes.

Leo had never said 'I love you' because he was saving it for Otto, *saying* it to Otto, whispering it in bars, in bed, in ecstasy. I could hear him now, that caressing dark-brown voice rubbing against Otto like the bristles of a beard. They were both tangled up in bed with me, cramping me, ignoring me, taking up all the room. I punched and kicked them out again. Better to be alone than be betrayed.

I lay in the darkness listening to the purr and leer of their departing car. It was cold and clammy in the nylon sheets. I had taken off the nightie because I didn't like the feeling of being wrapped from neck to toe in Janet. There was only one blanket, a thin, grudging sort of dishcloth thing she had probably bought because it said 'non-iron, non-crease, no-fuss', not to mention non-warm, no-use. I crept out of bed and opened the bottom drawer of the dressing-table. I hoped I'd find one of Adrian's sweaters which would come down to my thighs and smell of Mars bars and medieval kings and pencil sharpenings.

There weren't any sweaters, only a stack of baby clothes wrapped in tissue paper. I stared at the matinée jackets with their minuscule pearl buttons, the tiny Viyella nighties and midget woollen vests. There were three dozen towelling nappies, a white fluffy shawl, a muslin christening gown; two little bibs with bears on, even a bobbing bunny for hanging in a pram. Everything was white – white and dead like Janet's baby was. Opening that drawer was like ripping off a Band-Aid. I'd thought I was grazed before, but now my wounds all shrieked and poured with blood. Lucian, Lourdes, Ray, God; my cold, hope-less suitcase still shivering on the doorstep, Mike gasping and dying in a foreign hospital, Ray in mortal sin. And roaring, revving, honking through them all, Leo and Otto blazing into Kashmir with the sun shining on their wild and spoken love.

I picked up a tiny dress with smocking on the front and pink ribbon threaded through the sleeves. Janet had wanted a girl-child. She'd had a boy and I'd murdered him. These were the corpse's clothes. Increase and multiply, the priest had said and all I had done was kill. Leo was in Otto's bum in Kashmir, and Karma was in kennels, and Janet's baby was rotting in a hole. I didn't cry. It would only disturb Adrian as he nuzzled into Janet in the master bedroom.

I carried the baby clothes very gently in my arms as if they were still living. I laid them on the bed, spreading them underneath me like a nest. I kept the shawl to one side while I snuggled in and arranged my limbs against the towelling nappies and the little piles of vests. It was warmer now, and softer. I tucked the shawl across me and pressed the bobbing bunny between my breasts. I closed my eyes. The road to Kashmir dwindled, softened, slumped, until it was only a length of soft white baby ribbon curling through a sleeve.

I slept.

twenty-nine

Adrian woke me in the morning with a cup of tea. I refused to open my eyes. Babies sleep nineteen hours out of twenty-four. All I wanted was to be a baby – to lie on my back and kick my legs and crow, and shut out all the grown-up things like loss and sex and pain and God and Kashmir, which had come choking and screaming into the room when Adrian drew the curtains.

I took a sip of tea. He had forgotten I take sugar. I had been married to Adrian for six and a quarter years, with three cups of tea on average, every day, two spoonfuls per cup. I tried to multiply six and a quarter by three hundred and sixty-five, by three, by two. I'm no good at arithmetic but I knew it must be near a ton or so of sugar. And now, not even a saccharin. It was as if he had slapped me in the face. I could feel slow stupid tears sliding down my cheeks. I pushed the cup away – it was cold, in any case.

'Thea . . . *darling* . . .' He came and sat beside me on the bed. He was wearing a fuzzyish blue sweater which made him look cuddly like a child's toy. But above the neck, he was man. There were newly minted frown-lines running down his forehead, and on his chin a tiny glower of blood where he had cut himself shaving. He smelt of the sort of strong, cheap soap they use in public washrooms.

He laid his hand, palm upwards, on the bedspread, as if it were an offering to me, like a piece of toast or the morning newspaper. I was naked underneath the covers. The baby clothes had worked themselves down to the bottom of the bed and were now all creased and tangled with the sheets, the bobbing bunny just a hard lump in my side. I struggled up and took his hand. My breasts looked pale and puny against its broad, freckled tan. He dragged his sweater off and slipped it over my head. I felt his hands brushing down my chest, clumsy and tender both at once, as if he were trying to dress a baby. He left his arm around me. I could hear a bird singing one astonished note over and over in the laburnum tree outside. The sun was throwing gold-dust at the clouds. How could birds sing and suns shine when

Leo was in Kashmir and in love with Otto, and Adrian didn't belong to me?

'Adrian,' I said.

'Mmmm . . . ?'

'May I stay here? Just a week or two? *Please.* Just till Leo gets back.'

'He's . . . er . . . not *coming* back, Thea. I think you ought to know that.'

'Yes,' I said. Then 'No'. There didn't seem much difference between the two. I could see Leo growing old in Kashmir, hair white against his sallow skin, blue veins raised on frail, shrivelled hands. Otto wasn't older. Otto was still young, pale, flabby, narrow, sly – hair fine as a child's, eyes like runny eggs. Louis de Gonzague.

'I know it's hard, darling, but it'll be better in the end, honestly it will. Leo was never right for you. You can start again now. Find a nice little bedsit somewhere and a new job. I'll help you, Thea – you know I will.'

'Thanks,' I said. A cold wind from the Himalayas was cutting through my head.

'Let's have breakfast, shall we? – and try and make some plans. Janet's gone to work already, but she said goodbye and hoped you were feeling better.'

Goodbye. That's what Janet *would* say. Maybe she'd even left the details of a few bedsitters on the breakfast table. No – nothing there except the damask napkins, and some dusty looking starch-reduced wheatflakes and a slice or two of slimmer's bread which was so white and light it was like eating Aertex knickers. The wheatflakes weren't even in a carton, just measured out into two small bowls, so we couldn't pig ourselves. I glanced around the kitchen. Nothing was in its packet, as if manufacturers' wrappings were too bright and tawdry to be allowed to expose themselves. Everything had been decanted into matching tins and jars. No vulgar competitions, no shrieking advertisements. The six multi-coloured cereals no longer sat and juddered on the fridge. There wasn't even the judder. It was a new fridge which didn't need defrosting. Janet always bought things for what they didn't need. Perhaps she saw Adrian like that – her non-iron, non-feed, non-screw husband.

I tried to force the food down, but Leo and Otto's breakfast kept getting in the way. Hot, steamy, foreign things they were gulping down in bed, Otto dripping coffee on to Leo's naked chest, feeding him little morsels of goat's-milk cheese or bean curd, fingers touching lips.

'If I stayed *here*,' I said, spreading my bread with some low-calorie margarine which smelt like paraffin, 'I could help Janet in the house. I mean, if she's working in the City, she can't have much time to . . .'

Adrian put his knife down. 'She . . . er . . . *won't* be working much longer, Thea.'

'Oh?'

We both stopped chewing and there was a silence in which all the dumb, silent, stupid things like sinks and cupboards and draining boards started to writhe and shriek and wring their hands and I knew they were only waiting for Adrian to take a hammer to them and batter them to pieces.

He had torn his slice of bread into ragged little shreds, as if it were an unwelcome item on a newspaper. 'You see, Thea . . .' He put his knife down, picked it up again, jabbed it through the tablecloth. 'What I wanted to say was . . .' There was a little rent in the non-iron terylene, which showed through the dark wood of the table like a tiny smear of blood. 'We – I mean, Janet. She's . . .' He stopped.

'Pregnant,' I breathed.

'You *knew*, Thea?' He crammed all the bread bits into his mouth, almost in relief, and mumbled through them. 'You *can't* have done. She *promised* not to tell you and I . . .'

'No,' I whispered. 'I didn't know.'

I waited a moment while the kitchen stopped spinning and howling and tearing out its eyes. Stupid to be so hysterical. Pregnant was only a word – eight letters, nine months. Adrian wasn't her non-screw husband, that was all. He had screwed her through the stitches, maybe even at the hospital on the National Health. She had hardly recovered from the D and C, the patching up, before he had flung her on her back and ripped her apart again. The baby clothes I had creased and spoilt were for a *living* child. Janet was no longer a nine-to-five receptionist, but a full-time womb. That was her job, now. She would be at home with Adrian every minute of every single day, swelling and sanctifying a little more each month, rationing her husband while she and her baby grew to fill the house. There wouldn't be room for me. They'd need all the space for white muslin dresses and bobbing bunnies and cans of no-fuss baby food sitting on the non-judder, non-care fridge.

I tried to push the ceiling away. It seemed to have fallen in on me and was pressing on my forehead, so that everything was jumbled up together. Leo pregnant, Otto lying in his arms in a tiny muslin dress, both of them in bed making babies together, Adrian in the delivery room being stitched and sterilized.

'I'll just have a bath,' I said.

'Look, Thea, I didn't *want* you to know, honestly I didn't, but Janet thought . . . You're not *too* upset, are you?'

'No,' I said. 'I'm not.'

I knelt on the lino in the cold, cramped black-and-white tiled bathroom, which had little droplets oozing down the walls and three different types of bath-cleaner, each with a J-cloth folded neatly on the top.

'Bernadette,' I prayed. I knew she was listening. After all, she'd planned this entire thing – the loss of Leo, the long wait on the doorstep, Janet's pregnancy, the dead and living baby clothes. She was forcing me to see I didn't need homes or husbands or pregnancies. I was special, chosen, branded, however I might fear it. I had tried to run away from her, refuse to be a seer, turn instead to all the trifling tinsel baubles like love and babies and luncheon vouchers, double-barrelled offices, chocolate-coated toys. One by one, she had wrested them away from me, cut off all my bolt-holes. She had found me a job far more dazzling and exclusive than anything the Burton Bureau could offer, lifted me above the squalid pettiness of screwing and spawning, and saved me for her own high calling, to be hallowed, hallmarked, blest.

I knew now what I must do – follow her example and go back to St Maur's, to those simple dove-white nuns who had turned their back on earthly ties and dross. Bernadette herself had entered a convent, given up her friends, her home, her relatives. It hadn't been easy for her. She had sobbed all through that first bitter night away from home, pined for her Grotto, her father, the safe familiar life with her brothers and sisters in their cramped and cosy kitchen. She could have married and produced a string of kids. But God had made her fruitful in another way, filled her womb with visions instead of babies. Even if they were false visions, she was still famous, still allowed to flit about the world. I had tried to evade her, stamp her out, trample on her, call her just a nightmare, or an illusion, pretend she never happened. But I knew I had seen her more truly than I knew anything in my life. She was forcing me to accept it. She would pursue me and punish me, pounce on all my comforts and securities until I fell on my knees and cried 'thy will be done'.

I was on my knees now, the squiggled lino pressing into them, the steam from the bath I didn't want but which Adrian had run for me, coiling up to the polystyrene ceiling, like incense or a prayer.

'I'm coming,' I whispered to her. It didn't matter now that Leo was in Kashmir or Janet six weeks gone. I had my mission too, my goal, my labour. I would suffer birth-pangs for the Truth. I had no more need to demean myself, to trail around employment agencies and put up .cards for shabby basement rooms or answer ads for 'Fourth girl wanted, to sleep in dining-room'. I would return to the convent and soar beyond the world, live in a white nest at the top of a tree, with winged white nuns fluttering all around me. I pulled out the plug and let the shining, untouched water glug away. I didn't need to wash – I was clean now, uncorrupted.

I walked downstairs, coat buttoned, hair combed. I had even made my bed – returned all the baby clothes to their swirls of tissue paper. They hardly mattered now.

Adrian was tinkering with the waste-disposal unit. His back was bowed and leaden, as if he had grown older in an hour.

'I'm going to the hospital,' I told him.

'*What?*' He swung round. There were splashes on his shirt and one button had pulled undone. Despite the rationing, he was still too broad. '*No*, Thea. Look, if you're worried about that bill, I . . .'

'I'm *not*,' I said. They wouldn't charge me. They had accepted Bernadette without a dowry. I would pay in Truth, if not in fees. It would be an honour for them to shelter me. Several different convents had *fought* for the privilege of housing Bernadette.

'I've got to see Sister Ursula,' I explained. 'I've something to tell her – something vitally important.'

He tugged a piece of carrot out of the sink and stared at it as if it were a new type of vegetable he'd never seen before. 'She's . . . er . . . not *there*, Thea.'

I smiled. Janet had instructed him to say that. They were both shit-scared I was going to cost them more. They were so materialistic, so worldly, they couldn't see beyond bills and fees, scrimping and screwing, making babies on the National Health, eking out the Camembert all week.

'It's OK,' I said. 'They won't charge me. All I want is a fiver for the taxi, and after that I won't bother you for a cent.'

'I'll help you as far as I can, Thea – you know that – but you're *not* to go to St Maur's.'

I wondered now how I could ever have admired him. He was so *limited*, so narrow, floundering around among his ha'pennies and his cash-books, not realizing that souls and truth come free.

'D'you know the number of a taxi firm?' I shrugged. I was already thumbing through Janet's ready-reference book which was full of plumbers and discount houses and hairdressers called Maison Victor.

'Thea, *listen*, they're pulling down the hospital. It's going to be demolished. I didn't want to tell you, but . . .'

Amazing the lies Janet would resort to. She'd pull whole buildings down, just to pay me back. She'd probably spent the night polishing up her stories, then passing them on to Adrian after they'd finished screwing, instructing him to confuse and con and frighten me.

'Look,' I said. 'I'm getting out of here.' Next thing I knew, she'd be telling Adrian to inform me they'd demolished Kashmir.

'Thea, *please*, you *can* stay – just for a day or two. I'm sure it'll be all right. Janet's only a bit on edge because she's nervous about the baby and feeling sick all the time and . . .'

'Oh, horrid,' I said. I remembered it with Lucian. 'Tell her I'm sorry, will you.' I *was* sorry. Who *wanted* to be pregnant, with all that morning sickness and cramps and swelling ankles, and only pain and death at the end of it? I didn't even want to go to Kashmir. There would be flies and germs and roaring feverish roads and gaunt suspicious border-people who couldn't speak your language. I had a white nest waiting for me, quiet and uncorrupted, a Calling.

Adrian turned his back on the waste-disposal unit. 'Why don't we go out together? Take a little walk, or have a cup of coffee in the high street. I'll buy you a skirt or something, if you like. You'll need some decent clothes if you're going to get a job.'

'I've *got* a job,' I said. 'And I don't need anything.' The nuns would give me my robes and daily bread.

Adrian still had the piece of carrot in his hands, picking at it, shredding it, littering Janet's floor. His face was strained, taut, wary. The drop of blood had congealed on his chin, but he looked as if he might bleed again all over, if I even raised my voice. No point in talking to him about souls or saints or nuns – he'd never been religious. Religion for him was just another string of isms – Deism, theism, Judaism – explored in his neat scholarly handwriting in essays and dissertations, and then contrasted with atheism, rationalism, materialism. He couldn't understand that I might crave bread and wine and sackcloth rather than coffee and a skirt. I knew I'd have to lie to him.

'It's all right,' I breezed. 'I know what I'll do – I'll go to Patricia Jane's. She said I could stay with her. She'll even find me a job. Her father runs a kennels and he told me once I could help him with the dogs.'

I had kennels on my conscience. I'd never liked Karma, but I knew he'd droop and die without his master. Everyone would *loathe* him in a kennels. He was far too big, for one thing, and too opinionated. He hated other dogs and refused to fawn on people. They only like dogs who wag and squirm and grovel and *conform*. I could see him standing tall and proud and suffering, refusing to eat or drink or knuckle under, his black non-Afghan ears pricked to hear Leo's footsteps on the path. When he didn't hear them, he'd just lie down and wait for loss and pain and hunger to snuff him out.

'Well, *that's* a relief,' said Adrian. 'You're talking sense at last. Look, where does Patricia live? I'll take you there, if you like. Perhaps we'd better phone her first, in case she's . . .'

'No need,' I said. 'There's always someone in. She's got an enormous family – cousins and aunts and brothers and sisters and things. I'm always welcome. I don't even have to knock. "Just walk straight in" her father says. He's *wonderful*, her father. He . . .'

Adrian dropped the last shred of carrot and took my hand instead. 'Thank God for that, Thea. You need to be with normal decent people. I've been worried sick, if you really want to know. I've never liked you shacking up with Leo.'

I wished he wouldn't say that name. It was like wheels running over and over me on a ten-lane motorway. 'Just lend me some money for the train fare, will you?'

'I'll come *with* you, better still.' He was already turning off the extractor fan and bolting the back door. 'Make sure you arrive there safe and sound. And I ought to have a word with them about your job. People tend to exploit you, you know, especially if you work for friends.'

'No, really, Adrian, I . . .'

'I'd like to, Thea. Please.'

'No.'

'Well, just to the station, then.'

'No.'

I still had his sweater on. I didn't hand it back – it would be the one last link between us. I knew I wouldn't see him again. I kissed him very slowly and solemnly on the lips. He tasted of low-calorie marmalade and Janet. I could feel his heart beating strongly through his chest like an efficient and well-regulated machine. *Rationalism. Mechanism.* We stood for a moment holding hands, while the bird in the laburnum tree called 'Bernadette, Bernadette', and at last I pulled away and walked slowly down the hall.

The last I saw of him, he was standing at the door, still sweaterless, calling out final, hopeful, new-start sort of things after my dwindling form. I think it was his way of telling me he loved me.

He had also given me two dirty ten-pound notes.

thirty

I sat slumped on the taxi seat and stared. The driver had tried to warn me, but I'd thought he was simply one of Janet's stooges and hadn't listened when he'd gone on about redevelopment and demolition men. I'd been planning my campaign with Bernadette and couldn't be bothered to chat to taxi drivers.

'Just look at *that*!' he said.

I looked. Three brutal yellow cranes towered above what had once been the middle section of St Maur's. The roof had already gone and most of the outside walls. You could see right inside, into bare, gaping rooms with all their skin scraped off. The hospital looked as if it was having an operation on itself. It had been drugged and anaesthetized, then opened up and gutted, all its vital organs wrenched out, tubes and scaffolding shoring up its body. The surgeons had sauntered off before bothering to stitch it up again. They'd left it sick and bleeding, switched off its life-support system, declared it a hopeless case. A gang of looters was snatching all its treasures, the rings from its fingers, the gold from its teeth. Beside it stood a towering pile of rubble – iron bars and wooden frames, twisted piping, broken bricks – its own guts and entrails shovelled out of its belly and flung into a slop-bowl.

One of the cranes gripped a huge iron ball in its yellow teeth and was crashing it into what was left of the walls. Two tons of Portland stone crumbled like sugar. It was a child's game, knocking skittles down, dismantling houses made of cards, except this time, it wasn't wood or paper, but a hundred-year-old fabric built to outsmart man and time. Elegant stone pillars, slim and white and gracious like the nuns, had snapped in half like matchsticks, triple-bonded walls sunk to their knees with no one to help them up again or drag them to a convalescent home.

'Blimey!' said the driver, as another storey bellowed to the ground in a shroud of dust. I had paid him, tipped him, over-tipped, but I still sat there in his cab, like a numb and stupid chunk of masonry myself, unable to move my limbs. I turned my back on the window, but the view from the other one was even worse. A huge whooping fire was gobbling up window-frames and floorboards, its gloating flames leaping to the sky, showers of sparks singing against the charred, distorted corpses of bookcases and bedsteads. It was like a sacrament – fire and smoke and incense pouring up to God, and instead of gilded and embroidered priests, a gang of demolition men in filthy dungarees, with picks and spades for gleaming chalices.

The driver had opened his door and was staring out across the carnage. 'Bloody hell!' he muttered. 'Bloody bleeding hell.'

'I was a patient here,' I faltered, turning back to the other window and watching the cruel iron ball shatter a marble portico as if it were plywood. 'I'm *still* a patient here.'

'Don't think you'd stand a chance, Miss.' He laughed. 'Only terminal cases, I'd imagine.' He lit a cigarette and settled down in his cab to watch the larger blaze. 'They told us·down at the Plough they were going to pull it down, but I never dreamed this quick. Hey, gov,' he called to one of the demolition men. 'What the hell you up to?'

'What d'you *think* we're up to? Having a party? The place was rotten, cracked right through like a teacup. A danger to the public. Would have cost thousands to restore. No one *had* thousands, so . . .' He shrugged.

'It *was*n't cracked,' I shouted from the inside of the cab. 'Or rotten. You're *lying*! It was never a danger to the public. Janet only said that because . . .'

I shut my eyes. Leo was responsible. He hadn't paid the bill when they needed thousands. It was the final, crippling blow. Leo's fist was slamming into that building, his bare hands wrenching out whole stone staircases, his strong, steely shoulders buckling walls. I knew he was powerful, violent even, but now he had turned into a Samson and was tearing down my temple, destroying the only refuge I had left. Where was my cool white sanctuary, the top part of my tree? I couldn't see any trees at all. They must have felled them before they even started. Three months ago, I was lying in that hospital, with nuns and nurses ministering to me, fawning on me. And nobody had mentioned a word about demolition. They must have *known* they were doomed. They'd muttered a bit about staff shortages and lack of funds, but never the cruel reality of iron balls and bulldozers, cranes and flames and death throes. I remembered the word summonses. How could a pile of rubble issue summonses? How could a hospital roar and fume and threaten when it was only a stretcher-case itself, too weak to let out a groan? And what about the nuns, and Father Sullivan? Could you demolish twenty-six white nuns and one black chaplain? Batter them with a crane, toss them on a fire, strip them down, scrap them? I almost hoped Sullivan had been crushed by falling masonry. It would be his punishment for screwing me in the confessional, refusing me Absolution. He'd never returned, never inquired about me. And yet we were told to call him Father. I'd had enough of fathers. Deserters, liars, Wildmen.

I opened the door of the taxi. The air slapped hot, smoky, frightening, against my face. I stumbled across the rough, uneven ground. I was looking for the maisonettes, the neat little garden paths, the crew-cut privet hedges. Gone. Only a hole in the ground now, a ragged patch of dandelions pushing through the scrap-iron. I plucked a flower and laid it on the ground, trying to find the spot where I had made my First Confession and pay my tribute to it. It was like a wreath on a grave – Ray's grave, God's grave. The coffin was the packing case where Ray had sat and given me Absolution.

'Where are the nuns?' I shouted. 'What have you done with the nuns?'

The foreman grinned at me from the cosy fug of his site hut. 'We packed 'em in a tea-chest and shipped 'em off to heaven.'

'*Heaven?*'

'Well, Lacock then. It's not much different really.'

'Where's Lacock?'

'Wiltshire way. I may have heard wrong, of course, but someone said they've bought a house down there and set up shop in the country.'

'*Shop?* You mean another hospital?'

'No, just a convent, luv. There's no place for nuns in hospitals. Not now they're building these new, fancy places with transplants and scanners and the like. Nuns don't hold with transplants. I saw one on telly once, arguing with a doctor. Told him off, she did. If the good God made you, she said, then He don't want you doctors adding new bits and pieces He never bargained for.'

'But didn't they *know*?' I anguished. 'I mean why did nobody *tell* me? I was a patient here, yet no one breathed a word. In fact, I'm *still* a patient. They're expecting me. I've got a room here. They kept it for me. It's sort of . . . permanent.'

He wiped his mouth with the back of his hand and spat. 'Must be some mistake, Miss. They've known for *months*. The surveyors came in over a year ago. It was a fire risk, on top of everything else. They took in patients up to February, but even then, the place was running down.'

'It *wasn't*,' I shouted. 'It couldn't have been. Not at a hundred pounds a day.'

I felt a wave of fury break over me like a flame. A rotting mausoleum cracked and fragile as a teacup, a fire risk on the demolition list, a danger to the public. And then they'd had the cheek to issue summonses while they sat safe in Lacock, forcing Leo to flee the country for a sum you wouldn't charge if you owned the Ritz, let alone a clapped-out pile of debris. It was they who should pay *him* – as compensation, hush-money, restitution for all his worry and fear and travel expenses, for Karma's kennels, Karma's funeral.

Religion again – that's what it was – metal jugs and priests' tithes screwing the last shivering cent out of cringing congregations, great granite churches pressing down on tissue-paper men. Busy-body bishops setting up frauds and shams and miracles so that gullible people would pour into a sleepy one-horse town and make it into a metropolis. No wonder Bernadette had looked so stricken. They'd used her as a stool-pigeon, battered on her simple trusting soul, turned her into the biggest money-spinner after the Sistine Chapel and the Eiffel Tower. Right – I'd help her. Even without the hospital and my safe white sanctuary, I'd still pass on her message, dethrone the Blessed Virgin, shatter Lourdes. I'd be the iron ball on the crane, the dynamite, the bulldozer, tearing down that whole deceitful town until it was only a handful of shacks again, a few scrawny sheep grazing on a mud patch, a dot on the map so small you could flick it off like dust.

It wouldn't be easy – not without the nuns. I'd have no means of livelihood, no soft white Sisters to feed and shelter me, or lend me books and give me introductions to the bishop. I'd be back to bedsits, dole queues, loneliness. Penances again. Fasting not because I wanted to, but because there was nothing in the larder; shunned by society as a wrecker and a scourge. There was wreckage enough already. I gazed around at the bruised and bleeding masonry, the whimpering hulk of the hospital, dying beside its own twisted guts. The sky pressed down on it – white, bland, totally expressionless. No colour, no hint of sun. It could have been any season. Spring meant nothing here.

One small, stupid chair sprawled on its face in a rubbish tip, the only human object in a pile of slag and sweepings. I stared at its crippled legs, its gashed cane seat. It was *my* chair, the one that had watched beside my hospital bed all the hours I'd been there. It was still alive, still breathing. Leo had sat on it, and Ray, and Adrian and Sister Ursula. I could almost hear them calling out to me.

I blocked my ears, turned away, ran towards the fire. Heat and light rushed into everything. Even the sky was live and scarlet now, dipping its cold white fingers in the flames. Little flakes of ash were drifting and curling in the air, falling on my hair, turning me grey too early. The flames made wild, leaping patterns on my clothes, the whole horizon blazing and crackling in front of me. A gang of workmen were sitting round the fire, brewing tea, their faces ruddy from the flames, their bodies bright, solid, dirty. This was the real world – those loud, brawny men with their legs and cocks and raucous laughing mouths and huge calloused hands, swapping stories, telling jokes, stretching out their bodies to the heat. *They* weren't crippled, battered, deported to Kashmir. They weren't even rationed. There was a whole five-pound tin of sugar at their feet and they were gulping tea not from prissy little teacups, but from cock-sized, pint-sized milk bottles filled sweet and scalding to the brim. This was where I belonged. I'd seen those men before, or others like them – greasing and steaming in the workman's caff, flinging ketchup on to fry-ups and custard on to stodge, cackling and swearing in the public bars, wiping froth from their lips or sperm from their overalls. I envied them. They knew each other's names, knew which ones took sugar and how much, knew what they were doing with their lives. They took their orders from a four-square foreman who didn't speak in riddles. They belonged together, were free to spend their lifetime taking tea-breaks. Bernadette had never cocked them up, forced them to give up sex and peace and leisure, to fight for barrenness and truth. I inched a little closer to their circle, stood trembling on the edge. I could feel the fire panting in my face, the men's own heat and sweat and friendliness melting into mine.

'Thirsty?' asked the tallest, holding out his bottle. He had dark tufts of body hair pushing through the rents in his tee-shirt. His hand grazed mine as I took the bottle. He grinned. White teeth. Fat lips.

The tea scalded down my throat, the glass hot and hard between my hands. I held the bottle close against my chest, then inched it lower, lower, down. It was so long since I'd had a man, a proper man, and here were twelve of them – big dirty blokes, with bulging fore-arms, slurping mouths, legs sprawled wide apart, huge trampling boots.

'What's yer name, luv?'

'Bernadette.'

'Come again?'

'Bernadette,' I repeated, louder. One of the men was stripped to the waist, a scarlet eagle tattooed on his belly, which fluttered as he moved. His navel was deep and secret like a tiny chalice. You could have stored sugar in it.

'Fancy sort of name. French, isn't it? What's your Mum call you? Bernie?'

'No,' I said. 'She doesn't call me anything.'

One of the men cackled, showing stained and broken teeth. 'Run away from your Mum, then, 'ave you? Come to join us? Can you work a crane?'

'No,' I said. I knew I could learn, though. I longed to stay with the world, the heat, the rough, the purple, to play groupie to a gang of demolition men; to live in a hut and drink from bottles, to lie with navvies who smelt of filth and fire, to lick the sweat from their stomachs, to have my cunt tattooed. I didn't want babies – bad-tempered wombs which botched their job, morning sickness, swollen breasts. Or marriage with its damask napkins and its ration-books, someone else's initials branded on my birth certificate, somebody else's smell trapped inside my skin. All I wanted was to sprawl beside a fire with a gang of workmen who couldn't read, or write, or reason, or play pianos, or reassess medieval kings. Men who'd use a piece of Ch'ing to piss in, or tear up the *Listener* to wipe their arses on. Men who lusted after women, not crawled and slavered after other men, men who'd jeer at Otto as a nancy and a perv.

'Let's see yer 'ands, luv,' bawled a red-haired Londoner. 'You can always tell a worker by 'is 'ands.'

I put down the bottle and spread out my hands on the slab of concrete they were using as a table. I had always thought I had large, ugly hands, but now they looked small and delicate. They were dwarfed by the huge hams stretching all around me, hulking hairy wrists, cracked and calloused palms, filthy broken fingernails. Hands had never looked so beautiful. I could feel them clawing down my breasts, dragging off my clothes, hauling me back and down and powerless while they grappled down my thighs.

'You'd never make it,' grinned a stocky man with a red woolly cap over his matted thatch of hair. 'Not with 'ands like that, mate. You gotta be tough in this job. It's bloody good pay, but they don't take weaklings.'

'You could always make the tea,' said Eagle.

'Or scare away the ghost,' chipped in the Irishman.

'*What* ghost?' Despite the fire, I shivered.

'Some nun, they say, creeping around the corridors with her head in her hands. Load o'rubbish, I call it. I don't believe in ghosts. I never trust what I can't see plain with me own eyes.'

'There's *loads* of stuff you can't see, but it's still there, i'n it?' That was Red-cap. 'I mean, what about electricity?'

'I *seen* the ghost. Last week it was. It rapped my knuckles when I swore!' Loud laughs.

'Don't scare the girl. She's pale enough already.'

'Looks as if she's seen a ghost herself.'

More laughs. I crept towards the laughter. It was a hot, bright, reassuring sound. I needed to escape from ghosts. Bernadette kept tapping me on the shoulder, pale and chill and sullen like the sky. I had slipped down and was lying on my back. Above me soared the white, uncalloused clouds. That was where the saints lived, pure and clean and shining, with no blokes, no entanglements.

'Just once,' I begged her. 'Just one last taste before I leave it all.' She must have heard me because suddenly everything blurred and snarled and darkened and I could feel my voice choking through a sort of purple fug. It was as if the sky had somersaulted and trapped me in its underside, dark and hot and feverish. There were no clear outlines left, only flickering shadows, hungry groping flames. I could hardly tell where earth ended, and fire and air began.

The man with the eagle seemed to be bending over me, its cruel scarlet talons only inches from my crotch. I could smell his hot raunchy body, his rancid underarms.

'So you want to join us, do you?' As he grinned, I glimpsed the gap in his teeth, the dark blur of his tongue.

'Oh, *please*,' I breathed to Bernadette. She was still there somewhere, although she didn't answer. The world had contracted to the black crevice of my cunt.

Eagle was already fumbling with his jeans, while his mate grabbed my wrists and held me down. He pinioned my arms so fiercely, I couldn't feel much else. It was over in a minute, anyway. He was zipping up again before I even knew he'd come. Then he and his mate swapped places. The mate was rougher and took his time about it. He was a dark, swarthy bloke with bluish stubble and oil stains on his face. He started off just staring at me, peering closely at my body, as if it were some new piece of machinery which might be dud or dangerous. Then he moved against me, almost insolently at first, as if I wasn't worth the effort. I was so annoyed, I bucked and back-jumped underneath him. He soon fought back and I came at least three times before his one. He still clung on, though. He was shouting now, calling out words in some wild foreign language which sounded thick like Czech, and threshing with his heels against my buttocks. I knew he wanted to outdo me, so I let him come at least twice more, and then again, the back way, before I kicked him off. Even then, his cock was still half-stiff and wouldn't fit back properly in his jeans. He left them open while he stood there watching, jeering, as the third one clambered on.

He was just a stripling, thin and shy and jumpy, who dribbled when he kissed. He had long greasy hair which dangled in my eyes and a little nervous cough. He sweated so much, he made all my body wet. After three minutes, he was hauled off by the Irishman who came before he'd even entered me and then said, 'Jesus, Mary and Joseph' and spat contemptuously on the ground. I watched the little gobbett of spittle froth and shiver by my hand. Red-cap was the best. He kept his woolly hat on and almost all his clothes, but he knew how to move against me and he bit my breasts so hard, I almost fainted.

After that, they came in twos and threes. I soon stopped watching – just shut my eyes and let all the wild sensations trample over me. Things were so distorted now, I hardly knew if I was real or not. I reached out my hands and tried to touch the sharp, consoling edges of the world, but a workman must have shifted them. There was nothing left but fear and noise and grab. A Band-Aid scratched across my stomach, a sneeze exploded in my ear. Stubble chafed and pricked my breasts, calloused hands criss-crossed up and down me. Other men were leaving their machines and running over, wiping their hands on their overalls, tearing off their belts. I had long lost count of all the pricks. Some hacked and bucked and bull-dozed, others merely dabbed. Somewhere in the background, I could hear crashings and groanings from the wounded hospital as bits of its limbs fell off, angry splutterings from the fire, sudden shouts from the men who worked the cranes.

I squinted through my eyelids. The world was so bruised and bleeding, someone must have mugged it and flung it in the gutter. I was lying there beside it, with six or seven men fighting for a cock-hold on my body. Their skin glowed red and livid in the fire, their limbs were charred black branches, their eyes hot and spitting coals. The sky was even darker now, soggy with clouds which were only bloody swabs and pus-stained bandages. I could feel it pressing down on me – soiled, polluted, stinking – like the workmen's bodies.

'Bernadette,' I shouted. 'Bernadette.'

She couldn't hear me. I had lost her in all the thrust, the heat, the roar; the sweaty vests flapping against my stomach, the heavy boots trampling on my hair. I could see furious messages scrawled across the air, smell smoke and sin and darkness. Ordinary things like spades and pickaxes were grinning horribly, my own body split and cracked across its surface like a broken vase. I had no idea if I was vase or flesh or dream. Perhaps I was crushed against the galloping flanks of a nightmare, or tossed into another (bloodier) life like Louis de Gonzague. All I knew was I wanted to wake up.

I opened my eyes and crawled on my hands and knees towards the fire. Someone had restoked it, so the flames leapt even higher now, licking at the floorboards of the sky. I was torn, exhausted, filthy. I needed fire to purify me, burn me down to ashes. Things were always burnt in winter, to make way for the spring. New buildings built on the charred cinders of the old ones. Even here, a new, shining hospital would rise from all this scum, soaring like a phoenix out of flame. Scanners out of scrap-iron, transplants out of nuns.

'Lord,' I cried. 'Look upon the flame that lights our darkness, the fiery pillar that sweeps away the murk of sin.'

The words of the Easter Vigil were jumbling, leaping in my head. The Christians had begged their God to bless the Fire, so it would cleanse their bodies, cauterize their souls. The pagans before them had flung sin and death and darkness on their funeral pyres, until the whole sky roared and sung with light. Only fire could heal me, purge me, light me; burn away my sin like a blow-lamp, melt the workmen's pawmarks off my cunt. I must blaze and kindle with the hospital, be cremated with it, until our cold, fused ashes lay white and ghostly on the ground. I didn't replace my clothes – just walked naked, trusting, praying, towards the fire.

'Watch out!' shrieked the man with the tattoo. I knew his voice because it sounded shrill and powerful like the eagle's.

I didn't stop. The whole horizon was blazing like a beckoning red carpet which God had laid out in my honour.

'Come away!' yelled Red-cap. 'You're crazy! You'll kill yourself.'

I fought and shook him off. Already the flames were licking down my thighs, stretching out their fingers to my breast. The open wound of the hospital streamed and wept with blood. My mouth was full of lava, my eyes were scarlet holes. The yellow crane was towering over me, its sharp teeth splashed with blood.

No, not blood. The iron ball had turned into a paperweight and the red was only peonies gleaming on the glass. I stretched out my hands towards it, and as we touched – fingers, bodies, mouths – the whole blundering, dazzling, loving universe burst flaming into flower.

thirty-one

'Please,' I murmured. 'Could I have white curtains? The blue ones hurt my eyes.'

'That's right, dear,' said the nurse. She was also dressed in blue. There's very little white on the National Health. I was in a side-room off a ward which had cornflower curtains and a grey and yellow speckled floor. I had burns on my face and body and bruises where I'd struggled with the workmen when they'd dragged me from the fire. They didn't hurt – not now. Nothing hurt except the blue.

They seemed to know who I was. They called me Mrs Morton and even had all my notes and X-rays from St Maur's. It seemed odd that my notes should be saved when so much else had gone. I didn't eat – there was no more need to, really. They gave me pills which they said would make me sleepy. My body dozed – heavy and lumpy like a fat white bolster, but my mind was laser-sharp. It was as if the fire had burnt off all the dross and left me fierce and light and pure.

I thought mainly about Bernadette – not just her message, but the fact of seeing her at all. It was only now I realized what it meant. Somehow, I had missed the most important thing about it – that since she had appeared to me as a living breathing person, then there couldn't be any death. According to the books, Bernadette had died in 1879 – more than a hundred years ago – and yet I had seen her as young, as fresh, as childlike as in her photographs – not aged, not ghostly, not marked by time at all. That hundred years had been nothing but a sneeze, a flick of the fingers, a puff of smoke. Bernadette had dropped into the present as if the towering granite walls between the centuries were merely matchstick fences you could topple with a finger. Adrian kept centuries very stiff and separate in his leather-bound textbooks – *England in the Thirteenth Century*, *The Hundred Years War*, *The Twelfth-Century Renaissance*. But clearly he was wrong.

I lay in my three-foot bed in my eight-foot cubicle with the blue curtains drawn around me and a pale blue ceiling blinking down, and all time spread out before me like a smooth white counter-pane thrown across my bed – past, present, future, all sewn together like little squares of patchwork. I'd always seen time as a book before, heavy and serious like one of Adrian's tomes, divided into chapters (centuries), with a beginning and an ending, and page numbers plodding steadily and logically from one to six or seven hundred. Now I realized it was just an enormous piece of parchment which you could roll up or spread flat, covered not with footnotes or boring complex arguments, but with huge leaping pictures, splashed one on top of the other, and where all the footprints of all the different peoples were jumbled up and criss-crossed, so that the Blessed Virgin or John of Gaunt or Josie Rutherford were all racing and tumbling on one shining stretch of sand.

It was as if all the leaves of all the world's books had floated out of their covers, wriggled free of their indexes, and fused into an endless sheet. Ancient Chinese Emperors sat dicing with Adrian's medieval kings (Henrys and Edwards without their numbers now, and medieval meaning nothing) and with towering American presidents not yet born. Louis de Gonzague took tea with Bertrand Russell. Ming and Ch'ing were sold in Habitat, sharing the shelves with 1980s mugs. There was no time, no death. And if there was no death, then I couldn't be a murderer. Janet's baby was still kicking and crowing in its cradle, my own child kicking in my womb. Lucian four months or forty months – it didn't matter any more. If he had once been living, then he was *always* living, and I was still pregnant with him, glowing and plump and blest like Janet was.

The nurse was fussing with my hair. They'd had to cut off most of it. I didn't mind. I didn't bother with mirrors any more – there was too much else to look at. I'd discovered that small, secret things like safety-pins or sticking plasters had whole worlds rolling through them.

The nurse put my brush and comb back in the drawer. 'It's growing jolly fast,' she said. 'I'll be plaiting it next week!' When she smiled, I felt whole mountains crack. I'd stared at her apron once for half an hour and watched the Alps form in its snowy folds and creases. Another time, she brought me a small green pot-plant (from Adrian, I suppose). It grew into a tree with great tangled roots and towering branches, which blocked out so much light, I had to ask her to remove it.

When she'd gone, I pulled my nightdress up and laid my hand lightly on my stomach. I felt Lucian stir and flutter underneath it. And not just Lucian. All the babies who had ever lived (or died) were there inside me. We were all one, all fused, all sharing the same father.

A second nurse came in with a cup of tea and a miniature swiss roll wrapped in silver foil. I didn't touch it, didn't need crawling comforts any more. There was so much white and light and growth inside me, food would only muddy it. I was trying to clear away everything which weighed me down or soiled me, all the distractions which kept me bound, gross, caged. I had one last job to do – that's all – to pass on Bernadette's message to the world. Even that was easier now, because I knew who had appeared to her. It wasn't the Blessed Virgin, it was Janet.

I had been so stuck in time, so obsessed with birth and death and dates and normal life-spans, it hadn't occurred to me before. But now I saw there *was*n't any time, the whole thing clicked. Bernadette's Lady could have come from *any* century, even ours. She could just as well have been a modern person, living in what we (wrongly) term the present. The only limitation was that she called herself the Immaculate Conception. No problem there – I realized now that Janet herself was almost certainly conceived immaculate. She hated sin and sex and imperfection and would never have stood for someone like the Blessed Virgin being freed from sin, while she herself was stuck with dirt and squalor, messing up her soul like dirty fingermarks. It fitted with her whole blameless upbringing, her Devon Cream childhood, her goody-goody father, the badges she had won for Good Behaviour.

Another point was, Janet had blue eyes – the same deep flower-blue which Bernadette described. The Blessed Virgin couldn't have – coming as she did from Galilee where everyone was dark. It was obvious, really, Janet would be special, one of those exclusive one-percenters who had keener, sharper eyesight than the blurred and groping ninety-nine per cent of us, who had to put up with dark eyes.

The words she spoke were utterly in character. She asked for penance – Janet *would*. It was part of her whole policy of rationing people and confiscating toffees and her everlasting economies and rules. At the eighth apparition, she had forced Bernadette to kiss the ground for sinners. That was the sort of thing she made *me* do – not literally, perhaps, but through a score of small humiliations. She was also hot on sinners, which meant anyone who had different opinions from herself, or who wore dungarees or boob tubes, or didn't use a napkin. She requested processions in her honour and a chapel to be built. That was also typical. Janet expected homage all the time, not only from Adrian, who was forced to trot round Sainsbury's with her every Saturday morning, totting up the prices on her pocket calculator, but also from all the tradesmen who had to deliver meat and vegetables and know their place and call her Madam. Even at work, people bowed and scraped to her and a special girl came in from Contract-Bloom and put fresh flowers on her desk each day, as if it were an altar.

What finally convinced me, though, was the ninth apparition when the Lady commanded Bernadette to wash herself in a spring. Hadn't Janet asked much the same of me? Well, not in a *spring*, perhaps, though even that would have saved her precious water. Janet was obsessed with washing. She put a full load in her Hotpoint Liberator every single morning, and made Adrian shower before and after anything connected with food or sex or Sunday. The Mother of God would hardly come down all the way from heaven and waste her apparitions nagging people about their washing habits. Only Janet could be that finicky. In fact, the whole of Lourdes is fixated on the Baths. There's no other place in the world where people queue for three or four hours just to immerse themselves in freezing water and where even the sick and dying are carried to the wash-house.

The statue in the Grotto even *looked* like Janet – the marble-smooth complexion, the sanctimonious expression in the eyes, the gaze fixed heavenwards to avoid the squalor (and the prices) down below. The more I thought about it, the more convinced I was that Janet had not only been conceived immaculate, but had probably experienced a Virgin Birth as well. That meant she'd produced her baby (*both* her babies) without a man involved. It was obvious she'd approve of Virgin Births – no fuss, no mess, no man, no sperm. And *I* approved. A Virgin Birth meant Adrian had never screwed her, never *known* her, as the Bible puts it. Which allowed me to discount her, to even try and like her. She wasn't a rival any more, she wasn't even Adrian's wife. The Holy Ghost had fathered both her children and Adrian was mine.

'Aren't you going to eat that nice cake?' tutted Nurse. She had bustled in to take my tray away.

'Later,' I said. I wished they wouldn't speak. There wasn't room for words. Even Janet was taking up too much space. Once I'd announced her as the Lady, I'd leave the rest to her. I no longer wished to fight or challenge people, or rush about the world, or mix with priests. Janet could do all that. She could go to Lourdes herself and master-mind the change-over from Blessed Virgin Mary to Blessed Virgin Janet. The French might even welcome her. They've always been anti-Semitic and Mary was a Jew. Janet is pure Aryan, a natural blonde with breasts. She would also suit the famous Gallic thrift. She could ration the Holy Water and charge an entrance fee to the Grotto and the Baths, and insist on discounts for bulk-bought statues of herself.

'Sleeping again, Mrs Morton?' Sister was holding a vase of spring narcissi. Since the pot-plant, no one sent me flowers, but some of the other patients died before their flowers did, so the nurses passed them on to me. I didn't want them really, but I tried to smile. They seemed to like me smiling. At least the flowers were white. There was so much white inside my head, I preferred the room to match it.

'Mr Mackenzie is just on his way to see you,' Sister said.

'Mr *who*?' I stared into the open mouth of a stiff narcissus and saw Kashmir crouching in it. She might have muddled up their names. Rzevski and Mackenzie share some of the same letters.

'Mr Mackenzie. He's our dental surgeon.'

'Oh, I see.' The narcissus was drooping now. 'Why *dental*?'

'We plan to do something with that mouth of yours. The rest of you is healing up so nicely, we thought we ought to make you as good as new. Ah – here's the dentist now.'

His shoes boomed so loudly across the lino, he made the vase tremble. He was dressed too vividly for a hospital. His suit was a jabbing navy and there were dizzy red dots on his tie which kept hurling themselves against my eyes. Even his voice was brightly coloured, like those pinks and yellows you get in liquorice allsorts.

'Well, Mrs Morton, we've decided to keep you in a little longer and do a wee operation on your mouth.'

I nodded. I had almost forgotten that I had a mouth, but there was no point arguing. My body wasn't mine any longer. It belonged as much to Mr Mackenzie as to me, and his to Nurse and hers to . . .

'I've already discussed your case with the dental surgeon at St Maur's . . .'

'Oh, so he was saved, then?'

'I beg your pardon?'

Perhaps they had all been saved – nurses, doctors, Sisters, priests – bedsteads, bedpans, even the hospital itself. Perhaps I had only dreamed the demolition. I glanced at the marks on my hands – they seemed red and real enough. There was even one last dressing on my arm. I touched it very gingerly with a finger and the pain shuddered a little underneath.

'A Dr Davies also telephoned me . . .'

I couldn't remember any Dr Davies. He was probably something to do with the accounts.

'I don't think they told you much at the time. You were very shocked, I understand.'

'Oh, no,' I said. I think he was muddling me up with someone else. The world was too quiet and shining for it to shock.

'Well, you're doing very nicely now, my dear. The burns are healing well. There's no infection. We're all very pleased with you.'

I smiled. It was so easy now to please people. I had only to lie still and white and silent and let them peer at me and scribble on my chart and bring me things.

'Your front teeth have already been fixed, of course – and very well too, by the looks of them. All you need is a new permanent denture which fits a little better. We'll look after that, but what I want to work on first are the two *adjoining* teeth. I'll have to remove the tips of both those roots. They were fractured off, you see. I believe you had a blow.'

'No,' I said. 'I fell on stone.' I couldn't remember falling. It seemed so long ago, I couldn't really remember anything. It was only words, anyway. *Stone blow odd acquaintance Wildman shoe boxes blancmange.* They didn't have blancmange on the National Health. Or bills. Even the drugs came free.

'Unfortunately, the roots didn't break cleanly, but were fractured on the oblique.' He spoke very slowly and loudly as if I were a deaf or stupid child. 'That means at an angle. Do you understand me, Mrs Morton?'

He drew a little sketch on his notepad. The fracture was just a wriggly line and the root looked like a prick. I turned my head away. I was finished with pricks for ever. It seemed strange that teeth had roots. It made them sound like trees. There were no trees in this hospital. There weren't even any windows. I didn't mind. I could see everything I wanted in my head.

'In order to remove them, I'm afraid I'll have to cut out a piece of the upper jawbone. It won't be much – just a tiny fragment. I shall also excise the . . .'

'Excise?' I murmured. I picked up the word and put it in my word collection. I'd show all my new words to Leo when he returned. *Oblique, Mackenzie, plasma, haemoglobin.*

'That simply means cut out.' He smiled. '. . . excise the lump on your lower inside lip. We thought it best to do the two together. It means one anaesthetic less, and no one likes anaesthetics, do they?'

His smile was still hanging across my bed, bright and damp and shimmering like a rainbow.

'Is that all right with you, then, Mrs Morton?'

I nodded. I didn't really mind what they cut out. Mackenzie was standing up now, six foot blue of him breaking up the rainbow.

'I'm afraid you'll be a little sore, my dear. I'll have to put a stitch or two in each of the affected gums. There'll be some swelling, bruising, but we can give you something for the pain. There's no need to suffer, is there, not these days.'

'No,' I murmured. I wasn't listening, really. I didn't want priests or doctors any more. They came, of course – prayed or probed or chatted, sat on my bed and fussed. Sometimes I soared above them, above my own body even, looking down on it as if it were a tiny speck floating in huge white space. Other times, they dwarfed me. Their hands were huge steel pincers, the words they used battered against my face like sharp black stones. Their breath made dirty footmarks on the white space in my head.

I preferred to lie on my own and think about Kashmir. One of the nurses had brought me in some maps and leaflets from the Indian Tourist Office. The Kashmiri place-names were liquid poetry on my lips – Shankaracharya, Manasbal, Chashma Shaki, Shalimar. I read in a guide book that the Vale of Kashmir was known as the Valley of Happiness. That's because Leo was there. I saw him, sometimes, wandering among the dark ruins and shining waters of Srinagar. Otto wasn't with him. I doubt if he ever was.

There was a little tap on the door. I didn't bother with visitors and the nurses never knocked. I squinted through my eyelids. There was a blue blur which was Staff-Nurse and a brown blur hovering a pace or two behind her. I knew its name, but somehow it looked different, so I closed my eyes again.

'This is Mr Mackenzie. He's taking over Mrs Morton's case . . .' Nurse was introducing someone. I heard them mumbling greetings to each other.

'How is she?' whispered the someone. His voice was male and quite familiar.

'Oh, *much* better. In fact, I'm glad she's got a visitor. It'll take her out of herself. She's been a bit . . . withdrawn, you know. We're going to operate in the morning – just a minor op – finish off that business with the teeth. But you can stay an hour or so. It'll do her good.'

More whispering, then retreating footsteps and a softly closing door. I lay there a moment, allowing the silence to soak into my eyelids like the soft white cream they rubbed into my bedsores. When I opened them again, there was only the brown blur left. It moved a little nearer and shifted into a man in a brown serge petticoat with a shout of red on top.

'Ray,' I said.

thirty-two

'You've got your dress on,' I murmured.

'Yes.'

'It suits you.'

'Yes.'

I sat up slowly in bed and stared at him. I could see what he meant about the Franciscan habit. It didn't look poor at all. All those yards of shining stiff material must have cost much the same as a top-price suit. The design was almost fancy, with a wide cowl collar and broad flowing sleeves. I couldn't see any trousers underneath, but perhaps they were well rolled up. The girdle round his waist was fat and white and decorative instead of a scrappy piece of string. I had always pictured St Francis wrapped in shivering rags and tatters, like those tramps you see on Charing Cross Embankment with wads of dirty newspaper tied around their feet. Ray had new brown shoes on – not moccasins or sneakers, but conventional lace-ups from a bourgeois shop like Peter Lord. He looked fatter in his robes, and somehow older. His hair had been pollarded and some of the fiery red seemed almost tarnished. Only the spectacles were old and chipped and still familiar.

He didn't hold my hand or even sit on the bed, just took the chair Mackenzie had been sitting on. I didn't mind. I knew at least he wouldn't shout or hassle, or stare at my scars, or ask stupid questions like when was I going home.

'Don't . . . talk,' I said.

He shook his head. The silence was thick and white like snow. I think he was praying through it. I crept all the way to Kashmir and then on to Saskatchewan. There were no seas or mountains in the way.

When I got back, Ray was still sitting there. He was so still and solid, he looked like a smooth brown stone. I remembered vaguely, long ago in some shadowy foreign room, he'd tried to approach a woman. He'd talked a lot beforehand and then had sex with her. I couldn't recall the details, except there was also a boy involved.

'How's . . . Leo?' I asked. No, that wasn't the right name. I struggled to remember. 'Was it *John* – the one who . . . ?'

'Mike, I think you mean.'

I nodded. It wasn't Mike, but at least the name sounded safe and ordinary. 'Yes, Mike,' I said. 'How's Mike?'

'I'm afraid he died, Thea. Very peacefully.' (I smiled, to reassure him.) 'How are *you*?'

'I'm fine.'

He looked away. He was fiddling with his girdle. I knew he wanted to say things, ask things, comfort me, hold my hands, reach out and touch my soul. I tried to keep on talking.

'Are the other boys OK?'

'Yes.' He cleared his throat. 'Thanks.'

He shifted on the chair a little. I could see lines on his face which he'd never had before. 'Actually, I . . . won't be working with the lads much longer.'

'Oh?'

'No, I'm . . . er . . . going up north. That's really why I came, Thea. I wanted to say goodbye.'

'You're going *home*?'

'Oh no.' He smiled. 'Further north than home. All the way to Glasgow.'

'*Glasgow?*' It sounded almost as exotic as Kashmir. 'So you're leaving the Franciscans?'

'No, no, I'm re-joining them. Properly, I mean. I'm going back to live in the community. Not my old one, but one of the smaller Scottish houses.'

'Working with thalidomides?' I asked. The robe didn't suit him really. He should have been taller or had holier coloured hair.

'No, not this time.'

'More handicapped?'

'No.' His voice was softer. Everything was softer, bourgeois, better quality.

'A slum, then?'

'No, not really. It *used* to be a slum, but they've rebuilt it all.'

'*Paper*work?' I said. The word sounded slick and almost treacherous.

'Yes, paperwork.' When he grinned, he looked almost like the old Ray. 'The Vicar up there was taken ill and had to go into hospital. It was all very sudden and they're still in a bit of chaos, so they want me to help them out. I'll be doing the administrative stuff – you know, writing letters, paying bills, making sure the roof's OK and the place isn't falling to pieces.'

'But I thought you said . . .' I stared at his shiny toecaps, the thick folds of material which cut him off from people and had to be dry-cleaned.

'I *did*.' He was smiling still.

I remembered the story he'd told me about St Francis tearing the roof tiles down. His homeless, roofless founder had actually *wanted* the place to fall to bits. I wondered if Ray would have also to check the kitchens – stockpile the dainties, order the prime pork chops.

'Three meals a day?' I muttered. It was more an accusation than a question.

He nodded. I couldn't see his socks. Would they be best brown wool rather than thin green nylon?

'And coffee in the lounge and wine on feast days?'

'Quite possibly.'

'And stereos and Dunlopillo mattresses and . . .' I stopped. Despite the robe, the haircut, his face was still the same, still pinched and plain and radiant. He seemed as eager now for the Dunlopillo life as he had been in denouncing it. I tried to picture him scribbling sums in carbon-copy cash-books (ruled like Adrian's), checking coal and oil supplies, choosing coffee beans; but all I could see were his burning, shining eyes, blinking earnest and distorted through his spectacles.

'I'm even going to be helping with some fund-raising. You see, Glasgow's a sort of powerhouse for the Missions. They send forty thousand pounds a year to Africa – *fifty* thousand last year! That's more than all our other houses put together.'

I wondered if I'd heard right. Here he was totting up the lucre, when before he'd all but trampled on it.

'You mean, you're going back to church bazaars and bingo and writing begging letters and all those other things you said you couldn't *bear* to . . . ?'

'Thea . . .' He was sitting closer now. 'I was *wrong* about all that. Ridiculously wrong. I'd turned my vow of poverty into a sort of vow of self-importance – having to be poorer and holier and shabbier than any of my brothers. And denouncing the cash which other folk and other countries were genuinely in need of, just because it clashed with my so-called principles.' He stretched out his hands and left them lying on the bed like a pair of gloves. They were still rough and red and holy. 'In fact, I made a cock-up of *all* my vows.' His fingers twitched a little as if they were embarrassed. 'One of the reasons I came, Thea, was to try and tell you . . . how *sorry* I am. I mean, about that . . .'

I remembered now – the boy's name was Lionel and he'd screwed me in a toilet, although he was a priest. Ray had come round afterwards and made his apologies for him. He couldn't make them himself because he was deaf and dumb.

'You *said* sorry, Ray – at the time.'

'Yes, I know, but, I wasn't sure if . . . I mean, now I'm going away, I thought . . .'

'You already *explained* about Lionel – don't you remember? – how he didn't really mean it and . . .'

'*Lionel!* It's not Lionel I . . .'

'It doesn't *matter*, Ray.' It didn't, any more. I had moved into a space where sex was only an echo, an old stain from something I'd spilt months or years ago which had dried to a faint white film.

'Thea, you're a good girl. Truly good. You've taught me a lot, you know. See this girdle?'

'Mmm.' He was flicking the two ends of it to and fro between his hands, almost nervously. It made the whole room spin.

'There's three little knots in it. See them?'

'Mm.' I wished he'd keep things still. Stillness was important now.

'They're not just decoration, d'you realize that? They stand for our three vows – poverty, chastity and obedience.'

I nodded. Things always came in threes: mummy, daddy, Rutherford – Adrian, Janet, baby – Leo, Lionel, Ray.

'D'you know, Thea, I was so concerned with the first two, I hardly even *thought* about obedience. Well, not until that . . . night. It was you who brought me back to it.'

'*Me?*' I'd given up my own vows. They were only noise and self.

'Yes, I was so disturbed about breaking my vow of chastity and the harm it did you – I mean, seeing you so pale and shocked and obviously upset, and then Mike dying the very next night, almost like a punishment, in fact. When I got back from his hospital, the first thing I heard was that you'd rushed off back to London before I'd even said goodbye. D'you know, Thea, I just sat down and cried. Stupid, isn't it? I don't know whether it was shock or exhaustion or whether I was crying for you or Mike or my own sinful doltish self. I haven't cried for *years*, not since I was a kid of six or seven. It really shook me up, made me think – I mean, *really* think. It was as if I was looking at my life from the outside like a stranger passing judgement on it. It was only then I realized that I'd broken my vow of obedience far more often and more seriously than my vow of celibacy, and I hadn't even *seen* it. All those so-called scruples and ideals I swamped you with were almost arrogance, petty treacheries – rebellion, if you like, and rebellion is just a more glamorous name for disobedience.'

I shut my eyes. He still didn't understand. He hadn't mentioned Bernadette, or grasped that God and Mike and Glasgow were no nearer or further than the span of his own hand, or that words like disobedience were only strings of letters with a frown on top.

'Forgive me, Thea. I'm rattling on again. I don't want to tire you out.'

'You're not,' I said. I was watching Mike, still alive and shining, kicking a ball about on that endless sheet of parchment.

'I shouldn't be talking at all – not when you're unwell. But I'm leaving, you see – *tomorrow* – and I wanted to be sure you understood that . . .'

'I *do* understand.'

'It's funny, really, but when we make a move, or change office, it's actually *called* an Obedience. That's the Franciscan word. You see, Thea, it doesn't *matter* how we dress or what we work at – paperwork can be just as sacred as caring for thalidomides. As long as we do it willingly. St Francis was always on about the "littlenesses" of life – those tiny, daily, footling things which lead us to God if we do them for His sake. Even if we're only sorting jumble or scrubbing out the bath, that's just as much a calling as preaching in St Peter's or shepherding whole *bus*loads of the handicapped. You knew that all the time, Thea – that's the crazy thing.'

'Hush,' I said. There was no such word as littleness, not when the world was throbbing in my hands.

'I'm sorry, Thea, I'll go now. I know you want to sleep. Just let me say that if there's anything . . . I mean, if I can ever *help* or . . .' He slipped a piece of paper on to the bed. 'That's my new address. You can write to me there. Even phone me, if you like.'

He stood up, touched my shoulder. His hand felt hot and tense and awkward, as if he were frightened I might slap it down. 'God bless you,

Thea,' he murmured. He looked almost like a stranger in his habit. There was no point talking any longer. His God was brown and harsh and handicapped, whereas mine was white and quiet and boundless and neither blessed nor cursed.

I scooped a white narcissus from the vase and pushed it in his hands. 'Please,' I said. 'Take it.'

The stem was dripping water down his robe. He stood a moment, nervous, at the door. 'Look, Thea, even though I'm going, I . . .' The flower was already drooping. He was clutching it too tightly, stifling all its sap. I listened to it die. 'I mean, I'll still be there if you . . .'

'Goodbye, Ray.'

When I opened my eyes again, he'd gone. I unfolded the piece of paper which was ruled and narrow like his life was. His writing hadn't changed. It was still small and cramped, as if it had grown up in a slum and knew it mustn't spread itself, or leap into fancy swirls.

'St Francis,' I read. '407 Cumberland Street, Glasgow.' He'd even added the postcode and the telephone number.

I opened my hand and let the Glasgow house, St Francis himself and the whole order of Friars Minor flutter gently to the ground.

thirty-three

In the morning, everyone spoke softer and there were no more cups of tea. I was going up to theatre at eleven.

Sister brought my letters in. They came in dribs and drabs from Notting Hill. I supposed Adrian or someone must be forwarding my mail. He was probably keeping my accounts as well, and sending in my sick-notes. I rarely read the letters. The one with a second-class stamp was from my mother and the other said 'Good News from Brentford Nylons'. I dropped them in the waste-bin without even slitting the envelopes. The third one was a postcard. On the front was a brilliant Eastern bird with sweeping tail feathers and hot scarlet plumage like tongues of fire. Its wings were flexed and soaring, its head bent back and gazing at the sun. Trembling, I turned it over. All the writing had been smudged and blurred, so there were only mangled stumps of letters bleeding and writhing on the back, an indecipherable black stain, as if the rain or God or Time had blotted it out. There were two brightly coloured stamps – foreign stamps – one with a lotus on, and one with a turbaned craftsman at a loom. The postmark said Srinagar.

I held the card like an icon in my hands. It didn't need words or writing. I knew already what it meant. The bird was a *feng huang*, so Leo was telling me the vase was mended and peace restored to the universe, that a Golden Age had come. I stared at the preening beak, the blazing wings. Adrian had nagged and niggled about Leo not apologizing. But now he had offered not merely a brief and grudging 'sorry', but had sent me the symbol of peace itself, so that I could hold it bright and breathing in my hands, the bird which was too gentle to peck at a grub or tread on a blade of grass, which flew away in wartime and returned only when gods smiled on the earth.

I turned it over and stared at the print again. Although it was distorted, I recognized Leo's bold black fountain pen. The address was so fogged and fudged, it astonished me that all the post offices from Srinagar to London had passed it so confidently from hand to hand. I knew, then, it was blessed. It would have arrived on my bed, had Leo simply tossed it blank and unaddressed into the air from some high peak of the Himalayas.

This was the 'sorry' I had waited for almost four long months (all my life, perhaps), the one Leo had never entrusted to anyone before, not even God or Otto. Only his sorry could heal me – I was healed. I could feel his remorse bandaged round my body, hot like a poultice, soothing like a balm. It was as if the phoenix had nestled on my breast and wrapped me in its feathers. Leo had held that bird. His breath had warmed it, his fingers ruffled it. Therefore Leo's breath and hands were against my own.

I knew what he was saying, knew what he had written on that card. It could be one thing only. Hadn't he told me the *feng huang* symbolized the perfect union of man and woman?

I traced my finger along the tangled mess of print. 'I love you,' I spelt out. It was easy, really, once I understood. Leo had written those three short endless words and the rain and wind had rubbed them out again and the customs men excised them, but I could still read them as plainly and simply as if he had daubed them in shouting scarlet letters on the hard white skull of the world.

I smiled. I knew he'd say it in the end.

He had tossed his love in the air like a homing pigeon and it had scorched a trail across the sky. All the way from India to England, I could see whole countries stunned and reeling with it; the landscape branded with Leo for ever – his nails clawing up and down the fields like furrows, the sharp angles of his body sculpted into the hills.

I closed my eyes. His love was so violent, it was like a fist smashed in my face. Leo had never hit me – all he had done was tell me that he loved me and I had bled with the jolt and wonder of it.

'Wakey, wakey, Mrs Morton! We're ready for you now, dear. Be a love and give me that card and those dirty Kleenex, will you. We want to tidy you up a bit.'

I passed her the Kleenex, but not the card. She tried to coax it from me, but I held on tightly while she fussed around. I'd waited so long for Leo's love, I wasn't going to be parted from it now. I let her take my temperature, instead.

I'd already had my bath and enema. I rarely shitted now without assistance. There was nothing left inside me – no food, no faeces, nothing base or low. I was clean and white and empty like the inside of a flower. I had only one last thing to do – to pass on Bernadette's message to the world. I knew I mustn't delay too long. Pilgrim planes were screaming into Lourdes, nation jostling nation for their holy water and their miracles, Mary's name instead of Janet's on a million million lips.

'Excuse me,' I said. 'But there's something I've got to do before my operation.'

'You've got to spend a penny, dear, that's for sure. Out you jump, and I'll tidy up your bed while you're out of it.'

I suppose ordinary nurses couldn't grasp I had a Mission, so I walked on, past the bathroom, and knocked at Sister's office. She must have understood because she escorted me back to my room with two assistants and dressed me all in white. It was like a ritual stripping. I was naked underneath. They took away my squalid bra and soiled pyjamas and robed me in a pure white vestment like an alb, with my hair coiled up beneath a spotless coif. I was a nun now – no hair, no cunt, no curves. They even removed my jewellery – the tawdry plastic bangle, the tuppeny-ha'penny chain. They left my wedding ring, but taped it over with a piece of sticking plaster. A ring meant nothing now. I was neither married nor divorced. I wasn't even separate. A ring could only bind two separate people.

They eased my denture out and dropped it in a dish. I wouldn't need it any longer. I didn't intend to eat again, or kiss or bite or talk. I had already renounced my possessions. My room was bare, my locker empty save for the box of hospital Kleenex and the water jug. Even that, they took away. They left me parched and fasting. Nuns always fast before they take their final vows and priests before their ordination. I was nun and priest at once, man and woman fused, like Leo and the *feng huang*. They folded my counterpane away and left only one white blanket and the sheet. If I wriggled down the bed a bit, I was wrapped totally in whiteness, white sheet pressing on my eyes, white hands folded on white breast. Bernadette had died like that, garbed all in white, lying on a white bed with white curtains pulled around her. She had called it her private chapel. I shut my eyes. I was lying in my own chapel, dressed in a robe which was both shroud and wedding dress, and with my handmaids all around me.

The handmaids spoke in whispers. Even they wore white now. They had changed out of their blue and put on dazzling uniforms – white cuffs, white caps, white dresses. Their voices were white to match.

One of them was standing over me with a sacred vessel in her hands. 'Just a little prick,' she smiled. 'You'll feel a bit woozy, but don't worry, I'll be popping in and out.'

A needle pierced my arm, but I hardly felt it. Leo loved me, and since there was no time nor space nor boundaries, he was with me still, the child of our love leaping in my womb. The phoenix sat soft and sheening on my breast, its feathers ruffled round me like a shield. I lay back and listened to it sing.

All things were mended now. St Maur's was standing whole and unmolested, stretching its white arms up to heaven. Even Adrian's ancient temples which I had seen as only heaps of weeping stones with weeds and picnickers sticking up between them, were now raised high and proud again, incense smoking from their singing mouths.

Leo had sent me not just peace, but flowers. There was a vase of white narcissi on my altar. The blossoms were drooping a little, but they still spelt life and spring. I watched their slow white throats breathe in and out. They had tiny dots of yellow in their centres, which swelled into huge round suns, so bright they blinded me. I tried to stare only at the vase, but it was so vast and glittering, the whole room roared with light. Even if I closed my eyes, the brightness dazzled them. I realized, then, it was coming from inside me.

'All right, my dear?'

Someone had swum in again – a handmaid, probably. I could see her mouth gaping like a vast black jewel-box lined with scarlet plush, and one hand crouching on my blanket with all its struts and girders sticking up. Next time, there were two of them, but all their different parts had floated away from each other and were scattered around the room. They must have been in pain, but they still kept smiling. The smiles themselves had cracked into tiny fragments which fell on my bed like hail.

'We're taking you up now, Mrs Morton.'

I nodded. They all understood about my Mission now, because they had sent a man with a litter who lifted me high on to it and wheeled me out of my room along miles of white, shining corridor which smelt of God and ether. White walls reared up in front of me and then fell away again, white doors yawned open and closed effortlessly behind me. People bowed and whispered as I passed.

'Careful with her now.'

We had stopped a moment and they were cramming me into some

grey metal box with wrought-iron gates which clanged so loudly shut, I could feel the echo like a sharp knife cutting through my skull. There was a sudden judder and the earth fell right away, and we were soaring up, up, up, so fast some of my limbs were left shuddering behind. There was a pause, a jolt, and then up again, until suddenly my head grazed against the sky, and we had pierced right through it and were streaking past the higher constellations in black, rushing space.

When we stopped, the air smelt purer and we were in some high shining room where the gods wore green and huge glaring lights stared into my eyes like planets. Fuzzy white angels kept curving towards me and retreating. I felt so light, so radiant, I must have become pure soul. Solemn white faces were bending over me and I could hear the heartbeat of the universe roaring through my veins.

I knew now, this was the place and moment for my message. I could see sacred vessels gleaming in glass cupboards – tubes and chalices, syringes and phials. Important people were gathered round my litter, tense and reverent, hanging on my words.

I struggled up, but part of my body was missing and its hinges wouldn't work. A green archangel came and held me down.

'S . . . something to tell you,' I stuttered. 'Message for the world.'

'Tell us *later*, dear. Plenty of time when you come round.' She didn't sound like an angel. Her voice scratched and chafed against my soul. I tried to push her away and lift my head. I knew it must be now – there wouldn't be a later.

'What's the matter, Mrs Morton? You really must lie still, dear.'

'Bishop,' I gasped. My voice had turned from solid into gas. All the same, they must have heard it, because a tall lordly figure was striding towards me, a man in a dress with neither legs nor hair, but robed all in green and transfigured like a god. He was holier than a bishop because he wore his vestments even on his face. All I could see were two piercing eyes and a blaze of light behind him like a halo.

'Must . . . tell you . . . something,' I mouthed.

'All right, my dear, you go ahead and tell me.' His voice was beaten bronze, his eyes as deep as the Saskatchewan Lake.

'Listening?' I whispered. It was essential that he caught my words. My voice was only a vapour trail dissolving into space.

He nodded. Behind him, I glimpsed other faces, faces behind faces, distorted in shining silver surfaces, reflected in mirrors, cut and branded by the light.

'It wasn't' – I paused – 'the Blessed Virgin.' I could feel the whole world drawing in its breath as I scooped up the last fluttering feathers of my voice. 'It was . . . Janet.'

I glanced at the tall green god to make sure he had understood. 'Janet,' I repeated, as the glory of a task fulfilled broke against my body like a wave.

He was nodding, smiling. 'That's all right, my dear. Nothing to worry about at all. We'll take care of everything.'

Relief roared and thundered in my brain. I felt a peace so deep, I longed for it to close above my head. I had done it, said it, kept my tryst with Bernadette, and now the burden had been lifted from me. Other, stronger powers would shoulder the toil, the fear, the anguish, the conflict with authorities, the struggle with the priests. All I had to do was lie back and let all things pass. I didn't belong in Lourdes or London any longer. I had reached that place where words and work and turmoil were just an interruption of the light. The green god's hands were hovering over my arm. Blue rivers flowed slowly to his fingertips, dark forests sprouted on his wrists. He was so strong, he could topple Lourdes with just one finger, break up all the marble and mosaics, and set up Janet in some new, no-fuss, no-nonsense shrine.

I closed my eyes. The last dregs of my body dropped away. I could see the whole shining, singing universe from Kashmir to Saskatchewan spread out like Leo's postcard in my hand, all centuries shaken up together, all continents scattered like a drift of petals in one small cul-de-sac. There were no boundaries any longer, no marriages, or birth certificates. We were all one, all joined. Lucian was Leo's and Leo Lucian's, and Louis de Gonzague was only the unborn child of Otto's father alive and smiling among his shoe-boxes.

I stared at the small glass bottles in the cabinet, the rolls of bandages, the lengths of tube. I felt them leap and breathe and quicken as they shouted up to heaven that they were as vibrantly alive as I was. My shape and outlines were already blurred and merging, until I was glass and bandage with them, star and stone. This was my Communion, communion with all things. It didn't matter any longer that I had never been a ticked and slotted Catholic, or that my so-called First Communion had left me choked and disillusioned. There were no more shrill religions feuding with each other across their barbed-wire walls. We were all priests, all gods; all absolute, all light. Every smallest, humblest object, whether pin or pot or thumbnail, blazed and hymned with light. There was only light. One light, one singing life.

All creeds dissolved, all colours fell away. I could hear the sound of whiteness surge slowly through the room. I recognized it. It was Leo's music, that safe, soft, healing music he had played when I returned from hospital, but now it was the *feng huang* who was singing it, pouring out its hymn of peace and light and harmony, fertility and grace. I climbed on the sound and soared. I was a phoenix now, a white one, rising from the flames of pain and violence, flying away from purple, from the colour of pomp and penance, the shades of Lent and sin. I had left pain and death behind, scorched through fire and furnace, and come out hallowed on the other side where the pure cold light of heaven smote scalding on my eyes.

Somewhere, far below me, the green god touched my arm. 'We're going to put you to sleep now, Mrs Morton.'

I smiled. Of course I couldn't sleep. Even if I closed my eyes, the radiance would startle them apart again. And I wasn't Mrs Morton. All names had been rubbed out or whited over – Elliott, Rzenski, even Wildman. No deed polls now, no Babel, no baffling, battering words to show me up or shout me down. Not even any different languages. *Feng huang* meant phoenix now without any mistranslation, and I was simply, only, Thea, which meant goddess and divine.

An angel pushed my white sleeve slowly up my white arm. I had no sleeve, no arm. I was so high, high, above them, I could see the door of heaven opening slowly in the sky.

The shadow of a streak of silver fell across the light, a javelin gleaming in the green god's hands. He was trying to pierce me with it, but I had already flown too far. The sky came hurtling forward, and as I soared, roared, rushed to meet it, I saw my father sitting up in heaven, holding out his arms.

Find out more about Penguin Books

We publish the largest range of titles of any English language paperback publisher. As well as novels, crime and science fiction, humour, biography and large-format illustrated books, Penguin series include *Pelican Books* (on the arts, sciences and current affairs), *Penguin Reference Books, Penguin Classics, Penguin Modern Classics, Penguin English Library* and *Penguin Handbooks* (on subjects from cookery and gardening to sport), as well as *Puffin Books* for children. Other series cover a wide variety of interests from poetry to crosswords, and there are also several newly formed series – *King Penguin, Penguin American Library,* and *Penguin Travel Library.*

We are an international publishing house, but for copyright reasons not every Penguin title is available in every country. To find out more about the Penguins available in your country please write to our U.K. office – Dept EP, Penguin Books Ltd, Harmondsworth, Middlesex UB7 0DA – unless you live in one of the following areas:

In the U.S.A.: Dept DG, Penguin Books, 299 Murray Hill Parkway, East Rutherford, New Jersey 07073.

In Canada: Penguin Books Canada Ltd, 2801 John Street, Markham, Ontario L3R 1B4.

In Australia: Marketing Department, Penguin Books Australia Ltd, P.O. Box 257, Ringwood, Victoria 3134.

In New Zealand: Marketing Department, Penguin Books (N.Z.) Ltd, P.O. Box 4019, Auckland 10.

In India: Penguin Overseas Ltd, 706 Eros Apartments, 56 Nehru Place, New Delhi 110019.

LACE

Shirley Conran

A million dollar bestseller and a publishing sensation – *Lace* is the novel that teaches men about women . . . and women about themselves.

'Which one of you bitches is my mother?' This question sears through the thoughts of the four women summoned so mysteriously to a glamorous New York apartment, unlocking the past and a secret – a secret that has enmeshed their lives and dogged their success, and one that lies at the heart of this scorching, sensational novel.

The story of four women. Judy, Kate, Pagan and Maxine, who took life as they found it and dared to make it a success. Against an international backdrop of the rich, the famous and the depraved, these women – bound together by ties stronger than love itself – created legends.

LESSONS

Lee Zacharias

'I went home from my first solo contest bedecked, deflowered, betrothed, and depressed . . .' Jane Hurdle's musical gift lifts her above the ordinary. But in her struggle to become a musician, through her husband, lovers and family, she finds that life and art are often at odds . . .

'Symphonic . . . wonderfully readable' – *The New York Times*